Mr. Bluestick

by
Michael Aloisi

www.AMInkPublishing.com

www.AMInkPublishing.com

AM Ink and its logos are trademarked by *AM Ink Publishing*.

Also by
Michael Aloisi

Fiction
Fifty Handfuls
White Ash

Non-Fiction
Unmasked
Arm Candy
The Killer & I

As Michael Gore
Tales From a Mortician
Skeletons in The Attic

Foreword by The Author

One day, heading back on the Metro North train from New Haven Connecticut to NYC where I was living at the time, I saw something out of the window that I just could not explain. It was night and I was staring mindlessly out of the window as the dark world sped by, thinking of nothing in particular. Then, suddenly in the middle of the pitch-black woods, I saw a brilliant slash of blue light. Instantly I sat up, craned my neck and tried to see what it was, but in mere second, we were half a mile away.

The image was burned into my brain and I tried desperately to figure out what on earth could have caused a blue light in the dead middle of the dark woods. The thought bothered me so much, I took out my laptop and started writing. After having just released my first novel, *Fifty Handfuls*, I was already working on several new stories, but this image would not leave my head. I abandoned everything I was working on and focused on explaining to myself what the blue light was. And with that, *Mr. Bluestick* was born.

Done with the book, and having personal success with self-published my first book, I put this story out in the fall of 2006. It did well for an independent book and it found many avid readers even in its poorly edited state. As my writing career took off, I abandoned my old self-published books and left them as a piece of the forgotten past. Then, when a fan of my newer work told me how much she wished she could get a copy, I realized it was time to give it new life.

At first I wanted to re-write the entire thing as I feel it shows my young adolescent writing that could be better, but then I understood that it shouldn't be changed. It's a snapshot of my life and the world I wrote it in. Changing it would be, changing my past and I didn't want to do that, I merely wanted to let this story enter the world again.

Going back and reading it now, while I cringe at some of the writing, I still enjoy it and hope you do as well. I may never find out what that blue light was that I saw so many years ago, but in reality, I never want to find out, for the story I created around it, has a life of its own.

Enjoy the book,

Michael Aloisi

For My Mother.

There is no way I could ever
express my gratitude for everything
she has ever done for me.

Without her
I would be nowhere.

1

"I hate you, I hate you both! I'm not going!"

The door slammed, sending the plastic clown mask off its hook and onto the floor. The sight of the childish clown face fluttering to the floor caught her eye, but she ignored it and flopped onto her bed. Lilly's face slammed into one of Larry's button eyes, her once favorite teddy bear. With anger, she tossed it aside and buried her head in the soft pillow. *Stupid childish things.* As much as she tried to be a grown-up, she couldn't stop the rush of hot tears that poured out of her face, wetting the jumping sheep pattern of the pillow cover. A light knock came upon the door, just a few seconds later than she thought it would.

"GO AWAY!" Lilly lifted her head just enough to shout. She *knew* it was Dad. He was always the one to cave first and try to bribe her with something, anything to make her happy. This time though, there was *nothing* that would make the fact of moving any better. It didn't matter; she would refuse to go. Lilly could hear the door handle turn slowly. Man, she wished she had a lock, but her dad said "no way" to that a long time ago. She cracked one eye open just a bit to make sure it was him, because if it was mom, she would throw a fit. Over the sheet and through blurry tears, she could see the shadowy figure of her dad. He was a large man with salt and pepper hair styled just like any other dad.

"Lil, can I talk to you?" It was more of a whisper than anything.

Lilly didn't respond, her eyes were shut tight once again as she heard the door close. She could tell he was still in the room though. Dad always shut the door to talk to her when she was mad at Mom…which was a lot. Suddenly, but slowly, she felt the bed sag near her stomach from him sitting down. Next came the hand on her head, *petting*. It made her furious.

"Don't pet me like I'm a dog!" she screamed and squirmed as far away as the twin bed would allow her.

"Look, honey. You're going to love Lakeheath. I know it's far from here but it's soooo cool! I promise! Besides Mom and I already decided to let you finish the school year here so you won't have to enter a new school in the middle of the year."

"I don't care; I'm not going. I'm staying here with Aunt Lorraine!" Lilly squeezed the pillow closer to her face, waiting for a lecture about how she couldn't do that.

"I know there is nothing I can say that will make you feel better right now, and I know you're going to be angry for a while. But you have to know this is best for the family. You'll be happy there, I promise. Now, if you want to have a sundae with Mom and me, we'll be in the living room."

The deep impression rose, lifting Lilly back up as he stood. It was followed by a quick kiss on the head that she tried desperately not to receive. After hearing the door shut, she lifted her head to suck in some cool fresh air. The crying had stopped but she was still mad.

Getting up, she flicked on her Doc McStuffins desk lamp to admire the collage she had made in art class. The assignment was to show things you love. In the center of the red paper was her parents hugging and smiling (though she would have cut Mom out if it wouldn't have made Dad mad). Around them, amongst her Reese's candy wrappers and cartoon characters were pictures of her two best friends, Sara and Toni. There were at least half a dozen pictures of the three of them; they were inseparable. She stared at them now, *knowing* she was going to have to leave them. The tears fought to come back.

There was only one month left of school. That was *not* enough time. She couldn't leave her friends. They already had so many plans for the summer! And Lakeheath was three states away, not exactly down the street. A plan was in order; *she had to run away.* Sara and Toni would go with her; she just knew it.

--

"She stop her crying yet or what?" Tom sighed and rolled his eyes at his loving wife. He plopped on the couch and put his head on her plump lap. He could feel her stiffen, but he kept his head there anyway. Loving her was hard at times, but he was sticking to his vows, even if he didn't understand what the hell was going on in her mind.

"So, tell me again how you're the one whose job is taking us to another state and I'm the one she's mad at." Sandy said.

"Because, she's Daddy's little girl!" He said trying to make light of the situation.

A quick swat on the cheek made him roll over and face her gray eyes, the eyes that were the first thing he noticed about her, the first thing he fell in love with, the same eyes his daughter had, that were now crying upstairs. Tom arched his neck up for a kiss. Reluctantly and as if she was about to swallow some sour medicine, Sandy gave him a quick peck. Getting anything besides hate from her was getting harder and harder.

"It'll all work out. A month after being there she won't even remember this shitty house," Sandy said matter-of-factly.

Tom looked around the house and thought about what his wife had said. "But this is *our* home, our first home. You used to love it here." Tom sighed.

"Oh, spare me the water works! Yeah, lots of memories, but you know what? A two floor, four bedroom house beats out any memories this two bedroom shack has!" Sandy replied sourly. Tom desperately wanted to fight for the honor of their house, to try and remind her that they had good times, many of them there, but he knew it was pointless. Shutting his mouth he hoped the fresh start and her new meds would make things better… they had to.

--

Leave now or wait until they're packed? That was the question running through Lilly's mind as she paced around her room. What would she take? She had way too much stuff to bring; she couldn't possibly take everything. Where was she going to stay? That was the biggest question. She thought of hiding out at one of her friends' but that wouldn't last too long. She remembered seeing an episode of "Boy Meets World" when Cory hid his best friend in his room. They found him in a day, things like that never work, *this* was never going to work.

Giving up on making a plan, Lilly felt her stomach rumble as she remembered what her father said about having a sundae. Back when mom was normal, "Sundae, Sunday Night" ice cream parties were always her favorite days. As long as she could remember, she had a huge sundae with all the fixings while watching TV with her parents before going back to school the next day. She really wanted one, but the thought of eating it with mom made her almost sick. After a second tummy rumble, she decided to not let it stop her, she would just make one for herself and come back to her room and play online.

Lilly marched into the kitchen to see everything on the counter ready to go except for the ice cream. She pulled out the rocky road and dropped it hard on the counter. Being less than four feet tall made it hard for Lilly to make stuff in the kitchen without the help of Dad or a stool, but she was determined to accomplish this task on her own, even when Dad raced in the kitchen ready to help. But when the scooper got caught in the ice cream, she gave up, faced the other way and pouted while he made the biggest sundae she'd ever seen.

"You know, Lil, tomorrow we are going to take a ride to see our new house. Let's make a deal. If you're good, when we get there, you can pick any room in the house to be yours, even the biggest one." Lilly refused to answer, but the idea of having a bigger room and the sight of the amazing sundae in front of her did change her mood.

2

They left early the next morning. Lilly was still grumpy, and a giant sugary pancake breakfast did nothing to cheer her up as it usually did. She ate in silence, practically ignoring her parents the entire time. The ride after the meal was *long*. Lilly played with her tablet and half-heartedly read some cheesy teen novel. Finally, a bit after eleven they saw a sign reading "Welcome to Massachusetts!" Her father yelled hooray while Lilly rolled her eyes.

"Are you excited, Lil? It's only a few miles over the border, so we're almost there!" her father said to the rearview mirror.

She closed her book and started to look out the window. Might as well see what the place looks like. The town wasn't much different from theirs - stores, trees, houses, same old, same old, just like anywhere. *Yippee*, she thought.

As they drove, fewer and fewer houses were rushing by the windows, more and more trees were. This piqued Lilly's interest. She loved the woods, unlike Sara and Toni who never wanted to get dirty. As the car took a left onto a brand new street her father proudly proclaimed was their new home, Lilly tried to catch the name but she couldn't read it as they sped by. She wanted to ask her parents what it was, but she still refused to speak to them. The few houses they passed were huge, but not yet finished being built. The only ones that looked somewhat complete were theirs and the one next to it. The front yard was still nothing but dirt.

The three of them stepped out of the car without speaking. It was eerie, like a ghost town, equipment everywhere but no noise at all. Tom went over to Sandy to proudly put an arm over her shoulders. Lilly watched them but her mom didn't respond to the act at all. While that irked her and she was already in a bad mood, the site of the house did ease some of t was huge, well, compared to their old house. Two floors, two-car garage, a porch that wrapped around the whole front and half of the left side, but best of all, it was blue, Lilly's favorite color!

"Dad, it's, pretty awesome," the tiny voice squeaked out from behind them. This time her Dad hugged her shoulders and squeezed tight. He then crouched and met her eyes. Lilly brushed her straight brown hair aside to see him better.

"Wait until you see your room… whichever you pick that is."

She gave him a halfhearted hug, and caught her mom's disgusted glare over his shoulder.

"Come on! I'll race you to your new room!"
The two ran to the door and right in it. Being still under construction, the door wasn't locked. In fact, it didn't even have a knob yet. The stairs were just inside the door. They ran up them two at a time, ignoring the downstairs, Lilly in the lead.

"Ha, ha, I'm going to beat you. You don't know which room is yours!" Her dad sprinted by her and into the first room on the left. "I win!"

"Nope, because this isn't the one I want!" Darting out of the room Lilly dove across the hall into another room and abruptly froze. The walls were still just sheetrock, but on the sidewall was a bright blue plastic sign reading "Lilly's Pad"! Lilly instantly loved it and the room, even if she hadn't really picked it herself, because she would have anyway. It was huge, at least three times the size of her old room. Heck, the closet was the size of her old room. But the best part of it was the huge bay window with a built-in seat, just like Punky

Brewster's, from that old show she watched on TV Land reruns!

"Sara and Toni are going to be so jealous!" Lilly squealed with excitement. Maybe moving won't be so bad after all, she thought to herself.

"You know, hon, they can come and stay any weekend they want with you."

Sandy finally strolled in. Lilly turned to get a hug. She grabbed her mother's legs and squeezed tight. Sandy hardly reciprocated.

After searching every inch of the house and loving it, they had a picnic in the empty dining room to christen their new home. Sandwiches, chips, pickles and Ring Dings for dessert. Lilly was back to her old self, talking and laughing with her parents. Of course, her parents knew this was just an up of one of the many ups and downs that would be coming in the next few weeks. Finishing her Ring Ding, Lilly asked to check out the back yard, the one place they had yet to see.

Mom said she would clean up. Hardly hearing the end of her sentence, Lilly and her Dad sprinted out through the back sliding door. Once on the dusty ground she stopped running and put her hands on her hips.

"Hmmm, Yup! Definitely could have a full soccer game here!"

Her dad laughed and offered to build a goal for her. Of course this pleased her to no end. They casually strolled around the perfect square, just under one acre property. Tom thought how it was like a cookie cutter yard: The neighbors had different houses, but the same size and shape yards that all ended at the woods. As Lilly made her way to the edge of the woods, Tom thought about how much the dozens of bushes or fencing needed to separate the yards was going to cost him, an expense he wasn't counting on.

"DAD!"

The sudden yell made his heart jump. He had lost track of where Lilly was. Tom spun around, fearful of what he would see. A branch through her leg? Rabid dog attacking? Sprained ankle in a gopher hole? Thankfully, none of them was true; it was a yell of excitement. He turned to see her jumping up and down and pointing.

"Dad, Dad! I think there is a stream over there! Can we go look?"

He smiled and joined her across the border and into the woods. Tom fondly remembered when he was growing up, playing in the woods and always wanted Lilly to have the same experience. Unfortunately, where they lived now was so overdeveloped that a few bushes on the edge of the road was the closest thing to woods they had. He knew Lilly's friend Sara (the rich kid, he called her) had plenty of woods at her house but she would never go in them with Lilly.

The density of the woods surprised him. There were some paths but they were overgrown. Lilly would probably fix that soon!

"Are your feet ok?"

"They're fine Dad!" Lilly was wearing her favorite sandals that gave little protection the crunching sticks underfoot.

"Well, when we live here you can't be wearing those when you go exploring."

Lilly rolled her eyes. Sure enough, after a few yards, she could see glistening water rushing by in the distance. She started to run until her Dad yelled to slow down and wait for him. She obeyed and held his hand as they stepped over a rotting log.

The stream looked as if it once had been a river. The bank was at least twenty feet wide with an eight-foot slope to the water. But now it was only a three-foot trickle. Lilly looked thrilled, Tom looked horrified. The thought of his daughter falling down the slope, getting knocked out and drowning, burst through his mind. Tom had never been a worrywart, that is until Lilly was born. Then the whole world seemed to change; it became meaner, edges got sharper, and TV shows got dirtier. He felt like an old man with such worries but he didn't care. His daughter was his world and keeping her safe was what mattered.

Lilly started to make her way down the slope. Tom's heart began to pound. Some major rules were going to have to be put in place. He followed after her, trying not to get too dirty. Lilly plunked a hand in the water, pulled it up and watched the water drip off as if it was something she'd never touched before. Tom watched silently, enjoying her youth and curiosity. Lilly then looked downstream towards the house. It took a sharp left and disappeared. Next, she looked upstream and that's when she saw it - a crumbling old brick building about half mile up the way. A massive wheel tilted towards the water, broken off the building, only a huge rock kept it from falling. Her eyes lit up. The endless array of games she could play thee bounced through Lilly's head.

Tom turned to see what was catching Lilly's eye and that is when he saw the mill. In his eyes it was the furthest thing from a playground. It was a crumbling death trap, full of broken glass and rotting wood. "Dear Lord, no," Tom thought.

"Dad, can we?"

Tom's gut was too busy doing flips to answer quickly. "Not now, Lilly, we've got to get back before Mom gets worried."

Lilly looked heartbroken. After asking two more times, she reluctantly clawed her way back up the bank.

As soon as they got back to the yard, Lilly sprinted to the house to tell Mom the good news of what she found. Sandy pretended to be excited while holding back laughter at her husband making a crying face behind their daughter. After Lilly was done raving about it, Tom kissed Sandy to whisper in her ear about how dangerous a place it must be. She didn't seem to care; in fact, she seemed a bit pleased. Shortly after, the three packed up and headed back to the house that none of them wanted to return to.

3

The next few weeks dragged by for the Boyer family. They all thought time would fly by in a blink of an eye but instead it never seemed to end. All the packing, waiting, good-byes, and everything else daily life had to offer made time stand still. But it was now finally upon them. Moving day.

Lilly, Sara and Toni had spent the night sleeping on the floor together in what was soon to be Lilly's old room. They laughed, ate and cried all night. It was hard for them to say good-bye. They had been friends since their earliest of memories.

The morning sunlight hurt Lilly's eyes as she opened them to the empty room. Realizing moving day was finally upon her, tears started to form once again. Sara was still snoring but Lilly could tell Toni was only pretending to sleep. She got up and peed. On the way back to the room, her mother stopped her without a big hug like Dad always gave her in the morning.

"Better wake those two up; we leave in an hour."

Lilly could only nod. She wanted nothing more than to leave right then in her pajamas and not have to say good-bye to them. It was going to be too hard.

At the door she could hear the two whispering. She cupped her ear on the door to hear but couldn't make out anything. Giving up and biting down the urge to just run and hide in the moving truck, Lilly pushed the door open. The two gave her puppy dog eyes. Lilly ran over to them and they all hugged.

For the next hour they hardly let go of each other. At eight AM Sara's mom arrived to bring the two home. That's when the water works began. Tears streamed out of all six eyes. After a ten-minute triple hug, the three had to be physically pulled apart. Lilly felt as if her heart was being ripped out of her chest. She'd never have friends like them again. She just knew it.

It took more than half the ride for Lilly to stop crying. Her Mom kept telling her that everything would be just fine, they already had a trip planned in two weeks for the girls to come visit and she could always talk to them on the phone. But that didn't matter to her. She was leaving them. Only two things gave her comfort: the thought of decorating her new room and exploring the old mill and woods.

This time pulling up to the new house was a different experience. The whole street looked different. Pretty much every house had been built and green grass was everywhere. But to Lilly's horror one major change had taken place. Around the whole house was a white plastic fence. How would she get to the woods? How could her dad do this to her? She wanted to scream at her dad and ask him why he did this but he was in the U-Haul truck. Mom would have to do.

"Ma! How could dad put up a fence around the yard! How will I get to the woods?"

"Calm down, honey, I didn't know a fence was going to be put up either. I'm sure we can figure something out. Now, don't go giving your dad trouble. He's stressed out enough."

Lilly sat fuming in the passenger seat. It was already a horrible day and now the one thing she was excited about was ruined! Mom let the U-Haul pull in first then parked in front of it. Lilly stormed out of the car the second it stopped and ran to the side of the house to check on the fence in the back.

To Lilly's surprise, smack in the middle of the far fence was a gate; on the gate was a sign reading "Lilly's Playland". Her mood turned from rage to joy. She really did have the best dad! Fast as she could she ran to give him a thank you hug.

"Ahh, you deserve it, honey. We just have to go over a lot of rules before you can go exploring out there. OK?" Lilly scrunched her face to pretend she was thinking before nodding.

Sandy lectured the movers on where to put each box, while Tom started to search through them. Lilly sat on her window seat patiently in her new room, waiting for her boxes. Gazing out, she could see a good distance into the woods. The stream occasionally shot a glimmer her way. It must be a better view during the winter, she thought. Straining her eyes she tried hard to see the old mill. She wanted so badly for the movers to bring the box up with her Mickey Mouse binoculars inside of it.

Just as she was feeling confident that the view was etched in her mind, an overly sweaty behemoth of a man clomped in with a box that he placed down not too gently. If Lilly hadn't met him early today and learned his name was Todd, she would have screamed at the sight of him. He wore white painters pants and a white tank top stained with what looked to be soda. Pretty much every inch of him was dripping with sweat. He faked a smile for Lilly. Wiping his forehead with a red rag he produced from his pants, he turned and left. Lilly waited a second to hear his footsteps on the stairs before diving into the box. She hesitated opening it at the site of still wet sweat marks on the sides and top.

To Lilly's disappointment, the box was one of the many that was filled with dolls and toys. Her binoculars were in her fragile box. While rifling through the dolls, looking for one to show the view to, a stampede of steps started on the stairs accompanied by shouting. It must be something heavy. Lilly retreated to the window seat to stay out of the way. Sure enough Todd was back, but this time with Tito, a man half his size. They carried Lilly's white dresser and she was overjoyed to see it. Finally the room was going to start turning into hers.

By two o'clock, the movers had left and the house was a mess of boxes, bubble wrap and foam peanuts. Again the three enjoyed a picnic in the house; only this time they sat at the dining room table that was covered in boxes. It took effort to catch one another's eyes over them.

"Dad, can I go explore the woods after we eat?"

Tom, who was starting to look as sweaty as Todd the mover, sighed. "Sweetie, we need to unpack first. Okay? Tomorrow afternoon, I promise. Let's just get settled in tonight so we have beds to sleep in."

Lilly started to pout but she understood. She did want to arrange her room. It's just the old building held such surprises that she couldn't wait.

The sun was starting to set as Lilly was hanging up a poster of Jessica Simpson. Her mom walked in and helped her straighten it.

"So what do you think, kid?"

"I love it, Ma. I just hope there are a lot of kids on the street."

"Well, we'll find out soon. The realtor said that most of the houses have been sold and the other families should be moving in within the next few weeks."

The thought of having to make new friends terrified Lilly but she wasn't going to let her mom know it, Dad maybe, but not mom.

"Are you ready for your first shower in your new home?" Sandy tried to make it sound fun. She couldn't figure out why it was so hard for her to be close to her daughter. There was no doubt she loved her. Well, at least she knew she had to love her, yet she always felt awkward around her. She had never been good with kids her whole life, but she thought that would change with having one. But it didn't. When Lilly was a baby, it was much easier but ever since she was five, she found it hard to talk and open up to her. It was a problem that bothered her tremendously. One she never talked to Tom about. He was just so good with Lilly, hell, any kid for that matter. He had wanted a second kid so bad but she purposely made excuses and sabotaged efforts of becoming pregnant because she was just too scared to have to deal with another. There were times she felt like she might die from the guilt of it alone.

"It really does have a seat in it, huh, Mom?"
Sandy was too busy sulking to hear her daughter. Lilly looked at her and rolled her eyes. Mom always did this to her, just zoned out. Dad never did though.

Since the shower had a seat, she played with Rex, her showering buddy of five years, for an extra long time. Grandpa gave her Rex right before he died. At first she didn't want a dinosaur toy but when he died, it became special to her. A toy she figured would always shower with her. Now, still somewhat wet, she wore her yellow Tweety bathrobe brushing her hair in her room. Bored, she strolled to the window to check out the night view. She could barely make anything out except for the pale purple sky. It was just too hard to see with her light on. Ready to give up looking, something caught her eye. She stopped brushing her hair and got closer to the window. There it was again. Between black slashes that must have been trees, something was glowing. White? No, no. Blue. Yes, it was definitely blue, and glowing, and it was coming closer to the house.

4

"DAAAAAAAAAAAD!"

Within a second Tom was in Lilly's room, razor in hand, face covered in foam, towel wrapped tight. "What, what is it?" On the short rush over Tom's overactive mind was racing once again - bookcase fell on her, robber, or scissors injury. But luckily, as always, she wasn't bleeding or in pain, but she did look awfully scared.

"There's a ghost in the woods!"

Tom darted to the window and looked out. Barely able to see through the glaring gold of the setting sun, he shaded his eyes and searched harder. For a second he thought he saw something but he couldn't find it again. After a few seconds he pulled his face away leaving a fading breath stain and a small smudge of shaving cream. "What did you see honey?" He started to crouch down to his daughter but quickly realized he would expose himself.

"It was blue, Daddy! Blue! And it was coming towards the house."

"What do you mean by blue?"

"Glowing, it looked like the big glow sticks you buy me at the circus."

Tom knew those glow sticks well; they cost more than the tickets themselves. He turned back to the window for another glance and once again saw nothing. "Well, it could have been someone with a flashlight walking through the woods." The instant he finished saying that, he felt uncomfortable at the thought himself. Someone in his backyard? No, no that would not do. Why would anyone be out there though? Maybe it was just her imagination.

"You sure you saw something honey?"

Lilly gave him her well practiced please *believe me, it's true daddy e*yes. Tom leaned over and picked her up for comfort, whether it was for him or her he didn't know.

The curtains in her room had yet to be hung up. Standing now half naked with his daughter in his arm he felt vulnerable. He always avoided standing by a window when it was dark out and he had the lights on. Someone could be standing ten feet away and you would never see him. But he could see you clear as day. This Tom knew, as a kid he had a neighbor who never closed his shades at night. If it had been a young girl his own age, Tom would have been thrilled. But it wasn't; it was a three hundred pound, very hairy single man who had no problems walking around in his underwear.

"You know what, sweetie? When we get back from dinner, we'll put your curtains up so you won't have to look out."

Lilly couldn't figure out how curtains would stop a ghost from killing her but she knew when to stop arguing with her dad. She hated making him feel bad; he always wore his hurt on his face.

That night in bed with the curtains up, Lilly could hardly sleep, not because of the blue light but because it was a new place. On vacations she always got scared and slept in the same bed with her parents. She wanted to now but she needed to prove she was a big girl or else Dad wouldn't let her explore the woods alone. That was another thing keeping her up, being excited at the thought of going into them tomorrow.

Per order of Dad, Lilly put on sweat pants, sneakers, and a long sleeve t-shirt. Of course, she made them all match, with a blue and charcoal colored theme. Even though it was pretty warm, her dad wanted her to wear it, so she did. He must be worried about her getting cuts from bushes or something. Confident she met the requirements and looking good, she nodded to herself and headed downstairs.

Sandy was laughing at her husband when Lilly walked in. She couldn't help it, he was a dork. Not only had he dressed for a thousand mile hike, he had also packed a survival kit that could help you live through a nuclear attack. It was times like this that she questioned her ill feelings toward him.

"Your dad is a dork!"

"Tell me something I didn't know!" Lilly blurted. The comment them all off-guard making it even funnier.

"Well, are you ready to go, my little explorer?" Tom flung his overly stuffed backpack onto his shoulder over several layers of shirts.

"You do realize we're just going into the backyard, right?" Lilly smirked. Tom looked at Lilly and rolled his eyes jokingly before marching out the back door.

At the gate Tom stopped and looked down at Lilly. "Now, my young cadet, during this journey you will be given many rules. Rules you must follow if you want your wilderness privileges to stay intact. The rules are put forth for your own safety and my peace of mind. Do you promise to follow the rules?"

Looking up at her father, she wanted to act as if she didn't care, but she did. She wanted to be able to explore and play anytime, maybe with new friends. "I promise, sir!" Lilly yelled with her best army guy impression.

After taking a second to consider the promise, Tom started again. "Rule number one! Never, ever, ever go into the woods without telling your mother or me first."

She nodded to agree.

"Hep, hep, hep two, three, four!" Tom started a goofy march that Lilly followed giggling.

Tom didn't really know which way to go at first but figured it would be best to head for the stream and follow it to the mill since Lilly would want to go there the most. After stepping over branches and crunching old leaves, they reached the stream edge. Tom guessed it was about forty yards from the house. Since there wasn't a path right to it, he made a mental note to clear one so his daughter wouldn't scratch up her legs. He took off his pack and placed it on the ground. "Whew I'm tired, should we take a break?"

"Daaaad! We just started!"

"I'm just teasing!" He pulled a white, inch-thick rope that was smooth and soft to the touch out of the backpack. He had gotten up early to go to Home Depot to buy it and some other items. Lilly looked curiously at him while his eyes darted from tree to tree. After a long determination, Tom picked a thick old tree several feet from the bank edge and started tying the rope around it. He was never good at tying knots so he made five of them, just to be safe. The rest of the rope he flung over the edge of the bank. A few feet of it splashed in the water and started to flow downstream. Carefully he held on tight to the rope and backed down the red rock. "See that, honey? If you're ever going to come down to the stream, I want you to use this rope; that way you won't get hurt."

Lilly went down the rope the way her father did. At first she wanted to yell at him and say she didn't need a rope, but it did make it pretty easy so she decided not to. Tom cut the excess rope and pocketed it while Lilly looked around.

"Well, which way next, partner?" Lilly pointed to the death trap, just as he expected. They started to walk along the clay bed towards it, glass crunching under feet every so often. Tom wanted so badly to forbid Lilly from stepping foot in the stream but he knew it wouldn't work. That's why he put the rope up. At least if she's going to go down here it would be a tiny bit safer.

"Hey Lil, never take your sneakers off down here, OK? I know the water might be tempting in the summer, but there is way too much glass."
Lilly half heartily said OK while trying to hop from rock to rock.

In a matter of a few minutes, they were at the mill, factory, or whatever it used to be. It must have been massive once, but now half of it was in rubble, the other half looked decrepit but intact. Just before the giant old wheel, the clay streambed turned into concrete. Tom's breathing started to speed up at the thought of his daughter playing on the wheel and it finally letting go after hundreds of years. He told her to never touch it. Again he got an absented minded *okay*.

It took no effort to get back up to dry land. An old staircase sat crumbling, but usable next to the mill wall. Once up the stairs they walked to the front. Vines covered almost every inch of the ancient bricks, and, judging by the trees that were growing inside its structure; parts of the building had to have collapsed some time ago.

5

Walking along the outside of the building, Tom was baffled to not find an old road that led to it. It seemed to be in the middle of nowhere. From the outside it looked as if it was built in the eighteen hundreds. He made a mental note to look it up on the Internet.

"Dad! Look!" Lilly was hunched down next to a pile of bricks three times her height. He walked over and looked down at what she was examining. It was a fire pit with a half-burnt *Hustler* magazine. The cover was half burnt off and a shot of a woman's bald crotch stared up at him. Tom quickly kicked it out of view.

"What was that lady doing?"

Tom avoided the answer by picking it up and throwing it farther away. Lilly knew it must have been one of those magazines they keep behind the counters. Quickly Tom scanned the vicinity for any more items he should shield Lilly from, but didn't find much more. The area looked to be a frequent party zone for teenagers; makeshift log seats, trash, and dozens of beer bottles. Tom remembered areas like this well from growing up. Again his paranoia kicked in, what if Lilly came out here when a group of kids stoned out of their gourds were sitting around? The chances of them being out here before dark were slim, but still. . . .

At the far end of the old mill, one whole part of the structure still stood. It looked to be three stories high and in good condition. Lilly immediately ran for the doorway. Tom couldn't help but think how the stress of being a dad would kill him at an early age. He bolted after her and stopped her just inside. There he pulled out two flashlights and took a firm grip of her hand. The inside was oddly dark for such a sunny day. Tom and Lilly walked slowly and carefully. Every step was taken only after a light searched the dirty, dust-covered floor. Tom was surprised that it was made out of wood, it felt strong though. After a few steps, Tom figured the room was a complete square, barren of anything. It must have been a reception area. The only thing he did see, but hid from Lilly, was a sleeping bag along the far wall. Teens will do it anywhere, he thought.

Lilly's flashlight found the entranceway into the mill first, then Tom's light shone on it as well. His heart raced wondering if they should go through the massive archway. If he didn't let Lilly explore the whole place, he knew she would come back alone someday to satisfy her curiosity. Their clasped hands were starting to sweat. He could feel Lilly taking shorter and shorter steps. That was a good sign. If she became scared of this place, she'd stay away.

He searched the edges of the archway and concluded to himself that a door had never been on it. It was two feet thick and had no hinges. He then shone his light through the black frame. Within a second he felt as if he was in a horror movie. For the beam of light revealed a long hallway with so many doors that the beam just died out half way down it. Objects of all sorts strewed the hall; desks, chairs, sheets, papers, clothing, but oddest of all - dozens of light bulbs, most smashed. Tom could feel Lilly backing away, he wanted to as well.

"Dad, it's scary."

"There is nothing to be scared of, hon. It's just an old building."

"But what about the ghost I saw last night? What if it lives here?" Tom felt the hair on the back of his neck stick up, for fear of a ghost but more so of a drug addict or some wacko who called this home. He tried to rationalize with himself. This was a safer town, which was one of the big reasons for coming here. This town had no bums, or druggies, did they?

"Do you want to go back out, Lil?"

"Yeah." Her voice was tiny and filled with fear, not one Tom wanted to ever hear again. He started to back away from the hall but his eyes stayed fix on it, almost mesmerized. Finally he started to turn back to the outside door. That's when it caught his eye. A tiny streak of light flashed in the hallway. It was so sudden that he couldn't even be sure what he saw was real but that didn't lessen the fear it caused. He forced the panic down and tried his best to slowly walk back to the outside door, which seemed to be almost a wall of white light since his eyes had adjusted to the dark.

Once outside Lilly finally let go of Tom's hand to rub her eyes, just as he was doing. Lilly walked back over to the party zone and sat on the well-worn log.

"Can I have some water, Dad?" Tom sat with her and pulled out the water. As they sipped it, Tom glared at the building, desperately wishing it wasn't in his backyard.

The rest of the woods seemed pretty boring compared to the mill. It seemed a bit funny to Tom how the actual nature part of the woods seemed humdrum and the man-made part was exciting. As they explored, Tom set out a strict guideline of how far each of three ways Lilly was allowed to go into the woods by herself. The basic rule was she had to be able to see the house. Tom wanted to take back that rule when Lilly climbed up on a pile of bricks at the mill and blurted out, "I can still see the house!" But he was now confident that her fear would keep her out of it, for a few years at least.

At the end of the tour that only took an hour and twenty minutes, Tom stopped Lilly by the gate to the house. He knelt down to speak to his daughter, eye to eye. "Now, I know you're a big girl. . . you know the rules and I know you'll follow them. But here is the last one." He took off his backpack and started to rummage through it.

"Anytime you go in the woods alone, you have to take one of these with you." Tom handed Lilly a Motorola walkie-talkie. It was a good one, or, at least, it should be for how much he paid for them this morning. Lilly's eyes widened.

"That's for me?" She excitedly grabbed the blue talkie and pushed the button; it let out a loud squeal being too close to the other one. Tom took a few steps back with his.

"Roger Wilko, are you there?"

"Sure am, Dad!" Lilly thought of it as a great toy to play with, Tom thought of it as a life saving device. As long as she left one in the kitchen and took one with her when she went in to the woods, he could always keep in touch with her. Tom was feeling better about letting his only child play in the woods, but he still wished he could stop being such a paranoid person. Then again, what's the harm in being safe?

6

The rest of the day Lilly spent playing with her walkie-talkie even though she was only talking to herself. By bedtime Dad forced her to leave them in the kitchen to charge. She wanted to take it to bed and leave one in his room, but Mom wouldn't allow that.

After getting tucked in by both her mom and dad, Lilly couldn't fall asleep. She was fully unpacked, (her parents had weeks of work ahead of them) leaving her with nothing to do tomorrow. Lilly laid in bed not knowing what the next day would hold. It was officially summer break and she had no friends. Upset, she left her bed and headed for the window seat to pout, just like Punky did in the show. Only it wasn't raining out as it always was when Punky was upset. Lilly twisted the plastic stick to let in the soft moonlight through the blinds. This time she could see the yard much better since her light was off.

Just when she was finally getting sleepy and bored of looking at nothing moving but branches in the wind, the blue light appeared again. Fear shot through her body. It was much worse than earlier in the day when Dad wanted to go down that hall. This froze her, she couldn't move. Not even a blink. The light traveled slowly through the woods, appearing and disappearing behind trees. Lilly wanted nothing more than to let a scream out. No, she was a big girl, a grown up, they don't scream. Even if there was a ghost outside?

This time the light did not disappear as it did the night before. She sat there watching it move for several minutes. Slowly the fear released its grip just enough for her to blink and wet her eyes. Mickey Mouse! Her binoculars! She left them out just in case the ghost came back. Remembering this enabled her to burst from fear's grip and run to her dresser where they lay waiting. Without hesitating she ran back to the window and found the light was much closer to the house. The plastic was cold against her eyes. Without success she tried to find the light through the eyepiece, but she could only see darkness. It took six times of looking back and forth before catching it through the toy lens.

It was brighter and bigger than she thought but she still couldn't tell what it was. Her fear of it being a ghost had left. It wasn't wavy like a ghost should be, or so she thought it should be. It looked solid and strong. Like a glow-stick. But much, much bigger. Closer. It was almost to the fence, and for Lilly that was as brave as she could be.

"DAAAAAAAAAAAAAAD!" She darted out of the room and down the hall. Her parent's room seemed to be ten times farther away than in the old house. It used to be right next-door, now three doors lay between them. Before she even hit the closed door it swung open, stopping Lilly in her tracks. The image of a monster already gotten to her parents flashed in her mind, something big, drippy and green chewing on their arms. But nope, just Dad in his blue striped boxers, scared and concerned.

"What is it, baby?" Lilly resumed her run and attached herself to his legs, crying.

"The light is in the backyard again!"

Tom picked her up and did a half jog to her window. He sneakily peaked out of the slats making sure not to scare whatever it was away.

"Where was it, honey?" Lilly pointed. But it was gone. Tom tried to find it for a solid two minutes, during which Sandy snored down the hall. Finally, he gave up and tried to put her back to bed.

"It was probably just your imagination, honey."

Lilly put on her angry face. "NO, I saw it!"

Tom sighed. "I believe you. Who knows, maybe it's a giant firefly!"

She did not find that humorous, Tom could tell by the way she crossed her arms over her chest. It took another ten minutes for him to convince her to go back to bed. She refused, wanting to sleep with them. Of course, Lilly won and got to sleep in their bed. She didn't want to, big girls sleep alone. But she was scared, really scared.

The next three days Lilly didn't step foot in the woods. Not only because she was scared but also because her parents kept her busy with other things around the house and exploring the town. The nights, on the other hand, were different. She spent them all in their bed. Each night the same thing happened. Lilly would try to sleep in her room, see the light, and then run to their room. Sandy was starting to get really annoyed, she needed her sleep. It didn't matter that she didn't have a job yet and could sleep to whenever she wanted.

After the fourth night Tom and Sandy discussed what to do. Tom was the one who decided it was best to let her stay with them for a while, much to Sandy's disapproval. He rationalized by saying how a new house and a new town can be hard on a kid. He knew there wasn't really a light. It was just her way dealing with the move. At least that's what he wanted to think.

"Two more nights, NO MORE!" Sandy had bargained with Tom. What was wrong with her? She knew the kid just needed attention and love, yet she kept finding herself being snotty to her and pushing her aside in the bed. She really was the worst mother ever. She thought to herself.

The last night that Sandy was going to allow was upon them. Like clockwork, Lilly burst in. Up until last night she would ask permission to stay with them, not now. She just ran and jumped right in the middle. Sandy propped herself up on one elbow and kissed her daughter goodnight for the sole purpose of giving her husband a dirty look. Tom got the message and tried to talk Lilly into staying in her room. She refused. Tom, being the good guy peacekeeper, as always, suggested he stay with Lilly in her room. Grudgingly, Lilly agreed.

Lilly entered her room like a scared cat in a rocking chair factory. She stayed as far away from the window as possible. Tom tucked her in and checked outside to make her feel safe. He glanced around half-heartily, knowing he wasn't going to see anything. And he didn't. Little did he know that the blue light was out there, just not on.

7

It took a few more days of not seeing the light before Lilly started to forget it and feel ready to explore the woods alone. Dad was starting his first day at his new job. He did something that Lilly couldn't really understand, all she knew is it had to do with money and computers. Mom was inside painting the extra bedroom. She gave her the walkie-talkie and headed out. Following the rules she put her pink sweat pants on, even though the June heat was starting.

Lilly stood at the gate trying to delay going in. Even though with the bright daylight it was far from scary. She re-tied her shoes twice, put her hair up in a scrunchy and did a few jumping jacks for no reason. Then she was ready. She casually walked on the path her dad recently cut for her to the stream. On the way she picked up a perfect walking stick. Long, smooth and sturdy. Like most people she loved to have a stick in hand whenever walking through wooded areas, it made her feel more comfortable, secure. At the water Lilly tossed the stick down the edge and used the rope to help herself down. She splashed the stick in the water for a bit, felt around for slimy, cool rocks, found a few and put them in her pocket.

Lilly realized fast that the woods, which held such promise, were, well, pretty boring when you're alone. She started to get depressed and angry with her parents again for making her move away from her friends. They were probably together right now, dancing in Sara's room. She wanted to be there more than anything. Bored and angry, Lilly tossed her stick back up the hill and started to climb the rope. Her feet slipped a few times since it had rained the day before and the clay was still moist. After failing to make it three times, she let go of the rope and dried her now sweating hands on her shirt. Satisfied that they were dry, she took a solid grip on it again. If she didn't make it this time, she was going to have to look for another way up or radio mom for help. Her feet still slipped a bit but she started to make headway. All of a sudden it felt as if the rope was being pulled up. But it couldn't be. After another step she knew it was being pulled up; she hadn't moved her hands yet she was farther up the hill. Panic overcame her. Who - or what was pulling her up? Should she let go, fall down the hill? It might be safer than what was up there.

"Mom, is that you?" There was no answer. The top edge was coming closer. Lilly glanced at her walkie-talkie wanting to use it, but knowing she'd have to let go to do that. She could almost see over the ledge now. Lilly decided to let go and take her chances down by the water, but her subconscious fear of falling backwards, getting cut up and maybe even smashing her head open wouldn't let her. She was now at eye level with the ground; thousands of leaves came into view. Lilly quickly scanned for who or what was pulling her up, but saw nothing. The rope disappeared behind the tree it was tied to.

Lilly tried to think of a time she had been more scared but couldn't. The fear of wetting herself was also creeping into her mind. She clenched her bladder best she could. Two more tugs and she was able to let go of the rope to grab dirt. Without hesitation, she threw her leg over the edge safely up on the ground. Breathing heavily, covered in leaves and dirt, Lilly feared looking up at whatever just helped her up. She could hear the squish of wet leaves as someone or something came towards her. Tears started to leak out of her eyes. The squishing stopped and Lilly knew whoever it was, was right in front of her. Then she saw it - a brilliantly bright blue stick came down fast to the ground, two feet from her face.

8

Lilly tried to slip her hand down to the walkie-talkie. That's when the hand came towards her face. It was gloved in dirty white cloth. But instead of pulling her hair as she expected, it scooped her up by her armpits, gently. Within a second she was on her feet being brushed off. She wanted to scream but, after seeing the eyes, she knew she didn't have to. They were gray, not a sad gray but a kind, loving, caring gray, sort of like hers. Lilly instantly felt calmed and mesmerized by them.

What the old man was wearing, on the other hand, was not as settling. The tuxedo must have been over a hundred years old, wrinkled, ripped, dirty, pilled, and just plain shabby looking. It was hard to pick the oddest part of the outfit. It had to be either the black sequined bow tie, the cloak or the overly tall top hat. His features were odd as well: a big crooked nose, gray bushy eyebrows and a six-inch-long white goatee.

"Well, now! Look at how soiled you are, Lilly!" Still scared and confused, hearing her name made Lilly's head spin. Did she know him? She sure as heck had never seen him before.

"I do fear it was my fault you got soiled. I just thought you could use some assistance climbing up; the bank can be mighty slippery, you know."

Lilly just stared at him, wide-eyed and confused. The strange man felt awkward and started to straighten out his frilly white bow tie.

"Who... who... are... you? Are you the ghost? How do you know my name?"

A crooked smile crossed the man's face as if satisfied at the girl's choice of questions. "I know everything and everyone that enters these woods. They have been my home for as long as I can remember. As for being a ghost. . .". The man rapped his chest with his fist a few times.

Lilly seemed to giggle a bit. "What's your name?" Lilly inquired.

The man resumed his speech with one hand holding the lapel of his coat and the other skillfully swishing around his glowing cane. It was spoken as if he was putting on a play. "As for my name, my dear Lilly, I do not know."
Lilly looked at him genuinely puzzled. She was so interested in this strange man that she had completely forgotten that she was talking to a stranger alone in the woods, which broke her dad's rule number 12. "How could you not know your name?"

This question seemed to puzzle the old man, he arched one eyebrow then the other. Finally he answered. "Well, it's a long story. How about you call me whatever you want."

"Mister, I don't think I'm allowed to name you."

"But, of course, you are, Lilly, I'm giving you permission."

Lilly was intrigued by the idea of being able to name a grown-up herself. All sorts of names ran through her head - Bob, Justin, Rumplestilskin, Prince, Thane, Tom, Bubba, but none seemed to fit him. The man started to twirl his stick in the air, making a magnificent glowing blue circle. "That's it! I'll call you Mr. Bluestick!"

He thought for a minute by tapping a finger on his chin. "I love it!" Mr. Bluestick offered his hand to her.

The fear of talking to a stranger finally set in. She remembered seeing some show at the mall once where they told her to run far away and tell her parents if a stranger ever tried to touch her. But was he a stranger now? She did name him after all, and he seems so nice. Lilly took his hand. It felt as if his hand was made of plastic, it was hard and rumpled. It was odd but only for a second as Lilly forgot about it quickly. It was a fast, hearty handshake. Then Mr. Bluestick tipped his hat to her.

Both of them smiled at the thought of making a new friend. There was silence between them. If it were two adults, it might have been awkward but for them it wasn't. Finally, after several minutes of examining each other thoroughly, Lilly spoke. "How come your cane glows?"

Mr. Bluestick picked up the cane with both hands, raised an eyebrow and suddenly the cane went dark. Lilly clapped, and he gave a little bow before making it go back on. "It is illuminated in the color of my home. I miss it there and this helps remind me of it."

Lilly was confused by the answer but didn't want to be rude and ask again. Besides, it always made her feel dumb when she had to ask things again. She gave a smile and nodded.

"So, you were what I saw outside of my window? Not a ghost?"

Mr. Bluestick had a deep laugh to go with his deep voice. "You thought I was a ghost? I'm so sorry, my dear! I just like to go for walks at night, I used to stroll through a big clearing where the deer would graze at night. Sometimes they would come right up to me and eat out of my hand! It was right where your house is now. So I still walk by it some nights to see if there is any."

"Wow, deer? In my backyard! That's so cool!"

Again the silence crept up upon then. This time it was much shorter though.

"Where do you live Mr. Bluestick?"

He smiled again. Lilly couldn't tell if it was a happy smile or a polite one, like how her mom always made her smile at her relatives' houses. " Why you visited my home not too long ago, you and your father!" With the cane he pointed to the mill.

Lilly's heart sank a bit. How could such a nice man live in such a scary place? Maybe he wasn't so nice.

Mr. Bluestick saw Lilly's face scrunch up in disgust at his home. He quickly spoke to put her at ease. "Oh, my dear! You didn't see anything of my home. What you saw was what I call the creepy walkway! It's there to keep people away. My place is clean and wonderful, hidden deep inside."

Lilly's face seemed to lessen a bit, but he could tell she was still scared. "Don't worry, my dear, someday after we have become good friends I'll take you there."

At the mention of friends her smile came back. "I'm your friend?"

"Well I sure hope you will be my friend, Lilly!" She smiled big, it made him smile.

"Of course, I'll be your friend! You'll be my first friend I've made here!"

The two celebrated with big smiles and giddy movements until Lilly's walkie-talkie crackled. "Lilly, Lilly, honey, come in for lunch." Mr. Bluestick looked curiously at the device on her hip.

"That was my mom, I'd better get going. How will I find you?"

"No need, I will find you whenever you play out here."

Lilly said bye and excitedly started to run home to mom, not wanting to wait to tell her about her new friend.

9

Lilly held her mother's attention for around thirty seconds. Sandy was thrilled to hear she met a new friend, but once she heard his description and name she tuned out. No need to listen to a child's imagination. She finished the peanut and butter jelly sandwiches and placed then in front of Lilly. She kept giving her daughter *uh huh's and oh's* absent-mindedly, all the while watching "The Makeover Story" on TLC. Lilly could tell that her mother didn't care. She didn't let it ruin her excitement.

It was a few more hours until Dad came home and Lilly could hardly wait to tell him the news. He would care. She occupied the time by calling Sara and Toni; of course Toni was at Sara's. She started to tell them about her wonderful new friend but she kept hearing giggles in the background. "Who is that?"

"What? Oh, that's the TV. So, anyways, he has a. . .blue stick?" Toni replied with a giggle. Lilly started to feel silly and stupid for telling them. She heard a rustle on the phone and she instantly knew someone else was on the line besides the three of them.

"Sara, I know someone is there. Who's over?"
Saying that brought laughter from the three girls on the phone. Toni snorted, Sara giggled and the mystery girl cackled loudly. Lilly felt like a fool, someone else had taken her place. She should have known it, too. The way they acted the other week when they came up to visit. They were totally different, acting as if they didn't care about anything. At the time Lilly just figured Sara was jealous that someone finally had a bigger, better house than she did. But now she knew that it wasn't that it was a new friend, she was no longer needed.

Lilly hung up the phone, not finding out and pretending not to care who the new friend was. Immediately she assumed her familiar crying position, face buried in the pillow. Tears flowed for the next hour. Her two best friends had betrayed her. They knew her better than anyone in the world. They promised to be friends forever. Now, just because she moves away, they replace her? Lilly heard footsteps at her door. She'd deliberately not closed it so mom would see her like this.

Sandy almost felt as if she was having an anxiety attack. Her daughter was bawling her eyes out and she had to talk to her. She was no good at this. Carefully she placed her steps on the carpet, trying not to alert Lilly of her presence. Having her spin around and talk to her would be too quick of an assault to handle. She needed to take this slowly.

A solid two minutes went by while she stood like a statue listening to the quiet whimper. She felt so bad for Lilly. She vividly remembered those days as a kid, crying her eyes out because someone picked on her at school. But her mom never came in to talk to her. Nope, one good yell of *"Stop your damn crying and do the dishes"* would always fix her. And she turned out fine, right? Slowly she raised her arm to glance at her Timex. Twenty or so minutes and Tom will be home. He can handle this. Just as carefully as she came in, she snuck out backwards. Lilly heard her mom leave and cried a little harder.

It wasn't long after that Dad arrived in her room with open arms. She quickly attached herself to him, not letting go. It only took ten minutes of Dad talking for her to settle down. Lilly was still bitter and angry but at least the tears had stopped, for now. Finally calm, she told her dad about her new friend, her only friend here.

"I swear, Dad he was so cool!" Tom's gut was twisting in a knot but he tried to relax it, knowing she was just using her imagination. Lilly always had a vivid one. But this story was odd compared to most of her stories. Usually they ranged from monsters to ghosts in the woods, but an old man in a tux? The story made Tom uneasy, but then again he remembered reading an article about how young kids her age often make up imaginary friends to deal with life changes. It's very common. Maybe this will be good for her. So being the good father he tries to be, he entertained her imagination.

"Really? Wow, I wish I had a friend like that!"

"I'm sure you can meet him sometime! He said anytime I go out there he'd meet me!"

"That's fantastic! See, and you were worried you wouldn't make any friends here!" In her excitement Lilly pretty much forgot about Sara, Toni and the mystery girl.

Trying to cheer her up even more, Tom suggested pizza for dinner even though Sandy already had one planned. Lilly ate with vigor as she rambled on and on about Mr. Bluestick. Tom warned Sandy ahead of time to go along with whatever she was talking about.

Lilly kept giving her mom odd looks and Sandy felt guilty. It was too much for her to take. The guilt has been building from the day she found out she was pregnant, but today she hit her lowest point ever. Leaving her kid to cry alone, what kind of mother was she? As Tom and Lilly laughed at some childish joke, Sandy stood up with tears in her eyes.

"I. . .I. . .I." Sandy said with gasps in between each before sprinting out of the room.

10

Tom was in shock and Lilly was pretending that nothing had happened while she ate her slice. He looked at his daughter as if she would have an explanation as to why his wife ran off like she did. It took him a long thirty seconds to unglue himself from the chair and run after her.

The bedroom door was locked just as he figured it would be. As he lightly knocked on the door, he wracked his brain trying to figure out what he did. In a muffled voice, she told him to go away. Without even looking, he reached up and retrieved the small key-like piece of metal from the doorframe. As he crouched down and stuck it in the tiny hole, he thought of how stupid these locks really are. You can pick them with anything, or, if you turned hard enough, they snapped. No good for protection, just to keep people from seeing you naked, he guessed.

The door slid open slowly, making Sandy even more upset. The last thing she wanted now was her overly understanding husband to use a soothing voice to try and coax what was wrong with her. She pulled up the yellow flannel cover over her face. It was something she'd done her whole life. Anytime conflict arose and a serious discussion was at hand with her parents or a lover, she couldn't look at them. She would hide her face so they couldn't see her. Yes, it was childish but it gave her tremendous amounts of comfort. She could recall one particular fight she had with a boyfriend (long before Tom) that ended in a physical fight because she couldn't look at him. It was over something stupid, too; the topic slipped her mind but the fight didn't. After twenty minutes under her pillow, Jack, who was three times her size, tried to take it away from her. She held on with all her might and ended up getting thrown, by accident, into the end table, causing her to get twenty-three stitches and a nasty scar on the back of her neck which she now hides with her hair. All that and yet she still stayed with him for another six months.

"Sandy, what's wrong?" The soothing voice shot through her like a bullet, sending anger to her arms, making her choke the pillow some more. Then she could feel him sink onto the bed and shimmy over to her. She tensed up even more. There was no way Tom was getting this out of her. No way. His arm went across her body attempting to embrace her. She moved to the edge of the bed, signaling him to stay away. Tom thought he was in big trouble even though she often backed away from him.

"What did I do?"

Sandy felt even worse now. She didn't want him blaming himself, though in a way it was always his fault. He was such an apologetic man that he would end up waiting on her hand and foot the next three days if she told him that it was her fault. Hell, he should anyway - having a kid was his fault.

"Look. . .I'm. . .uh. . .just getting my period and I'm. . .emotional. With the move I'm just stressed that's all. Please, just give me some alone time, okay?"

Tom didn't believe it for a second but knew when to leave her alone. She would tell him what was wrong when she was ready, or after he pestered her for five hours when she was in a better mood. He caressed her hair for a moment, kissed her hand that was turning white from squeezing the pillow, and got up. Before leaving he looked back and commented on how she looked. "You know, that is one trait Lilly definitely got from you, except she usually hides on her stomach." Tom then quietly snuck out of the room and shut the door to hear the sobs return, louder than before.

Lilly quickly got bored at the table alone. The pizza was delicious, extra pepperoni her favorite. Originally she worried about not having good pizza here but that now was no longer a worry. Not being entertained by eating alone, Lilly decided to stroll around the house while munching on a slice. Room to room she walked around humming and biting. Some pieces of pepperoni fell off but she quickly picked them up, being a good girl. She was going to watch some TV, but that was one of Dad's rules that he actually stuck to, no TV watching during dinner, no exceptions. So instead the walk continued past the TV and to the back door to look out into the yard.

To her wonderful surprise the former ghost, now friend, was out there. She could see the blue stick bouncing around. At first her stomach dropped, it was hard to not think of it as a ghost. Thinking Mom and Dad would be gone for some time, Lilly ran back to the pizza box to grab three slices; she piled them messily on a thin paper plate. Then it was off to the fridge to get a can of Coke.

Lilly had a hard time opening the door with her hands full so she didn't bother closing it as she sprinted across the lawn. Nearing the gate she could see that Mr. Bluestick was heading away from her. She shouted out his name. The light stopped moving, spun around and started to come closer. Lilly had to keep telling herself it was just her friend as the light came closer. It was a scary sight. A glowing stick bobbing and weaving through the air in dark night. If she didn't know it was him, Lilly would have peed her pants.

"Well, hello there, my little friend! I didn't think we would meet again so soon."

"I thought you might like some pizza," Lilly said, proud of herself being able to offer someone something.

"Pizza? Now what might that be?"

Lilly was confused that he had no clue what pizza was. "You don't know? It's my favorite supper," Lilly said unsure.

"Well, Madame, in that case I shall taste it."
Leaving his white gloves on, he picked up the top slice from the wrong end. Lilly giggled and showed him how to pick it up. Mr. Bluestick bit in, chewed and moved the food around as if it was fine wine. His eyebrows danced as he evaluated the taste.

"Well, I must say Madame has a wonderful palette."
Lilly handed him the plate and put the soda on the fence post for him, giggling at the odd word he just said. He eyed the can with interest.

"Hmmm, I have seen the receptacles before but never have tasted its contents." Lilly knew he must have been teasing her. Everyone has eaten pizza and drunk soda before!

"Lilly!" A shout came from the house just as Mr. Bluestick was about to take his second bite. Instantly the stick was shut off, the sudden darkness unnerved Lilly.

"That's my dad. Want to meet him?"

Mr. Bluestick started to back away. "No, no. Not yet, my dear, not yet. May I take this nourishment back with me?" Lilly nodded and he stuffed the can into his pants pocket and started back into the woods.

"I thank you a million times, my dear, until we meet again!" Lilly waved bye and ran back to the house, disappointed that Dad wasn't going to meet her new friend.

"Dad, Dad, Dad. . .Mr. Bluestick was just here! You just missed him!" Lilly looked back over her shoulder to see if his light was back on - only darkness. Tom looked very displeased that she was by the woods.

"Lilly, you know the rules!" Tom said sternly, trying to be the tough dad he wasn't.

"But dad, it was Mr. Bluestick!"

He let her in, shut the door, and locked it. For a long few seconds he stared into the woods, he knew it was just her imagination but it was still nerve-wracking. Why can't she just have a fuzzy bunny that lived in the fireplace as an imaginary friend? Not some old man who lives in the woods.

Tom ushered her back into the dining room and was surprised to see most of the pizza was gone. He questioned her and she went on and on about how Mr. Bluestick has never had it before and he loved it. It settled his fears of the imaginary friend being real, but at the same time he was still upset. It was going to be his lunch tomorrow.

11

The next day at work Tom wasn't in the best of moods. Sandy, who was wandering around the house like some restless spirit, kept him up half the night. She still didn't tell him what was wrong even in the morning when her eyes were red and puffy from lack of sleep and crying. Worrying about her was distracting him and putting him in a bad mood.

Being the new boss of the IT department was stressful enough. Sniping at people during the first week didn't leave a good impression either. He did his best to calm himself and be professional. Staring at the family portrait on his desk relieved some of his troubles. That's when his boss came in, Gary - old, fat, and money hungry. It took three weeks of negotiations on his salary before things had been made final for the move. Gary wanted to pay less, but Tom stood his ground and finally won out with a happy medium.

"Tom, how are things running? Getting used to our way here?"

It took him a second to snap out of his daze. He smiled and answered back. "Running smooth, Sir!"

"Good because I. . ."

Tom's cell phone rang. Gary looked at him annoyed. Tom figured his boss was calculating the amount of money per minute he was spending on him and how much was going down the drain to a personal call. He looked at the caller ID, not wanting to answer it. It was his house. Knowing Sandy would call his office phone, he knew it had to be Lilly and answered it.

"Daddy. . .Mommy left the house three hours ago. She said she'd be back in five minutes. I know I'm not supposed to go in the woods alone, but I'm getting sooooo bored. Can I pleaaaaase Daddy?" The familiar plunge of panic started in Tom's stomach. But instead of the usual small rock dropping in the acid, it felt like an anvil. Sandy would never leave Lilly home alone for that long.

Gary, seeing Tom's face go pale, sat down in front of the desk respectfully, not interrupting as he normally would. He liked the kid, hell, better love the kid for how much he is paying him. More than anyone else here, but he is the best at what he does and worth it. He just hoped everything was all right. He couldn't afford not to have him around. Gary didn't care what anyone here thought of him, so he stared right at Tom, trying to judge what was wrong. He listened intently at what he was saying.

"Honey, don't leave the house until mommy gets home, okay? Make sure the doors are locked. I'll call her cell right now and call you back in a few minutes. Just check the caller ID and don't answer unless it's me, got it?"

Gary watched the sweat start to bead on Tom's forehead. That was one thing that was mentioned in his recommendation - Tom is a worrier, but that worry usually gets the job done better, or so said the letter from a previous boss. He couldn't help but wonder if there were bottles of Maalox or Tums in the drawer.

Tom hung up and apologized to Gary, who seemed to be judging his every move. The boss told him to make his other call, the business could wait a minute. Having his boss stay there and stare at him made it torture. How was he supposed to talk to Sandy? He dialed the number anyway. As her cell rang, Gary stared at him, not even blinking. Tom wanted to swivel his chair to face the back wall but knew it would show a sign of weakness. There was no answer. The anvil was joined by a whole flock of them, splashing one after another.

"Hmmm, no answer. So what. . .uh. . .so. . .how can I help you, Mr. Strum?" It took Gary a few seconds to answer. "Oh, nothing. Just wanted to see how you're adjusting to the job." Tom was aggravated that he sat through the phone calls making him more of a nervous wreck for nothing.

"It's going great, just great." Gary nodded and walked out of the office, saying nothing more. Tom figured it was a way of showing power, but he didn't care about that right now. His wife was missing and his daughter was home alone.

Tom took an early lunch break to look for Sandy. Having only been in town for a few weeks, everything was still pretty new to him. He had no clue where she would go. And that's just what he was telling himself - she *was* somewhere, not in an accident, somewhere probably having a coffee. If this happened back in Maylor, which it never had, Tom would instantly have gone to Cup O' Joe's, the local coffee and Keno hang out. Sandy didn't gamble but her best friend Alyssa was addicted. She would spend hours on end in the smoky, cramped diner waiting for her numbers to come up. Sandy would sit with her back to the TV and be supportive, trying to breathe in as little smoke as possible.

The grocery store, the diner, and the drug store, the only three places Tom knew that Sandy had gone to more than once so far, showed no sign of her car. He kept calling home every five minutes to make sure Lilly didn't leave and Sandy wasn't back yet. No such luck. After twenty solid minutes and only thirty left to his lunch break, the fear and panic he held back so well started to leak out. Horrible images of Sandy's body crushed inside her silver Altima shot passed his thoughts, followed by her raped body in the woods out back. Tom was never too creative. It was times like these that the tiny bit of imagination he did have worked though, and he wished it didn't.

With twenty minutes left to lunch break, he headed back to the house. Just about to pull into the driveway, Tom saw Sandy's car out of the corner of his eye. It was past the house in the half circle at the end of the road, just sitting there, two houses down. Tom parked and got out. His first instinct was to run to it in case she needed help but his legs wouldn't follow his demand. Instead they slowly led him towards it. Against the gleam of the windshield he could see a person. He prayed it was Sandy. She wasn't moving.

Heart pounding, stomach churning, sweat spouting, he put his hand to the door handle and opened it. Sandy was motionless. Tom had a hard time telling if she was breathing. He sunk to his knees; a few sharp pebbles dug into them. As he reached for her face, Sandy's head turned towards him. He jumped and almost laughed. Her eyes looked so troubled, red and swollen.

"I. . .need help Tom. . .I do." Tom started to cry and buried his face in her neck.

12

Lilly sat by the side window watching the movers unload all kinds of furniture and boxes into the house on the right of them. She had yet to see who lived there. The excitement was overwhelming. The first new neighbors! If this had been a week ago, she would have been crossing her fingers, hoping for a kid to play with. But, now, she didn't really care. She had Mr. Bluestick. Who else did she need as a friend?

Unfortunately, she'd only seen him once since the night she introduced him to pizza. It was quick, they only talked for a minute. For some reason Dad had radioed her to come back because they had to take Mom somewhere. It was some doctor's office and the waiting room was terribly boring. No *Highlight* magazine, only adult ones that were stupid. Luckily she brought her Harry Potter book. It seemed as if they were in there forever. When Mom came out, she looked as if she had been crying.

Usually Mom never paid much attention to her stories but lately she hadn't even talked to her. Dad said she was sick and just needed to rest for a while and not to bother her if she didn't have to. So now, sitting at the window watching the movers, Mom was upstairs in her room. She'd hardly left it in the past few days, only for meals and bathroom breaks. But that only meant Lilly could do pretty much what she wanted in the house, Mom wasn't over her shoulder ready to yell.

Ready to give up waiting to catch a glimpse of the neighbors, Lilly saw a big black SUV pull up. She ducked her head a bit to make sure they didn't see her peeking out the window. A tall, skinny man that reminded her of a scarecrow bounced out of the Navigator. She squinted hard to see the man was much older than her dad. She waited until he reached the front door before she gave up on anyone else coming out of it. Oh, well, she thought, one neighbor down, six more to go.

Lilly walked by her mom's room and yelled to her that she was going into the woods. No response, she didn't expect one. She clipped on her trusty walkie-talkie, picked up her sturdy walking stick that she kept by the door and headed out. Mr. Bluestick had to be there somewhere and she was going to find him. Twenty feet into the yard she heard someone shout but ignored it.

"Hey, little girl." Now she knew it was for her but was angry at being called a little girl. Turning to face whoever it was, Lilly yelled back. "I'm not little!" She put her hands on her hips to show she meant business. The man she saw getting out of the SUV was leaning on the fence, smiling big.

"Sorry, I mean, excuse me, Miss." Lilly was still upset at the comment and didn't budge from where she was.

"Are your parents home? I'm moving in today and would love to introduce myself. I might as well meet you while I'm at it." Lilly had to think about whether or not to go over to him or not. Technically, he was a stranger, so she could get in trouble for talking to him. On the other hand, he was their neighbor and Mr. Finney back home was always nice to her. She decided to walk over. As she got close to the fence he stuck out his bony hand to greet her. Lilly shook it lightly.

"Shawn Daggerty, nice to meet you, Miss." She shook it and introduced herself. He asked again if her parents were home.

"Mom is home, but she's sick." Lilly didn't like the way the man looked; she felt uncomfortable near him. She couldn't think of a skinnier person she had ever met. His hair was graying, receding and short. He started to talk to her about something else but she couldn't take being near him anymore.

"I've got to go, I'm meeting someone in the woods." The man looked baffled.

"The woods, huh? You play out there all by yourself?"

"I have a friend that lives out there but Daddy makes me wear this anyway." She pointed to the walkie-talkie.

The man smirked. "Well, you tell your dad to stop by when he gets home. Have fun with your friend." Finally, free of the man, Lilly turned and ran to the woods. She couldn't get away fast enough.

Lilly could feel Mr. Daggerty staring at her back the whole way into the woods, at least that's what she thought since she was too scared to turn around and see. Finally out of eyesight, she turned and looked to make sure no one was following her. Then she made her way right towards the old factory to find Mr. Bluestick. Finally at the mill, Lilly took a seat to wait. He'd show up, she just knew it. Every so often she would stare at her neon pink Swatch watch to see how long she was waiting. After a solid ten minutes, she decided to yell out his name. Once. . .wait ten seconds, again, wait five seconds. . .then once more. Nothing.

Lilly was thoroughly upset and decided to head back. If she left now, she could still catch TRL on MTV or maybe even some Sponge Bob. Ten feet into her journey home, she heard a voice.

"Going home, so soon Madame?" The smile spread across her face fast and big. She knew it was him. Finally! She turned around and jumped a bit, being surprised at how close he was.

51

"Hey, Mr. Bluestick! I haven't seen you in a while."

"Well, my dear, I have been working extremely hard at making my Chrimsawheel!"

Lilly frowned, she'd never heard of such a thing.

Once again Mr. Bluestick could judge her face and answered before she could ask.

"Lillian, my dear, please take a seat and let me explain my invention." Lilly took a seat on a stump that was a bit squishy from decay. Mr. Bluestick stood in front of her, leaning both hands on his cane as if ready to put on a show.

"Now, Lilly, what I'm about to tell you might be shocking. It might be hard to believe. But I swear to you, my fair lady, it is all the truth. Now, as I told you bits before, I am not from here." He gestured with his cane in a big circle.

Lilly put her face in her hands, excited to hear a story. Mom would almost never read her one. Dad used to every night but lately he had been too tired at night. It was much needed attention.

"Now, I don't remember all the details of this story, but I will do the best I can to elaborate on it for you. You see, many years ago, I got stuck here on what you call Earth."

Lilly interrupted. "Wait a minute! Are you trying to tell me you're not from Earth?" She gave him her best "come on!" look she could.

"No, no, dear, not at all, not at all! You might not believe me now, but you will, Lillian, you will. Now, as I was saying, I got stuck here some thirty-odd human years ago. Now I would like to say I was some great intergalactic explorer searching the galaxy, but I cannot. I was merely a young, what you call, man exploring that simply got lost. You see, I loved my creators. . .err. . .or what you call parents, dearly but I got in a fight with them one day and decided to teach them a lesson and use their teleportation machine.

Little did I know your planet did not have one that could send me back!"

Pacing back and forth, he now stopped to convey sadness by putting his head down like a true vaudevillian would do. Lilly, still on the fence whether or not to believe him. Regardless if it was true she felt bad for him.

"So for the past thirty years I have been here working on different machines in attempt to go home. The latest one, my Chrimsawheel will work! I just know it shall! You see, it's a complex configuration of goniometrical pulses of light...You don't want to hear the technical stuff."

Lilly looked at him, thought, then exclaimed. "You're like E.T.! He was just trying to go home too! That's so cool!"

Mr. Bluestick tilted his top hat and thought about the letters. "Hmmm... I do not know this E.T. of yours but I would like to meet him."

Lilly rolled her eyes and giggled. A million questions came to her mind. One after another they started to shoot out of her mouth fast.

Mr. Bluestick shook his head. "Dear, dear. One at a time, one at a time."

Sandy lay in bed and tried to count the plaster swirls on the ceiling for the hundredth time that day. It had only been a few days since she started to take several medications, two she couldn't pronounce, and one that had a commercial on TV that ran every ten minutes. Every time it came on and the dopey music would start to play, she would throw a pillow at the TV. She threw the pillows so often that the only exercise she was getting was getting up to retrieve them.

It felt as if her mind was turning to mush. Her thoughts were cloudy and confusing to her. She was definitely depressed but it was almost as if she couldn't think of why, must be the drugs. Screw Tom for making her go to the doctors. Only if the drugs worked as they did in the commercial, she'd be out in the backyard gardening with a Jack Nicholson sized smile on her face. If only.

The doctor visit and breakdown in front of Tom had been painful enough. Now she couldn't even face her daughter. In fact, she couldn't remember the last time she looked at her, let alone talked. She had no clue what to do. Tom was being overly supportive just as she suspected. The pain showed horribly on her face making her look ragged; it was another thing that made her feel horrible. Tom smiled every time he looked at her but she could tell he was thinking, "How the hell could you not love your daughter, you cold hearted bitch." Luckily for her, suicide never crossed her mind. When she was sixteen, her closest aunt hanged herself; Sandy found her. Then came her first experience with a psychologist. A frightening one.

Dr. Blanchard was his name. He took her on for free since her mother couldn't - more like wouldn't - pay for her to see a shrink. She had said to suck it up. She'd lost her sister and was fine, and it's only a damn aunt to you. So through a friend they found Dr. Blanchard. The first visit was fine. She actually felt good about it and wanted to go again soon. The second visit was a different story.

Sandy lay on the couch like the first time, but for some reason his chair was much, much closer. He started right off the bat asking her stuff about her sex life and what she liked and what she had done, which at that point in her life was pretty much nothing. Uncomfortable and scared, she knew what he was asking her was wrong, but in her day, you were taught to respect doctors and elders. . .always. So she answered with minimal responses and tried to redirect the questions to no avail. Then he put his hand on her thigh.

After that visit she pleaded with her mom not to go back though she didn't tell her why. But, of course, her mother refused and made her feel guilty about how she was the one who wanted to go. Then came the third, fourth and final visit. Two hours of her life she never thinks about, never told anyone about, two hours that ruined her trust of doctors forever. Two hours that attributed to her lying in bed right now.

"So… you're not from another planet, you're from another universe? I'm confused."

"Don't wrack your brain too much, dear. The details are not as important. So, tell me more about this television you talk about so highly. I would love to see it someday."

"You can see it now! Want to come over? We can catch some of Sponge Bob." Lilly jumped up and tugged on his sleeve to go.

"Pleeeeeeaaaaassssse! You can meet my mom. She's not that cool but. . .my dad will be home soon and you'll love him!"

He pondered it for a moment. Then patted the stump next to him signaling for her to sit back down. "Sit, sit. You see, dear. People like your parents don't take too kindly to me. You see, they tend not to believe in such things, whether they are true or not. They'd rather live their daily lives and not have to worry about fantastical things. Younger adults like yourself still have the ability to see the truth. When I first came here, I explored your world for a while. When I tried to tell people where I was from and that I was trying to get back, they laughed at me and said I was crazy. Can you believe that?" He paused as if trying not to cry.

Lilly placed her hand on his and he nodded in appreciation before continuing. "After a while I was chased out of the town, forced to hide here in the woods. But it's okay, I like it here, it's quite. . .peaceful."

"Well, don't you worry, Mr. Bluestick, I'm your friend now. I won't let anyone chase you. I believe you! And I'll help you get home!" Lilly hugged the man harder than she hugged her mom, and much longer. Mr. B closed his eyes and smiled at the comfort of the small hands around him.

13

That night at dinner it was just Tom and Lilly once again. Tom himself was starting to get depressed seeing his wife in this state, and she seemed to be getting worse. Not having the mental power to cook a full meal, Mac and cheese was served once again. Lilly, not surprisingly, was happy. It was much better than the veggies Mom cooked with every meal. Lilly was eating fast and greedily while Tom slowly forked two or three noodles into his mouth at a time. Lilly started to tell stories about Mr. Bluestick but stopped noticing that her usually over enthusiastic dad was acting strangely like mom. Amidst the squishy sounds of the macaroni being stirred around by Lilly came a loud chime. Tom was more than surprised but less than excited about their first ever visitor, whomever it may be.

Tom got up and dragged his feet to the front door. He put on a fake smile and pulled it open. Tom was greeted by Shawn Daggerty's large, crooked smile. In his arms were a bottle of wine and a six-pack of beer along with a small blond haired doll with a pink dress on.

"Mr. Boyer, I presume. Shawn Daggerty, your new neighbor." The excited feeling of having a possible new friend in this town gave Tom a tingling feeling in his spine that was instantly doused at the thought of his wife upstairs. Embarrassment was the first thing that came to his mind. He was going to have to start off a friendship by lying to this man, saying his wife has the flu. But what else could he do?

"Nice to meet you. Lilly told me she met you today. I was going to stop over later tonight." Another lie to start off with. Tom hesitated and then invited him in. The house was a mess; dinner - an embarrassing one at that - was still on the table, and, of course, Sandy upstairs.

Lilly heard the creepy man's voice echo off the hall wall and into the dining room. It gave her goose bumps. Hearing her dad invite him in, she shoveled a few more bites of pasta into her mouth in an attempt to make a quick getaway. Carefully she eased out of the front entrance to the dining room and that's when Tom called her name. Dang it.

"Lilly, come in here and say hello to Mr. Daggerty." She heard some mumbling.

"To Shawn." No escaping today. It was now Lilly's turn to drag her feet to meet Mr. Shawn. The sight of him made the goose bumps rise some more. She didn't bother with the fake smile as her dad had done. She pouted.

"Look what Shawn brought over for you. Isn't it really nice of him, Lilly?" The tone Tom used was his way of saying "Lilly, you'd better be nice and polite even if you hate it."

She did. She didn't play with dolls anymore - or at least she didn't let anyone know she did. And even if she did, this one was hideous. Shawn crouched down to greet her with the doll. She avoided eye contact at all cost. Biting her tongue, she gently took the doll from him and hardly mumbled thank you.

The two men sat at the counter. Shawn apologized for stopping by unannounced and offered a beer. After some prodding Tom accepted the Bud Light. After what Lilly thought was long enough, she silently snuck out of the room.

As much as Tom wanted to clean up the dishes, tuck in his daughter and try to mend what he could with his wife, the allure of a beer sounded wonderful. It had been ages since he drank and, hell, it was a Friday night, why not? Almost instantly the two became like old buddies. Lilly, every half hour or so, would sneak into the adjacent room and listen in. It horrified her to hear them getting along. She didn't know why but he sure scared her. Maybe he reminded her of one of those bad guys in a scary movie she wasn't supposed to watch, yet saw at Toni and Sara's.

It was 2AM by the time Tom's new friend left. Tom was tipsy himself. He felt guilty for being drunk in the same house as his daughter, but, hell, he deserved it with all the crap that has been going on. Besides, he tucked her in when he was supposed to. When he finally snuck into the bedroom, he was surprised to see Sandy in a nightie sitting in the chair by the bed. It was the red one that he bought a few years ago on Valentine's Day, his favorite even though he had only seen it on her once. She looked good, shockingly good after the way she's been. She must have taken all night getting fixed up. Tom shut the door and locked it.

Sandy got up and did her best "I'm going to rock your world" strut to her husband and planted a wet, hard, lustful kiss on his mouth. Tom was over-joyed. Sandy was as well, but for a much different reason.

14

Thank God for Mr. Bluestick. If it weren't for him, this summer would be dragging. The past two weeks have been odd, fun, and boring. Odd, Mom had suddenly been treating Lilly like a golden child, smothering her with kisses. Fun, Mr. Bluestick and Lilly met most everyday. They played all kinds of games and soon he said she could come into his fortress to see his secret Chrimsawheel in action. Boring, three more families moved in on the street, one with teenagers, another with twin babies and the last one was two women together.

The worst part of the past two weeks had been Mr. Daggerty or Shawn, as he keeps saying to Lilly with a hand on her shoulder. Dad and he have been best buds hanging out whenever they can. Lilly has been getting used to it, sort of, but only because she had to. Lying in bed now, she could hear both her parents downstairs laughing with Shawn. She pulled the blankets over her head.

"So now let me get this right. Lilly says there is man. . .from another planet who wears a suit with a top hat, and he lives in the woods!"

Shawn had a hard time getting it out without cracking up.

"I know it's crazy. She has such a good imagination. But for now we're not going to say anything to her about it. All the books I've read on parenting said it's perfectly normal to have imaginary friends at this age." Sandy nodded in agreement with Tom's statement.

"So, Shawn, you said you had two boys, right? Did they go through that phase?" Shawn's face went slack for a second, then tightened up again. "I. . .wasn't around for much of their lives. In fact, they won't even talk to me now."

Tom and Sandy looked at each other. Their curiosity was through the roof, two-weeks of talking, this was a first. But was it too early to prod for more info? They both said they were sorry and Shawn changed the subject back to Lilly.

"What did you say her imaginary friend's name was?"

"Mr. Bluestick." The two said in unison.

"Bluestick huh? Why so?"

"Supposedly he carries around a glowing blue cane! No clue where she got that one!"

"Really. . .uh. . .I could have sworn the other night that I saw a blue light in the backyard. . . weirdest thing. Must have been over-tired."

Tom's mind immediately went into panic mode. The two times that he thought he saw a light flashed back to his mind. It wasn't just his imagination! But what could this mean? Mr. Bluestick is real? No way. No way at all. For one thing how could there be a man living in the woods wearing a tuxedo? For another thing . . . damn it, he couldn't think of another excuse for Mr. Bluestick to be imaginary. He needed to though. The thought of a man playing with his daughter alone in the woods all this time. . . Jesus. "You say you saw a light. What was it like?" Tom wanted to blurt out that he saw it too, but didn't.

"Gee, I don't know. It was definitely blue. . . or bluish. I was going to the bathroom before going to bed, had the light out since I ain't got no shades up yet. Just happen to glance in the back. Saw it only for a few seconds. Seemed close to the house though."

"Who wants another drink?" Sandy said, changing the subject. It worked and the three resumed their meaningless debates and discussions on politics, shows, life and food late into the night. Meanwhile Tom couldn't get the comment out of his head.

The next morning Lilly was up way before Mom and Dad. She made herself a bowl of Count Chocula cereal (the one mom refused to buy but dad would to make her happy) before watching some Saturday morning cartoons. After an hour or so, she got bored of waiting for permission to go out and play. She got geared up, strapped on her walkie-talkie and burst into her parent's bedroom. The door was always open, except for every once in a while it would be shut for an hour, usually when Mom was in one of her moods.

"Daaaaaad," she whispered into her father's ear. He grunted in response. "I'm going to go and play with Mr. Bluestick. It's past nine."

"Uh...oh...sure, Hon."

Lilly placed the house walkie on the nightstand next to the watch she bought him last year for Christmas then quietly crept out.

She was hoping that today would be the day she finally got to see the Chrimsawheel! She was so excited about it. Mr. Bluestick has been talking about it a lot lately, saying his trip would be soon. Her feelings have been torn lately. On one hand, she wanted nothing more for him than to make it home to his family, but, on the other hand, she wanted it to not work so she could keep her only friend.

Heading through the backyard as of late had been a chore. Mr. Daggerty seemed to love to be in his, and every time she tried to make it across he would stop her. Usually just a hello, but every now and then he would ask her questions. Today was one of those days.

"Morning, Lilly! Say, your parents still asleep?"

With her head down, not stopping her walk she answered back, "Yes, Mr. Daggerty."

"Why don't you come over here, I've got a favor to ask. And what did I say about calling me Mister?"

Darn it, only a few yards from the gate. She almost made it. Slowly she turned to his yard, and was surprised to see he had no shirt on. His bony elbows rested on the fence.

"Come here, I'll lift you over the fence. I just need your help for a second."

"He's going to put his hands on me? Yuck! It's going to be worse than the stupid hugs I've been made to give him." Lilly thought.

Reaching the fence, he prodded her to come a bit closer. Then so quick she let out a gasp, his stick like hands sunk into her armpits - thumbs on her chest - lifting her over the fence and placing her back down. She could now see he was only wearing beige shorts, that were too short. Yuck, again.

Shawn strutted in front of her to the cheap plastic chaise lounge chair that was alone in the middle of the yard. He sat on the edge and gave her a big smile. "I need some sun! Don't you think?"

Lilly, being a kid outside most of the time, looked almost ethnic compared to him. He was beyond pale. Moles, stray white and black hairs, wrinkles and various other gross things that Lilly was too scared to look at long enough to identify were all over his emaciated body.

"Just need ya to rub some suntan lotion on my back. Don't want to burn, right? I can put some on your legs and arms, too, if you want before you go out and play in the sun all day."

Lilly was shocked. There was no way she could do it. He handed her the Banana Boat SPF-45, laid on his stomach and grinned up at her. Man, his grin was huge and hideous. It sort of reminded her of that singer Dad really liked. She

63

couldn't think of his name but he yelled a lot and had really big lips.

"Make sure you don't miss a spot." She didn't dare look at his back anymore, she might vomit. What to do, what to do? She looked to the woods hoping to see Mr. Bluestick and be able to run to him. Nope. Then to the house, no help there either.

"What ya waiting for, Lil?"

"Uh. . .well. . .um." Run? If only, Mom and Dad would give her hell, right? Think! Think! Think! Then it came to her. "Mr.. . .Shawn, I just remembered, I think I'm allergic to this kind. I break out in a rash." Genius! She was congratulating herself for being so smart.

"Nonsense, Lilly. I bought it the other day when I went shopping with your mom. She said it's the same kind you use, a little higher SPF but the same brand."

Her stomach rolled. She looked at his back knowing she had to do it now. His spine stuck out so much it looked like a row of snow-covered mountains in a valley of dry skin. Nope, can't do it. Plan B.

She'll catch hell for it but at least she won't have to touch him. Lilly dropped the bottle onto his back and sprinted for the woods. Shawn didn't have a fence in the back of his yard so she had easy access. He didn't bother to get up, merely turned his head and watched her run and disappear.

Lilly ran fast and hard through the path she now knew by heart. She was scared, not of Shawn but of her father. When she was in trouble, he was never mean, hardly yelled and never, never hit her. But his face. His face hurt her heart more than anything in the world. It was the last thing Lilly wanted to deal with today. Today was supposed to be a great day. The day she finally gets to see the ChrimsaWheel.

Out of breath, she slowed down when the old mill was in sight. Mr. Bluestick would usually appear within a few minutes of her arrival. How, she had no clue. She assumed he watched from an old window but he swore he didn't. He said people on his planet had a good sense of when things were happening. She plopped down on her favorite stump, trying to ease her breathing.

Mr. Bluestick was in fact watching from the second floor window, as the gentle child looked frantic sitting on the stump. So fragile he thought. He truly had come to love Lilly over the past few weeks. How couldn't he? She was the only friend he'd had in ages. The only contact with the outside world. He was nervous about bringing her to see the ChrimsaWheel. No one has ever seen it but him. Once she saw it, there is no going back. But what worried him most was the thought of her father finding out.

Tom looked like a nice enough man. Mr. Bluestick had come to that assumption after watching them night after night from the backyard. Loving, caring, good father and husband. But that's what made him nervous. If Tom finds out that he is real, he'll take Lilly away from her. He couldn't let that happen.

Tom rubbed the crunchy sleep crud from his eyes. Saturdays were wonderful. No alarms, just take it at your leisure. He loved his job but not as much as sleep, like most people. Most people's first reaction is to look at the clock once they open their eyes. Not Tom, he always turned toward his wife to make sure she was there and all right. It's something he'd done since the first time they spent the night together. He just couldn't believe he was with her, he had to see if it was real. After a while it just sort of became habit.

Next, Tom would always turn to the clock to check the time. Today, though, he couldn't see the clock. A walkie-talkie was in the way. Mind still cloudy, it took Tom a few seconds to register the meaning. Once it clicked, he sprang up from bed, almost fell putting on his sweatpants and grabbed the walkie. Pushing the button, he wanted to scream at Lilly to come back, but scaring her would do more damage than good. She might start to run home and trip and get hurt. Then, again, she might already be in harm's way. The imaginary man might just be real! He could have her right now.

Deep breaths. Three. That was enough to take the edge off. Click, with the button deeply depressed, Tom talked like the good dad he was.

"Lilly, sweetie, it's Dad. Where are you? Over and out. Roger." Their little way of agreeing on ending a transmission. Lilly thought of it after watching an old G.I. Joe episode on the Cartoon Network. Tom waited, heart thumping as usual. He wondered how much damage his body has taken over the years from all the stress he put on it. He wondered at what age the heart attack would come that would take him away from his family. That was something he knew would happen. Just as he knew that certain days he was going to come home and find the house burnt down, but didn't. Just like he knew some sicko was violating Lilly right now.

After a solid forty seconds of dead air he sent another transmission.

"Lilly. Please respond to me. . .it's not funny. Over and out. Roger."

Even though Tom always thought something was wrong, he always knew he usually was just overreacting. But this time it was different… she actually wasn't answering. This time he didn't wait for her to respond. He finished getting dressed and within seconds rushed out . Halfway down the stairs he radioed her again. By the time he got to the back yard she still wasn't answering.

Lilly's heart was beating just as hard as her father's was, but from excitement and just a bit of fear. She held Mr. Bluestick's hand; it still felt weird. It felt strong and comforting but the soft, dirty white glove was making her hand a bit too hot. They were in the same hallway that she and Dad backed away from on their first trip here. It was scary. But she trusted him. He told her not to worry. He wouldn't let anything happen to her and that it only looked scary to keep bad people and things away from it. After a few feet into the hall, she couldn't see anymore. It was so dark, it made her eyes hurt. It made her think about how her mom told her once that cats can see in the dark. She thought she was joking with her until Dad agreed. She wished she were a cat now. Lilly hated not being able to see. A few times she thought she heard her radio click, but decided it was her imagination.

They passed dozens of frightening doors, too many for her to count. Her eyes started to adjust and she could see a bit better. Yet she kept her head down, eyes on the floor. Even though Mr. Bluestick was with her, she was still too scared to look into the rooms. At the end of the hallway, which seemed to take forever, they took a right. . .another really long hallway. They only went past a few doors before entering the one on the left.

"Now you won't be able to see at all my dear, but don't worry, I can." Lilly wanted to ask how and if he was related to cats. A ball of fear in her throat stopped her.

"There is nothing on the floor. You won't trip." Surrounded by complete darkness, she took tiny steps. Finally he stopped walking. Scratching followed by three clicks, a rattle then a "kachunk" came from in front of her. Then her eyes were hit with the sharp pain of sudden bright blue light - his cane came on. Why couldn't he have turned it on before? Through the open door she could now see a staircase leading to blackness. Mr. Bluestick's face glowed with a weird blue that somehow made him look not as friendly.

"Just down the stairs, my love, and we'll be home!" The wording sounded odd. He had never spoken like that before. *My love? We'll be home?* Lilly started to second-guess going down the stairs. She eased back a tiny bit, but he held her hand firmly, not letting her go back.

Racing through the woods Tom tripped and stumbled every few feet. The trees were a blur as he kept his eyes fixed on the decrepit old building in the distance. He almost fell more times than he cared for, though it didn't slow him down much. Thirty yards away he tried one more time to call her. . .no answer. Finally, close enough to the building he started to look for signs of her, something, anything. But nothing. Just the usual beer cans, chip bags and burnt magazines. Giving up on the radio he began to yell. He screamed his daughter's name so long and loud it burned his throat. For a second he thought about how he never knew he could yell so loud, then his mind instantly went back to finding her.

The crumbling building looked ominous. But after searching all of Lilly's favorite spots outside of the mill he had no choice; he had to go in. Lilly had to be more scared of going in there than he was. This meant only one thing. She wouldn't have gone in alone.

For the second time in one day, Lilly found herself in a tight spot. What to do? It was spooky looking down the stairs. There was no way she was going down. But she couldn't just run away as she had with Mr. Daggerty. It was dark in the hall, it would be impossible to find her way out. Once again she was going to have to try an excuse.

"I have to go pee!" His face seemed to contort in the light, making the deep lines on his face into canyons. The look was close to the one she was expecting to get from her dad tonight - hurt, upset, and disappointed.

Then his eyebrows raised and lips stuck out. "You can use mine, it's clean, I swear to that. Just down the stairs, past the ChrimsaWheel to the right."

Lilly was realizing that lying wasn't doing her any good. Well, he would never hurt her anyways, right? And with his cane he should be able to protect her from anything. . .right? She thought of her choices. Go down and see the ChrimsaWheel she's been so excited about or run into darkness? Down was the answer.

Mr. Bluestick smiled and led the way. One step at a time. He seemed to take them too slowly, almost as if they were covered in ice. The walls were old red brick, or so she assumed, since the blue light made them gray. Once at the bottom, she looked back up - it was the scariest site she had ever seen. About twenty steps flickering with blue-gray light...then nothing beyond. There was no going back now. He let go of her hand for the first time and searched his pockets. Lilly wiped the sweat off her hand. With the warm moist feeling gone, she started to feel vulnerable. She grabbed his pant leg for comfort. Finally he produced keys; four locks in all were opened, then another hallway. After a short walk Mr. Bluestick produced another key and slid it into a hole in the wall. She heard a loud click behind her, from up top.

"Just in case we have been pursued, my darling." He knelt down to face her. Lilly's could feel her eyes bug out. She knew he could tell she was scared. She tried her best not to show it, but it was no use.

"Now, Lillian. . ." Lillian? That wasn't even her name! On the birth certificate it was Lilly! She was angry at being called that and wanted to tell him, but words wouldn't come out.

"I need you to shut your eyes - not that I don't trust you - in case someone ever makes you come back here to show you my secret. Don't worry, I won't let you trip."

Lilly shut her eyes, but the lids fluttered with nerves. She jumped at the feel of something cold and smooth on her face. He was blindfolding her! All the stories her Dad told her many times about how to stay away from strangers. The things that he told her could happen came flooding into her head. But what could she do now? The door was locked, it was dark! In a matter of a second it was tied around her head and she couldn't see at all.

With slow, steady steps she followed him down the hall, turn after turn. She remembered the story of how a woman in a trunk remembered all the turns the car took after she was kidnapped. The little information led to the arrest of the bad guy. Left. . .straight, right, right, left...no, no, right. . .. Lilly tried the best she could but with his constant humming and the butterflies eating away her stomach she couldn't remember all the turns. It was no use.

They stopped, locks clicked, chains rattled and finally a door opened, a few more steps, the door shut, metal slid, more locks. It was getting harder for her to breathe. The air was warmer and sticky in this room, making it even harder for her to catch her breath.

"We're here! Just keep it on for one more second. Here, hold this railing and stay right where you are! Let me get everything ready for you to see!"

The flecks of chipped paint stuck into her palm as she moved it back and forth on the railing. She could hear clicks and buzzing electric noises. He was still humming to himself. It wasn't a song she knew. Then he came back near her. He didn't speak but she could feel him right behind her – he wasn't far at all. They stood in silence for what seemed like forever. Then both of his hands were on her shoulders, every so lightly. Mr. Bluestick started to hum again. This time it was louder. After a few seconds he changed it into a drum roll sound.

It was thick and heavy yet fit in the palm of his hand. Tom whacked the stick against a tree to make sure it wouldn't break on contact. Not only did it not break, it stung his hand from the vibration. It would be a good weapon. He just prayed he didn't have to use it. Holding it up high like a baseball bat, he stepped into the building wishing he had a flashlight, his cell and a million other things. He was always so prepared. . .not today. His haste got the best of him. Now he was alone with a stick and nothing else.

It was so dark that his eyes ached from the sudden change. He stepped over the broken glass and trash to enter the hallway - the hallway he was petrified to go down with his daughter, the hallway in which he thought he saw a blue light. Slow, shaking steps he took. Eyes adjusting, he could barely make out the doorways along the hall. He instinctively wanted to yell out her name but gulped it back for fear of alerting the kidnapper - if there was one.

Tom didn't bother to look in the black doorways. He couldn't see enough to tell if she was in there. Hell, a circus could be in there and he wouldn't know. Instead he listened the best he could. At each doorframe he tilted his ear and strained to hear breathing, movement, anything. After a half dozen doors he realized it was taking way too long. Every second was too precious to waste. He had to speed up his search.

Risking a whisper, Tom started to say his daughter's name every few steps, steps that were now quicker and longer, less cautious. Several times he almost tripped on a beer bottle, papers, chair and dozens of other things he couldn't see that were licking at his feet. Little by little his whisper grew louder.

After what seemed like a thousand doors, Tom hit the end of the hallway. At first he was relieved thinking there couldn't be much more to go. Then he looked right and left. Both ways were black. For all he could tell they didn't end. "A flashlight, a flashlight, a God damn flashlight! Why didn't I think of that? I could have searched this whole place by now," Tom thought while leaning against the wall trying to decide which way to go. Before he knew it, tears were wetting his cheeks and fueling the scream that was bubbling in his throat.

Mr. Bluestick's gloved hands were now working on her blindfold. Lilly gripped the railing so hard she thought the paint chips were going to make her bleed.

"Ta Da!" The blindfold was whipped away. Lilly immediately squinted, out of fear or from the bright lights she didn't know. Slowly she started to open her eyes. It was almost like she was expecting a kickball to be flying at her face.

"Weeeeeeell! What do you think!" Lilly didn't understand the question yet. Then she saw it. It was the greatest thing she had ever seen. It was like a theme park in a room. Thousands of colored lights were everywhere, some blinking, others chasing each other through bent tubes. Her mouth dropped as she took in the sight of the. . .ChrimsaWheel! It was beautiful. From the railing she looked down at the ten-foot high structure of a wheel. Sort of like a Ferris wheel but with only one chair, one chair that was stuck on the base of it. The chair itself looked like one of those thrones that Lilly seen in some movie about a king, except it had lights wrapped all around it. One arm had blue lights, the other red. The wheel itself had more colors than Lilly could name. Straight lights, curved ones, circles, flashing ones, it seemed like every light was a different color. Hundreds of wires (most with lights on them) ran from behind the chair into a big box next to the wall.

"Mr. Bluestick, it's so cool!" Finally being able to pull her eyes away for a second, she looked back at him. His smile was huge! Then down the stairs she ran to explore this new wonderful place. Mr. Bluestick carefully followed her around making sure she didn't push the wrong buttons. Lilly checked out every inch of the enormous square room. The walls were painted different colors with large circles that looked like planets with no details. Wires, boxes and all kinds of doodads were strung about. But she saw no bed or bathroom.

"Where do you sleep?"

"Well, my dear, I have another room separate from here. You can't be too safe you know. That way if someone finds me living here, hopefully they won't find the ChrimsaWheel!"

"Can I see your room?" He looked a bit flustered and his eyebrows danced a bit.

"Not at the moment my dear. This is a big enough step for today!"

Satisfied that she'd looked at everything in the room, Mr. Bluestick started to explain how the machine worked. Most of the words were too big for her to comprehend but she nodded anyway. The basic idea, as she understood, was that the wheel spins around creating a force field that would open a door in time and let him travel to his home planet.

Sitting in the ChrimsaWheel chair now, she couldn't believe how worried she had been. That's when she heard it. It was low but unmistakably she heard her father calling her name. The sound had traveled through an orange vent with the words *security system* painted above it.

"It's my dad!"

Mr. Bluestick's face looked serious, not scared. "No problem, Lilly, my little confidante. I'll simply slip you out the emergency escape." He ushered her to the far back corner where a large pink curtain was. He moved it aside to reveal a circular metal door also painted pink. Then it was open.

"This tube will let you out by the stream in the back. Just think of it as a big slide. Don't worry, I take it all the time myself, it's oh so safe. When you get out there, holler for your father and just tell him you were out back playing by the water. Remember! Don't tell him about me! He wouldn't understand!"

Lilly was scared. If he found out she was in the mill, which would mean big trouble, on top of the trouble she was going to get in for the suntan lotion this morning.

Mr. Bluestick helped her up into the tube. Once sitting on the edge it looked frightening, like the water slide she waited to go on in Florida for over an hour then chickened out.

"Now, now, Lilly. It'll be fine," He said, sensing her fear to go. They both turned as they heard her dad yell again.

"You must go, Lilly! Please!" He let go of her, hoping she would slide, but she held onto the sides like a cat not wanting to go into water. He gently worked on removing her fingers while trying to coax her into it.

"You know, once you do it, you'll be begging me to let you do it again and again," he said in a chipper voice. Giving up on the fingers, he resorted to a quick tummy tickle. Worked like magic. Lilly instantly let go and started to slide down, but before she got too far she tried to grab hold of him, knocking his top hat off. Before he realized what was happening he could only watch it slide down after her.

It was faint, tiny, distant and unclear but the greatest sound Tom had ever heard - Lilly's voice. She was alive, but safe? Wanting to sprint to her but not knowing which way to go, he strained to hear it again. There it was "Da...back...."? Dad? Out back? Tom sprinted into the darkness he'd come from, not worrying about what he might trip on. Amazingly he made it to the tiny spot of light at the end without harm. He burst through the door ignoring the blinding pain of the sudden light change. He took the right too quickly. Feet sliding out from under him, he hit the ground hard, arm under him in an unnatural way. The popping noise registered in his head before the pain got there. Rolling onto his back, his crooked arm flopped onto the ground. It was the first bone Tom had ever broken. Tiny spots of bright light, which Tom thought looked like fairies, danced in front of his eyes. Next came a sudden urge to vomit. He tried to sit up but doing so moved his arm. Pain kept him flat on his back staring up at the fairies that seemed to be taunting him. Then the walkie crackled.

"Daddy, I'm behind the old mill looking for rocks. Where are you calling me from? Over and Out, Roger."

Jesus! How could he have forgotten about Lilly? Thank God she was all right. The fear and hard pumping heart in his chest didn't calm knowing she was okay. They seemed to get worse. With his left arm he grabbed the walkie off his belt and raised it to his sweaty lips.

"Honey...uh. . .Da. . .Daddy's in the front. I need your help. Come up here."

"Okay Daddy, I'm coming. You forgot to say Roger out! Roger out."

Numb with pain, he realized that maybe it wasn't a good idea to have his daughter see him like this. She might get scared and not be able to get help. Picking up the walkie again, he pushed the button and began to speak, but it was too late. He heard the crackle of his own voice somewhere behind his head. Then came the child's scream.

"DADDY! Oh no, oh no, oh no."

Somehow Tom managed a smile, a delirious one, but a smile nonetheless. He still couldn't see Lilly. She must be behind him, he thought. With his good arm he raised it and waved, trying to make her laugh. It didn't work.

"Baby. . .I'm going to be just fine, but I need you to go get mommy, okay? Take your walkie to her so I can talk to her."

Lilly was sobbing, no words were coming out. Tom was getting frustrated that he couldn't see her.

"Come here, baby. It's okay." The fluttering spots had settled down to a few now and then. The vomit feeling was gone too, but it left his mouth dry. Out of his peripheral vision he could finally see his daughter, the one he thought was in trouble, which ended up getting him into trouble. Her steps were gentle and careful, the steps of someone approaching too fast. He looked at Lea fearing he would break some more. Sweat was now in his eyes, making his vision of Lilly a little blurry but he could have sworn she was holding a large top hat. He tried to raise himself up a bit to show he was okay. The tiny movement sent pain right back into his body, inviting a whole new party of fairies to dance before his eyes. He was close to passing out and he knew it. "Honey. . .hurry, go get mommy."

Lilly dropped the hat a few feet from him and started running. Tom stared at the hat while the fairies waltzed around it just before he passed out.

15

Tom opened his eyes hoping to see a medic above him ready to help. He saw no one. Just a few birds chirping and one of those odd-rattling bugs you only hear when it's hot out. Then he remembered the hat. The man must be real. He quickly turned to examine it, but there was nothing. He turned both ways, nothing. It was there, wasn't it? He didn't imagine it. He saw it. He knew it. The urgency to find this hat took over. He tried to sit up but the fairies came back to take him on another trip to darkness.

The next several hours were choppy, blurry memories that Tom would never entirely remember. It wasn't until his arm was fully cast and plenty of pills were plopped into his stomach that he started to think clearly again, well, as clearly as you can on heavy painkillers.

Sandy had that odd plastered-on, fake smile she'd been wearing the past few weeks, Tom thought. It was odd but he liked it much better than the weeping Sandy who wouldn't talk. She was holding his good hand. Lilly was sitting at the edge of the bed, her head down, face still rosy from crying. Tom looked at his cast. It covered from his palm up to his elbow. Wiggling his fingers wasn't an option. They were restricted, besides it hurt.

No one in the little curtained room had said anything yet. He wasn't sure if they already had and he just couldn't remember.

"Sandy could you get me a pen out of your pocketbook?" Without a word Sandy obliged. Lilly stayed still hoping that if she didn't move he wouldn't see her. Sandy handed the thick black ink pen to him.

"Lilly, honey. Would you sign my cast?
" Lilly looked up, bewildered. She looked to her mom as if to ask if her dad was all right. Sandy nodded to her. The little

girl slid off the bed and plopped onto the floor. Eyes on the ground, she made her way to her father's side.

"But. . .Daddy. . .it was my fault you got hurt." Tears followed the tiny voice. Tom wanted to wipe them away but his good arm was on the opposite side.

"Honey, this has nothing, nothing to do with you. I tripped, that's all. It's not your fault. I'm not mad at you, no one is." Lilly still looked confused.

"But if you weren't looking for me, you wouldn't have fallen."

"Nooooo, if I wasn't a clumsy old man, I wouldn't have fallen!"

The comment got a little smirk from the girl before she reached across and grabbed the pen. She asked where to sign and what. Tom told her both were her choice. In big letters across the middle she wrote *I love you Daddy, Lilly.* Tom watched her carefully write the letters out as if they were art.

The drive home seemed long. No one spoke. Tom stared out the side window and contemplated what to do about work. The thought hadn't occurred to him until Sandy mentioned it on the way out. Now he couldn't get it out of his head. His entire job was typing and writing. There was no way he could do any of that. What will Gary say? He's only been at the job for a little while. He's already taken too much time off while Sandy had her episode. He was sure to fire him, he just knew it. Six, if not more, weeks without being able to type. Then even after that he would have to have therapy. The break was so bad they actually had to do a surgery to put a metal rod in. Who knows if it would ever heal right. He was useless. Jesus, if he got fired what would he do? They already can't afford the house.

Tom sank deeper and deeper into his seat and depression. Pulling into the driveway, he didn't want to get out of the car, let alone move. But he had no choice. Sandy and Lilly were right there to help him out, as if he was some sort of invalid. He resented the attention but tried not to show it.

It was still early in the day by the time he was settled into a chair in the living room. Lilly propped up his feet. Sandy made him lemonade. They were being as nice as possible. He hated it, he much preferred being the person doing the serving. Never in his life did he feel as if he deserved attention like this. Whether it was Father's Day or his birthday, he always felt awkward. Today was no exception. Finally he had to ask them to stop. He wanted to be left alone to call Gary. He asked them nicely, and they reluctantly left the room.

The phone felt oddly cold in his hand. He wondered if Sandy had lowered the a-c for him. He dialed Gary's home number that took Sandy a half hour to find in the online yellow pages. His heart pounded again for the hundredth time that day. He dreaded the call. The day was already one of the worst he'd ever had. All he needed now was to top it off with losing his job. Sandy urged him to call tomorrow after he rested, but Tom refused. He couldn't take the stress of wondering and worrying.

On the third ring the chipper voice answered. He'd never heard Gary sound like that before. Then again, he'd never talked to him on a non-work day. He apologized profusely for calling on a weekend. Almost instantly the chipper voice turned back to the gruff one he was used to. After explaining the situation, there was a long silence only accompanied by deep breathing on Gary's end.

"Tell you what, Tom, I like you and I paid a lot to have you come all the way out here. I must say your work is impressive. Your problems are not. Take two weeks off, straighten out everything, and I mean everything. When you come back to work, I'll have an intern help you until the cast comes off. But when you are back, no and I mean no more leaving work, Tom. You understand? I think I'm being more than generous here."

Tom, feeling relieved, thanked him over and over again. The man snapped at him to shut up before hanging up with out a good-bye. Tom hung up the phone, reclined the chair and fell asleep.

While her dad napped, Lilly sat in her room trying to read her new *Teen People* issue, but she found it uninteresting, mostly because she couldn't get out of her head the sight of her father on the ground with his arm bent the wrong way. The guilt was stinging her heart. She'd never seen her father hurt before, let alone cry and she never wanted to again.

What a day - she finally gets to see the most amazing thing that she's been waiting forever to see, and what happens? She almost kills her dad. If only she'd listened to him and not gone into the mill. But then she would never have seen the ChrimsaWheel, which she was dying to see again. Lilly threw the magazine on the floor, bored, not knowing what to do.

"Hey! What did that magazine ever do to you?"
The voice startled her almost enough to scream. It was Dad, looking much better than before. The nap must have done him some good.

"Sorry, Dad."

"Don't be sorry to me, it's your magazine!"

She could tell he was trying to be chipper so she herself tried not to sound so glum, but she couldn't help it. Her eyes were glued to the cast and her big writing on it. Lilly had to hold back the tears as the guilt and vision of her father on the ground shot back through her mind.

"Lilly, it's okay. Really it was just an accident." Tom sat next to her for another round of counseling.

Sandy stood in the hallway listening to her husband counsel Lilly. Leaning up against the wall, she couldn't believe Tom's compassion. The man just broke his arm a few hours ago, and it was Lilly's fault. Yet he's in there telling her it was all his. She was amazed at how he did it, how he was never in a bad mood, never yelled. Thinking about how amazing he was made her feel bad for what she was about to do in a few days.

Tom and Lilly had been much more accepting to the new Sandy that she decided to be after days on end in her room, the new Sandy that wasn't going to be around much longer. After being so miserable, it just all became so clear one day. She tilted her head a bit more to hear the conversation. Lilly was giggling now. He was good. She figured tonight that she would please him and maybe one more time before Thursday she could grin and bear it as she has for so many years. Anyway the bastard won't have any for a long time after that.

After reassuring his daughter and cheering her up a bit, Tom gathered his courage to ask her the question he was dreading. "Now, Lilly, I have an important question to ask you. You have to tell me the truth, okay?"

Lilly instantly knew what it was going to about. She had no clue what to answer. The only thing that came to mind was, *he's gross.*

"Now, you know the difference between real and make believe. I know you do. I have to ask you if Mr. Bluestick is real or someone you made up."

The statement took her by surprise. She really thought this was going to be about the suntan lotion this morning. *This* was much worse. How could one day go from horrible to great and horrible again so many times? Lilly stalled, trying to think of an answer. She already promised Mr. Bluestick that she would never say anything, but, at the same time she had never lied to her father. Even as much as she wanted to, she just couldn't. Mom was a different story.

If she said that Mr. Bluestick is real, her Dad would forbid her from playing in the woods with him. Mr. Bluestick would probably never talk to her again. She couldn't have that happen; he was her only friend. On the other hand, if she lied, her dad would be able to tell right away. Again she found herself in a dilemma, for the third time that day. Her young mind couldn't take such stress and confusion. She wanted to run again, but how do you run from your dad? Where do you go? The only choice was to lie.

"Dad. . .there is no Mr. Bluestick. I made him up. I have no friends here so I just wanted someone to hang out with."

Tom instantly put his arm around her. She looked sad but he wasn't fooled at all. It was a lie. Eight year olds aren't that good at them; it takes age to perfect lying. Instead of accusing her and starting an argument, he set his mind in motion to take care of things in a different way.

"Ok, Lilly, just wondering. Thanks. Well, you know what? I have the next two weeks off from work. You won't have to go into the woods alone once the whole time!" Lilly didn't notice the smile cross his face, just as Tom didn't notice Lilly's eyes widen.

The next day both Lilly and her father slept much later than usual. But Lilly still woke up first, . She needed to get in touch with Mr. Bluestick. She had to tell him that Daddy was going to be with her all the time and she's sorry if she couldn't see him for a while. She wanted to see him bad too. The ChrimsaWheel was so amazing she had to see it again. Maybe if she wore Dad out one day, she could go back out alone to talk to him. She couldn't risk that, though. If only she had a way of leaving him notes?

Rushing to finish before Dad woke, Lilly wrote a note to Mr. Bluestick, telling him what was going on and asking what happened with the hat? Did he take it back? He really must not have wanted Dad to know he was real. Just as she was folding it, she could hear Dad peeing. It always made her giggle to hear the loud splashing since mom and she never made much noise. Boys are odd.

"Morning, sweetie." Her dad groggily grumbled a few seconds later. Usually he was much more chipper. Lilly examined his stubbly face and half- closed eyes before looking at the cast that she still felt guilty about. Not wanting to see him in a bad mood, she ran over to him for a hug. He was less than receptive and even let out a small grunt. He patted her lightly on the head before disappearing down the stairs.

Lilly gave him some time to wake up before loudly stomping down the stairs to alert the house of her presence. To her surprise Dad was in the living room alone. Mom was nowhere to be seen. Cautiously she approached him.

"Where's Ma?"

"She went out to do some shopping. Why don't you watch TV for a bit, then we'll go to a movie later on."

Lilly tried not to cringe her face too much. A movie? She wanted to go to the mill! She hadn't gone to a movie in a long time but, still, the woods beat any movie, hands down.

Seeing his daughter's reaction and in too much pain to do much more, he gave her a puppy dog look before pleading. "Come on, Lilly, we haven't seen a movie in ages! I'm too tired and sore to go into the woods today, maybe in a day or two, okay? So go online and pick out what you want to see."

Lilly put on a fake smile that looked more like misery than anything and left the room.

No music, no sing-a-long, just silence. Lilly felt scared to be in the car with her own father. Body Snatchers? Lilly never saw the movie but with her vivid childish mind she was able to picture some slug-like creature sneaking into her dad's body so that the man next to her wasn't really her father. He was never, ever like this. He didn't even bother to shave. Lilly just sat far away from him as she could, wondering if it was really him or not.

Tom had never been in a worse mood. The pain was relentless, he was exhausted and his wife was MIA. He felt horrible for treating Lilly badly. But each time he was about to apologize, the pain in his arm would change the track of thought. Putting the car in gear was a challenge. He was surprised he pulled it off since he needed his left hand to do it. For a long moment he thought maybe he shouldn't be driving with one arm. Is that against the law? Then again there are paralyzed people who drive, so why not with a broken arm?

Tom was baffled at how Sandy had slipped out of the house without him knowing it this morning. He only slept for a few minutes at a time. Did she wait for just the right moment? Or was it just a coincidence? And what is up with the note she left? One word "Shopping." Nothing else. She'd never done that before. When he called her cell, she didn't answer, as he expected. For a split second he thought that maybe she was getting a surprise for him. Then the male mind took over. The thought that she was having an affair beat out all other possibilities. It only added to his foul mood.

The movie theater parking lot was shared with a half dozen other stores in a strip mall. Tom hardly glanced at it while parking. It was Lilly that saw Sandy's car. Parked right in front of *Getaway Now* the local travel agency. She pointed it out for him. He followed the line from Lilly's little hand to the car. After eliminating the possibility of her going to any of the adjacent stores, Tom felt his face fill with blood.

Lilly watched her father/alien's face turn bright red and his lips tighten. Definitely a body snatcher. What do you do in a situation like this? Mr. Bluestick would know. He wasn't from here. For the umpteenth time today Lilly wanted to run from him, a feeling she was getting sick of. There was also a new feeling. She wanted to be with Mommy more than Dad. That was a first.

Tom tried to control his rage. Being cool and calm in any situation was his one born talent, which was not kicking in today. He tried to blame it on the broken arm and recent events. For a split second he thought that Sandy was planning a trip for them. But she knows he has no vacation time after these few weeks. Maybe she was going to take him away this weekend. That thought still made him mad; she knew they couldn't afford a vacation. Then the other thoughts flooded in. She's running away, she's having an affair with one of the agents, and several other crazy ideas. This was all new to Tom. Of course he'd been jealous in life, but he was the biggest optimist he'd ever meet. No matter what. Not being able to shake this mood was driving him crazy.

"Lilly, stay in the car. Here are the keys; listen to some music, lock the doors I'll be right back." He handed her the keys without looking at her. Lilly, terrified, hopped back into the car without hesitation. She watched her father start to walk the long distance across the lot towards her Mother's car, the car that she'd rather be in.

Sandy walked out with the small bag of information. Instantly she saw her husband. It was odd how you can recognize someone from over a hundred yards away. But it was undoubtedly him. The almost duck-like walk, the body shape, and of course, the bright white cast. Panicking, not wanting to be caught, she pretended not to see him when he picked up his pace. Fast as she could, without being obvious, she got in the car. Turning the key, she started to back out before the engine even finished revving. It made an odd grunt of disapproval. She didn't care though. She needed to get away and have some time to make up a story that was believable.

By the time she was driving, Tom was running towards the car. Sandy kept her vision straight forward, trying her hardest to act natural. Green, green, green she chanted in her head, praying it would help change the light at the exit. It would make all the difference in getting away. Red. She started to slow down, knowing Tom would be at her window in a second. Why is he running so fast? He must be on to her, but how? GREEN! Yes! She gunned the gas and sped through the light and on to safety. In the rearview window Tom stopped and put his hands on his head trying to catch his breath. She better make up one hell of a story. Hell, she might as well not even go home.

16

Lilly couldn't tell if the movie was good or not. She was too busy watching her alien dad. He spent most of the movie staring at the wall and ceiling fixtures. Summer camp, maybe that's what it was about. Who knows. . .the only thing that mattered right now was how her dad was acting odd. Lilly had never seen him run like that. And when he got back, he didn't say a word. Only two sentences have passed his lips since he slowly walked back. One was to ask for tickets, the other for the popcorn.

On the way home again, Lilly was stuck looking out the window in silence. She crushed herself up against it hard. Pulling into their street, her dad suddenly hit the brakes. Lilly pitched forward and felt the sting of the belt across her chest. Looking up she expected to see a squirrel in the road but there was nothing. She looked farther and saw her mom's car was in the driveway. Was that it? Why would that shock Dad?

Tom was shocked to see his wife's car in the driveway. He figured she was on a plane trip to Tahiti with some buff young guy. He kept the car in the middle of the road, fearful of the confrontation. A tiny bit of him wanted to just turn around and take Lilly out to dinner, but that would only delay the inevitable. It took courage to ease off the brake.

Once parked, Lilly got out of the car quickly and shut the door. For a long minute she waited for her dad to follow. Yet he sat with his hands on the wheel hardly blinking. Glad to be away from this alien dad, she ran into the house. Mom was cooking dinner - odd. Was Mom an alien too? She hardly cooked anything that wasn't boxed or frozen. And it looked like a big meal too.

"How was the movie, hon?" The question sounded phony but Lilly played along.

"It was good."

"Where. . .where is. . .uh. . .your father?"

Lilly tried to peek into the pot to see what was for dinner but couldn't get high enough on her tiptoes before Mom swatted her away.

"He's in the car still," Lilly said over her shoulder as she headed to her safe haven away from all these aliens.

Sandy watched her kid walk up the stairs and made sure she was totally out of sight before gasping for air. Her body was shaking. She was petrified of the confrontation that was coming. Apparently Tom was as well. She hunched over and tried to breathe normally. It was a hard decision to come home. But it was Tom, the man who had pretty much never yelled at her, let alone hit her. If anything, he would rationally ask her what she was doing. She'd say that she didn't see him and was picking up info on a Disney World cruise that she was planning on suggesting to him tonight. Dinner would have been closer to ready if she hadn't had to drive around for an hour to find another travel agency to get brochures on it.

Hearing the door handle, Sandy stood up with a bolt, turned to the pots and absent-mindedly started to stir. Time to use the acting skills she didn't really have. Giving Tom a few seconds to get in the door, she turned with a smile to greet him as if it were a glorious day.

"Why hello, my. . ." Seeing how awful Tom looked stopped her sentence cold. Messy hair, unshaven, bags under the eyes. This was not good.

"Thomas! For heaven sakes, are you all right?" Sandy was genuinely worried (for her sake not his). Tom instantly noticed that she was *too* concerned. A foot before her outstretched arms could touch his face, Tom grabbed her wrist with his good arm. His eyes bored into hers.

"No lies. No stories. I know you saw me. What were you doing there?"

The grip on her wrist was actually hurting. Sandy couldn't believe it.

Masterfully tuning her radio to the Disney channel, Lilly jumped a mile at the shout. It was her mom. She's heard her yell plenty of times but only at her for not cleaning her room or something. Never at her father. The words were hard to understand, but she could easily tell they were said with anger. Her dad yelled next. Her heart sank in fear as she shut off the radio. Dad yelling? Uh Oh.

Lilly slid off her bed onto the floor and against the wall, as if it would somehow protect her from hearing this. The yells lowered for a second and she could only hear low murmurs. The day was already odd thinking Dad was an alien. She knew it was just silly to think that but now it seemed almost real. Her father would never act like this. She had to march down there and set them straight! Tell them to stop acting like kids, it was almost dinnertime!

Then came the crash. Lilly jumped and immediately wanted to go under her bed, but couldn't because too much stuff was under it. The closet was the next and only hiding place in this room. She cautiously stood up. Something behind her outside caught her eye. A blue streak in the setting night. Forget the closet, she thought, as she rolled her window open a crack.

"Mr. Bluestick, don't leave, I'm coming out!" The wand waved to her almost as if it was a living creature itself.

It was almost dark out. Flashlight! Last time she wished she had one. Grabbing her backpack, Lilly threw things in it as if she were leaving on safari. Flashlight, gum, bug spray, candy, magazines, clothing, hair clips and, of course, her iPod. Lilly had no more of a plan than to just get away from the yelling going on downstairs. At least this way she'd be prepared, regardless of how long she was gone.

Packed and ready to go, Lilly had to build courage to go down the stairs. It sounded as if they were still in the kitchen, which would leave the front hall clear for her to escape. She'd have to go out the front door but that wasn't a problem. A quick trek around the house and she'd be home free.

Standing at the top of the stairs, she was actually upset that the yelling was again a low murmur. She needed to wait until the yelling was loud enough for her to leave without them noticing. Slowly, one step at a time, she crept to the door. With hand on the knob, she waited for the yelling. Then it was there again but it was different now; she could hear the words. Trying to ignore it and listen in at the same time, she unlocked and opened the door. About to shut it, home free, she heard something she wished she hadn't.

"I HATE YOU!"

It was Mom, yelling at Dad. It made her freeze with the door open just an inch. There was a long pause before her dad's yell snapped her out of the daze. She shut it and ran.

Not thinking, Lilly ran to the left side of the house to make her way to the woods, Mr. Daggerty's side. Next to the house, jogging quietly, she saw Mr. Daggerty looking down at her from the upstairs window. Did he hear her parents, too? She hoped not; she was embarrassed as it was. She only looked at him for a second. He had his shirt off and he didn't wave. He looked dazed. Did the aliens get him, too? She only hoped they didn't get Mr. Bluestick yet, but he was already an alien, so they couldn't take him over, right?

The sky was still gray, unlike the woods, which looked like a wall of black. Lilly stopped at the mouth of the woods, hesitant. She looked back to the house. Two figures paced back and forth angrily. She looked to the woods— black. Then, like a beacon from a lighthouse, came the blue light she so loved. It was a good fifty yards in. With some effort Lilly dug through her backpack to find her own light. As she walked following her white beam, she wished she could change the color. It was only a matter of seconds until she was shining it on the tuxedoed man. He raised his gloved hand in protest.

"Now, now, Miss Lilly, please turn that off!"
Lilly obliged, thankful that his cane gave off enough light to illuminate the ground and his face. Strange, just yesterday the light made him look evil and threatening. Now it made him look like an angel. Mr. Bluestick looked at her face inquisitively, trying to judge the mood. Her eyes were starting to fill with tears as she ran over and hugged the cloaked man.

"Now, now, dear. What's the matter?"

Lilly began to explain the entire past two days' events, starting right off where she went down the slide. As she spoke, the pair sat down on an old log. Mr. Bluestick covered his cane on one side with his cloak to shield it from view of the house.

The entire time she spoke he did not look away from Lilly's eyes. She loved how intently he listened. When her story was finished all the way up to seeing Mr. Daggerty standing in the window, Mr. Bluestick put his thumb and forefinger on his face to show he was thinking.

"Let me see your hand(s)??." Without even thinking about the odd request, Lilly stuck her hands out, palms up. With his gloved hands, he clasped them gently and started to pore over them like a palm reader.

"Do your parents' hands look like this as well? Smooth, that is?" Lilly thought for a minute and nodded.

"Well, then, you have nothing to worry about. You are human, and so are your parents. Now as for aliens having taken over their bodies. . . impossible! I remember a class on humans when I was young. You are practically impossible to take over. You know, Lilly, you'd be amazed what. . . pain...can. . .." He started to stare off into the woods, his brow furrowed as if a painful memory was punching around in his head.

"You'd be. . .well, he broke his arm, Lilly my dear. Pain can change a person." He seemed bothered by the statement. Closing his eyes, he shook his head. It must have thrown the thought right out since he then crossed his arms and nodded as if to say *see*.

Lilly looked a bit relieved. "But how can you tell by looking at my hands?"

Mr. Bluestick smiled a Cheshire grin as if he was waiting for the question. Cautiously he started to look around to make sure no one was near.

"I'm going to show you something, Lilly. All the people on my planet are the same way. It may not be the prettiest to you. But for me it's normal."

Lilly edged closer, intrigued. He expertly gripped the cane between his knees and stuck his own, gloved hands out. Slowly and almost painfully, he peeled his left hand glove half way off to reveal shriveled, bumpy, misshapen skin. Lilly couldn't tell what color it was since it shined blue, but the sight made her own skin crawl, mostly since it reminded her of Freddy Kruger, the scary claw guy from the movie she accidentally saw part of on late night TV. The movie had given her nightmares for weeks. After a second of looking at it, though, her repulsion faded away. This was her friend. She's held this hand many times now; a few wrinkles wasn't going to change that. Carefully she touched it with one finger.

Donning a genuine smile, she looked up at him as if to prove she wasn't scared of it. Her smile quickly faded when she saw the big wet tears in his eyes. Suddenly he covered his hands back up and shoved them in his pockets.

"Missing home?"

Mr. Bluestick looked off into the woods. "Yes. . . something like that. You should go back home before they get scared, Lilly."

She thought it was an odd statement and was worried she'd done something wrong.

"I want to stay with you for a while, at least until they're done yelling."

Silently he nodded. One last tear ran down his cheek.

Crack! The snapping branch startled the two of them. In less than a second, the blue light was doused, leaving them in total darkness. *Crunch*. Lilly was picturing a big hungry bear ready to eat them only yards away. The darkness would have terrified her if it weren't for Mr. Bluestick's hand on her shoulder. Her mind wandered to the sight of it. It was repulsive, but he was her best friend, which made it all right. She repeated that over and over in her head until there was another snap somewhat close this time.

Warm, hot air flowed into her ear, freezing her stiff with fear until she realized it was Mr. Bluestick's breath before he whispered to her.

"Climb onto my back, quietly, my dear. Under the cloak. We need to get out of here quickly."

"Is it a bear?" Lilly replied in her lowest whisper possible.

"Worse, a human, now don't make a noise."

Lilly thought of all the broken beer bottles near the mill and wondered if it was one of those older bully kids you always see in movies, the ones with leather coats and chains. They always had knives. What if they tried to hurt them? She climbed up under the cloak and wrapped her little arms around him. Luckily he was skinny enough that she could grab her own wrist and hold on tight.

The rise from sitting was shaky. Mr. Bluestick's legs wobbled under the extra weight of the small child. It took a solid three steps before he adjusted to the little girl being there. Slow steps, making almost no noise, then faster, still almost no noise. Behind him he could hear the crunches, snaps and scrapes of someone not used to the woods following them. It was going to be a challenge to shake him. Usually he could lose anyone in a matter of minutes but with Lilly, this was going to be difficult.

Zig, zag, left, right. Mr. Bluestick raced through the woods fast, hoping not to topple over. After several minutes the sounds of the predator were hard to hear. He paused to listen and judge which way to go. It was hard to hear over Lilly's panicky breathing. He shushed her, she held her breath. The steps were far enough away. He had to make a break for the mill. Though he was on the opposite side of the woods, he made it into the mill entrance in a few quick minutes.

Entering the small, pitch-black entryway, he let Lilly slide off his back. She kept clutching to his legs. His legs were turning into Jell-O. Taking a step, he almost collapsed.

It was the hardest workout he'd had in years. With a click he had the room glowing blue. Lilly released her tight grip and came out from under the cloak, letting Mr. Bluestick fall on top of a broken desk to relax. The two sat in silence, making sure they had lost their pursuer.

Tom sat in a lawn chair out back too angry to cry. Crying was something Tom was not afraid to do. As a kid his father yelled at him about how men don't cry when he used to get upset. Then his mother would come in and console him saying it's okay to cry. He could use her now. He missed her. Getting his mind back on track, he replayed the argument over and over in his head. He said the lines back and forth, thinking of the things he should have said, and the things he regretted saying, the things that sent Sandy, with tears in her eyes, running to the bedroom and locking the door.

It was the last place he wanted his wife to be right now. The week she spent locked up there scared him to death. She'd been an absolute angel the past few weeks. A new woman. And now he's gone and ruined it. Who knows how long it will take her to come out this time. No doubt about it, it was the worst fight they ever had. Tom totally admitted to himself that if it weren't for the lack of sleep and the pain he was in, he'd have been much easier on her. But he couldn't help it, he snapped for the first time. Jesus! He even knocked things over! What the hell was wrong with him? He could feel the tears coming now.

"TOM!" The deep loud yell stopped the tears from coming out. Disoriented, Tom stood up to see where it came from.

"TOM, TOM!! Quick!"

The backyard was so dark he could barely see the white blotch running towards him. He balled his one good fist defensively, not knowing what was going on. The blotch was coming closer. Tom stood up to meet it on level ground. It was Shawn! He un-balled his fist and relaxed a bit until he saw the frantic look on his neighbor's face.

"Christ, Shawn, what's the matter?" Shawn's eyes were wide with panic and he gasped as he tried to explain what was wrong.

"Lilly! It's Lilly."

All the events of the day disappeared upon hearing his daughter's name. He looked over his shoulder at her window. He just assumed she was there. "Slow down, slow down. What are you talking about?"

"I looked out back and saw that light, you know the blue one?" Tom's gut fell like a rock dropped into it. He swallowed hard trying not to vomit.

"Well, I came out to see what it was, and, fuck, Tom. It's some strange ass guy wearing a tux."

"Dear God, so he's real. . ." Tom stared back at his daughter's window, but Shawn quickly grabbed him by the shoulders and looked into his eyes.

"TOM! She's not up there. Lilly's with the man."

The world stopped. Sound, time, everything. It was yesterday all over again, but this time it was real and much, much worse. He felt dizzy and weak. For a second he wanted nothing more than to be in bed sleeping. Shawn shook him, more from his own panic than to snap him out of it.

"I, I followed them for a bit. But I lost them. I didn't have a flashlight and I was afraid that if I yelled it would spook him and he'd hurt her. Tom, he was carrying her."

It's amazing how one second something can be so life altering and emotionally painful yet the next second it's insignificant. Tom started to race for the woods in a craze with nothing more than getting his daughter back on his mind. But as he formed his hands into fists to run, pain shot through his bad arm, instantly reminding him what being unprepared can do. Stopping, he turned to Shawn. "Go get any flashlight you have, and a weapon too."

Not even finished speaking, Tom darted into the house. He grabbed the emergency flashlight that was plugged into the kitchen socket before scrambling through drawers to find a weapon. He chose a large meat tenderizer over a knife It just felt more comfortable in his hand. Next, he raced up the stairs and kicked in the bedroom door like some action hero saving the girl. Sandy screamed seeing the weapon in his hand. Tom paid no attention to it.

"Lilly has been kidnapped by the guy in the woods. Call the police. Shawn and I are going after her."

He started to run again but paused when he noticed that Sandy was packing. His heart stung. They glanced at each other, fear and pain in their eyes.

When Tom got back outside, Shawn was already there. He had one of those million watt police lights and a flimsy steak knife. Tom nodded to him and the two raced into the darkness. Beams of light bounced through the treetops as they jumped over sticks and logs, ignoring the footpath to take a more direct route to the mill.

"Sandy is calling the police," Tom yelped while leaping over some pickers.

Shawn suddenly stopped running. "Police? No, no. Tom, we can handle this. You've got to tell her to call back, tell them it was a false alarm."

Tom didn't slow down or even look back at the man. Whatever the reason for his odd comments, he didn't care. After a few seconds, Shawn caught back up to him and kept pace. Nothing more was said until they reached the mill, which looked ten times more ominous in the dark. "The place is like a maze. What do you think we should do, stay together or split up to cover more ground?"

"You even sure they'd be in here, Tom? He was heading the other way with her."

Tom stared at the mill as if the mill itself was evil. "Positive."

They entered the door that Tom had walked through twice before. This time was different, he could see. The lights quickly checked each corner before heading down the hall.

"There are dozens of doors. Christ. I'll check the ones on the left you check the ones on the right."

Holding the flashlight with his broken hand was sending unbearable pain through his arm and into his shoulder. But he had no choice. If he was going to be effective with his weapon, he needed it in his good hand.

Room after room – nothing, just trash of different generations, the ex-workers of years ago and the partiers of weeks past. The journey that took Tom five minutes last time took them only a minute tonight. They reached the end of the long hall. Two ways to go.

"You feel safe going that way alone, Shawn?"

Shawn, who was spending more time looking back towards where they came from rather than in the room, nodded. Tom didn't know and didn't care if Shawn was checking for the police or covering their backs. The two started off in separate directions.

SHIT! Tom thought. Why didn't I bring the walkie-talkies! Again, unprepared. He looked back over his shoulder and watched the light bounce around in the distance. He was glad he wasn't alone again. In a few minutes the cops would be here as well. Tom shone his light down the hall to see ahead. The tunnel of light just disappeared in the endless blackness. His gut sank as he cursed the size of this place.

Sandy sat on the edge of the bed, phone in hand. The computerized operator was telling her to hang up and try again. Her jaw was shaking more than her hands were. *I am one sick fuck, what the fuck is wrong with me! Dial the fucking phone! FUCK YOU! FUCK YOU!* Sandy argued with herself in her head. Tom ran out the door ten minutes ago. She's been sitting there with the phone in her hand for nine.

Sucking on a lollypop, Lilly was humming a tune while Mr. Bluestick was pacing back and forth in front of the ChrimsaWheel.

"Come on, Lilly, my dear, you must go. We must get you home before your parents find out you're gone."

"But what about the man in the woods? What if he is still out there?"

Dang her! That was the exact reason he hadn't rushed her back yet. Whoever it was posed a definite problem. He could catch him and expose his hideout. Or worse, what if the man attacked? Lilly could get hurt. He wasn't willing to risk that. His mind hurt from thinking of ways to get Lilly back quickly and safely.

"I've got to pee!" Lilly said with glee.

Mr. Bluestick looked over to the little girl who was smiling widely, lips red from the candy. She looked so happy sitting there on the ChrimsaWheel! His heart ached with love. He just wished he could take her back with him when he left. What a minute! Pee, liquid, water! That's it! "You're a genius, my love!"

Lilly giggled before replying. "But of course!"

Mr. Bluestick ran to the wall and grabbed an old boat oar that was painted pink and studded with blue beads. "The stream! It's high enough today that we can take it back to your yard and get off. We could sneak you back home and no one would ever know! Of course, I'd have to find a way back, but I can do that no problem!" He looked back at Lilly, only to find that she was now frowning.

"I don't want to go home, Mr. B. I want to stay here."

He walked over to her and patted her on the head before crouching down. Halfway his legs burned. How sore they're going to be tomorrow, he thought.

"Look Lilly, I want you to. . ."

A faint mettle *tink* stopped his speech. Lilly went to say something but he put a gloved finger over her lips to shush her. *Tink, tink, tink.* The noise came closer. He stood up with some trouble and walked over to the wall. Looking up at a small four-inch hole in the wall, he put out his hands and caught the tiny metal ball.

"What's that?" Lilly said, a bit too loud.

He immediately put both hands up to shush her. With two fingers he motioned her to come close. She tiptoed over.

"Someone is here in the halls. I set up an alarm system. When someone brushes against it, they have no clue but it sends a tiny ball down here to warn me."

Lilly thought it was so cool but realizing that it was a threat, her interest changed. Holding hands, the two ran to the lights and shut them off. Mr. Bluestick picked Lilly up, this time in his arms, his legs still protested though. Almost silently, he scurried over to the tube. He placed her down next to it and clicked on his cane.

"Now, Lilly, I don't want you to be scared, okay?"

"No, no, don't make me go down alone. It's dark out!" She hugged him and wouldn't let go.

"Don't worry, I just want you to wait here. I'm going to go see who it is. But if you hear me yell, I want you to go down it and run home, okay? It's very important, my dear." Mr. Bluestick could feel her little head nod against his chest.

"But it's dark, I need my flashlight."

Within a second he retrieved it and brought it back to her. Lilly turned it on.

"I'm going to give you something very special, Lilly, it was mine when I was a child. It will protect you in case you have to go out there alone, okay?"

She now looked at him with fear and interest. From under his cloak he produced a strange looking object. He handed it to her. With both hands she took it. It sort of looked like one of those hand weights that mom used when she went walking. It was oval but on one side four different color jewels stuck out. Mr. Bluestick guided her fingers through it.

"You see, slip your hand through the circle. You have four buttons by your thumb, each one lights a different jewel. Try it!"

Pushing the first button lit up the red jewel. The sparkling light covered the whole wall. Lilly smiled broadly and tried the others, green, yellow and blue.

"Thanks! I love it!"

Mr. Bluestick gave her a quick hug, clicked off his cane and disappeared.

Still off the hook, the phone was now across the room. Sandy hugged her knees sitting in the middle of the bed. She glanced to the clock. Twenty-three minutes had passed. Her half packed suitcase was still open next to her. Getting up, she angrily grabbed some more underwear and crammed it into the case. Then it struck her - if she didn't call and something did actually happen to Lilly, she could get in trouble herself. Twenty-four minutes. Shit.

Sandy dove for the phone, shut it off, waited several seconds and clicked it back on to hear the familiar dial tone. Plotting out in her head what to say she hesitated while beginning to dial the three numbers. Nine, *I have to act frantic,* one, *my husband just ran to find her,* off button.

Deeper into the mill than ever before, Tom searched the rooms more slowly. To his horror some of them led off into other halls, making the search painstakingly long. After every step he paused and strained his ears, praying to hear his daughter's laugh, cry, yell, anything. Room after room nothing. From time to time he was hearing crunching and clattering in the way off distance but he could only assume it was Shawn.

One particular room he entered seemed a bit odd. The thick years of dust and dirt didn't seem to cover the floor as much. And though there were piles of trash on the floor, none of it seemed to be in front of this one door, a huge metal, rusting door. Tom tried to open it, locked. Feeling like a detective in an old movie, he leaned down to examine the keyhole. Clean and shiny. He started to lose his breath. This was it, this was it.

Lilly waited and waited. There was almost no noise, making waiting in the dark even scarier. She had to stop herself from turning on her new light band, but couldn't. It was so cool! With her left hand she kept covering the light so she could see its radiant glow with out exposing herself.

Would it really protect her? How? Did the lights actually have powers? It did come from another planet.

Feeling brave enough to shine the light around the room, Lilly held out her arm like Wonder Woman and clicked on each different light, one by one. *Ca-Thunk.* The noises echoed in the room. Lilly doused the light and scrunched against the wall some more. It had to be the door. Someone was trying to get in! Dear God, who was it? Why would someone want to hurt them? Where was Mr. Bluestick?

First her eyes shut tight, then she screamed at the light that appeared only inches away from her. It took three full seconds for her scream to die before she realized it was just Mr. B.

"Shhhhhhhhhhh!"

She could hardly see his face but knew his finger must be in front of his mouth to help get the point across. Lilly wanted to yell at him for scaring her so much but she was shaking too much.

"LILLY! LILLY! ARE YOU IN THERE!"

Before Mr. Bluestick could explain who their intruder was, the scream from her dad came booming through the door.

"Oh no! What do we do?"

"The slide again, it worked last time. Just use your normal flashlight once outside so he won't ask where you got that." Lilly had all four colors shining now, making Mr. Bluestick's face look an odd shade of puke red.

"In the woods, my dear. It was that foul neighbor of yours who followed us. He must have told your father," he said, pausing several times to allow for Tom's yelling.

"Just get outside, yell for him. I. . . I don't know what to tell you. But just, uh...well, my love. If you must tell him of my existence, just don't tell him about this room and my machine. Just tell him I'm an old man living here. He just won't understand the true story."

Lilly was ready for the slide this time. She got in on her own and with a quick hug she was off. She couldn't understand why Mr. Bluestick looked so sad. If dad would only meet him and talk to him, then they could all hang out. But for some reason Mr. B seemed scared. Once outside she quickly switched lights and started to make her way to the front. At the side of the mill she yelled for her dad.

The hug hurt. It was so tight and long Lilly thought she was about to be crushed to death. Dad's hard arm cast dug into her back; it was definitely going to leave a bruise. After what seemed like an eternity, he loosened up and she saw Mr. Daggerty striding over with his arms out. Ewww. Lilly tried her best to get away from the hug but couldn't, Dad was still holding her. The bony sweaty arms stuck to her like gum on a sneaker. Lilly shivered.

"Lilly, this is very important. Where is the man that kidnapped you?" Tom said placing her down on a makeshift seat. Shawn behind him was taking up guard, knife far out in front of him.

"What? Kidnapped? What are you talking about, Daddy?"

"LILLY! This is no time to fool around, you don't have to be scared anymore either. You're safe now and we'll take care of him."

Lilly made a mean scowl and yelled back. "Scared! I left the house because I was scared! I feel safer here with Mr. Bluestick!"

Tom felt as if it was a punch. He wanted this whole week, hell, this whole summer to redo. He'd stay in his little box house. It was always fine there.

"Lilly, look I'm sorry mom and I got in a fight. It's just like when you and your cousin Bill argue over who gets to use the slip and slide first. It was no big deal."

She raised an eyebrow to show how stupid of an analogy it was.

"Look, Lilly, did this man touch you, or hurt you?"

"HE WOULD NEVER! He's my best friend."

Tom couldn't believe what he was hearing. It was weeks ago she first mentioned this magical man and he just played it off. He was furious with himself. Interrupting their talk, Shawn cut in.

"Hey Tom, I don't hear sirens yet. And we have no clue what this wacko might have in there. I, uh. . .why don't we get out of here while we can."

Tom hadn't thought of that, a mix of emotions was running his mind right now. Anger at himself, fear for his child, and desire to kill the man who kidnapped his daughter were in the forefront. Actual danger to himself was nowhere to be found.

"I guess you're right, we'll come back and search with the police later." Tom tried to pick Lilly up to carry her but she kicked and screamed. Back on the ground, she wanted nothing more than to run back to the ChrimsaWheel and sit in the big comfy chair.

In the back yard Shawn made a halfhearted excuse to leave and scampered off. Tom ushered Lilly with her head down into the house. Instantly he yelled for Sandy. No response. The cops should have been here by now. Again he yelled for Sandy. Lilly sat glumly at the table while Tom locked the back door and drew the curtains. Again he yelled for her.

Not waiting for her to come down, Tom stomped up the stairs. Their door was closed. He didn't have to turn the handle since he broke the lock last time. There she was, sitting with her back against the bed, phone in hand, eyes and face red. Hands trembling. Tom looked around the room cautiously before approaching her. "Sandy?"

His wife didn't budge and hardly blinked. Tom was numb, not worried, scared or angry. Nothing. He sat down beside her and gently took the phone. Placing it on the bed he put his good arm around her shoulder. She still didn't move. He wondered if she even knew he was in the room. Was it fear of losing her daughter? Anger at him? Tom was too exhausted to think anymore. Tears started to flow. Lose his wife, win her back, lose his daughter, find her, and lose his wife again. It was becoming a vicious cycle.

17

The rest of the night was much calmer. Tom apologized to Lilly and explained that he loved her and tomorrow they needed to have a long talk. He then scooped his wife up and placed her into bed. Lilly slept in the middle of the two the whole night. It made her happy and she felt loved. Mom didn't say anything but she smiled and kissed her twice on the head. Dad would hardly let her go. And, for some reason, he put a chair in front of the bedroom door.

Tom woke to a jolt. Panic raced through his cloudy mind. Lilly! He turned and found both the women in his life next to him sound asleep. It felt good, it was after nine, and amazingly he had slept for some time and actually felt refreshed. Staring at his child, he wanted to wrap his arms around her and squeeze as hard as he could. But he didn't dare disturb her.

It was an odd mood, Tom thought. He was ecstatic that he had his daughter and wife safely next to him. At the same time, though, he was going to have to face talking to the police and explain why they didn't call last night. Then, to top it off, he had no clue how Sandy was going to be today. But, most of all, he knew the hardest thing was going to be telling Lilly she couldn't hang out with Mr. Whatever-his-name-was.

Tom snuck down stairs and started to make batter for pancakes. Halfway through whipping the frothy liquid, Sandy, looking refreshed, entered the room in a robe. She looked nothing like the woman from last night. She smiled at him and opened the fridge for some orange juice. Tom was baffled but happy. Carton in hand, she shuffled sleepily over to him and planted a kiss on his cheek. Odd again.

Minutes later Lilly peeked around the corner, wondering if she was in trouble.

"Get in here, girl! You got a mountain of hot cakes to eat!"

"Daaaad! They are pancakes."

With syrupy smiles, the three of them laughed and ate with big appetites as in the old days. Well, actually, better than the old days. Sandy was much warmer. So much so it made Tom nervous. So much unresolved, but for now that was just fine.

After breakfast Lilly ran to watch cartoons as if everything was normal, leaving Tom and Sandy alone in the kitchen to clean up. Sandy kept smiling. Tom piled plates on top of each other, trying to build courage to talk to her. Placing the dishes next to the sink where Sandy was filling it up with soap, Tom thought about just forgetting everything and just letting this fake perfect family thing go on long as it can. Then he glanced out the window that was above the sink. The woods looked ominous for the first time. He had to do something. There was a crazy man out there.

"Sandy. . .." Tom watched her smile falter a bit then regain its wide stature on her face. "There's actually a guy out there that Lilly has been playing with."

Sandy soaped up the sponge and squeezed it out several times before responding. "So what do we do?" The response had little emotion.

For fear of making eye contact, they both watched the bubbles in the sink build up on top of each other. Tom let out a sigh and walked back to the table. A moment later he heard the running water shut off, allowing the low murmur of Sponge Bob's laughter into the room. The fantasy family lasted shorter than he thought it would.

"Well, I'm going to have to go to the police. We just can't have Lilly playing with some old bum in the woods." The fingers on his shoulders made him jump a bit, they were wet and unexpected.

"Why don't you try to meet him first, maybe he's not that crazy. If you call the cops, they'll arrest him and Lilly will go crazy. We should wait until we know it's necessary to call them."

The statement sounded oddly rehearsed. Tom mulled it over. She was right, but the thought of that man being normal seemed impossible to him. "You think so?"

"Think about it. Lilly hasn't been hurt yet and she seems to love the guy more than us lately. The cops will take him away right in front of her."

That's what he wanted, to have him taken away. Far away from his daughter. Tom started to chew his lower lip.

"Please, Tom. For Lilly. If he seems dangerous, then we call the police."

Tom wanted to rebut but she was starting to massage his shoulders, wreaking havoc with his thinking process. The light pressure seemed to make the idea okay.

"Okay, okay. I'll see if Shawn will go with me. I'll have to talk to Lilly, though, and find out where he stays. That place is a maze." Almost instantly after agreeing, the fingers stopped massaging and he heard small splashes of the plates being put in the sink. No response, nothing. If only he could figure out what was going on in her head.

Sandy started to mindlessly wash the syrup off the plates. But her hands were shaking too much. In an attempt to stop the trembling she sank the plates into the hot water. It was almost too hot for her to keep them submerged, but Sandy cherished the stinging pain. The urge to vomit was even stronger than the one to stop the shaking.

Hearing Tom talk about calling the police was almost too much to take. Scream, run, cry, a lot of things ran through her mind hearing the word *Police*. Yet, once again, she amazed herself by being calm (well, enough to trick her husband) and lying for the umpteenth time. She really had no choice though. Cops coming here? No way could she handle it. Tom, yes. But police, no way. They would be all over the place, asking questions, looking through things. It would spoil all the plans she had.

Tom stood behind Lilly, waiting patiently for a commercial break to make his move. Watching Sponge Bob try to catch jellyfish, Tom ran through the lines he'd been working on for the last fifteen minutes. He was going to go in with sugar, acting as if he wanted to meet the guy just to be friends and nothing more. Finally, a cereal commercial came blaring on. Lilly snapped away from her hypnotized state and acknowledged her dad with a smile.

"Hey, sweetie! Can I talk to you?"

"Sure! Make it quick, though! The commercials are short." Tom grinned and plopped onto the blue beanbag chair shooting her out of her comfy little nook with a giggle.

"Daaaad!"

"Whoopsie Daisy!" Tom sighed and watched another commercial, building up courage as they both squished around comfortably. "Look, sweetheart, I've been thinking it over and I really want to meet your friend."

Lilly's eyes bulged with excitement as she jumped up and hugged him. The sudden movement made Tom sink to the bottom of the beans. The hug felt great, but best of all genuine.

The show came back on. Lilly paid no attention. She just kept going on and on about how great Mr. Bluestick was. When Tom finally asked how to find him, she casually talked about how he made her not look as they went through the halls. This whole idea suddenly didn't sound so good.

An hour later Tom headed next door to Shawn's house to thank him for last night and yet again ask him for help. Walking next door, he noticed all the windows were shut tight and his car had a cover on it for the first time. Odd. Tom knocked on the door and waited. He had an eerie sense of being watched. As he was about to leave, the door finally opened a crack.

"Uh, Tom, hey." Shawn's eyes darted everywhere but at Tom from behind the chained door. "What's up?" For the first time Tom realized that he hadn't been into Shawn's house. Random crazy ideas started to dart through his mind about his new best friend. But they needed to take a back seat to the task at hand. Just as he was about to speak, the door shut, startling him. Within an instant it was back open. Shawn jumped out and shut it once again. What is it with everyone? Tom started to feel as if he moved to some parallel universe. "Hey Shawn, I just wanted to thank you about last night."

As he spoke, Shawn's beady eyes stayed on the street until Tom got to the part about how he hadn't called the cops. Eye contact. After that Shawn seemed to relax and was more than willing to help. Tom made sure to make a mental note to find out more about him when this whole ordeal was over.

Tom dug around in the tiny shed that was filled with packing boxes of yard items yet to be hung up. It was dusty and nicked up but sturdy. His trusty old baseball bat from his youth was hanging on a hook. Shawn had a billy club that looked as if it was from the twenties. Tom didn't ask where he got it. With the final items in place– walkie-talkie to radio the house, cell phone, flashlights, and weapons, they were ready for the task at hand.

Turning back to steal a look at the house, Tom caught Lilly watching them. She jumped back. Holding the bat made him feel safe, but now at the same time guilty. She was obviously nervous, even from this distance he could see it in her eyes. Before he had headed out, she had begged to come along. Tom stood his ground and said no with a promise to be nice to the old man. Now with the bat at his side he could only imagine what went through her head.

The walk was slow and awkward, nothing like the night before. Crunching leaves and cracking sticks was the only noise between them. Tom was thankful for wearing the cargo shorts. All the items fit nicely, leaving his injured hand free to rest. Oddly he was more scared of hurting this mystery man than he was of getting hurt. The way his emotions had been lately he didn't know if he would be able to control himself. Hopefully, Shawn would keep him in check.

Lilly wanted to sneak out and run the long way around the woods to beat them to Mr. Bluestick, but Mom, today, was actually acting like a mother and keeping an eye on her every move. For the first time she was wishing her mom wouldn't be motherly. The bat kept popping into her mind. Why did dad need that? Did he really think Mr. Bluestick was a bad guy?

After watching Dad and the creepy guy disappear into the woods that she loved so, Lilly shuffled her feet to the living room to turn on the TV and click around. Mom followed her in and sat next to her. Odd again. Maybe the family *had* been taken over by aliens. Things have just been so weird since moving here.

Sandy looked at her daughter-studied was more like it. Scanning every inch of her face , Sandy desperately looked for the tiny bit of resemblance to herself. Nothing. She didn't get it. Everyone from checkout clerks at the grocery store to relatives said they looked so much alike. They had to have been just being polite. Not one hair looked similar.

My daughter, my ass! She thought while holding back the look of disgust. Anger welled in her. For the longest time she has fought all the thoughts, the voices, the plots that constantly bugged her. Not anymore. Finally they have won out. It was a wonderful feeling to let them run free, to not have to fight or think anymore. They'll run the show now.

Two more days, two options. Her mind clicked back and forth between the two decisions she had made. One was worse than the other, but both seemed viable. A woman had to do what a woman had to do, right? What other choices did she have? How is a child yours when really you were just an egg donor, drugged by your husband for God knows what reason or how many times. She could hardly think of the things he must have done to her without getting the shakes. No more, though, the sick bastard won't get another chance.

Almost an hour searching the dark, creepy, disgusting halls turned up nothing. Tom was having a hard time finding the door he was at last night. Of course, soon as he started the search for it, he realized a crow bar should have been on his list of items. If they find it, there was no way he was going to get in. Several times he contemplated

Aloisi

giving up and going back but his instinct to protect his family was too strong.

Shawn had disappeared into a room up ahead as Tom leaned against a wall thinking about the tiny house and crappy job he left. They seemed so much nicer now.

"BINGO!" Shawn's voice came booming from the door.

Tom dashed ahead to see what he had found. The empty room was completely empty, which was odd since every other one in this whole place had some sort of trash in it.

Shawn was working at prying a large steel door open with his fingers, carefully holding his flashlight in his armpit. "Give me a hand!" Shawn gasped.

Tom just looked around. He wasn't positive but he could have sworn the door he was at last night was on the other side of the hall. The left, definitely it was on the left. Wait, what if he had been coming from the other side, though? It didn't matter for now. It was a door, the first one they found that was locked from the inside.

With his one good hand, Tom joined in on the effort to make it budge. It was useless. Fifteen fingers weren't going to pop open a steel door. "We ought to look for something to use on it." Tom sighed, staring at it as if he had heat ray vision that would melt the locks off.

"You could just use the key, good chap!"

Tom let out a half laugh, thinking it was Shawn putting on a fake accent.

"Would you gentlemen care for some tea?"

Feeling his hair stand up on the back of his neck and sensing Shawn was feeling the same, Tom grabbed his bat and preparing to turn around.

18

Spinning around, unbalanced but ready to fight, Tom clumsily raised the bat, making the flashlight drop from his armpit. The man who spoke was all in shadows and hard to see. His light went out with a clank then he could see Shawn's light bouncing around trying to find the target.

"Gentlemen, gentlemen, no need for the panic. I am unarmed and harmless. Here. . ." With a twang, the room was suddenly filled with an eerie blue light. Tom couldn't believe his eyes, his bowels gurgled and he felt as if he was in some horror movie. Here they were in an abandoned mill, trapped in a room with no exits, staring at a man dressed in a tuxedo from the twenties holding a giant blue light. Surreal.

Shawn and Tom both stood their ground, weapons in hand, speechless, waiting for the mad man to attack.

"Shall we have the tea now? Do follow."

Suddenly the light was bouncing down the hallway. The pair looked at each other, trying to read the other's eyes and to see if what was happening was real or not. Finally they decided to follow, slowly. In the hall the man was waiting several doors down.

"In here!"

They followed the voice and the brilliant blue light in the distance. In a low voice that hopefully only Tom could hear, Shawn whispered to him. "What if this is a trap?"

The thought hadn't occurred to him. He was too fixated on wondering if this man had touched his daughter. Rage was building inside him. He had to go after him, regardless of what was in that room.

"True, here, take the walkie and stay here. If I yell, radio back to Sandy to call the police."

Shawn seemed nervous and reluctant but obliged . Tom started down the dark hall to the door that was now glowing with normal light. He held the bat high and wished his other arm was good to give the bat more strength behind a swing.

Staying against the far wall, Tom slowly peered into the room. He was really expecting a pendulum to swing out and cut him in half, but all he saw was an old man sitting at a table with three cups of tea set out. With tiny steps Tom entered the room.

"Ahhh, good of you to join in!"

The hand holding the bat was getting sweaty and he was worried it might slip, but it was too late to dry it. Feeling like a S.W.A.T. agent, he quickly scanned the room for anything that might harm him. Nothing, oddly the room was more than welcoming. Two couches, an old TV, microwave, stove, sink and the walls—the walls were painted glorious colors like a tie-dyed shirt. It almost felt as if he was transported to another building entirely. How could something in this good shape be in here? How did they not find this room before? And how the hell did he have electricity?

"Please, sit, sit. And invite your friend in. I know you must be horribly upset that your daughter has been playing with me, but please let me explain."

Lilly! The bastard! Suddenly the fantasy room wasn't important anymore. Never in his life had he wanted to hurt someone so much. He could only imagine the things he did to his daughter out here. It would feel so good to just swing the bat at his head right now.

"I swear to you, sir, I would never harm your precious Lilly. She has been a friend to me and nothing more. Now I know I may look a bit odd to you. . ."

"You son of a bitch!" Tom could feel the sweat

pouring down his face as he raise the bat a bit higher, preparing to swing.

Shawn was by the door listening carefully, walkie-talkie in hand, even though he knew he wouldn't use it no matter what was to happen. Hearing how angry Tom was, Shawn smiled. Perfect. Just perfect he thought, before jumping into the doorway to calm his "buddy" down.

"TOM! Relax!" Tom turned to see Shawn standing in the doorway. Another second and he would have done it. He would have swung and swung until he couldn't anymore. His mouth fell open and tears started to well in his eyes. Defeated and emotionally exhausted, he shuffled over to the farthest couch, away from the man and sat. Staring at the floor, he thought to himself over and over again, "What the fuck is going on, this isn't real. How the hell has everything gone to shit?"

Strangers to each other, they locked eyes with concern for Tom. Shawn broke the gaze and cautiously walked to Tom. "It's okay, buddy. It's okay. Nothing more is going to happen." If only you knew, Shawn thought, as he placed a hand on his shoulder, all the while keeping an eye on the man sipping tea.

"Please, why don't we all just have some tea and a civilized talk? I understand how you must feel. A crazy old man, wearing a tuxedo, living in an abandon mill. I must look like some child molester. But I swear to you, and Lilly will, too, that I have never touched her. And never would. We merely have been keeping each other company playing games! Lilly has been terribly lonely here in the new town. I'm just being a friend."

Tom listened to the strange, nervous rambling. A powerful headache was starting to build behind his eyes from the stress.

Mr. Bluestick couldn't remember a time when he was so nervous. For crying out loud, they almost found his ChrimsaWheel. Then how would he get home? His plans to leave were now going to have to be pushed up, especially if Tom gets the cops involved. There were only so many days he could hide out in the mill without being found. It had been a tough debate with himself this morning about whether or not to hide. But he knew it was too late for that; they had much too much proof he existed. They wouldn't have stopped until they found him. Best to try and defuse the situation, which he knew would be practically impossible.

When Tom had that bat above his head, he desperately wanted to trigger the collapsing ceiling trap to protect himself but this is Lilly's father and if he was hurt more, she'd be crushed. He'd rather take a beating than see her hurting. Thankfully, that odd chap saved him. Lilly was all too right about this sticky man. A bad vibe just poured off him like bad body odor. Besides, when he watched from the woods at night, Shawn seemed to be doing some odd things.

Sitting in silence once again, Mr. Bluestick wondered if he would have rather never met Lilly. No, the girl's friendship was worth this. Was it worth the chance of never getting home, though? He started to let out a large sigh but stopped himself. Why won't Tom just speak? He found himself frustrated, wanting to ramble on, but knew too much talking wouldn't be good.

"What's with the outfit?"

Ah wonderful words. Mr. Bluestick grinned before replying. "Why, I think it looks rather good, don't you?"

Tom gave a huff. It was tough to tell whether it was a laugh or annoyance. "How long have you lived here?"

"Well, a long time now, well over twenty years, I would say."

Shawn thought Tom was crazy for actually talking to this whack job. He couldn't be sane.

"Tom, I think we should just go."

Tom gave Shawn a blank look and shook his head no. "Why do you play with Lilly?" He asked behind gritted teeth.

"Your daughter is a wonderful girl. So full of imagination and life! When you get to be an old man, you crave youth. Haven't you ever seen how close grandparents get with their grandkids? It's a way of reliving your childhood. You'll see someday. It's completely harmless. I never had children...um...sorry. Uh, in a way, playing with Lilly is like letting me experience what I never could."

Tom was touched and impressed by the man's cool, calm and professional delivery of each line. But it did nothing but make his mind swirl more with a million questions. Who is he? Why has he lived here? How does he get food? Though they were all on the tip of his tongue, wanting to jump off, he fought them back and stood up. The bottom line was, no matter how nice this man seemed, he was crazy. No one else would live in the woods and wear a tuxedo for twenty years. He may be harmless but that was not a chance he could take.

"Look, I'm trying my best to be nice here for the sake of my wife and daughter. I'm not going to call the police on you but you better stay away from Lilly. If I find out you talked to her one more time, I'll have this place swarming with cops. You'll be in a loony bin for the rest of your life!" Tom stated this while standing up and brandishing his bat.

Shawn walked out the door first, Tom followed but turned back . "And if I see that blue light behind my house ever again at night. . . Shawn and I might just have to skip calling the cops!"

Walking down the hall, Tom's heart was thumping. Never in his life had he threatened someone. It felt good yet totally wrong at the same time. Carefully he made damn sure he remembered the path to that room, just in case he ever had to get there fast again.

19

Like the proud hunters of yesteryear, Tom and Shawn tromped through the small gate back into the yard feeling victorious. This time the walk back was filled with plenty of talk, mostly about how nuts the guy was. Finally arriving, Lilly was in the downstairs window looking out like a sad kid on a rainy day. Tom smiled , proud he protected her. She gave him a wide smile back. That's when he realized his mistake. He wasn't going to let her see the old man again. This wasn't going to be good, not at all.

Before they could even get to the door, Lilly burst through it. Wrapping her arms around his waist for a hard hug, she blurted out, "Isn't he cool, Dad? Don't you just love him! Now he can come over for dinner and we can watch movies! It'll be so, so, so cool!"

Shawn had to hold back a smile. Tom patted her head, not ready to have the talk just yet. If he did tell her, she just might run off again. This was going to be tricky. For the next few weeks they won't be able to let her out of sight.

"Let's go inside, honey, and talk, okay?"
The ecstatic girl let go of her father and looked up, suspicious. Her gaze then went to Shawn. As always, the sight of him made the hair on her neck stand up. He smiled at her with a wink.

"Good to see ya Lilly." She ignored him.

"Dad, wasn't he cool?" Tom tossed the baseball bat into the grass.

"Come on, Lilly."

"DAD!"

"Hey, uh, Tom, I'm going to head home. If you need something,   let   me   know."

"Thanks again, Shawn. I'll come over tonight and talk." Shawn nodded and walked away.

Lilly liked seeing the man leave but that didn't explain her dad's reactions. How could he not think Mr. Bluestick was fun and amazing? She looked at the multicolored light in her hand and felt a pang in her stomach. She knew it was fear of losing her best friend.

The door slammed with such force that Tom cringed and waited for everything to fall off the walls in the house. Nothing did. His fist went to knock lightly and use the soothing voice that he always used to coax his way into the room, but he stopped himself. Not tonight. He was too exhausted, so much happened this past week, too much. All he wanted now was his wife, the wife he used to know, to hold, to kiss him and tell him everything is all right. The chances of that happening were slim.

After setting up a string tied to a chair leg with cans on it to alarm him of an attempted escape from Lilly's room, Tom retired to his own. He wanting badly to shower but did not want to risk leaving a window of opportunity for Lilly to run off into the woods again. Sandy had been reading or pretending to, at least. Her eyes didn't move from one spot in the book, some cheesy paperback romance novel called *Fifty Handfuls* or something like that. He could hardly imagine what lame premise it had. Without being overly obvious, Tom slid under the sheets and lay closer to her than usual. He rested his head on her arm. Amazingly her eyes still hardly moved. Lightly he nudged her arm with his head, once, twice and finally on the third time she broke her gaze and gave him a lame smile. Tom gave her his best *I need to be held* puppy dog look. It seemed to work, she tossed the book aside, not even marking the page.

"Crazy night, huh?"

"Week!"

Sandy slid down from her propped up position and let Tom nestle into her armpit. Tom wondered whether he should spoil this rare moment with talking. Sandy answered that question by putting a finger on his mouth to hush him. In a matter of seconds, Tom found himself fighting not to fall asleep.

Sandy couldn't help but admit to herself that it did feel good having Tom snuggle up against her. But then again it could be any man really. She couldn't see his face and without him speaking she could imagine it was anyone she wanted to it to be. And that is exactly what she did. It was amazing how easy it was to picture sandy-colored hair, a sharper jaw and more muscular body under her arm. Just like Mark. Soon she wouldn't have to imagine him being under her arm, he'd actually be there instead of this . . . this foul bastard.

Lilly plotted. She could tell by now that her parents were asleep. There wasn't a sound in the house except for the regular creaks of it settling, or so that's what her dad had told her that those noises had been. It had been a good hour since her tears had dried up. Why doesn't dad like Mr. Bluestick? It made no sense, none at all. He was so cool and nice. Maybe dad was just jealous that she spent so much time with him?

Getting out of bed, Lilly scrambled for the window wanting more than anything to see the light, the light that once was so frightening and was now so comforting. Straining her eyes she scanned back and forth trying so hard to see it. But nothing. Earlier she had strained her eyes looking for two hours straight. Depressed and ready to give up for the night, she saw something red. Red light? It couldn't be Mr. Bluestick, could it? Cupping her hands on the glass she focused with all her might to see what it was. It seemed to be a letter. *L? I? L?* It kept changing, and . . . and it was spelling her name! It instantly made Lilly think of some old movie that dad loved where these soldiers sent Morse code with flashes of light, except this was much easier to understand. Not wanting to miss a letter but knowing she needed paper, Lilly dashed to her desk and grabbed her Brartz notebook and pen.

Back at the window the red flashing letters were now on the letter *Y*. Good, she hadn't missed anything! The next letter came up and she almost forgot to write it down, she was so amazed how it was happening. Was it all different lights that he had? No that would be too much to carry out here. Maybe it was like the time when she went to the Fourth of July fireworks and a few kids had these toys in their hands that spun around really fast and said, "Happy Fourth!" with little explosions after it. Yeah, that was probably it. Oh no, he was on the second letter. *D. . .O. . .* It took almost fifteen minutes for all the letters to be spelled out. Lilly read back the note. *Lilly, don't worry. Meet me at 11 at night on Tues. in front of the mill. Flash twice for yes, once for no.* Lilly read it, confused, but excited at the prospect of seeing Mr. Bluestick again. She instantly put on her light band and flashed all the colors twice and waited for a response. Shortly after came *B. . .y. . .e.*

Lilly finally climbed in bed with a smile. She was happy that Mr. Bluestick wasn't mad at her and she was going to get to see him again soon. But something seemed wrong. It didn't seem like him to ask her to meet late, especially having to go into the woods alone. And what was with the red light? How come he never turned on his blue light? He knows how much it comforted her. The weirdest part was why Tuesday? That was almost a full week away.

Maybe it was because Dad went back to work then. Oh well, it didn't matter, she was going to see her best friend again soon.

The light was heavy and much more expensive than he ever imagined. Amazingly it had worked. That was his biggest worry, spending so much money and not even having it pay off. But when he saw that weird child's toy light flash, it made his entire body get the chills. It was like a full body orgasm without actually coming. Ever since he saw the little girl, he knew he wanted - no - needed her. It had been killing him to hold off so long.

Years of running and a dozen fake names later, Shawn Daggerty thought he was over his obsession. After seeing Lilly for the first time, the urges came back full force. He often still fantasized about children, but he thought it was in check, that he controlled it. But moving in next to one was too much, much more than he could handle, especially one this cute, this ripe.

For the first few weeks he thought he'd be content at just watching from the window and touching himself, but, day by day, it got less satisfying, making the need for this plan more and more important. Not until tonight when he was driving back from Spencer's Gifts with the two hundred dollar light banner did he realize he was in trouble. After a long talk with himself, he realized that it wasn't his fault. God (who saved him from hell and put him on the right track) put her here, in front of him and dropped this perfect plan in his lap as a gift to him, for doing so well.

20

Once again Tom woke to an all too strange world. Sandy was already downstairs making breakfast and Lilly, amazingly, was at the table, not watching TV. Both greeted him with a hug and a kiss. This house really was turning into the twilight zone. And yet, once again, reluctant to spoil the mood - even if it was a fake one again - Tom sat and ate heartily, shocked that his daughter was talking to him.

Lilly could see that Dad was confused and tried to hold back a smile. After long thought and two journal entries, Lilly came to the conclusion that lying to her Dad and pretending he was right was the way to go. The more she protested, the more he would keep an eye on her. If she kept pretending to go along with not seeing Mr. Bluestick, maybe he would let her play in the woods again alone. Then she would be back to the days of fun.

It was just like the time that her old best friends Sandy and Toni weren't allowed to play with the older kids on the block. After a week of fighting they told her mom that she was right. Two days later they were outside playing with the older guys. Of course mom was right and after the guys picked on them one too many times, they didn't hang out with them again anyway. This was the same thing . . . sort of.

Mark, beautiful, sexy, muscle-bound Mark! Soon, so soon. Less than a week and she was going to leave this sham of a life behind. No more cooking, cleaning, and, best of all, no more of that damn kid. All the trouble lately had been driving her nuts! Why can't the girl be like her? Probably because she wasn't hers in the first place. Bastard, Tom.

It's going to be so wonderful . . .sun, fun, adventure, and amazing sex, she assumed. How could it not be amazing, he's gorgeous. So what if he's never actually talked to her, they were meant to be.

In hopes of keeping this façade going, Tom offered to bring the family to the local water park. Sandy frowned and declined, saying she had a nail appointment. Lilly, on the other hand, was ecstatic. And so the week went by. Lilly and her father became closer than they had ever been, swimming, hiking, shopping, going to movies, and playing games. Amazingly, the family even had two different game nights that week alone. Lilly won in Monopoly but Tom won more games of Uno. Sandy lost both but just seemed happy; in fact she seemed to be glowing.

Finally, on Sunday, Tom felt a pang of regret that he had to go back to work. His arm felt much better. The cast will be off soon, but, best of all, his head was clear and his heart was thumping with joy. All the thoughts of Mr. Bluestick were washed from his mind. For all that mattered, it never happened. He was happy.

Lilly had a fantastic week! Dad was so cool that she almost didn't care that she had been forbidden to see her best friend. Dad was also going back to work tomorrow. On one hand, she was happy, since it meant that she got to see Mr. Bluestick again; on the other, she had been having fun. Now she'll have to be alone with Mom. Though she has been fun this week, too, which is really odd since she couldn't remember the last time she was. Oh well, regardless of anything, it was still summer for another month!

Summer's End
Part 2

1

Monday dragged for everyone. Lilly was excited about seeing Mr. Bluestick tomorrow and sad Dad was gone. She killed time playing video games, reading and drawing. But nothing seemed to extinguish her excitement long enough. Mom, on the other hand seemed to be on cloud nine, she was humming! Humming? Mom has never done that before and she has been treating Lilly all day like a princess. "Can I get you something to drink dear?"... "Cookies?"... "Would you like to rent movies?" Lilly had no clue whether it was because Dad wasn't home or whether she was just becoming the mom she should have always been. Whatever it was, it was creepy.

"Oh what a beautiful moooorning, oh what a beautiful daaaaaay!" Sandy sang to herself as she cleaned the house . It was nice having the house somewhat to herself. It put her in an even better mood. In fact, she was in such a good mood she couldn't help but be nice to the little brat. Well, more than one reason was behind that. It was fun to see the skanky little girl looking confused at the offering of cookies and it was good practice for becoming an actress. By God, she was going to win an Oscar someday! The performance she had pulled off this past week had been superb! If it were a daytime drama, she would have an Emmy by now! What a wonderful life it's going to be! The amazing actress and her hunk of a man! All she needs to do is wait until Thursday!

Exactly what he was afraid of, chafing. He knew it, the last thing he wanted to ruin his perfectly planned event was a chafed, sore dick. But what else was he to do - walk around hard all day not being able to concentrate on the necessary plans that needed to be meticulously set out? The only option was to satisfy the pulsing need. Each time he did just that he thought of the dozens of different things that he would do to that sweet, perfect angel. As he looked down at the red, raw skin he grew angry with himself. He had to force the amazing images out of his head so he could get some work done. There was a lot to do between now and heaven.

The pain was less, but the itching was getting worse. Tom was almost tempted to use the massive scissors on his desk to cut the cast off. And he would, too, if it weren't for the drawing that Lilly had put on it. It was a crude child's sketch of a house with the two of them in front of it. When he asked where mommy was, she said getting her nails done. He couldn't help but laugh at that.

Getting back to work was easier than he thought. Same old crap. It was amazing, though, how time off will make you hate working, even when you love a job. It was probably because everything was finally perfect. The house he always dreamed of, a wonderful daughter, and a wife that was treating him great. Even if she was acting like a Stepford Wife, it was still nice to be loved again.

Surprisingly, Gary, the gruff boss, was welcoming this morning. He looked a bit ruffled and clearly relieved that Tom was back.

"Welcome back, now get to work and don't pull any you-know-what." It would have seemed sarcastic but it was followed by a tiny, rare smile that said so much more than any words the tough man could ever express.

In a way, Tom was glad the whole fiasco of breaking his arm and almost losing Lilly happened. Without it, everything might still have been a mess. They always say it takes a tragedy to bring a family together and though Tom knew it wasn't a tragedy, he hoped it was the closest thing they will ever have to one. If only he were that lucky.

Monday was dragging for Mr. Bluestick as well. Sitting on a stool, he snickered at that fat earth cat that hated Mondays. The name escaped him but he vaguely recalled reading a cartoon several times before he stopped visiting the outside world. That thought, along with a dozen others, were just a distraction from the obstacle at hand. Finishing the ChrimsaWheel.

Ever since the run-in with Lilly's father, he knew his time here was limited. The outside world now knew too much about him. Before he knew it they would be after him. He'd lose his home and his life's work, which just happened to be his last hopes of making it home someday. Even worse, they'd probably try to dissect him. Time was short.

Feverishly, almost never leaving the mill, he worked day and night on the wheel, hoping more than anything to finish it before it was too late. He was getting close, too, until one fratula wire burnt out in a test spin. It meant he had to go back to the drawing board, the board he now sat in front of, puzzled. A solid two days now looking at the large old chalkboard that hadn't seen a wet sponge in a decade. Nothing has come to him, no answers. So, instead, his mind would wander. Mostly it would wander to the one thing that had made him happy - since. . .since as long as he can remember - Lilly.

Though he wouldn't admit it to himself, he missed Lilly more than his home planet and his family. He tried to justify it by saying it was because he hadn't seen his family in decades and Lilly was so recent that it was okay to miss her. Just as much as he contemplated how not to burn out the fratula wire, he pondered whether or not it was worth going to see the girl he missed most. Maybe he should, no . . . no. Can't risk it. What about just a glimpse? No one would even know he was there. That might be worth it, and not nearly as dangerous.

2

As the sun was setting on Tuesday night, moods were much higher than normal. Tom sat with Shawn out front of the house, admiring the purple, pink sunset while chatting about baseball, even though neither of them really cared for the sport. But it didn't matter, the two loved to chat. They could go on and on about any subject with each other for hours! Tom nursed a beer. He never drank during the work week but he didn't want to be rude to Shawn who had brought over a twelve pack of Bud Ice to celebrate his going back to work.

"Come on, drink up! Things are good again, my man!" Shawn egged on.

Tom, wishing he had more balls than he did so he could have declined, polished off his first. Before he could place it down, Shawn had slapped a cold, wet one, already opened, into his left hand. Tom chuckled and raised an eyebrow as if to say, "What the hell." It was a bit weird, though, Shawn was such a wine drinker that this brew-ha-ha seemed odd. Maybe he had a bad day? There was still so much he didn't know about this man.

Every time Tom tried to talk about Shawn's personal life, he'd be given a crumb, then the subject would change quickly. "What did your ex-wife do again? - "Lawyer. . . Hey, did you see that new show on Fox?" That was the way it would go every time, no matter what the question. Whether it was about his family, why he is retired, where he moved from, anything. The man liked to keep his personal life just that, personal.

So far the plan was going well, inebriate threat A. With Tom drunk and passed out, he would not be able to come to the rescue of his little daughter. It was a shame that he had to do this to such a nice man. Shawn thoroughly enjoyed these long talks with him. He only knew too well that this would be the last. After losing a daughter, talking about baseball will probably become very meaningless, not that it wasn't now.

He had no intention of killing Lilly. Yes, he would if necessary. For if he had to then it was God's plan. The plan was to make her his wife of sorts, well that is until she couldn't satisfy him anymore. They all did that eventually. His twisted mind rationalized that it was okay, in fact, good to do this. That way he would have a constant release and not need to go after more children, just this one. It was saving lives, which is why God gave him this gift.

Tom was only on the second beer when Shawn looked at his watch, not bad, he was doing fine. He needed to get a few more in him, though, and he seemed to be slowing. Chug contest?

"Hey, Tom, when you were in college did you ever do a chug contest? See who could slam the beer the fastest?"

Tom searched his old memories, smiled, then looked over his shoulder to make sure no one was near the door. "I was damn good at it if I say so myself!"

Shawn pulled out two more beers, popped them open and placed one in front of Tom. He smiled widely.

"I can't man, I'll get sick! I'm not young anymore."

"Ahh, come on, I'll bet you one lawn mowing that I can beat you. You win, I'll mow yours and vice versa."

Tom started to slowly nod. "You're on." After going through a comical routine of warm ups, neck stretches, arm rolls and even cracking knuckles, Tom was ready.

"One, two. . .chug!" Shawn called out.

Tom opened his gullet to the max and started sucking the amber liquid down hard enough to have it dribble out of his mouth. Shawn, on the other hand, chose the calm swallow method. Of course, his was easier to drink, being water and all. It was all too easy. Fill the cans and super glue the openings shut. Tom never noticed that he was only drinking from the ones on the right side of the cooler. Part one of the plan was working all too well.

Lilly waited patiently in bed for Dad to come and tuck her in. Mom already had, kissing her on the cheek and all. Lilly just stared at her as she did it. Weird. Dad was usually here by now. He'd been sitting outside with creep-o for hours now. She so wished he wasn't friends with him. But she wasn't complaining; her relationship with Dad was great right now.

Thirty minutes went by, it was now almost ten. Dad always went to bed at ten. This made Lilly nervous; she needed him fully asleep to make her getaway. Ready to go and play the tired, sleepy kid needs a hug routine to get Dad inside, she heard the footsteps on the stairs. Usually she could tell who it was instantly. It sounded like Dad but there was such a pause in between each step it made her wonder. Finally, Dad was in the doorway, looking goofy.

"What are you still doing up, missy!?"

"I can't sleep until you tuck me in Daddy!"

She was good at playing him. He puckered out his lower lip and over-exaggerated a frown as he headed over to her for a big hug.

"Sorry, baby, Daddy lost track of time talking to Shawn."

Lilly responded with a yucky face to show disapproval of his breath and the fact of being with Shawn.

"Well, I better tuck you in then!" Clumsily Tom tucked every blanket so tight around Lilly that a caterpillar would be jealous. Lilly giggled uncontrollably as Dad made it tighter and tighter.

"Hmmm . . . is that tucked in enough?"

"Dad! I can't move!"

"Good. Then you won't fall out!" He bent over and gave her a rapid-fire dozen kisses on her cheek. Again she giggled. He left and closed her door halfway.

Lilly relaxed for a bit in her cocoon. It was comforting. She had to be careful it wasn't too cozy, though, she had to keep herself awake for another forty-five minutes.

Lilly suddenly jumped awake! No! She fell asleep! No, no, no! Wiping the sleep from her eyes, she prayed it wasn't past eleven. The clock was a bit blurry, but the green numbers slowly focused. Five of eleven! Whew! She was going to have to rush to get there. Jumping up, she reached under her bed for her pre-packed backpack and outfit she had laid out beforehand, pink sweat pants and a white t-shirt with strawberries on it. She was dressed and ready quicker than a cadet at boot camp. Then she switched to stealth mode creeping on all fours into the hall to make sure Mom and Dad's light was out. Check. Now, onto the stairs.

Over the past week, in her boredom Lilly tested each stair thoroughly to find out which ones squeaked and where. Left, middle, left, right three times, left twice, then middle the rest of the way. Success! Not even a cat could have done it more quietly, or so she liked to think. The back door wasn't a problem, being a sliding door and so far away they wouldn't hear it even if it slammed.

Running through the backyard, under the stars, Lilly felt invigorated! It was thrilling to be doing something you're not supposed to. Then she froze halfway, petrified and angry with herself that she forgot to see if Shawn was up and looking out, as he usually is. She turned quickly and scanned his house. All the lights were off except for the living room that was flickering blue from the TV. Whew. She kept her run up. A hundred yards into the woods and she would be able to click on her light, which she contemplated not using since the moon was so bright tonight.

Getting near the water, she slowed her pace. She didn't want to be too out of breath for Mr. Bluestick. The moonlight looked so pretty shining off the water like a moving mirror. The water was significantly less than the last time she was out here. It had dried up by over half since the drought started. It was hard for her to understand that she couldn't play in the sprinkler because it hadn't rained in a while. Why not just use more water for the lawn then? Water is everywhere. Parents are weird sometimes.

The mill was finally in sight! She scanned back and forth looking for the blue light she so missed . . . nowhere. Oh well, he's probably playing it safe and waiting until she gets there to turn it on. Thirty yards away she saw something move near the door. At first it startled her. She was so excited to see Mr. Bluestick that she didn't even realize how scary the woods used to be to her at night. It had to be him though. A light came on.

It was definitely a blue light, but more like a flashlight, not the cane she loved so much. Lilly clenched her palm light and flashed a series of colors at the odd light, hoping it would brighten up the figure, revealing what she was hoping for. Through the dim colors Lilly could see a top hat and cape. Her stomach started to churn. Mr. Bluestick was much bigger than this man.

3

Lilly, like any girl her age would have, froze. Her mind searched for what to do. Run, that was it, run. She was fast and knew the woods like the back of her hand. She'd be back home and able to get Dad up in a few minutes, way before this, this, whatever it was, got her. What was it anyways? Did a monster take over Mr. Bluestick? Maybe it was him? Yeah, it could be, he could have gotten a cold and lost some weight, but that wouldn't explain the light.

The shadowy figure spun the light around in large, wispy circles as if to say, "Ohhh look at me! I'm magical!" Lilly couldn't help but stare. He was still far enough away to run without getting caught. With the ease of lifting a case of bricks, Lilly picked up her left foot, swiveled her ankle and put it back down. The right was next, it took more effort but she got it off the ground. She can do this. Time to run.

"Lilly! My dear, it's so good to see you!" A corny, vaguely familiar voice came from behind the slowly approaching light just as Lilly was about to turn and run. It slowed her retreat, though she did start to back up step by step. The light was coming faster now. Trying to build up courage, Lilly started to count down in her head. Five . . . four . . . three . . .. Then it appeared like a holy vision, the blue light, the real blue light.

From the second story window the light shone bright enough to reveal some bricks near it, but nothing else. It didn't matter, Lilly knew it was him.

"Mr. Bluestick!" Lilly yelled almost too loudly.
The shadowy doppelganger responded. "Yes Lilly, darling, ohhh how I have missed you!"
Lilly ignored him, now wanting to run in a different direction.

"Hurry! He's getting closer!"

The approaching blue light stopped and spun around just in time to see the much better light disappear, but only for a second. If this were a magic show, the audience would have gasped at how quickly the light appeared at the ground floor door. Lilly wanted to run to it, but avoiding the ominous obstacle in between seemed impossible.

Though Lilly hated the stupid movie she couldn't help but think of that *Star Wars* film where they fight with the light sabers. All she could see was two floating lights, slowly starting to circle each other. She couldn't hear anything except for careful, crunching noises coming from the two illuminations. Why aren't they speaking? For several minutes nothing changed except for a few inches each way. Lilly watched in awe. The light she loved tried ever so carefully to edge its way towards her, but the light she feared kept moving in the way.

"Lilly! Are you all right?" The voice came from the good light.

"Yes! But what is the other light? I'm so scared!"

"Lilly, listen to me, run home, get your father."

"NO! You leave here Lilly and your precious Mr. Bluestick will have that light coming right out of his skull!"

The voice! Lilly now knew who it was. She didn't even have to think about it, the hairs standing up on the back of her neck always told her who it was.

Shawn suddenly felt stupid. It had nothing to do with the cheesy tuxedo, top hat and gloves he was wearing, nor did it have anything to do with the crappy kid's toy light he was holding like a sword. It was merely the fact that he underestimated this crazy old bastard. Before donning this sweltering outfit, Shawn had set up a series of traps and alarms to alert him of the old coot's approach. Strings tied to cans, carefully placed logs tied to strings, he even barricaded the two doors he thought were the way into his lair.

Of course he had plans for taking care of him if he did show up, but they were emergency plans, and they were based on notice. This was not in the plans. Worse, Shawn now felt like an idiot for revealing himself (whether it be voice only or not) to Lilly so soon. Now she won't trust him. Letting her go get Dad would be fine if, that's if, he wasn't wearing this outfit. Plan B, if all else were to fail, was to knock out Mr. Bluebastard, then accuse him of trying to kidnap Lilly again. If the girl had her own story, it wouldn't matter. He'd be a hero once again. Of course he would be miserable that he didn't get what was rightfully his, but he was in no danger of getting arrested. That was not an option.

What to do now? Lilly seemed to be staying for fear of harm coming to her odd friend, so that shall be the method. But whom do you grab first? The decrepit old man or the frail little girl? Who would be the better bargaining chip? Lilly. Lilly would be easier to handle, smaller, easier to move. Besides he'd rather have his hands on those beautiful shoulders.

"Lilly, get your ass over to me. Now! This man is crazy. You shouldn't go near him. He could hurt you. I saw that he sent you a message the other day and figured I should come out here to protect you."

Lilly wasn't fooled for a second. Shawn had given her the creeps from day one. She never thought he was dangerous, just creepy, so why would he be out here? Does he really think he is protecting her? Then why would he wear that outfit? Why would he try to be like Mr. Bluestick?

"Why are you dressed like Mr. B.? And why did you say you'd hurt him."

The warmer voice cut in, louder and more meaningful than she had ever heard it. "Lilly! Please, I'm begging you, get out of here! This man is nothing but trouble! I can handle myself with him."

"Don't listen to the old man, he's weak, Lilly. I'll snap him in half. I'm not playing anymore games, Lilly, now get the fuck over here." Shouts of *get over here, leave, run, now, go, I'll kill him, please Lilly,* and others were muddled together, overlapping with anger and fear as the two tuxedoed men yelled. Lilly started to panic for the first time since seeing Mr. Bluestick. Knowing he was there made her feel safe, but he was telling her to go. If she went, what would happen to him? The woods suddenly seemed enormous and frightening at the thought of running back through them alone, leaving Mr. B. in harm's way. Flashes of the day her dad broke his arm because of her flooded over every thought. If Mr. B got hurt because of her leaving him now, she just couldn't take that.

He could feel himself trembling as he gripped the steel rod in one hand and his trusty blue cane in the other. Fear for himself wasn't the issue right now. It was the thought of Lilly getting hurt that was making him want to vomit. She was the one thing he loved in life, the daughter, the family, the friend he had been missing for so long. He couldn't let anything happen to her. All she had to do was run, just run. For God's sake, just run!

Lilly did run, just the wrong way, right into Mr. B's arms. It felt so good to have her tiny arms wrap around him. For a few seconds he wasn't in this situation, he was happy. That moment passed quickly, though.

Shawn was pissed. "Lilly, you stupid little bitch, you do realize that the harder you make this, the worse things I'm going to do to you." He hated to call his angel names but he needed to do what he had to, to get her.

Mr. Bluestick's gut fell to the leaf strewn ground. The shaking stopped, his fist tightened around the pipe, and he gritted his teeth, ready for battle, something that would never happen on his perfect plant. Lilly seemed to have caught the shakes that he just shed so he crouched down to her and, in a tiny whisper, he coaxed her, saying, "Lilly, you must go, get your father. This is too dangerous."

"I can't leave you, I don't want you to get hurt."

"My darling, he's merely human. I have a lot of advantages on him."

Mr. B kept his eyes glued to Shawn who was now shedding the hat, cloak and gloves with such anger that he couldn't help but get them caught. It was the perfect time to strike if only Lilly would release her suction-like grip on his leg.

One quick glance at the girl and he could tell she wasn't going anywhere, fear had set in. With a fast snap of the antique clasp his cloak came off.

"Lilly, listen carefully, darling: This cloak will protect you; wrap it around you and you will become invisible to all night monsters. Use it to run home. If you can't make it, at least go into the trees behind me and cover yourself in it so he won't find you. I'll be right here."

Shawn still struggled with his costume as Lilly quickly wrapped the cloak over her head. Before scuttling off, Lilly gave Mr. B. such a sad look that it felt as if a knife has been plunged into him, a knife just like the one Shawn was pulling from his boot.

Shawn was furious. Was this another test? Did God want him to kill the old man? Did he have to fight for his prize after already earning it? It didn't make sense. All the planning, the preparing, it was gone. How would he salvage this?

"Lilly! You run home and I'll cut off his head, then go back and do the same to your dad!" Hopefully that will keep the little precious prize, his prize from going too far. Old man first - he posed more of a threat. Technically he could kill him and easily get away with it. All he would have to do is change clothing and use the story that he was attacking Lilly and he saved her. But if the police did too much research on him . . . No! Killing him was out of the question; for his plan to work he needed this bastard alive!

"Listen, you old kook. You have two choices: Choice A . . .you go back into your creepy ass dungeon and forget that all of this happened. Choice B . . .I stab you several times, tie you up and make you watch what I'm going to do to Lilly. If I were you, I'd choose A."

Shawn dried the sweat on his hand, trying to grip the knife better. This wouldn't be half as nerve-racking if he could just see the nut better. The moon gave him a faint outline, but the light rod he had was blinding bright, making it nearly impossible to see anything near him that it lit up.

"Shawn, I know you're really a gentleman and mean no harm, so I'm choosing option C - I stay here until you leave Lilly and me alone."

He couldn't help but snicker at the man's eloquent way of speaking. The words seemed to flow out like an actor's on a stage. "Fine, you dumb fuck. Get your brains bashed in!" Shawn took a step towards the light, trying to intimidate more than anything.

"Sir, I apologize but I forgot to mention the rest of option C! It involves four of my good friends that you haven't met, the ones that have you surrounded."

The sweat came more, his world was crashing down, Lilly could be home by now. Thankfully Tom would still be drunk and sleeping, but the time was ticking nevertheless. Keep it together! Damn it! The old man had to be bluffing. He was a recluse; no one would be his friend. It was merely a ploy to catch him off guard . . .well, it wasn't going to work.

"Right, old man, this is your last chance to take choice A." Shawn squinted as the light stick finally moved after being still so long. It floated up and started to spin in a slow circle. Slowly it sped up. Was he signaling them now? Impossible.

"Tsk, tsk my man, I'm choosing option C!"

Lilly crouched next to a tree, wrapped herself the best she could in the cloak. Whether or not she was really invisible never crossed her mind as she watched Mr. Bluestick circle his cane around, wondering what the two were saying. She knew that running home was the smarter choice, but what if she got there and Dad didn't believe her? He loved Shawn, so much so that he was late for tucking her in tonight, not to mention how she was forbidden to come out here. She'd be in huge trouble and by the time she got back Mr. B. could be dead.

Calm and ready, knowing what he had to do, Mr. Bluestick smiled widely to show he wasn't scared. He couldn't see Shawn's face and he had no clue if he could see his, but it didn't matter, he wanted to show he wasn't scared, make him think he wasn't bluffing. As he spun the light around, Shawn looked as if he was buying the act but playing it tough as well. With a quick flip he placed the pipe in his armpit then plunged the now free hand into his pocket. Please work, it's been almost a year since he'd tested them.

Shawn took another step closer, NOW. Mr. B popped open the lid on the small remote and hit the button. A second passed and his heart sank as nothing happened. Then another push, another. Nothing. That's when he remembered last year he set the setting to "hold," meaning the button had to stay depressed for several seconds. With a hard, steady push, he counted in his head. Exactly on three his plan went into affect.

To the right of Shawn, two trees over from Lilly, a light flickered on, orange and long just like his Blue cane. Shawn's head spun in disbelief. Lilly smiled broadly. Mr. B. kept his eyes on Shawn. Green was next to click on, behind and to the right of Shawn. He spun around showing his knife as if he wasn't scared. Then purple, sharply to the right of him and again he spun in awe to see it.

Mr. B. gripped his pipe and clicked off his own light. "Believe me now, sir? Be careful, Carl is the worst . . .and right behind you."

Shawn spun around just in time to see the biggest, brightest light coming blaring on. It was white and different from the others. It was a spotlight aimed a dozen yards off to his right at the fire pit. Staring up at the light, wondering why this man was aiming it away from him, it hit him, not the reason why, but a pipe.

Hitting the top of his shoulder with enough force to send shocks of pain to his fingertips. He dropped his knife. Shawn dove for the ground and spun to see the old man still wearing his top hat, holding a rusty pipe high in the air ready to swing again. He scampered backwards, then remembered that the so-called Carl was there. He was surrounded.

Putting up his hands in a plea, Shawn spoke. "I'm sorry, I wasn't going to hurt anyone, I swear!" Mr. Bluestick lowered the pipe a bit as if to contemplate the situation.

Shawn looked to see if any of his other crazies were approaching. His eyes scanned each light quickly. None had moved, not even an inch. He squinted some more and noticed that the orange light was in the tree, on a branch too high and thin for any man to have put it on. It was a trick! This made things different.

Mr. Bluestick had no clue what to do now. He had fooled the man and had rendered him safe. If he beat him he would go to jail, but if he let him go, he would still be a danger to Lilly. He had to do something. Tie him up? Whatever it was he had to do it fast, before he figured out the lights were just a fake.

He was proud of himself. Four years ago after a too wild party where Mr. Bluestick helplessly witnessed a rape, he had installed the lights. He felt so guilty not being able to help the young girl, but there were five men. Luckily only one did the raping, but he knew if he tried to stop them he would have gotten beaten to death. The endless parties never bothered him, but that did. So to prevent future catastrophes, he had installed the lights, along with a loudspeaker system he could access while watching from the second floor window. At the same time, he also installed an efficient but not all too safe fireman's pole for himself in case he had to get out there and help someone. The pipe he kept next to the pole. The system of lights had worked on five occasions so far, two were almost date rapes, one was to protect a dog from being killed by some sick teen that was alone and beating it, and the other two were stopping idiots from setting fire to the woods. He never thought the system would have to be used in a manor like this.

Rope, he needed rope, but it was inside. Was it safe to have Lilly get it for him? Was she even still here? What other choice did he have?

"Lilly, darling are you all right?" he yelled blindly into the dark.

"Mr. B that was so cool! You kicked his butt!" She came running out from under the orange light. He couldn't help but stare at her in relief.

Shawn eased his hands down as if defeated, one on his brow, the other carefully feeling around his beltline. Mr. Bastard may have fooled him but his trick will be much better. The cold can was right where he had put it. Silently it slid off his belt. Then with perfect timing, as if God was giving him a window of opportunity, the tuxedoed man turned to see the prize that was approaching. The girl was here, and the old man vulnerable . . . perfect.

The hissing noise came a split second before the burning. It was a feeling like none other, pure pain mixed with a lack of air. Whatever this evil liquid was that splashed his face, it seared his eyes, and scorched his lungs, and it came from Shawn. The pipe fell oddly close to his opponent's knife. The pain made him hunch over, involuntarily leaning on the cane's on switch. It flickered, revealing his suddenly swollen face. He wanted nothing more than to scream to Lilly to run, but that was impossible. The one sense he did have was hearing, though it was hard to focus on it through the pain. He heard crunching leaves and he knew Shawn was getting up. With his freed gloved hand, he tried frantically to wipe the pain away, no use.

"Run now, Lilly, and he's really dead! And if you move an inch, you'll get a mouthful of this, too!"

Shawn got up casually, knowing everything was going to be just fine. It may have been a scare but the gift was now his for the taking . . .back on track. Standing above the old man, he contemplated which weapon to pick up, his own or the old man's? The pipe! It would be so much more insulting and it won't kill him. Truthfully, he shouldn't hurt him at all, but he had to get him back. Picking up the pipe, he flipped it over and over in his hand, savoring the moment. Things were going to work much better this way. He can plant evidence in that moron's room, making it look as if he raped and killed Lilly. Of course, he'll have to make her bleed a bit.

What a perfect plan! Everyone will think the crazy old man had his fun with her and then buried the body somewhere in the vast woods. An open and shut case. No one would ever think that she was alive and miles from here being used daily as a sex toy! God was good!

"Where do you want it old man? Hmmm . . . the arm? The leg? How about the shoulder? Just like mine, which hurts like a bitch!"

"NOOOO, he's going to hit you!" It was muffled but Mr. Bluestick could hear the warning just fine.

Shawn raised the pipe as high as he could to put all the force possible behind it. Just as the pipe reached the apex of its swing, Mr. Bluestick moved, fast. First he started to turn back and to the left, making Shawn think he was about to flee, but that wasn't it. It was a wind up. The glowing stick was swung just like a pro hitter about to nail a grand slam. It was a blind swing but it connected none-the-less.

Lilly watched as the light she loved so dearly exploded right on Shawn's rib cage. It was such an intense explosion that she had to look away. Brilliant white, blue and orange sparks burst every which way, reminding her of fireworks. Mr. Bluestick fell to the ground next to some of the larger sparks.

Shawn stumbled backwards covering his eyes. The hit felt like a slap from a weak girl. The sparks and shards of glass on the other hand burrowed their way under his skin and into his right eye felt Amazon pinching beetles. Flat on his back he fell, frantically trying to pull out the glass. The only problem being he couldn't tell which spots of pain were glass and which were sparks smoldering on him.

"Lilly, are . . . what happened?" Mr. Bluestick asked, gasping. Within a second he felt the small hands on him. The worst pain in his life lifted a bit. He tried to smile to comfort her but moving his face in any way was a bad idea.

"Direct hit! Right in his chest!" It definitely wasn't a win then, it was only a delay. He knew they had to be quick.

"Lilly, I need you to be my eyes. Help me up and we'll go to your dad, my dear, but we must be fast!"

Lilly helped him up, then grabbed his hand. He could feel that the cloak was still around her. Trying to suck in more air through burning passageways, he smelled something. He paused and sniffed painfully again. It wasn't a good smell. Then he turned to his other working sense. The moaning from Shawn was loud, but there was something else he heard, crackling. Like a campfire. It was smoke he smelled.

"Lilly! Did the cane cause a fire?"

She hadn't wanted to mention it for fear of scaring him more. Besides it should go out on it own, right? It was small, only a few leaves . . . well, at first. It was heading to the brush.

"Yes," Lilly responded as if embarrassed for not saying anything.

Mr. Bluestick's mind swirled before asking his next question.

"It's getting big, isn't it?"

"Yes," again she said in a tiny voice. After a long pause he responded to her.

"We must get in the building then. The Chrimsawheel! That room is fireproof we'll be safe there. Lead the way, I'll tell you where to turn once we're inside."

Shawn, finally over the sudden pain, sat up and opened his one good eye to see himself surrounded by fire. Through the heat waves he could see the old man and Lilly disappear into the mill. God really wanted to test him tonight, to make sure he earned his prize. It was another crossroad. What to do now, chase after them and risk burning to death or run back and call the fire department before the entire woods went up in smoke. Damn these tests.

4

Through dreamless, deep, dark, black sleep, Tom heard his name. It wasn't too loud but it was definitely his name. The anger of being woken from such a restful slumber made Tom put his pillow over his head. Again, louder this time, it came. This time it was followed by a nudge and a whisper.

"Someone's in the house, Tom get up!"

Like a teen on the first day back to school after a too short summer, Tom wanted to dig a hole in the bed and hide, curl up and let the blackness come back over him, warm like a blanket, peaceful. But that wasn't going to happen.

"TOM!"

Loud and close enough to his ear, it forced Tom to remove the pillow and pop open his eyes. Up until this moment he had just assumed it was Sandy waking him up. Seeing blackness and a bright shining light at the door startled him. He sat up and his arm shot out to make sure Sandy was there. She grabbed his hand. Next was a quick look to the clock, twelve-fifteen. What the hell was going on?

The lights shot on, triggering a sharp thundering pain in Tom's head, a pain he knew all too well in college, but hadn't visited in a long time. Dealing with the headache and the sudden sight of his neighbor, dirty, scraped up, with one eye swollen shut and bloody, standing there with a flashlight was too much to figure out through the alcohol-induced sleepy haze.

"It's Lilly, Tom. For Christ sakes, the Goddamn woods are burning down. I barely made it out alive. She's in the mill with him. I tried Tom . . . I fucking tried and he did this to me!"

He raised his shaking hand to his ever more hurting eye. Nice touch, Shawn thought, adding the shake to his hand as if he was petrified. Yes, he was pissed, but scared, hardly. It was one of the hardest decisions he had ever made but he chose logic over lust. By the time he would have chased after Lilly and the old man, killed him and tried to leave with her, the place would be swarming with firemen and police. Try to use the alibi then!

Yes, the plans were ruined, but it was okay, he would have another, and another if that one failed as well. By coming back here battered he would be considered a hero! Lilly would be saved from the fire in that huge mill. They'd find and bring her to safety, all thanks to Shawn! The only problem was going to be making sure his face doesn't get on the news. As if he was a hero, the police wouldn't do a background check anytime soon. His alias would work just fine.

"I must have yelled for you a dozen times downstairs . . . I already called the fire department . . . I just don't know what else I could have done." Delivering such a stellar performance, Shawn recalled an article he once read on lying. It stated that the best liars were lawyers and actors. He couldn't help but wonder if he missed his calling.

Tom did not react. He sat there, looked at Sandy, who was clearly shaken but only because the neighbor entered their bedroom and might have just seen her naked breasts, not because her daughter could be dead, then he laid back down. The thought that this was all a dream crossed his mind, but only for a second. He wasn't that lucky. Shutting his eyes, he breathed deeply and slowly. Shawn and Sandy looked at each other baffled at why Tom had lain back down, both afraid to speak up. Luckily sirens spoke for them.

Soft and low, but definitely coming closer, the sirens wailed. Two, three? Tom couldn't tell, but if the whole woods were on fire, it might as well be a whole damn fleet.

Another deep breath, still not ready. As if the first two times losing Lilly was too much for a man to take, now this? Tom wondered if the courage was building up in him or if this was all too much to handle. Mentally he tried to play through what was going to happen next. Get up, run to the woods, firemen would try and stop him, he'd get burned and suffer smoke inhalation, only to find his daughter's charred body or perhaps find the crazy old man holding her limp and naked in his arms, refusing to let her go. Could he handle that? Did he want to? What choice did he have? Going to sleep, ignoring it, won't make this go away. He had to face whatever was going to happen. Tom realized that these few seconds, here with his eyes shut, lying on the too soft egg crate bed, was the calm before the storm.

With the sirens almost here, he couldn't hide behind his eyelids anymore. Tom shot up, threw on clothing and bolted past Shawn. Shawn stood there staring at Sandy. She couldn't tell if he was in shock or just hoping to see her breasts again. It wasn't until the engines' air brakes hissed to a stop that Shawn moved slowly out of the doorway. She listened for his footsteps on the stairs . . . none? Was he just standing in the hallway? Another air brake hissed as she waited to hear him go down the steps. A full two minutes after he left the room, she finally heard him on the steps allowing her to get up and dress.

Giving up on seeing Sandy's tits again, Shawn left to join the chaos outside. Before hitting the top of the stairs, he realized this was the perfect opportunity to build more evidence and get himself a treat. He slipped into Lilly's room and clicked on his flashlight. With the stealth of the pro criminal he once was, Shawn scurried over to the small bureau. Without having to search, he knew where to look; almost everyone kept underwear in the top drawer.

Silently pulling out the fake oak drawer, he had to hold in a gasp. So beautiful, so perfect. Two-dozen or so tiny pairs of underwear stared up at him. Strawberry Shortcake, Sponge Bob, Beauty and the Beast, Nemo, Flowers, dots, and solid colors. Too many to choose from! He grabbed a light pink one with purple flowers and stuffed it into his back pocket. The other pair didn't matter, yet he still hemmed and hawed at which one to choose. With lust he rubbed his hand over them all before realizing he better get out. That's how you get caught. Strawberry Shortcake it was! Into the front pocket it went. Drawer closed, light off, he headed back out of the room, trying to suppress a smile, not only because it would look suspicious, but because it hurt his eye like hell.

It was just like a movie - Tom always hated when people used that in interviews after a tragic accident. It's real life, for crying out loud. Yet the second he stepped out the backdoor, it was the first thing in his mind - *it's like a fucking movie.* As he sprinted through the backyard, he could see it in his head: him running in slow motion, the fire trucks tearing apart his lawn trying to get as close to the woods as possible while casting dramatic light upon his face. Then cut to the fire - roaring, massive, engulfing the woods that his daughter loved so. He'd never seen a fire like this except for, well, in a movie. The flames licked higher than the tips of the tallest trees that seemed to touch the clouds themselves. Crackling, trees falling, blindingly bright. And the heat, unbearable.

At the foot of the quickly disappearing woods, Tom was at a loss once again. What could he do? The fire was sixty or so yards away from their quaint fence entrance. Now, if this really were a movie, he would run into the fire, using his forearm as his only protection. Then a tense few moments later the music would swell and he would run out with Lilly in his arms. They'd both have a few smudges of ash on them, cough once or twice, but they would be perfectly fine. Too bad this was real life. He wouldn't make it ten yards before the flames and falling trees devoured and cremated him whole in a matter of seconds.

The only logical option was to let the firemen that he could hear galloping up behind him handle the blaze. Make them aware that his daughter was somewhere in there, not only that, she also was with a mad man! But when you've created a life, watched her grow from the tiniest of things into your child that you would give your life for without thinking twice, how do you just stand there and watch as the unspeakable could be happening to her?

So many noises from so many directions, popping, yelling, sirens, crashes, equipment jangling, all accompanied by the red disco lights behind him and the orange glow ahead… it was too much. All Tom could picture was a tiny charred body lying in the woods, a closed casket funeral. He was horrified that he let himself picture such images, the detail of which even shocked himself. Thankfully, a giant gloved hand pulled him out of his worst nightmare and out of the way.

The large, heavily equipped man dragged him back several yards before dropping him. He collapsed to the ground, weak, confused, not knowing what to do.

"Stay back!" demanded the man in the fireproof mask. It took him several more seconds again before he could shake the unbelievable burden and realization that there was nothing he could do. With the speed of an

Olympian, Tom dashed to the man who was now standing with an axe.

"LILLY!" Tom screamed as he spun the man around by the thick coat collar. Obviously shocked, the man's eyes were wide; they only became wider as he realized the meaning of the word. The mask came off, the man became human to Tom.

"OK, calmly, tell me, is there someone in there?"

Tom's eyes flooded tears that streaked down his face untouched. With a firm nod he responded. "Yes...my daughter, she's eight."

The man closed his eyes as if for a split second silent prayer before clicking his radio that was loosely placed under his coat. As he transmitted, he slipped away from Tom, victims was not his specialty.

Within a few seconds after clicking the radio, several other men surrounded Tom. Two were dressed in full fire fighting garb, the third was a bit older than the rest and the only one who wore jeans, boots and a hat, as if saying, *I'll help fight the fire! But only if absolutely necessary.*

"What's your name?"

Like that matters, Tom thought of the question from the half-ass fireman, yet he answered with a hard swallow. Looking past them, Tom felt as if he was on show. Everybody on the block, most of whom Tom had yet to meet, was now outside, approaching the woods, staring at the huddle as if they were the cause. Even closer he glanced at the well routined circus of ever-growing number of men planning their attack.

"Your daughter . . . she went into the fire?"

Tom knew the man had to ask the questions but that didn't stop his desire to punch him in his almost non-existent jaw. "She was already in there when it started. I don't know anything else. Ask him." All the men's gazes fell upon Shawn who was standing near the house, nursing his eye in an overly dramatic way.

Watching the men rush away, Tom's anger shifted from the half dressed captain to Shawn. How could that bastard let his daughter go into the woods? Why didn't he stop her? It took everything he had to stop himself from rushing at the man he shared too many beers with only a few hours earlier. Trying to douse the rage, he turned his attention to the woods. The fire was even closer now, ten more yards. The brutal images of Lilly started to come back. Not mentally able to fight them off, he slammed his hands on his head, in a moronic way of shaking them out.

Maybe Lilly was fine. The mill had so many rooms, so deep inside that she could have taken shelter, safe from the relentless flames. Even so, she was with that nutso. She might be safe from fire, but by the time they got to her, she might be raped, brutalized, in pieces. More vivid pictures he didn't want to see jumped up and paraded in front of his mind's eye. That sick tuxedoed freak, half naked, wearing the top hat, cloak, and tie on top of Lilly, laughing as he thrust. It was the last image he could handle. On his knees Tom vomited with the force of a hurricane.

Sweat dripped down his face un-wiped. Unlike everyone else a few hundred yards away sweating because of the heat, Mr. Bluestick was soaked because of fear. He crammed himself in the far corner of the massive, multi-colored room and just stared at the ChrimsaWheel. Since entering the room, his bravery had disappeared. He stood up to a demon and won, but he knew in the end it would be he who would be the loser.

"What's going on Mr. B.?" Lilly's voice was frail and cautious. The first three times she asked, he didn't respond. Soon as he got her in here, he asked if she was okay. She was and he went to the corner as Mom used to make her do when she was real little and did something stupid like spill juice.

She watched him hug his knees and start to rock, hardly blinking. The night was scary enough already, she needed him now. Scared but feeling as if she had no other choice, she approached him, staying out of his view and sat beside him. Taking a deep breath she could lightly smell the burning pine outside. "Are we going to be okay in here?"

No answer again. Examining his face, she couldn't tell if he was crying or if it was all sweat. Taking some effort, she pried one of his gloved, wet hands off his knees and held it with both of hers. The affection worked. With scared eyes he looked at her, his brow tightened with worry.

"I. . . Lilly . . . I hate . . . fire . . . I just hate it so much. Why couldn't I have finished the ChrimsaWheel by now?"

"I'm sure you'll finish it soon! Then you'll get to go see your parents, and maybe I can visit with you!" Lilly replied in her best chipper voice, trying to cheer up her friend.

"You'd really go with me? To visit?"

"Of course! That would be sooooo cool! How many people get to go to other planets!"

Mr. Bluestick finally cracked a smile. A split second later it was gone as the whole building shook with a loud bang, followed by two smaller ones. They grabbed hold of each other for protection.

"It's the fire . . . probably trees falling on the mill. Fire destroys everything, everything. It eats up every last thing, including your life."

The statement scared Lilly, not only because of its context but because Mr. B.'s voice changed. It sounded odd. Both their heads turned as a plume of smoke bellowed up from the secret escape hatch. Mr. B's face contorted with so much pain that Lilly thought he was dying.

"What is it? Are, are you okay?"

"It's just fire, Lilly dear. The most feared thing on my planet. It's worse than anything else."

Lilly was confused but didn't want to push the issue any more. After a long silence, Lilly herself started to cry as her young mind started to think of too many things a child shouldn't: Why did Shawn attack them? Is he burning up in the fire? What if the fire reached her house, burned all her things, or worse, hurt Dad? Another loud crash switched her thinking to herself - were they safe here?

"Are we going to die?" croaked out of her dry throat.

Mr. Bluestick looked back at her with sad eyes. "No, Lilly, we're completely safe here. This is one of the few rooms that didn't burn last . . .. We're safe, darling."

The two huddled silently, listening to the distant crackles and crashes as they waited, for what they didn't know.

By the time Sandy dressed and made her way down to the kitchen window, she could hear a helicopter-buzzing overhead. Looking out, she saw Tom down on his knees alone, a paramedic walking over to him. Several men, one of whom was attending to his eye, surrounded Shawn. This was not something she wanted or needed to deal with now. Shit. All her plans, with her luck the news crews will be there in minutes asking her how she felt about her daughter missing in a blaze. She should just shock the hell out of them and say, "Not bad."

It sure did feel good to not feel guilty over not feeling guilty anymore. It used to be such a hassle to feel bad about not caring when Lilly cut her leg on the end table and other stupid things. Tom would genuinely feel horrible, rush to her aid, feel her pain. What crap. Maybe this would be good. Getting rid of that little brat for good won't make her look like a bad guy when she up and disappears. Everyone would think it was stress. Then again, if she is toast, then she would have to stick around for a funeral, put up with Tom being a baby and worst of all, she'd have to put off her plans again. She's only two days away, damn it! This is why she hated the little fucker, always messing with plans.

Trying not to stress herself out over an outcome that she didn't yet know, Sandy composed herself and thought about what she had to do right now. Actress mode needed to be turned on. This time, though, she needed to turn it up a notch. Now, instead of playing Mrs. Brady, she had to play "Mrs. I lost my daughter", a much harder role. Should she play frantic and screaming or shocked and silent? Maybe a mix of both.

Sandy slid the screen door open slowly, gazing at the fire. In her peripheral vision she noticed some fireman eyeing her arrival. Eyes wide, she consciously flared her nostrils several times as she descended the steps. A small fireman, looking more like a little boy playing fireman, started to approach her, anticipating her freak out, which she did have planned.

Two steps on the grass, raise the hands a bit, shake them. Now! "MY BABY!" Run! Sandy sprinted in her best theatrical freak out. Screaming and crying, though no wet tears came. The tiny fireman was hardly an obstacle to avoid. With his oversized costume, he was slow. When Sandy was halfway through the yard, Tom got up, stumbled and blocked her from running to the fire, just as planned. Arms around each other, they clung like magnets, just like in the movies, firemen watching, fire raging as a backdrop.

After a few good sobs from Tom and fake sporadic breathing from Sandy, the half-ass captain, waddling from the big pants he now had on, made his way back over. Without an excuse me, pardon me, or even sorry, he started to talk in a business tone. "From what your neighbor tells us, I think your daughter has a chance. Supposedly the kook out there bashed Mr. Daggerty in the face, set a fire and ran into the mill. So she's most likely safe from the fire in there. Those old places can withstand a bomb attack. Whether she's safe with him or not is a different story. I'm going to get with the police chief soon as he gets here and get an attack force ready to storm the place. Just sit tight, folks, we'll get your kid out of there."

Every second made it feel more and more like a movie. Tom half expected to see a director nodding in approval of the speech off behind a camera somewhere. The knot in Tom's stomach didn't lessen at the news. His mind got rid of the charred body picture but that was about it. Knowing the fire was set by Bluebastard, Tom transferred his rage once again. Shawn did try to stop him. He was a good friend. He risked his life for Lilly. There are not many good people like that in the world.

Tightening once again, the knot in his stomach made Tom jerk a few inches in pain. Guilt was the reason this time. If he had done something about the nut before, none of this would be happening. He had himself to blame. He had to stop this! These thoughts. Amazing as your mind can be, it can also be your worse enemy, Tom thought, trying to shake it all out. A clear head was needed. He knew the building better than these guys. He was going to have to go in, guide them and save his daughter.

Arm around Sandy, Tom walked over to Shawn who now had a patch over his eye. He shook his head back and forth ever so slowly to say sorry.

"No, Shawn, you tried to save Lilly. Thank you." With his one free arm he brought Shawn in for a hug. The man hugged him like a child that had been away at summer camp for a month. It felt good having this support. It gave Tom a tiny bit more strength. The three pulled back a bit to see each other's faces, blank looks, awkward stares, casts, eye patches. They sure were beat up, but they had each other, Tom thought.

Sandy watched as a news crew was setting up in the road. A police officer kept them off their yard, thankfully. Tom scanned back and forth watching the brave people risking their lives to save a few houses that had already been evacuated, and to save his daughter. Shawn gazed at the fire's reflection in his bedroom window as he held back the smile that wanted out so badly. Maybe if he pulled his hand out of his pocket and stopped caressing Lilly's underwear it would be a bit easier to keep the smile at bay.

Fire Chief Thomas set up a makeshift command post on the hood of his government Jeep Cherokee. Flipping through a dozen maps trying to find one that had this particular woods on it, at the same time as shouting orders, he loved this. This is what he lived for. A fire roaring, threatening to kick his and his men's asses, but not letting it. Instead kicking its ass, all while being in the driver's seat.

Dozens of companies from three towns (and more on the way) were already attacking the fire, Thomas in charge of them all. It's been two years since they had something this big, the old apartment block on Sycamore St - damn owner thought he was slick - lost two men because of that bastard. As tragic as fire was, Thomas looked forward to them, no longed for them. Half a dozen cops were already on hand trying to help out with what they could, which, to Thomas, was nothing more than getting in the way. It was annoying but there was nothing he could do about it, especially with this fire, set by some crazy child molester. Story sounded fishy to him, but that wasn't his job. It was Captain Rudder's, the bastard who was probably taking his time brushing his teeth before coming here. Thomas' job was to kick this fire's ass and quickly, before any houses went up. So far they were doing a damn good job. The old stream should, hopefully, keep it from crossing over into the larger, vaster, thicker, harder to get to part. God he hoped the stream would hold.

Finally he found the right map. Barking out orders and using a thick red marker, he circled the farthest they could let the fire reach. Within two minutes of conversing about an attack plan with his underlings, they were ready. Not much more for him to do except watch and make sure everyone was all right. Watching his men deploy, he crossed his arms feeling like a general in battle.

"Thomas, you woke me up for a fire? Couldn't on-duty handle this?" said Captain Rudder.

Captain Rudder, yup, nice suit, greased up hair, even though it's the middle of the night, and shiny teeth. The mere presence of the cocky, vain dick would make Thomas's blood boil.

"Not just that, Captain, we have a suspected pedophile with a ten year old vic held up in an old mill. Supposedly he set the fire."

Rudder smoothed his hair and nodded with interest. Rudder was a big city cop in a small town, at least in his mind. Having such a small task force, he served as lead detective, captain, and occasionally had to go out on regular calls when someone was out sick. No matter what the title or day, Rudder wore a suit, doing his best to imitate his favorite TV detectives. Wearing the suit caused more trouble than it helped in a small town. People thought he was a jackass showing up to a domestic dispute wearing Armani, or shaking down twelve year olds for stealing candy bars wearing Gucci. It didn't matter to Rudder, though, since he planned on leaving this boring town one day, moving to Boston, New York, or D.C to become a homicide detective to solve a different murder each week, just like on *Law and Order*.

"Rudder!" Thomas barked to snap the man out of a fire-staring trance.

Rudder smoothed his hair to act as if his stare was him merely figuring out the whole nights events before even talking to one person.

"I'll go talk to the family, get the facts."

Stuffing his hands into his expensive pockets, Rudder felt a twinge of excitement as he strutted over to the small circle of distraught vics. This just might be a good one after all - child molester, big fire, could possibly turn into a murder. Yes, indeed, this might be a good one, one worthy of an episode of *NYPD Blue*. If only the fire was in a warehouse and that warehouse in a city, he'd be all set, the star of his own show.

Cold, manipulative, annoying and stupid, not to mention who wears Gucci to a forest fire? Tom once again had his anger focused on a new person. The man's sympathy for his kidnapped daughter was on par with the sympathy of a dropped ice cream cone. He might as well have said "Awe shucks, well you can always get another one." Tom was appalled but he held his anger in. If this man was going to be in charge of getting his flesh and blood home safe and sound, then he better damn well treat him nicely.

The questions were straightforward yet Tom had a hard time choking the answers out. Sally, of course, kept silent. Shawn helped by finishing most of Tom's half sentences.

When seeing Tom start to close up, Rudder crossed his arms like an old schoolmarm angry with her pupil for not knowing everything. Finally, he closed his custom black leather interrogation book that he had bought himself. "We'll do everything we can," the bastard stated, while glancing at the fire as if it was a fireworks display. He then turned and walked ever so casually with his hands in pockets again, back towards the fire chief, whom Tom now loved.

Without saying it, Tom knew they all collectively thought the same thing - dickhead. If he only knew his wife was fantasizing about Mark dressed as one of the fireman, stripping off the gear, all sweaty and taking her on the top of the fire truck while woods crackled like an audience cheering for their performance.

This is a good thing, thought Shawn. The guy was a dolt. Most likely he won't want to get his hands dirty at a crime scene, with wearing Gucci and all. With Dudder or Rudder, or whatever his name gone, it was back to awkwardness. They all faced away from the fire as if it was too much to watch. Staring at the ground a glimmer caught Shawn's eye. Water. A tiny stream of run off from one of the dozens of hoses that were spraying had made it all the way down between their feet, silent and almost unnoticed. For lack of anything better to do, he stared at it. That's when his mind formed a new plan, a new plan that made his old plan effective once again. It will be tricky, not to mention god damn risky, but if this is the flaming hoops that God wants him to jump through for his prize, then so be it.

5

Sitting on hard stairs, waiting to see if your daughter was a corpse or just plain mutilated was beyond any hell that Tom could ever have imagined. The hell in his mind had the fire and the pain. The only thing missing was a hot poker scoring him every five seconds. Right now he was so numb that it would probably go unnoticed. Shawn left his side some time ago with some lame excuse about protecting his shed from burning down. Tom figured he didn't want to deal with seeing them in this state anymore. Who would?

Amazingly, under the command of the half-assed dressed chief, whom Tom was starting to regard as a hero, the fire was rapidly diminishing, so much so that the team of officers were clumsily gearing up in some extra fireproof coats and hardhats, getting ready to make their venture into the unknown world of a psychotic, pyromaniacal, child molester's lair. Seeing this, Tom kissed Sandy on the head.

"Honey, I need to go with them. I know where his hideout is. If I don't show them how to get to it, they could be lost in that maze for hours." Tom stood up holding her hand, waiting for her to protest his actions. She didn't. Her sad eyes followed him before being buried into her own lap was all that Tom received. No good luck, no bring our daughter back, followed by a kiss like in the movies. Just simple shock.

Tom stood, ignored by Gucci guy while he de-briefed his men like soldiers about to go into war. Finishing his pep talk, which seemed a bit corny, he turned to Tom. First a suggestion, then pleading which led straight into demanding. Rudder smoothed his hair more than once as he declined to let Tom go into a burning forest to attack a mad man.

"This isn't a TV show, sir; you can't just go and save the day with the Officers. It's against regulations and too damn dangerous. I'm not going in myself, for crying out loud!"

Tom didn't care what the man was saying, he was going. Puffing up his chest, he gave his last argument, his best argument. "Do you have children?"

After a pause Rudder answered with an annoyed, "No".

"Then you have no clue what I'm going through. I am going in there. I know exactly where they'll be. All I will do is show the way. If you don't let me go, you're going to have to arrest me to stop me. Just think how that headline will make you look. Father of kidnapped ten year old arrested for helping. I'll make sure to add some other things about you in it." Tom couldn't believe his own bravado.

Rudder looked uncomfortable, smoothed his greasy hair, fixed the tie. "I'm not letting you, but what happens when I look away is not my responsibility."

The fancy suit walked away and whispered in the ear of what Tom suspected was the lead of the team. The leader approached. Thickly built with gray hair and rough face, the man gave Tom a smile that looked out of place on his face. "We're going to go in there and kick some ass. You don't leave my side though, and put on some gear. We leave in two." The man started to walk away then turned back to Tom, "Oh, and I have three daughters. When we get back tonight, maybe we can set up a play date for your kid to come over."

For the first time Tom had some hope.

Lights flickering everywhere, the room started to fill with a light haze of smoke. Mr. Bluestick knew it would be a matter of minutes before the power burst off. Like everyone this night, he was emotionally drained. The only thing that kept the horrors of his past from breaking through the door that he himself didn't know was locked away in his head was Lilly, sweet innocent Lilly, the daughter he always wanted, clinging to his side for safety. Dying now would be okay. He'd been a protector for once in his life, saved someone he loved. Dying wasn't an option just yet. Lilly had to be safe first.

The silence between them was filled with cracks, knocks, moans of warping metal, and an occasional sob. They'd be safe here, he knew that, but it didn't make it any less scary. Gazing at the ChrimsaWheel, wishing more than anything that it would work so Lilly and he could disappear, go to the perfect place he came from, be happy together, a slam occurred on the inside door, startling them. Lilly squeaked out the word, "fire." Mr. Bluestick shook his head no.

Again the slam came. The door was high up behind them and to the right, making it impossible to monitor. Three more rapid, hard slams. He got up, putting his hand out to keep Lilly in her place. Obviously he knew that it had to be a fireman searching for Lilly, but he could not be too cautious after tonight's events. Maybe that sicko Shawn hadn't given up. Open the door? Don't? Arm yourself? The next slam was accompanied by a cracking. Mr. Bluestick picked up an old, weathered hammer. If it was the firemen, who must already think he's nuts, he shouldn't have a weapon raised; they might attack him. He placed it ever so closely next to him on the table, ready, waiting to see who it was.

With a plume of smoke, the door burst open, revealing an axe-wheeling fireman. Through his large oxygen mask, he glanced back and forth through the room and spotted Mr. Bluestick, who had his hands up in a pleading gesture.

"I got a live one down here!" the yellow man yelled over his shoulder before descending the stairs. Instead of immediately rushing to Mr. Bluestick, he ran right past him, looking up and down the walls. Mr. B assumed he was checking for structural safety. He lost sight of him when the man walked behind the ChrimsaWheel. A few seconds later he reemerged seemingly satisfied that the room was safe. Spotting Lilly, the man rushed over and knelt beside her. With clumsily gloved hands, he grabbed her head and crammed on the extra victim-breathing mask. Lilly angrily shook it off.

"No! No, Lilly darling, dear. This man is trying to help you. Take a few breaths, okay?"
Listening to Mr. Bluestick she took a few deep breaths before the fireman stood and scooped her into his arms. Mr. B stood in the same spot since the door opened, watching Lilly being picked up and waiting for a bunch more of yellow, invisible-faced men to run in and tackle him.

Lilly tried to protest being carried, but again Mr. B talked her into it. As the man reached the bottom of the stairs with Lilly in his arms, Mr. B yelled, "Wait." The mask turned towards him. The glass was foggy with steam and smeared with soot. Mr. Bluestick could hardly see his face but he knew it must been one of disgust.

"Good-bye, my darling, I love you, Lilly, take care," he stated as he walked over and kissed her on the forehead.

Lilly's eye grew wide and confused. "Aren't you coming?"

"Yes, yes, go on though, I'll see you outside." Mr. Bluestick held back tears. There were two choices lying in front of him and neither involved seeing Lilly again. Physical death or mental death. If he chose to not accidentally die in this fire, society would eat him alive, say he's a nut, that he kidnapped Lilly, lock him up and laugh as big burly men in prison beat the hell out of the crazy child molester. Death seemed more appealing.

Fighting back the tears with everything he had, he watched Lilly be carried up the stairs and out the door, never to see her again. Defeated, knowing life was over, he shuffled to the ChrimsaWheel and plunked down in the useless seat, wondering how to kill himself before the flood of yellow coats ran down the stairs.

Tom really felt as if he was in a movie now, an entirely different one. Now he was an action hero. His heart was pumping with excitement and anticipation of saving his daughter. Wearing an uncomfortable plastic helmet and so much fireproof gear, he wondered how the hell he would make the walk out there before being exhausted. The fire was finally under enough control to allow the team to trek through the burning debris.

Eight men, counting Tom, gathered at the mouth of the woods, Chip, in the lead. (Tom learned from one of the giddy young bucks in the group that the man who gave him so much hope was named Chip, whether it was a nickname or first name, Tom had no clue.)There were two everyday firemen following, two police officers playing firemen sandwiched in the middle, and two more real firemen following behind. Putting their masks on, they formed a V-shaped pattern and started their march. Within a few seconds, they found themselves surrounded by fire. Tom looked back to see his home but couldn't through the heat waves and smoke. Fire was pretty much all he could see. He couldn't believe these men do this every day, and not only that, right now all of them were risking their lives for his daughter. Tom was amazed. Static, then a booming voice startled Tom.

"Okay, Pops, you guide the way. We might have to go around a lot of fallen trees but you'll still know how to get there better than we would."

Tom had forgotten about the radios in the helmet. Knowing everybody would hear him, Tom felt a bit of stage fright, but knew he had to be the guide. With a deep breath he steadied his voice and began to guide this hero squad through this burning, real-life hell.

Amazingly, they all arrived safely at the mill, which was in really good shape still. Being on the stream protected its backside. Only two trees collapsed on it, with little damage. And from the outside it looked as if nothing was on fire in it. On the way there, they had several close calls from falling trees but they were all trained enough that each one was spotted beforehand. Hopping over burning logs was another task Tom didn't take a liking to. Most of the guys made cowboy whoops while leaping over them. Tom carefully stepped over with the help of Chip.

After the tough guy cop ducked his head in and scanned the room with a flashlight and gave Tom a nod, they all entered it and took off their masks. The air was clear enough inside that they weren't necessary. Taking a breath of fresh air, smoky as it was, felt like heaven to Tom. No one else seemed to notice how good it was to have the mask off his face. The two officers removed their bulky gloves and replaced them with guns. Two of the fireman had axes, the other two had crowbars, Tom felt all too vulnerable with just a flashlight.

With the cops now taking the turn as leaders, guns ready, they started down the hall, Tom again was protected in the middle as if he was the president. They walked slowly, carefully checking each room before passing it. It was enough to drive Tom mad. He knew where they were and it certainly wasn't in this hall.

"For crying out loud! They're not in this hall! Could we speed this up?" The two cops gave him a dirty look, certainly annoyed that a civilian was even allowed to follow them, let alone try and bark orders at them.

"You positive you know where they are, Pops?" Chip asked. Tom nodded.

"Lanlin, you lead, straight forward according to Pops' directions. Bowerski, you follow behind with protection; we can't waste time checking these rooms."

The two cops bitched to Chip, stating that it wasn't his turf to tell them what to do.

"Yeah, well, fine, check the rooms if you want, I got a girl to save. My men will come with me. Have fun getting back through the fire." Chip boldly walked in front of everyone, axe firmly gripped with two hands.

Tom and the men followed. Seconds later the two cops took up positions, one in front, one behind. Tom was liking this Chip guy more and more.

Corridor after corridor the men picked up speed, racing to find the girl. Telling everyone that there was only one last turn, they all slowed down and stopped. Both cops came back to the front. One crouched low, the other stayed high, guns raised. It now felt like a monster movie. Any second now and the guy last in the group will get devoured by the drooling, bloody beast that they were so boldly hunting. Tom couldn't help but look over his shoulder. It seemed he wasn't the only one thinking that way. With shaky hands the once tough firemen were scanning the hall for the beast, ready with their blunt weapons.

On the finger count of three, the two cops burst around the corner. Tom squinted ready for gunfire. Instead he heard someone shout "Clear!" They all followed around the corner, slow as ever.

"That door on the left. . .you go in it and the door is on the right. It's a big steel door, I don't know what's behind it. He tricked us before and led us to a different room."

"So why do you think they are in there?" Chip asked making sure it was safe for his men.

"Because he tried very hard to keep me away from it."

Again the cops took up the stances outside the door. The real yellow jackets held back in a tight bunch, excited and petrified for a confrontation that wasn't a fire. Again, a finger count of three. The men disappeared into the room. The group had no choice but to watch the flashlight beams bounce around wondering what the hell was going on in there.

"Freeze!" followed by faint steps and a few other shouts that couldn't be heard. The men all bobbed, wondering if they should sprint after them as back up. Chip stutter-stepped twice, each time stopping himself from rushing in. No gunfire, no yells. They waited, avoiding eye contact at all cost.

"Chip!" Lanlin yelled as he emerged from the door.

"Room secure, we got the perp." Lanlin said slowly. His eyes went to Tom then to the floor. Tom felt his knees start to wobble. He couldn't see whom but one of the yellow coats grabbed and held him up.

"No sign of the girl, though there is something you should see Chip."

The group stood in the hall, having no clue what to do – follow? stay? Chip gave them a look that didn't help them decide as he disappeared into the room after Lanlin. Inside Lanlin gave him serious eyes.

"What is it officer? Is she dead?" Chip whispered through gritted teeth.

"No, like I said, we don't see her anywhere, and the old man keeps saying we already took her away. But there is this… you need to see." Lanlin shone his flashlight across the mildew stained wall and down to the dusty paper-strewn floor. Chip watched the beam, stomach churning over and over again as he thought of his own daughters safe at home, waiting to see what it revealed. Finally it landed on something very familiar to him. A pile of gear - fireman's gear and a dozen drops of blood standing out like lemons in a bowl of apples.

6

If Lilly weren't so hard to carry over one shoulder, Shawn would be skipping right now. A jolly old *I'm so happy that I can't help but skip a stupid skip, skip!* Grinning from ear to ear (making his eye hurt) he struggled through the dry riverbed away from the mill and the houses, stumbling on the slick algae-ridden rocks that hadn't seen this much air in years. God sure threw him a curve ball, but he reacted in enough time to still swing and hit a home run.

Shawn played it over and over in his head. He was a genius. Hardly anyone noticed when he disappeared. A quick walk down the dry streambed brought him into the heart of the fire but out of harm's way. Every ten yards or so he would scamper up the crumbly embankment to take a peek into the raging fire, looking for what he needed. After nine frustrating peeks, he found it: a lone fireman who lost his way. There was so much fire around him that he seemed almost to have a glow to him, an angelic glow. Shawn knew that this was not a coincidence.

With a little more play-acting, Shawn stumbled to the man acting as if he was harmed and smoke damaged. He was ever so careful to make sure his face was always covered. Wanting to be the hero he always dreamed of, the fireman instantly ran over to Shawn. With one quick swing the fireman was knocked unconscious with a large stream rock Shawn was concealing in his hand. Before the wannabe hero could even hit the ground, Shawn gave him a hard shove to push him over the embankment edge.

Back in the safe haven, he took his time undressing the man. Even though Shawn hadn't wanted to hurt anyone, he felt no guilt over this, it was too good of a plan. Even when he removed the mask and found that the man was merely a boy, no older than twenty-two, he didn't think

180

twice. With a quick yank, the microphone in the helmet came undone. After dressing himself in the man's gear, Shawn wanted nothing more than to look in a mirror and perhaps take a few pictures of himself as the hero fire fighter! Of course, that was out of the question, time was of the essence.

With such heavy gear it took a bit longer than he liked to get to the mill. Originally he planned to leave the woods with Lilly in his arms wearing this get-up, perfect cover. Sweating and struggling with the gear as he walked alone made him think twice. Reaching the mill at last, Shawn was relieved to find that no one had dared come here yet. Why the firemen hadn't thought to go down the streambed was beyond him. Using the map that he burned into his memory, he raced through the halls as fast as he could, which wasn't more than a brisk walk.

At the top of Mr. Bluestick's stairs he switched back into character, the hero once again. As he shouted to his pretend buddies and slammed the axe into the door he recalled watching DeNiro on *Inside the Actors Studio* talking about his method. He then pictured himself in the chair talking about his role as the hero in the Lilly saga. His heart pounded, not from nerves but excitement in having the girl in his arms finally. With Brando-like skills, he pretended to search the room for hazards when really he was planting a major piece of the puzzle.

When he reached the top of the stairs, the acting was done. He couldn't wait to shed the ridiculously hot outfit. Shedding the gloves, he set Lilly down. She looked shaken but not scared. Children are always taught to respect and trust firemen and policemen, making it an all too perfect disguise for any child molester. Reaching under the bulky coat, he dug into his normal coat pockets that he had stuffed earlier with necessary objects.

Within seconds Lilly was out cold. For a second he stared in amazement at the bottle in his hand, chloroform. It's been used in hundreds of movies and TV shows, so much so, that Shawn never thought it would work, yet it did!

Looking down at Lilly he could feel his pants grow tight as blood flowed to his crotch with excitement. It was a shame that he was going to have to wait a couple of days to enjoy her. With Lilly out cold, Shawn disrobed with the speed of a virgin who was promised to get laid if he could get naked in five seconds flat. The fresh air felt wonderful. He just wished he could feel it over his whole body. Again he plunged into his pocket, this time pulling out duct tape, with which he lightly wrapped Lilly's feet, mouth and hands, not too tight, just enough to keep her from running. She was only eight years old, after all.

Picking up Lilly was awkward and hard; dead weight is never easy to pick up. Ready to book out of the mill, an idea pricked his mind. So without delay he put Lilly back down on the ground and pulled out the jack knife. Taking a deep breath, not wanting to do it, but knowing it would be a great twist, Shawn sliced Lilly's finger open, just enough to bleed, nothing major. Holding her limp arms up, he squeezed the finger making sure the droplets fell right onto the coat. With a duct tape band-aid to cover the wound, they were off.

Leaving the mill, he was at first nervous at the thought of being caught. Then he realized he needn't be. He had the perfect alibi right in his arms. If anyone stopped him, he could easily just say that he snuck in and rescued Lilly. He would be a town hero! At the door he glanced around. About a hundred yards away he could see a few yellow figures morphing in the heat waves, approaching. Perfect timing. It would take them forever to search the mill.

Shawn was almost to his goal. He would follow the stream once again. It was a bit thicker here and the fire had hardly reached this far yet. Luckily, no, it wasn't luck but genius that he thought to follow the streambed. It was deep enough that even if a whole battalion of firemen were right above, they wouldn't notice him. Unless they walked to the edge for a peek. They would literally have to stand right at the edge and look down to see him sneaking off.

Reaching the fork in the stream, Shawn once again wanted to skip, or hell, dance, which is something he had almost never done. He took the right and was thankful that the car he rented under a fake name was still sitting where he parked it early this morning. Climbing up the banking was extremely hard with Lilly. In fact, it took so much effort that he tried four different ways before deciding on crawling up and dragging her behind. Hell, she'll get dirty, but that only means he'll get to bathe her.

With a quick chirp the trunk popped open to reveal the bed of pillows he had ever so thoughtfully placed there ahead of time so Lilly wouldn't get hurt in the bumpy ride out of the woods. The old road, which Shawn assumed led to the mill in a past life, before the wooden bridges fell into the ever-widening stream, was treacherous to drive. Two miles an hour was fast as he could go. Thankfully the fire had not spread to this secluded part. Strategically he had placed large, but not too heavy logs across the road to deter anyone feeling adventurous enough to go hiking this dry day. After twenty-four minutes, the tortuous drive was over. Shawn calmly pulled onto the much-welcomed smooth road only to hear thumping. His heart ached for fear that his little princess might get bruises from kicking the trunk too hard. Oh, well, she'll be in her new home in just a few minutes, safe and all his.

Tom went from a weak pile of mush to a strong piece of oak after waiting much too long without information. His daughter had to be in there. In a movie when the dad risks his life, the little girl is always waiting there for him with a sad smile. It couldn't be good news if they were making him wait.

They did their best to hold him back, but not wanting to hurt him, they could only hold him back for so long. Tom burst into the dark room to see a discarded pile of gear identical to his, the sight only added more confused wood to his fire. With strong steady steps, Tom marched through the glowing door to see an odd crazy man's world. He instantly thought of *Willy Wonka and the Chocolate Factory* because he had never seen anything outside of that and Disneyland that had so much color.

Surveying the room, taking in the color and walking down the stairs, Tom finally understood how this man could fool Lilly who had been tricked and lured into believing he was good and magical. The sick bastard was either nuts or a genius child molester. Rage built in Tom's gut as he pondered how many children the top-hatted fuck must have brought down here. The paint was clearly old. This must have been going on for decades.

Reaching the bottom of the stairs, Tom noticed his foe sitting in an elaborate chair at the base of a fake machine that looked like Wonka himself would sit in to produce sticky, gooey, delicious, chocolate, woppy pops. Seeing that he was uncuffed sent Tom flying, wanting blood, right at him.

Mr. Bluestick didn't even blink at the sight of Lilly's father racing towards him, wanting to kill him, for Mr. B himself was feeling the same pain of loss, but only worse. It was all his fault. He handed her right over to that bastard. Now no one would ever believe him. Even with Lilly to back up his story, it wouldn't matter. He was numb, completely numb. What could he do? He wanted to save Lilly more than anything in the world. He was just a crazy man though.

Right as Tom was about to fly into Mr. Bluestick's chest and rip out his heart, Chip, being the perfect father and hero he was, stepped in between, and caught him in a bear hug.

"TOM!"

Tom could feel his teeth showing like a rabid dog; he tried to ease his mood but couldn't.

"Relax! I want to kick the shit out of this freak asshole, too! But if we do, we'll never find Lilly. Once we find her we'll all turn our heads and you can do whatever you want. But Lilly first. You hear that, freak?" Chip shouted over his shoulder at Mr. Bluestick who nodded mournfully, not knowing what to do next.

It was a place of beauty. Shawn had rented it after the first debacle with "Mr. Blueballs," just in case he needed a place to run to and hide. Yes, it was only 2.6 miles from where he lived now, but no one would ever know he was there, let alone Lilly. It was an above the garage apartment owned by an old couple that had lived in the house for over forty years. Using the charm of acting, he rented the place from them under the name Lou Stone. The best part was no lease, obviously illegal, but to an older generation a handshake was stronger than a piece of paper. No paper, no evidence.

If for some reason he actually did have to run, no one would suspect him to be so close. They would be shutting off the roads at the border, not around the corner. And absolutely no one would be looking for Lilly in an old couple's garage, especially when there would be no doubt that the crazy top-hatted man hid her body.

Pulling into his parking spot, which was behind the garage, making his car invisible from the street, which was the selling point - he laughed to himself. Solid woods surrounded this place. The only neighbors were across the street and sixty yards down. The beauty of the old streets, big open yards, you don't find that anymore. Without a second thought, Shawn skipped to the trunk and popped it open. Lilly, face streaked with tears, looked terrified and confused at the situation. Seeing Shawn's face, her eyes widened, only to shut tight a second later as if not surprised to see who was putting her through this torture.

"Lilly, my darling dear, that guy was a real freak, sweetie. Don't worry. I saved you. You're safe now."

Lilly had no clue as to what was going on. Her head hurt but not as much as her feet from kicking the trunk. Did Shawn really think he was saving her? She highly doubted it. Though Lilly was scared at what was going on, she couldn't grasp the situation enough to figure it out entirely. She was still at the magnificent age when sex didn't exist in your mind. Yes, she knew what her privates were and that no one should touch them. Had she known what Shawn was planning to do with her, the fear levels would have been much higher. The only thing on her mind right now was getting the yucky stuff out of her mouth and making sure

Mr. Bluestick was okay. She couldn't figure out why, but for some reason she felt responsible for him.

Half-heartedly Lilly fought as he picked her up and tossed her with ease onto his shoulder. His bony shoulder pressed hard into her gut, making it even more difficult to breathe through her tear-induced, phlegm filled nostrils. And his hand, his hand balanced her by squeezing her butt much too tightly. Images of the day he wanted her to lather sun block on his emaciated body flashed through her head. It sent a chill down her spine knowing that disgusting skeleton was now holding her.

Remembering something that Patch the Pony had said in one of those silly videos they made the whole school watch in the gym once a year, Lilly toughened up and strained her neck up. Looking around she tried to find a landmark, something familiar. There was nothing, trees, gravel driveway, grass, the building she was being carried up to was brown, and in the back yard was a wishing well. That's it! A wishing well, they weren't too common. For a split second she was happy with herself. It faded fast, though, when the outside world disappeared with a slam of a door. The well was burned into her mind, though. All she had to do now was get to a phone.

Lilly couldn't think of a better feeling than being let off Shawn's bony shoulder. Just having his scaly skin farther away made this whole situation easier to handle. Shawn walked away from her, humming. Lilly wobbled a bit from the pain in her feet and the duct tape around her ankles.

Finally gaining balance, she scanned the room for a phone. Nothing. The room was practically barren. It reminded her of the time she went to visit Toni's grandmother's house years ago, old and creepy. The carpet must have been a brilliant yellow and frilly at one time; now it was matted down and stained here and there. The walls weren't much better, dark brown wood paneling, showcasing just one picture, a clown frowning with a flower that was crudely drawn. There was very little furniture, a couch, even browner than the walls, with two end tables and lamps that matched, no phone next to it as there should have been.

Washing his hands, Shawn took a glimpse out of the small serving window that gave you a view of the living room. He could see Lilly looking around.

"You like our new home sweetheart? Came completely furnished, didn't have to touch a thing. Well, your room, of course, I did a lot of work in there. Had to make it just right for a special girl like you."

Drying his hands with a paper towel, Shawn crouched down in front of Lilly with a warm smile. "Look, I'm going to take this out of your mouth and I want you to scream all you want because no one will ever hear you."

Lilly could feel her tongue stick to the cloth as he pulled it out. With her mouth clear, she sucked clean cool air deep into her lungs so fast that it almost put her out of breath. Ever so slowly she could feel saliva coming back while Shawn cut the tape from her feet. She didn't bother yelling, she was too angry.

"Ready to see your room? You've got to be excited." Shawn placed his icy bony fingers on her shoulders, making Lilly cringe once again, leading her to the back hallway. Passing the kitchen she did a quick scan for a phone. Bingo! Shuffling her feet two inches at a time she tried not to crack a smile at the sight of the black rotary phone. Turning back to the hall, she saw only two more doorways ahead. One had no door on it, revealing a blue on blue bathroom made of tiny tiles. The second door was shut until Shawn reached in front of her and swung it open to reveal nothing she wasn't expecting, the same walls, carpet, end tables and lamp, even another clown picture that matched. Someone was obviously a lazy decorator back in the day. The only thing different about this room was a small bed and dresser with only three drawers, one was missing.

Shuffling deeper into the room, Lilly couldn't imagine spending much time here, even if she was watching TV all day. Wait, TV, there wasn't one. Suddenly she got upset thinking of the shows she'll be missing. An odd thought to have in a moment like this but a concern nonetheless.

"Now, don't go getting all excited just yet! This is my resting place and soon to be play den for when I visit you. Your room, or shall I say living quarters, are over here." Tightening his icy grip, he turned her towards the once-closet. Where there should have stood a tacky sliding wood door, now stood a shiny steel one with several locks on it. Shawn released Lilly and pranced over to the door. With flair he presented the door like Vanna White. Then, after a complicated series of unlocking, he slid, with some effort, the door aside. "Beautiful, isn't it!"

Gazing at the tiny space she was about to be shoved into, the realization of what was happening finally set in. This was no longer just weird neighbor Shawn being mean and odd. This was terrifying.

7

With Lilly neatly tucked away and everything finally running as planned, Shawn pumped up the radio volume and sang along to an eighties song he hardly knew on his way back to the scene of the crime. This time he quickly stashed the car in a new location on the opposite side of the woods. As he had timed it before, the walk was only seventeen minutes back to his backyard. It was easy to slip in unnoticed. Perfect timing, too. Smoke was still everywhere but it was more of a smoldering wet smell now. The orange glow was practically gone as a group of warriors were exiting the woods with an evil, cuffed villain in tow. Or at least what they thought was an evil villain. Shawn stole one last smile of pure joy before having to act in another scene.

Captain Rudder strutted over to the group with a look on his face that made it obvious that sweat and ash disgusted him. "What's the situation?"

"He's not saying anything but pure shit. We did a quick search but found nothing. We need more men and plenty of lights to go through the whole building," Chip said with confidence as he thrust Mr. Bluestick at Rudder, who quickly jumped back not wanting to get soot on himself. The men chuckled.

"Where is the father?" Rudder asked as he looked Mr. Bluestick up and down with a sour puss of disgust and curiosity.

"He stayed to search with your boys, refused to go, don't blame him. She's got to be in there somewhere."

"You let a civilian stay and search a God damn collapsing building? In a fire! Not to mention the fact that it's a crime scene."

"Yup. Now I suggest you take your perp and pistol-whip his ass until he tells you where to find that girl while we get ready to go back out there. And if you don't get an answer in thirty minutes, then my boys and I will have to take over questioning."

Rudder's recently moisturized face was purple with rage as Chip and his men walked away with glares. After a few quick breaths, he yanked out an embroidered handkerchief and grabbed Mr. Bluestick's cuffed hands with it to lead him to the car. This was one fucked up night he thought. More procedures broken than in a cheesy Charles Bronson movie. This case was going to put his nuts through the ringer.

Gently guiding Mr. Bluestick to the car, Rudder's mind wandered to wondering whether or not his suit was going to reek of smoke. As he gently lifted his lapel to smell it, the perp made a run for it. Fuck this! It took him a second to prepare for a chase. It shouldn't be that hard, he's only an old man anyway. Turning to see what way he was headed, Rudder was confused. Wouldn't he run for the woods? Yet, instead, he was running right at the neighbor's house.

Shawn saw him coming, noticed he was cuffed and had a stroke of genius. Mr. Bluestick lowered his hatted head and rammed right at him. In an instant they were both on the ground. With a bit of overacting, Shawn screamed with faux pain before pretending to scurry away terrified. He put his hand over his already injured eye (which did hurt but not anymore than a few seconds ago) and screamed for help over and over again.

Mr. Bluestick rolled uselessly on the ground, trying to get up and attack the bastard who took away his everything. In his attempts he rolled over his hat, crushing it, doing more damage to the hat than he could do to Shawn.

"Help!! For crying out loud, get this sick bastard away from me!" As a slew of cops pounced on Mr. Bluestick, Shawn snuck him a quick wink.

"You have to believe me, he's the sick bastard! He is! HE IS!" Ready to spout more about Shawn, he was quickly cut off by an expert chokehold that brought him to his feet instantly. His eyes filled with tears of pain and grief as he watched a young cop cautiously help Shawn up. Everything was over. His life, maybe Lilly's, the poor girl's parents, all crushed just like his hat that now lay alone in the ash strewn yard.

The Aftermath
Part 3

1

Amazingly, Lilly slept soundly that night. The sheets were soft and clean. They smelled like hers at home. Dad used to say that Mom bounced them to make them smell so good. Lilly thought it was a silly comment and that Dad was joking. Oddly it was the first thing she thought of that morning. Rubbing the sleep out of her eyes hurt. They were still sore from all the crying and smoke of the previous night. It must have been what tired her out enough to sleep.

The few hours she was awake were spent first yelling, then crying, shaking and hugging the blanket that followed right before the sleep came. Waking up now, the tears were ready to come but she held them back opting to search her new miniature home for a way out. A few slivers of light snuck in here and there, giving Lilly enough light to see around. Quickly and carefully, she tried budging the doors. She pushed on every inch of the cold steel. Nothing. Next she went on to feeling the walls. A scream escaped her lips when she felt something cold, hard and tiny scurry away from her hand. When her scream stopped echoing, she could hear scraping. It wasn't a bug, was it? Putting her brave face on, she reached out again, this time grabbing whatever it was. With a quick yank, a light flickered on, the sudden brightness made Lilly quickly cover her eyes.

With the light beating down on her, Lilly finally got a full grasp of her new home. To an adult it was merely a walk-in closet, but to an eight year old it was a small room. Against the wall on the far right was the bed she slept on last night. Lilly could now see that it was just a few couch cushions sewn together. To the left of the bed was a small stack of children's books, a deck of cards and two dolls, one beat up Barbie wearing shorts and a tank top and one generic brown stuffed bear that must have been secondhand. The middle of the room was open with nothing on the old carpet. A tiny training toilet was in the far left corner. It reminded her of the one she had when she was a kid, only this one was yellow instead of blue and it had a large smiley face on it. Next to it was TP and a can of air freshener, the dollar store brand of lilac. Oddly, close to the toilet on the left were three bottles of Poland Springs water and a case of orange crackers, the kind with the peanut butter in the middle.

Lilly munched on the crackers while wondering what the heck she was supposed to do all day. First thing on her agenda was to yell and bang on the floor and walls. After several minutes that felt like hours her little hands and feet were sore from the pounding. What next? The books were stupid and too childish for her. What eight-year-old reads Golden Books anyways? She flipped through them and tossed them aside one at a time. By the time she cracked open the pack of cards, she had been up only forty minutes. Already boredom was on her mind over fear.

Sleep deprivation. Mr. Bluestick remembered reading about how it was used on spies to get them to spill their guts in wartime. And now he knew why. Because if he had anything to hide, he would spill it all for just a few minutes of sleep. Since they brought him in and booked him last night, they hadn't let him shut his eyes once. There had been five, maybe seven different people coming into the lifeless room to grill him over and over again. The last person left thirty seconds ago. He wanted to put his head down on the barren gray table and sleep. There wouldn't be much of a pillow since his hands were shackled to small eyeholes on opposite sides, making it impossible for them to get more then three feet apart. It wouldn't matter; a bed of sharp nails would suffice right now.

Sure enough the second his eyes shut, the door behind him swung open. It had ceased to startle him anymore. He couldn't help but wonder how many people were behind the ridiculously large two-way mirror that was directly in front of him. Was there a whole group fighting over who gets to go in and grill the crazy old man next? Mr. B waited for the stack of files to be slammed down to show their toughness for the umpteenth time. He was surprised when they were placed on the table and gently slid to the far chair that was strategically placed to not block the view from the mirror by a lovely woman in a brown pants suit. She looked kind. It brought a smile to him for it made him think of Lilly all grown up and becoming a woman just like her.

"Good morning, sir. I'm Sue Lamkins, the department psychiatrist. I was wondering if we could talk for a bit?"

"Of course we can, my dear, but I must apologize if I seem less than enthusiastic. I have not slept in over 28 hours."

"I completely understand and apologize, but you do know we are trying to find a little girl right now and we need your help to make sure she gets home just fine. You want her to be just fine, don't you?"

"More than anything. That girl has brought happiness back into my life. And if someone would just listen to me and go after the family's neighbor, Shawn, you'd have her back home with her wonderful father before lunch."

The woman made some notes in a pad. Mr. Bluestick tried to squint and read them but his eyes were too dry and tired to see much farther than his hands.

"Well, Mr. . .Is it Bluestick?"

He nodded with a smile. "Yes, Lilly gave me that name."

She gave back a warm smile that showed she cared. He knew it was fake and designed to make him comfortable but he didn't care, he had nothing to hide.

"What's your real name, Mr. Bluestick?"

He shook his head no as if trying not to laugh. How do you tell an adult that you're not from this planet, that you have no earthly name, and all you want is for Lilly to be safe and to be able to finally go home? Or do you lie? No one will believe his story anyway, why try and argue it.

"Mr. Bluestick?"

Thinking, his eyes wandered the room for something to stare at. There was nothing but grayness. His eyes glanced by the mirror but he dared not keep them there long for fear of seeing himself. He hadn't looked at himself in years and didn't want to now. His eyes went to the table. When he saw his ungloved hands, his eyes shut in a wince, only to open a few seconds later as if nothing happened.

"It's fine, we don't need to know it right now; we need to focus on Lilly anyway."

"Shawn, Shawn, Shawn," he replied in a calm steady voice.

"I don't want you to think that your comments are going unheard. In fact, Mr. Daggerty has already been asked questions and his house has been searched. I'm sorry, Mr. Bluestick, but they found nothing and the girl's father backed up all his stories. They said they have had a few run-ins with you before and that they have told you to stay away from Lilly."

Misery, frustration, physical pain from the beating last night and fear dropped on Mr. Bluestick like a car off a cliff. He slid down in the chair as far as possible and rested his head. Tears rolled out of his shut eyes as he closed out the world and let exhaustion take him over.

Tom was numb. His mind was blank. Sitting in the police station in an uncomfortable chair in the office of one of the detective's, he sipped what must have been his hundredth cup of coffee. He wanted to be out in the woods searching that damn mill with the two-dozen police and firemen but Chip had talked him out of it. He said if they found her, that he would personally take her immediately to him, that he needed to rest and that he could help more by being at the station answering any questions. Tom had reluctantly agreed even though he knew the real truth was they didn't want him flipping out if they found a body instead of his vibrant daughter.

When he first arrived at three in the morning, they asked him dozens of questions, most of which he couldn't remember now. From 5-8 AM they gave him a tiny room, which reminded him of his elementary school nurse's office. It was practically the same, right down to the tiny stiff bed they wanted him to nap on. The only thing missing was the three hundred pound nurse. He didn't remember sleeping at all but the time somehow went by oddly fast, unlike now. Now it seemed as if someone dunked the clock hands in molasses.

Getting up, his body was stiff and filled with exhausting pain. He walked around the room to stretch out. Doing so, he wondered why a small town that hasn't seen a murder in sixteen years needed so many detectives. From the offices he counted over nine. Whatever the reason, it didn't matter; he was glad they were here now.

Slowly walking around the desk, rolling out his shoulders, Tom examined the pictures on the desk. There were three. One showed a fat man in shorts, shirtless on a beach with a mask and snorkel on, with two shirtless kids, twins about five, clinging to his leg. The second one showed the same fat man with an amazingly skinny blonde at a Christmas party. Tom could recognize some of the other detectives in the background. The third picture was of just the two kids with tacky sweaters on, posing for the cheesy Sears photo. Tom sat down and looked from one photo to another. The bastard has no clue how lucky he is, Tom thought to himself. He's probably home right now on his day off, ignoring the kids, eating a high cholesterol breakfast while reading a paper. At that moment Tom vowed to never take anything in life for granted again. An annoying voice snapped him out of his trance.

"Mr. Boyer, can you follow me? We've got some leads." With the word *leads* Tom's heart rate jumped up sixty beats a minute, even if the information came from that dick Rudder.

Shawn sat impatiently in the Boyer living room watching *Animal Planet* with a young cop. Sandy was upstairs. He couldn't help but wonder what she was doing. She never seemed to care much for Lilly, or Tom for that matter. Hell, she didn't seem to care about anything. Even the few times he'd seen her pretend to care Shawn wasn't fooled. The young cop snickered at some dog galloping comically through snow. Shawn took it as his cue to leave.

The cop hardly noticed him get up and glide up the stairs. Shawn couldn't imagine how this guy was supposed to be protecting the family. At the top of the stairs, he paused and glanced into Lilly's room. The wait was killing him. Ever since he got her last night, it had been hard to keep his erection from being noticed. It had been years since he'd had such nice quality young meat as Lilly. He couldn't wait.

Shawn's focus went to the dresser from which he had snuck the panties. He wanted more, but now was not a good time to risk that. After adjusting his erection to make sure Sandy wouldn't see it, he proceeded to the closed bedroom door. He listened first, heard nothing, and then knocked. It took a few seconds but Sandy answered with wet eyes, though Shawn suspected they weren't real tears. "Just wanted to see how you were doing."

Sandy answered with a blank stare. She was a mess, wearing a sweatshirt and wind pants all wrinkled.

"Can I come in?"

Sandy really didn't want the slime ball to come in, but she didn't want to seem suspicious, so she opened the door for him. She plopped back onto the bed and Shawn casually sat at the make-up desk chair and examined the room he had never been in before.

"There still is no word. Tom's still at the station. Frustrating, isn't it?"

"Yeah." She replied in a faux frail voice. She watched Shawn cross his legs and touch the gauze patch over his injured eye. It made him look quite flamboyant.

"Sandy, I don't mean this as rude but you've never seemed too keen on Lilly." It was a huge risk but Shawn saw the opportunity and wanted to jump on it. He watched her face search for the right words, the right lie to cover up. Touching the patch on his eye for the hundredth time, he couldn't believe he had to wear it for two weeks. Finally she opened her mouth, but nothing came out.

"Don't worry. It's okay. I have three kids, haven't talked to them in five years now. At first I thought I should feel bad, but you know what? I never did. Just because society says you should love them, doesn't mean you always have to." It was a hell of a lie but it seemed to work.

Wondering what to do, Sandy's mouth closed. He kept his eyes fixated on her. She was staring at the floor now. If she didn't agree with him, then she would have protested immediately. Now all he had to do was keep talking. "I'm just saying it because, well, just in case, you know Lilly doesn't come back."

She finally met his gaze.

Tom entered the room of men in suits and felt out of place. Rudder gave a fake cough to warn the others that the dad was entering. Immediately they quieted. He motioned for Tom to sit down as most of the suits left the room. Only Tom, Rudder and another officer by the name of Pennski, who looked like Brad Pitt's ugly brother, remained. They sat across from him. It was the same room in which they had questioned him earlier. He was less than thrilled to be back in it, yet he couldn't take waiting to hear what the lead was. Please make it big.

"Tom, I know this might be hard, but do you know what underwear Lilly was wearing when she left the house?"

This definitely wasn't the type of lead he was hoping for. Leaning back in the chair, he tried to keep his mind off why they asked and concentrate on what she was wearing. Nothing came to mind. "I don't know. We've let her dress herself for some time now."

The two detectives looked at each other as if this was an incriminating statement. "Well do you think you could identify a pair of her underwear?" Pennski asked, using too many facial expressions as if raised eyebrows would get the question across better.

"I think I would . . . yeah."

Pennski got up and left the room without a word. Tom wanted to ask Rudder a dozen questions, but nerves and the fact that Rudder was examining his nails with such intensity stopped him. It made Tom look at his own nails. They were jagged and a few had tiny specks of blood. He hadn't even realized he had been chewing them, something he hadn't done since he was eleven.

Pennski came back with a plastic bag held low and covered just enough with his hand that Tom couldn't see what was inside. He tossed it on the table as if it were the convicting piece of evidence in a murder mystery movie. It pissed Tom off. Everyone was being so considerate and helpful but these two dicks, they were treating him like a criminal.

Settling himself, Tom lightly picked up the bag. Carefully he looked at the tiny pink flower print underwear. He turned it over and over to see if the one thing he feared was there, blood. Thankfully there wasn't, only some dust and dirt.

"Yes, yes these are hers," Tom said with confidence. He clearly remembered Sandy buying them at Wal-Mart. She tossed them in the cart without even looking at the pattern. Tom tried to argue with her to go through and pick some fun ones but she wasn't having it.

"Well, Tom," Rudder started, then sighed deeply while fixing his tie. "I hate to tell you this, but we found those in the suspects, umm, well, his . . . the mill."

Tom shut his eyes with force, trying to get every thought out of his mind. There were too many of them and not one was good. If the sick bastard had those, then something had to have happened. All the fantasies that he and Lilly were actually just friends and she ran away, scared of the fire, vanished. Opening his eyes back up, he saw the two detectives watching him with bored looks. "So how does this help find my daughter?"

They looked at each other wondering who should speak. Pennski went first. "Well, it's really more about evidence for any future trial. It's also something that might help us to crack that freak in there. If he knows there is solid evidence against him, he might come clean."

Tom nodded his head, wanting nothing more than to have five minutes alone with that sick bastard. Then he would tell where Lilly was. Fucking laws.

Two doors over, Sue Lamkins was still working on Mr. Bluestick, unsuccessfully. To Sue he was being more than uncooperative. She was doing her best to be the sympathetic therapist, but after they called her out of the room and she learned that he had the poor girl's underwear hidden away, she was having a hard time being nice. She had yet to confront him about it.

Mr. Bluestick - she couldn't believe she was actually using that name with him. She'd seen some nut jobs in her time but nothing like this, especially in such a small town. Maybe if he's a real tough cookie, she can get some papers published on him, hell, maybe even a book. The realization of potential behind this man, child molester or not, perked her up. "We found something in your home... something I want to talk to you about."

He looked up curiously. What could it be? He couldn't imagine what they would find of any interest to Lilly, besides the few drawings she made him. Maybe that was it.

"Now, we already know they are Lilly's. What I want to know is how you got them."

Getting a bit more interested, shaking off the pain and exhaustion, he sat up. Sue pursed her lips preparing for the reveal, right when the tiny light next to the door came on, signaling for her to come out. Damn it, she was just about to crack him. "I'll be right back, I'm sorry."

Opening the door she was met by Rudder's greasy hair a foot from her face. He was reading a fax. She squeezed by him and asked in a bitter tone what the problem was.

"Run on his prints came back, Doc! No more need for the pet names." With that statement he slapped the fax hard in his hand and presented it to her. On the front was a clean-cut young picture of one Edward Cotter, A.K.A Mr. Bluestick.

2

Sandy couldn't believe she was spilling her guts to the slime ball neighbor, let alone anyone. Not a soul knew her secrets. But for some odd reason she felt comfortable with him now. It did feel damn good to have it all off her chest though.

"So that's all of it. I was planning on leaving today. Then the little shit has to go and ruin it all." She cringed, wondering if that sounded too mean.

Shawn just smiled. "They're all a bunch of little shits, aren't they? I mean, I don't remember ever being so rude and disrespectful!" Sandy was smiling now too. She couldn't believe someone else felt as she did. This was amazing. No one ever understood her like this before. Damn, he left his three kids and wife behind. She could do it, too.

"How long do you think I should wait till I do leave? I mean, if I leave too soon, they'll be suspicious of me, no?"

Shawn squinted his good eye pretending to think. It was a bad choice, though, since pain shot through his bad eye like a freight train. It distracted him a bit but he got right back on track.

"You know, Sandy, this is actually the best time for you to leave. Well, I don't mean right this second, but soon. Think about it, you could blame it on the stress. You can say you can't be in this house, too many memories. It's perfect. If you just up and did it any other time, people wouldn't understand. Now they will sympathize with you. You're lucky, I didn't have so easy."

Sandy was grinning from ear to ear now. She hadn't thought about how perfect it was. He was so right! It would make her plan so much easier, too.

Shawn left after a few more minutes of stale chat. She had plenty of questions but he didn't bother answering them too much. The seed was planted; his job was done here. Walking by Lilly's room again, he stuck his head in and took a deep breath. It didn't really smell much like Lilly but he imagined it did.

Exhaling, he wanted to cry. It was all too perfect, way better than he expected it to go. He had been watching Sandy lately. Even followed her a few times. Which led to the realization that she was getting ready to leave. All he was hoping to accomplish by coming up here was for her not to care too much, which, in turn, he could turn into friction between Tom and her, which the cops would scrutinize and turn it into a conspiracy. Maybe they'd even blame them like the JonBenet Ramsey case. Everyone in the country thought they did it. Then ten years later and bang! They find the real killer. Only Shawn didn't plan on getting caught, not even in ten years. He never thought in a million years that Sandy was planning to bail! It was definitely an added bonus to his plan. Now a few days after things settle down, after they suspect that Lilly is dead, Sandy will leave and cause another uproar, keeping any and all attention off him!

Shawn hadn't planned on risking seeing Lilly for another few days but things were going so good it might be possible. His hard on was hurting so much that he walked right down the stairs, waved to the officer and headed out the door, right for his first taste of her.

"Edward Cotter. Born nineteen-thirty-eight in Tulsa, Oklahoma. Moved to New York City with his parents at the age of twelve. Grew up to be a prolific playwright. Won several awards, nominated for a Tony by the time he was twenty-nine. Was a rising star, yada, yada, yada.

Hollywood asked him several times to write film versions of his hit Broadway shows. He refused." Rudder sighed and skipped forward. "Let's see. Damn, this psychologist took too many notes. Ahhh, here we go. Bought property here in nineteen-sixty-seven."

The room looked like story time in a kindergarten class. Everyone was glued to Rudder's words as he read Cotter's patient profile from the old hospital records.

After getting the fingerprints, it took them almost forty minutes to find the file in the old storage unit three miles from the station. It was nothing fancy. In fact it was just a regular Rent-A-Space storage unit that all paper files over thirty years old were sent to once the new computer systems came in.

"Fuck this. He's never been arrested for anything but an accident and the charges were dropped. That's all we need to know; the rest of the file is useless. We need to spend time in the field searching. Jack, Tony and Lisa, you guys split this up, read through it and report back to me on it."

Rudder closed the thick file and rubbed his eyes, then gently patted under them to make sure he didn't produce any bags. The three rookies went for the folder and hesitated, not sure who should split it up.

Before any of them could decide to touch it Sue swooped in and grabbed it. "I'll look them over if you don't mind, Captain Rudder," she said with attitude. What did she ever see in him before? Thank God, she smartened up before she ever slept with him. It's amazing how you can go from wanting to despising so quickly.

"You can have it, Doc. I don't think it's going to do much good, though. The guy needs some pistol-whipping, that's what. And I'm going to go do the closest thing to it that I can."

She was ready to go off on him and comment on his little dick since she knew how sensitive he was about it, but she held back. There were more important things going on, a girl was missing, for Christ sakes.

Tom had heard everything as he pretended to be getting water from the cooler right outside the door. The guy was a playwright? How do you go from that to living like a hermit in the woods? Drugs? And what the hell was the accident he was arrested for? He didn't get it, he didn't want to, he wanted his daughter back.

Pretending to sip the water, he started to walk away as everyone was leaving the room. Out of the corner of his eye he saw Sue coming up behind him with the hefty file. Purposely, he moved to his right a bit to get in her way. She paused before trying to go around him. Tom turned into her. "Oh, I'm sorry," Tom said, trying to start conversation since he hadn't been introduced to her yet.

"It's fine, no trouble." Tom introduced himself and she reassured him that she was doing everything she could on her side to help.

"Well, you could help me a bit more." He looked around. "Can we talk in private for a bit?"

Sue really didn't want to get involved with a distraught Dad. She didn't have time to help him yet, but how can you refuse someone in need? "We can go in my office, but we must keep it quick. I'm close to wearing him down; hopefully he'll tell us where your daughter is."

Tom forced a smile and started to follow her down the one hall he had yet to go down.

"PENNSKI!" Rudder's yell stopped them both in their tracks. "Pennski, I'm going in there, I need you to hold me back!"

Tom had turned to see what was going on when Sue slammed Cotter's file into his chest for him to hold. She darted across the room, dodging desks like an obstacle course to get to Rudder who was loosening his tie outside of the holding room.

"Don't you dare go play tough cop with my patient. I'm about to get him to open up to me. If you scare him now, he might never come out of it," Sue lectured to the smiling grease ball. Everyone was now watching.

"Sue, he's my suspect. I only let you talk to him for fun. When I get the girl back and slap a twenty-to-life on him, you can poke around in his brain all you want, got it?"

"Listen here you small di ..."

Another woman in an officer's uniform put her hand over Sue's mouth and pulled her back. Rudder looked at her like some sort of pathetic dog. Sue didn't fight off the woman much. It was her best friend after all, looking out for her.

Confident that confrontation was over, Rudder gently and strategically messed up his hair before bursting through the door. Pennski followed, the door shut and the screaming began.

A solid hour. And it was glorious. Uninterrupted and too tired to dream. It was a bit uncomfortable not being able to move your arms and sitting in a hard chair, but being this tired made it feel like a king size bed made of clouds. That was until the door shot opened, followed by a quick kick to the chair legs. It startled Mr. Bluestick so much he actually yelped like a small dog. It took a few seconds before he could start to decipher the constant stream of screams into actual words.

"It's been thirteen hours, fucko! And I still don't have the girl! We know you did it, we found the girl's underwear. What were they, some sort of souvenir? Well, they'll add twenty years on to your sentence!"

Rudder quieted down for a second and sat on the table as close to him as he could. He looked at the scared man with a devilish smile. "Oh, and you know what? I found out something else. . .Edward." Rudder watched his face closely, waiting for the change, the guilt, the recognition. There was none and it pissed him off. Using his name was his fucking ace.

"Listen to me, Cotter! We know everything about you. We have enough evidence to put you away for good. And you know what? No jury will give you an insanity plea since it's an eight year old girl. EIGHT-YEARS OLD!" He shouted for the dramatic effect.

Pennski, who was standing behind Mr. Bluestick to add the fear of knowing someone was there but not knowing exactly where, nodded to Rudder for encouragement. "If you talk now, and depending what condition the girl is in, I'll do my best to see that you get put in a hospital, not jail, till your trial. Cuz you know what they do to old sickos like you, right?"

Cotter's face still hadn't changed. Rudder wondered if like himself he had seen too many cop shows and movies to know that this was all a line of crap said by thousands of actors each year.

"You want Shawn. Shawn, Shawn, Shawn, Shawn, Shawn, SHAWN!" screamed Mr. Bluestick. Finally some emotion, Rudder thought. He was sticking to his story but he was cracking.

211

Tom riffled through the files while the officer was calming Sue. Paranoid about getting yelled at, he only folded back corners with his back turned to everyone. He had no clue what to look for. What the hell did he care about the man's past for, anyway; now was what was important. For a quick moment he agreed with Rudder that yelling was the way to go, even though it went against his life philosophy of "you get more with honey than you do with vinegar." It was a corny cliché but Tom still believed in it. Just not this second.

Red-faced, Sue patted Tom on the shoulder, startling him enough to almost drop the folder. Shuffling it in his hands, Sue said to follow her to the office. That he did. It was cute, clean and comfortable. It reminded him of a school guidance counselor's office and in many ways it was the same, except for the chair with the eyehole hooks to cuff criminals to.

"I'm sorry about that scene; tension is high as you must know." Her eyes darted around the room as the redness in them faded ever so slightly.

Tom waited for her to calm a bit more before speaking.

"Mrs. Lamkins, I want to talk to Mr. Blue. . .um, Mr. Cotter. I think he will listen to me. I mean if he did do something to Lilly, maybe by seeing me, the guilt will come on stronger. You know, from the recognition."

Sue still looked distracted, but after a few seconds she started to nod. "You're right, I think it would work, but now that Rudder has gone and fucked. . .sorry about that. Now that he has messed things up, I need some time to do damage control, and, besides, Rudder will never let you in there. He's by the books."

Feeling a bit defeated and wondering what to counter with, Tom stared out the window. It faced the main entrance. Cars drove by with people going about their innocent lives, without a worry and with no clue what was going on in here. Leaning forward to look out more, he could see the tip of a news van, Channel 22, it looked like. His stomach did a flip. Rudder had warned him earlier that the press was going to get wind of this very soon, and that it was up to him if he wanted to make a statement or not.

Sue and Tom sat there, each in their own world, not even noticing the silence between them. Sue thought about the damage control she had to do with the patient while Tom started to think about how many times on the news he saw a distraught father on TV talking about his missing daughter, asking for prayers, for help. He thought about how many times he thought, "God that is awful," then went back to eating dinner and forgot about it.

"I'm sorry, Mr. Boyer, I really should get looking over these files. I'll see what I can do later on to get you in there. But, for now, is there anything else you want to talk about?" Tom didn't even hear the question, he just kept staring out the window.

Shawn left the Boyer house and made a quick pit stop at his. The police had already searched it and he wasn't worried a bit. When he planned all of this, he had rented a storage garage fifteen miles outside of town under the same fake name as the apartment. There he stored the dozens and dozens of child pornography pictures and videos. Over the years he had amassed a very large collection. More recently he had been using the Internet, but he wasn't worried about them searching his computer. Nope, he was too smart for that as well. That's why he kept a separate laptop computer, which was now in that garage. His home one was squeaky clean.

The laptop was the greatest tool in the world for a pedophile. When he bought it, he made sure that it had an airport card so he could get wireless Internet. Ever since then Shawn had been doing about three or four Wi-Bys a week. A Wi-By was simple, just put the laptop on the passenger seat and drive slowly around neighborhoods until you got an Internet signal. Most people who use wireless in their homes don't understand or don't bother to put blockers on their signal. Once he had access, he would simply park the car and surf the net.

It would only take Shawn a few minutes to find some choice kiddy porn he wanted. There is plenty of it out there. After downloading what he wanted, he would simply drive off, leaving no record of him being there, leaving him completely untraceable. Every time he drove off he giggled to himself, wondering if the FBI would plow down the door of some middle class home and search it for kiddy porn. It gave him such a kick.

After changing, Shawn was ready to go have his first appetizer. Looking out his window the place was still a zoo of police, firemen and now media, but he figured he could slip out without any trouble. He wasn't a suspect. All he had to do was stay away from the media; getting his face on TV was not an option. He might have impeccable false records but his face was still the same. If this story made national news and he was on it, he'd have to flee once again.

Luckily for Shawn, he had an attached garage on his house, which was also a great help when you're packing kiddy porn into a trunk of a car. Calmly, he slipped into the cheap Saturn and hit the automatic door button. Soon as the door was just high enough, he could see the media people scrambling to go after whoever was coming out. With a Patriot's hat pulled low, sunglasses on and collar up, he looked like either a celebrity hiding out from the paparazzi or a very guilty man hiding from his sins.

With a bit too much speed, Shawn backed out. The typical blonde street reporter woman was frantically waving over her not yet ready cameraman. Noticing the car, she reluctantly shimmied out of the way and put on a smile. As he sped past her, he could see her hand go from a missed knock to a desperate please-hold-on gesture. He smirked to himself. . .home free.

At the end of the road, Shawn, to be cautious, turned the completely opposite direction from where he was keeping Lilly. He kept an eye out for anyone following him and, for a while, he thought there was. To be safe, he went to the grocery store and bought a few non-perishable items. Next, it was on to Wal-Mart to pick up a few things for Lilly that he didn't have time to get earlier. In the parking lot he still felt as if he was being followed.

About a half hour after leaving the house, he was finally on the way to see Lilly. He drove cautiously, making a lot of unnecessary turns to throw off anyone following. Arriving on the street, he drove by the house first. It seemed to be all clear. On a side street he turned around and headed back. Pulling into the spot behind the garage was such a relief.

It was a bit hard sliding the key in the door with all the bags, but he eventually got it. Once inside he felt like a kid on Christmas morning. He could hardly walk; he had to run to the closet. Fiddling with the locks, he could hear Lilly gasp inside. He shouted encouragement not to worry.

Aloisi

The door moved aside, revealing the stench of stale smoke-covered clothing and fresh pee. Lilly looked a mess but to him it was a beautiful sight.

"Oh, Lilly baby, are you okay?" Shawn got on his knees in the doorway and spread his arms for a hug. Lilly put on her best angry scowl and pushed herself into the back corner.

"Lilly, it's okay. I'm going to take care of you from now on. It's just me and you." Her nose started to quiver. He could see the cry coming on.

From his past experiences with little girls, which was extensive, he had learned to coerce them, to make them trust him or else they would always fight. If he talked them into doing what he wanted, got them to think they were being good girls if they did what he wanted, they were so much more enjoyable. It was an amazing feeling having a nine or ten-year-old girl do anything and everything he said. Having to tie them down, tape their mouths, would still get him off, but not nearly as much as being able to lay back with his hands over his head, not having to do a thing. To get that, he was willing to take his time with Lilly. She was his now, after all.

"I got you some better food and a present. I've got an idea, why don't you take a shower, get all cleaned up and then I'll give you the present! Sound good?"

Lilly didn't want his damn present or his food. All she wanted was Dad to be hugging her in her own room.

"I want to go home."

Shawn put on a comforting smile and shuffled his way close to her. "Lilly, I didn't want to tell you this. But I think it will help you. So I have to." He sighed deeply and lay on his elbow. He fiddled with the carpet a bit then looked Lilly in the eyes.

216

"Your parents, well, they asked me to take you. They don't want you anymore, Lilly. They wanted to give you to an orphanage but I couldn't let them do that to you. It'll be just fine. I know you don't like me much, but give me a chance. You'll see in a while, you'll forget all about your parents, and it'll be just you and me."

Lilly was confused. The words hurt even though they had to be a lie, a lie, right? "That's not true, my dad loves me!"

Shawn put a hand on her leg. She tried to back away but couldn't go any farther. He caressed it, feeling the warmth of her tiny leg. He'd been hard since the ride over but now the blood was flowing so much it hurt.

"Look, why don't you take your shower and then I'll show you the letter your dad wrote. I was hoping that I would never have to give it to you but if you want to read it, you can. It might hurt though."

Lilly was starting to shake. She was having a hard time grasping and understanding that she was kidnapped to begin with. Now, having this thrown at her was too much for her developing mind to take. "Can I just shower now?"

The voice was so frail it made his heart jump. Maybe gaining her trust won't be so hard after all. He walked to the bathroom and showed her the Sponge Bob foam soap he bought her. She was less than thrilled. Lilly crossed her arms and waited for him to leave.

"Here, let me help you get undressed." She backed away and shot him a look.

"What's wrong? Your dad doesn't help you shower? My dad and mom helped me until I was at least fifteen!"

Lilly looked to the door and wondered if she could make a run for it, but she had already taken off her shoes. Can't get too far with no shoes, her dad used to always tell her when she wanted to go barefoot to the store. "I'm perfectly fine by myself, thank you!"

Shawn nodded OK and headed out of the room, making sure she knew to holler if she needed any help.

When he was finally gone, Lilly went to shut the door and realized, there wasn't one. She had no clue what to do. What if he walked by and saw her naked? She contemplated asking him where the door was but she knew it was no use. Turning on the water, she looked around to see if he was gone. Confident he was in the next room, Lilly started to undress in the corner, hoping to not be seen. Fast as she could, she wrapped around herself a yellow towel that still had the price tag on it.

Standing outside the door, Shawn silently unzipped his pants and pulled out his throbbing member. It felt like heaven to not be constricted anymore. Gently he stroked himself, until he heard the shower curtain close, then he sped up. With the caution of a cat, he then peeked around the corner. He bought six shower curtains until he found the one he could see through the best. It still didn't reveal as much as he would have liked but it was good enough for now. Seeing Lilly's tiny body, naked and wet through the blurred curtain was enough to make him finish in eight fast pumps. He closed his eyes and enjoyed the moment. Then he went right back to watching Lilly, until the water shut off. With a quick rub of his foot, he mashed his fluids into the carpet, zipped up and went in the kitchen to make his new love some food.

3

Sandy wanted to pack so badly but knew she couldn't, so she started to go through drawer after drawer, cleaning them out and organizing. That way she'd know what she wanted to take when she left. Originally she wasn't going to take anything, except for Tom's savings. But now, not having to disappear made things much easier.

Going through the dresser's bottom drawer, she found Lilly's baby box under some old sweaters. For a split second a bit of grief went through her and she doubted what she was doing once again. She had to close her eyes and remember how much the bitch ruined her life, how much Tom ruined it. She just knew the two of them plotted behind her back, she knew it.

None of that mattered now. She just needed to make it through a few days, put on one hell of a show, then off she'd be with Mark. He was a real man, a man that was going to take care of her, going to treat her right. God, he was beautiful. Missing him, wanting to hear his voice, Sandy tucked the box back in the drawer, but then she hesitated and pulled it back. It would make her look good if people thought she was lying here reminiscing alone! Opening the box, she placed some of the items – a lock of hair, hospital ID bracelet, and ink footprints - on top of the dresser. She smiled at it and headed for the phone.

Before she could pick it up and dial the all-too-familiar number of Antonio's Pizzeria, the phone rang. It startled her a bit. She let it ring twice since the officer had been screening the calls all day declining the news interviews, and keeping wackos at bay for her. On the third ring the officer picked up. A few seconds later she could hear footsteps coming up the stairs. She went to the door to meet the officer whose name she couldn't remember.

"Ma'am, it's your husband on the phone."

She thanked him and shut the door. She rubbed her eyes and headed for the phone, not wanting to answer it. It boggled her mind how all this had happened, not the thing with Lilly, but her emotions. How the hell did she ever love this man? It's because the bastard fooled her. He must have used hypnosis or drugged her for years. She would have never fallen for him otherwise. He must have been damn good at it, too, tricking her into getting married, having a goddamn kid! The bastard !

Sandy wanted to kick the phone, throw it out the window, shoot it, and set it on fire. Anything to not have to hear his voice. Well, he was good at fooling her once, but she wised up all right. Now it was her turn to screw with his mind. She shook out her body and prepared herself for some acting. In the saddest voice she could produce she answered, "Hello."

"Honey, how you holding up?"

Sandy did her best crying breath and sniffed several times before replying, "What do you think, Tom? Our daughter is missing. Missing!"

Was she laying it on too thick? She doubted it. This was a situation she could freak out in and still have it be acceptable. For a split second, she wanted to do just that so she could get off the phone faster, but she wanted to find out what the news was.

"I know Sandy, I know. Do you need me to come home? I think I'm helping down here."

"I'll be just fine. I feel like I'm sort of, well, waiting for her to just walk in." Oh that was a good one, she thought. Listening, she knew it hit a cord with Tom. She could sense the tears being held back.

"Well, I'm sure she will . . . soon."

After that they only talked for a few more seconds then said their good-byes. Sandy hung up the phone with a smile on her face. Damn, she did a good job, she thought. With a light plunk, she flopped back on the bed. This was going to be so good. First she'll get revenge, then she'll be free of this bastard and this hellhole of a life.

Tom hung up the phone, wanting to be there for Sandy. She was definitely taking it hard. She might act as if she didn't like their daughter, but when it came down to it, she damn well must! It killed him leaving her alone there, but Shawn said he would keep an eye on her at least. Thank God he had him; he had helped him so much. Jesus, the guy risked his life for his daughter. You can't get a better friend than that. When he got Lilly back, he was going to have to do something really special for him.

After a few seconds, he shook the distractions from his head and got back to the task at hand. After some clever manipulation and a few tears, Tom convinced Sue to let him help her with Cotter's file. It was highly unorthodox but she needed to get through them right away so she could go back in that room with full ammo. Besides she felt pretty bad for him.

The soft rustling of papers was the only noise in the room as the two read page after page. Sue made notes and Tom separated papers in order of importance, according to the few guidelines that she gave him. He found the guy's life fascinating. He was well on his way to being a huge celebrity, yet ended up being insane. Why, they had yet to find out. He couldn't help but wonder if Sue had those pages.

"This is it! This is what I needed to know. Finally found the doctor's diagnosis. It's all explained here." Tom looked at her with anxious eyes, waiting for her to explain, which she did not. She was too absorbed in reading to notice his eyes begging.

After mumbling to herself and scribbling notes as if her life depended on it, she finally spoke again. "The only thing I don't get is he has no history of sexual abuse, assault, or any crimes against him. It doesn't make much sense. The psychologist had all of his sessions transcribed and there isn't one sexually deviant thing in there that I can find."

Tom didn't really understand what she was talking about but was happy that they were getting somewhere. Finally she looked up from reading and noticed Tom. She seemed a bit startled for a second, as if she had forgotten he was in the room.

"I've got enough to go back in there. I just hope Rudder is done jerking him around. I think we've got something here, Tom. This could help break him." She took the papers from him, got up and left the room. Tom was left feeling useless once again.

Rudder had given up ten minutes ago. Sitting now in his office, he was planning his speech to the public to ask for more volunteers to search. The bastard wouldn't break. Yes, he cried and looked scared at the false threats of being beat, but his story stayed the same. He couldn't understand why it hadn't worked as it does on *Law and Order*. He even pulled the gang-rape-in- the-shower card but the guy didn't even budge. Maybe the fucko was so crazy he didn't even realize what he had done, maybe he believed his own stories. Pathetic.

Satisfied the speech was filled with enough emotionally powerful lines to get the softer hearted hicks off their asses to help, he threw down his pen and pulled out his desk mirror. It was an expensive one with lights built in and it had the ability to stand on its own. With his personal grooming kit on his lap so no one could see, he fixed his hair, trimmed his eyebrows and dabbed a tiny bit of make-up on a few blemishes.

Ready for the cameras! It had been a while since Rudder was on the news. Last time it was only a four second clip commenting on an arson case. This, this was going to be his big shot. It was to be broadcast live and in full on all the local news and radio programs, basically everything that carried the Amber Alert. Before leaving from his nap today, he had set his home VCR to record the most popular news broadcast. Also, Mom was recording another channel for him in case Channel 40 had better coverage.

Satisfied everything was ready, he put away the mirror, stashed the speech in his inside pocket (so he could look cool pulling it out) and went for the door. Catching his reflection in the over-polished glass, he adjusted his hair one more time and noticed a small crowd around the front desk. It seemed Dudley Do-Right Chip was back.

Chip's face was long, dirty, covered in stubble and clearly upset. No one would leave him alone. All he wanted to do was to get to Tom, to tell him the news first, but everyone was pecking at him for info on what he found. The answer was absolutely fucking nothing. But he didn't want anyone telling Tom but himself. Seeing Rudder come out of his office, he knew he was going to get in trouble if he didn't talk to him first. Acting fast, he barked to several people asking where Tom was. One of the secretaries told him Doc Lamkins' office. Luckily, it was in the opposite hall from Rudder.

With a quick turn, he avoided Rudder by twenty yards. Ignoring his shout, he scurried down the hall. His legs felt like lead. Only two thirty minute naps on the floor of the woods didn't help much when you're wearing your gear for God knows how many hours it's been now. Startling Tom, he burst into the room, shut the door and sealed the curtain closed. "Sorry about that. That dick Rudder is chasing me down."

Tom spun around with surprise and fear at seeing Chip's face. It definitely wasn't joy on it. There had to be bad news.

"Look, Tom, first off I want to tell you we haven't found her yet. But I wanted to be the first to tell you what the progress is." He made his way over to Tom who was watching with hawk-like attention. With a heavy plop, he sat down next to him. It felt amazing to be sitting. "Tom, we searched every single inch of that place, and the surrounding woods up to everyone's backyards. We didn't find a single thing, not even a clue." Tom squeezed his eyes shut, not knowing how to take this.

"Now, you know I'm not a cop but I would take this as a good thing. We figure that he either had help kidnapping her or hid her somewhere near by. We found a set of tire tracks on an old access road. The forensic guys are checking it out now." The door handle started to jiggle followed by a slamming fist and yelling. The two men seemed to not even notice it.

After a few more minutes, Chip opened the door for the red-faced man. He went on about how he was lucky he wasn't his boss. Chip just stared at him calmly and coolly. After Rudder's rant, Chip finally told him the news. Rudder thought carefully and wondered what he should change in his speech. "Well, we'll search again, and again. I've got to get to the reporters. Tom, do you want to say anything?"

Tom had been thinking about this for some time. He wanted to say stuff, a lot of stuff. But the thought of going out there, looking into those cameras made him uneasy or was it scared? Regardless, he didn't want to do it.

"Please just tell them how much my daughter means to me and how anything they can do will help." Tom wanted to say and please pray for us, but right now how the fuck could he believe in a God? Rudder nodded and walked out of the room. He would paraphrase and make it sound better.

Tom turned around to see Chip in the chair, rubbing his eyes, half asleep. "Chip, you have done so much for me already. Please go home to your family, tell them you love them and take a nap."

Chip looked as if he was about to cry as he stood up, shook Tom's hand and left the room.

Alone once again, Tom went to the window to watch the circus begin. It was hard to see from the sharp angle, but it was all too easy to tell what was going on. Rudder was standing on the small steps like some politician running for office. Several news crews were around him, though not as many as in the movies. After watching for a few more seconds, he didn't want to see any more.

Shawn made a peanut butter and jelly sandwich while Lilly got dressed in the generic Kid's clothing he bought her. Of course, every few seconds he snuck a peek down the hall.

Cutting off the crusts of the sandwich, he added some Cool Ranch Doritos to the plate and headed down the hall to her.

"I made you lunch." He placed it on the bed near where she was sitting. Lilly still looked frightened of him but she looked at the food with hunger in her eyes. As if trying to coax a bear out of a cave, Shawn pushed the plate close to Lilly, an inch at a time.

The sandwich looked so good to Lilly, but she didn't want him to think she needed someone to take care of her. If Mom and Dad didn't want her, she was fine on her own. The ugly pink sweat pants and shirt he had gotten her were super cozy, but two sizes too big and ugly. She just hoped no one saw her when she left the place.

Trying to conceal her hunger, she picked up the P and J, took a small bite and placed it back down, as if not caring. One chip was next, then back to the sandwich. She repeated the process while Shawn just stood there and watched. It reminded her of Mrs. Drinkwine, her second grade teacher. She used to make sure all the students ate their vegetables at lunch. If she thought you were hiding them, she would stand and watch you eat every bite. It used to be humiliating; she would stand right behind you, arms crossed. Everyone would stare at you and sometimes giggle. But for some reason this felt much worse.

Halfway through the sandwich, Lilly swallowed hard and asked if he had any milk. Shawn laughed and apologized on the way out the door. A few seconds later he arrived back with a glass big enough to swim in, filled to the brim. It tasted different from the one at home, thicker. When Lilly finished eating, Shawn patted her on the head and took the plate and milk back to the kitchen.

"Would you like your present now, Lilly?" Shawn shouted from down the hall.

Lilly responded with a less than enthusiastic, "OK".

With an odd hunch that made his spine show through his shirt as if he was one of those vegetable-eating dinosaurs Lilly couldn't remember the name of, Shawn came through the door backwards. "TA DA!" Turning around, he revealed a TV/DVD player combo and several movies.

She couldn't help but light up. She always wanted her own TV, but Dad said that it wasn't good to have one in her room, she was too young. It made her so mad at times but she learned to live without it. Dad said when she was ten she could have one. But look at her now! HA! For a second Lilly wondered if Dad was going to let her keep it, then she remembered Dad probably wouldn't care at all. Heck, he didn't even want to see her, right?

Shawn had to be lying. "Why are you lying to me! My Dad would never want to get rid of me!"

Shawn went from excited to disappointed, just like Lilly's expressions. He was going to have to pull out the big guns. With a gentle touch, he placed the TV on the bed and left the room again. When he arrived back, he noticed Lilly was examining the DVDs. She pushed them aside at his entrance.

"Well, I was hoping the TV would distract you, but, if you must see the letter, here it is."
He went to hand it to her but pulled it back right before she could snag it. Lilly looked mad.

"It's really mean. Lilly, I'm sorry."

In acting mode once again, he handed her the folded piece of paper. Pain and sorrow was on his face. It was a bitch holding back smiling, watching her open it. Her brow was scrunched as she read the first line; it scrunched more on the second line. By the third, her lips were pouted, the fifth, tears were building. By the end, she tossed it aside and dove for the pillows on the bed. Shawn let out the smile. He was good.

Silently he picked up the paper, examined his perfectly executed nasty letter that started off with "Shawn, for God sakes please take this little bitch off my hands." And that was the nicest part of it. Quietly, he folded it back up, scooted over and started to rub Lilly's back. She didn't cringe or even acknowledge his hand. Being ever so careful, he moved her shirt up just enough to show an inch of skin. Then on the rebound of the rubbing motion, he got the first feel of her young flesh. It was amazing, making him want the rest all the more.

Mr. Bluestick was relieved to see Sue come back in the room. She had been the only person halfway decent to him. The stress was killing him and he had no clue what to do. Not a soul was believing him. He needed to do something to help save Lilly. If anything happened to her, he would never forgive himself.

"Mr. Bluestick, I want to talk to you about your past. This might be really hard stuff but we need to get through it because I think if we do, we can help Lilly."

His past? Well, telling her that he wasn't from this planet was definitely a no go. Maybe agreeing with whatever she said was best thing to do for now.

Sue glanced at the mirror and hoped she turned on the camera correctly. She never could work those that well. Needing to make this as personal and friendly as possible, she pulled a chair right up next to him. It obviously made him a bit uncomfortable. Before speaking, she looked at his hands for a long time. It was terribly sad how grotesque they were. Shriveled, pink, purple, dry and flaky. The burns were unmistakable. She watched as he unsuccessfully tried to hide them. It was an obvious sore point, no wonder the notes said he had taken to constantly wearing tuxedo gloves.

"Do they still hurt, your hands, that is?"

He didn't really understand the question. Then he realized that she must have mistaken his skin, the skin that all his kind had, for an injury. "Ummm, no, no, not at all."

She lightly touched one hand. It shook as he tried to pull it away, but only got two inches. "Can I call you Edward, or how about Ed?"

Again he didn't know where this was coming from or why but he agreed with a nod.

"Ed, I want to talk about the fire."

Frustrated, hoping she was going to want to talk about something different, Mr. Bluestick responded as politely as he could.

"Mrs. Lamkins, with all due respect, I believe that Captain Rudder has drilled me enough on the events of last night. I cannot explain my deepest regrets that a fire was caused in part due to my self-defense. But I believe what is most important here is finding Lilly, do you not agree?"

Sue starred at him kindly, waiting for his frustration to fade enough for her to make the first attempt. It was always the hardest. This man has been living in a fantasy world for some time now. If she approached this incorrectly, he could hide from his past forever.

"Ed . . . Edward. I'm not talking about that fire, I meant the one that caused the burns on your hands."

His eyes turned to pin pricks. She could see him fighting the flood of memories, fighting to keep them hidden from everyone, including himself.

4

After pacing back and forth for way too long, Tom was urged to eat lunch with the officers. Kindly, he declined and kept pacing. He watched in awe as the place became almost deserted as everyone piled into the tiny, school-like cafeteria to eat the giant order of take-out food. It sounded and looked like a party in the crowded room. Did they do this everyday? Or was it just a special occasion, celebrating a missing child?

Tom scanned the room for Sue but didn't see her. She must still be in with . . . Cotter, was it? He walked towards the interrogation room door. No one was around. Being more daring than he had ever been, Tom turned the handle on the observation door. It was open. Pushing it in a few inches, he snuck a peak. Seeing no one, only a camera with a blinking light, some chairs and a large dry erase board with all kinds of papers stuck on it, he entered.

Silently, so not to alarm anyone or mess up the sound on the camera, he shut the door. The room was only lit by the faint glow coming through the two-way mirror. He crept to it and was surprised at how large a mirror it was. It came down practically to his knees. With a faint creak of fake leather, he worked his way into a chair right in front of the mirror.

There was Sue and Mr. Bluestick, the man his daughter loved, probably more than him right now. At first he felt incredibly awkward watching from such a voyeuristic angle. Every second he waited for one of them to turn and just look at him. It was like being at some sort of weird movie theater. After watching them talk silently for a few seconds, he searched the wall and found a knob that let him hear the conversation. It was to the left of the mirror. Level three was just loud enough for him to hear. Thank goodness for movies, how else would a regular person know so much about an interrogation room.

For the first few minutes with the sound on, he still didn't hear the words coming out. Tom was too focused on Mr. Bluestick's face. He thought about how his daughter might be dead because of him. He thought about how his daughter might have been raped by him. He thought about how much pain Lilly might have gone through or is going through because of him. The jagged nails he bit earlier were cutting into his palms as he stared. He wanted nothing more than to pick up the heavy metal chair next to him, smash the window, and strangle the bastard.

Shutting his eyes and rubbing away the horrible thoughts was the only real option. Going to jail for assault right now would not be helping Lilly. But if he did find out something bad, he was willing to go. Rub after rub, he made his eyes redder and raw. Finally being in so much pain he had to stop, Tom looked once again at the man. Pushing the thoughts out, he listened. It was hard, but, one by one, he let words slip into his vengeance-filled mind until they formed sentences.

Sue looked at Mr. Bluestick's barren eyes that avoided hers at all costs. She waited a few more seconds before asking again. "Ed, the fire that happened in the mill, can we talk about it? It's very important that we do."

Mr. Bluestick had no idea what she was talking about, but for some strange reason he felt like crying. Images and sounds kept invading his thoughts - flames, screams. He couldn't tell if they were from tonight or not. Some of them didn't seem to fit. It was starting to give him a headache. "I . . . can I please take a nap?"

"Soon as we get through this, Ed, you can sleep for a long time. So the quicker we finish, the sooner you can sleep."

Taking a deep breath in, he could still smell the smoke from the fire that took away his. . . no, the fire tonight, right? His mind felt as if someone was poking a stick in it and mixing everything around.

"Ed, I know everything that happened that night. It's all in your files. I know nothing was your fault. The pain and loss you went through was horrible. We need to talk about it to help us get Lilly back." Sue watched as he slowly started to rock back and forth in the chair, tugging at his cuffs. Needing him to be comfortable, Sue took a risk that she knew would get her in trouble if she got caught. Everyone was on lunch right now so she did have some time. And besides, what would it hurt to un-cuff him. He seemed non-violent. She had the panic button in the room, her mace and her collapsible baton, the two items she hated to keep with her but had to due to station regulations. She excused herself and arrived back in less than a minute. She had a set of handcuff keys in her office, which were used only once . . . for recreational use.

With a quick click, the cuffs were off him. Most people would rub their wrists and stretch, yet Mr. Bluestick automatically hid his hands in his armpits, as if they would disappear. Sue took the seat opposite him now, just to be safe with some distance. After a few seconds, he asked politely if he could stand and stretch his legs. She nodded. For several minutes he walked out all his cramps, never once letting his hands leave his pits.

"OK, Ed, we need to start to talk again. I did you a favor letting you out of the cuffs; now I need you to help me by talking."

He wanted to hide his face in his hands, but that would require having his gloves. He couldn't remember a day since he'd been on this planet that he hadn't worn them. Now they take them away from him and accuse him of being injured? He didn't understand this race.

"Ed, a lot of people died that night. It wasn't your fault."

People on the floor, gasping, flames crawling up walls, and Jessica. NO! Mr. Bluestick shut his eyes tight and started to pace again. Where were these thoughts coming from?

Seeing the wall crumbling, Sue knew now was the time to hit with the wrecking ball, to break through entirely. "Your wife died that night, too, Ed, along with seven friends of yours. I can't image how hard that must be."

Leaning against a wall, breathing heavily, he wanted to scream at her to shut up. Instead, he pulled his hands out from under his arms. They were shaking terribly. As if he never saw them before, he examined them. Terrified, he pulled up the sleeve to see the burns continued up his arms. Lightly, he touched his chest and stomach. They were there, too, weren't they? He slid down the wall and took a seat as he hugged his legs. "It was my fault . . . I killed everyone, everyone I loved." His mouth hung open as tears filled his eyes but didn't fall.

"Now . . . Lilly, for God sakes, I couldn't even protect her. That bastard took her. I tried so hard to protect her, but I messed up. Just like I did before."

Sue watched as the man stared at nothing while reality came to him for the first time in God knows how long. She couldn't believe what he was saying. When someone has a break, like this they tell the truth, they let it all out, unless they were completely faking. Having done extensive behavior research with FBI experts, no one could fool her with a lie (which is why Rudder got the boot after two dates). Edward wasn't lying. There was no doubt about it, but getting someone, anyone else to believe her was going to be a challenge.

Tom stood glued to the window, watching this man's story. For a few moments he forgot about Lilly and was totally absorbed in Mr. Bluestick's story, and what confused the piss out of him was that he believed him. Either this guy was the greatest actor since Brando or he was telling the truth. Or maybe he just thought it was the truth? It was driving him crazy.

It took two more clicks on the volume knob for him to hear the conversation when Sue went and sat next to him on the floor. Tom squinted to look at his face better. It seemed entirely different. The way he held it and his voice, it changed completely. It wasn't Mr. Bluestick on the floor anymore, it was Edward Cotter.

Tom got closer to the speaker to hear the pain-ridden words.

"You know why I loved Lilly so much?"

Tom watched Edward who was still staring at nothing. The line made him anxious, not knowing whether the next line was going to put him in a rage or relieve him.

"Because Jessica . . . she was pregnant. We were hoping it was going to be a girl." He breathed deeply and continued. "We were planning on announcing it that weekend ..." He shut his eyes again. "Lilly was what I lost, what I always dreamed of. A perfect little girl. Seeing her and playing games was, was like, getting a chance to live what I lost."

Tom clumsily flopped down into a chair. This man supposedly molested his daughter? Kidnapped her? He couldn't see it. Vomit found its way up into the back of his throat. He held it down. That meant that the man he trusted, the man he loved almost like family, the man he invited into his house on a daily basis, a man that he made Lilly hug every time she saw him, took his daughter away. It was too much for Tom to grasp. He couldn't believe it. There had to be a third party involved, there was no way Shawn could have done this.

The only thing that made Shawn nervous about getting caught was his car. If someone saw him leaving this driveway, it would be suspicious. He thought about keeping the rental car from the other night for good, and changing cars at a parking lot each time he came here. But that would be way too expensive and not having worked in the past six years, living off stolen money, he had to keep things tight so it wouldn't run out.

Not wanting to leave Lilly and terrified to pull out of the driveway, Shawn sat in the car, flexing his hands on the wheel. Before leaving Lilly behind, he emptied her potty, placed a bunch more food in there, and set up the TV/DVD player. Of course, he made sure she couldn't get reception first. Seeing her Dad crying on the local news would definitely ruin his plans. Lilly did put up a very big protest when she realized he was going to seal into the closet, but he explained that it was only temporary. He told her that her dad said he had to take her far, far away or else he would take her back and make sure she got put in an orphanage in China. So, being close to home, he had to make sure she was hidden until he forgot about her. Then, with a forced hug, he assured her that he'd be back soon and they would play some games.

A smile crossed his face as he sat in the parked car thinking about how it was too easy to trick her, easier than some in the past, yet a tiny bit harder than a few. Finally, he started the car. To his dismay, he noticed Mr. Broomhowsier coming out the back door with some garbage. Shawn wanted to quickly pull out and just give a polite wave but his nerves were stopping him. He cursed to himself as Mr. Broomhowsier finished putting the tiny trash bag in the ancient steel can. Maybe he won't come over, maybe just a wave. Nope.

With an old man shuffle, Mr. Broomhowsier made his way to the driver's window. Shawn put on his actor's hat and rolled down the window. "Nice day, isn't it, Mr. Broomhowsier!" The old man looked up as if he hadn't noticed yet. Then seeing half clouds, half blue sky, he puckered his lower lip and scratched his hairless round head. "I suppose so for a youngster like you. How is the apartment treating you so far? Haven't seen you around much."

"Oh, everything is fantastic, I'm still slowly moving from my old place. The lease there ain't up for another few weeks."

Still puckering his lower lip, he leaned on the door with his wrinkled old palms, showing Shawn that the conversation wasn't over. After an awkward pause, the old man spoke first. "Faucet running okay?"

Annoyed and wanting to leave, he replied it was fine, not even knowing why he asked in the first place.

"Seen the news? Seems some little girl got kidnapped. I don't think that's happened in this town in. . . hell, any town around here - in forty years! Damn world these days."

Shawn's heart sank to his feet in a split second. He could feel the blood draining from his face, leaving an ashen color. He knew he had to respond quickly or else the old coot would think something was wrong.

"You all right?"

Too late, he responded without looking at him. "Sorry, I, uh, it's just that. I lost a daughter myself a long time ago. That's why I'm a middle-aged man living on my own. Wife and I couldn't seem to deal with it afterwards."

The old man removed his hands from the car door and tried his best to squat his arthritic knees lower to meet him at face level. "Jesus, sonny, I'm sorry, I had no clue. Well, you know, they just asked for volunteers to help search on the news. I'll go look with ya if ya want."

Well, he got himself out of the moment but now what did he get himself into? "Oh, I would, you know, but I'm not sure if I could handle reliving all of that, you know."

The shriveled hand was suddenly on his shoulder at an awkward angle. The old man was obviously putting himself in pain to try and comfort him. "I understand. Well, if you need anything, and I mean anything, let me or Rita know, OK?"

Disgusted with himself, Shawn patted the wrinkled hand, thanked him and pulled out. The stress of this situation made the stress of driving off a lot easier.

The road was clear, thank God, and he pulled out. Now driving back to the circus that was at his house, he started to panic. Everything was so perfect until now. If Mr. Broomhowsier watched the news as much as it seemed he did, it made not getting on camera all that more important. For if that old bastard saw him, he would see he had two names and that he lived next to the missing girl. Hell, he'd call the cops in a second! Now he had to avoid the media at all costs.

As bored as she was, the day was starting to disappear into evening. Tom had been gone all day and didn't know when he was going to come home. No one had come to check on her, and the phone rang off the hook with relatives. She ordered the officer downstairs to tell them all to just go to the local search group and help; they were no good to her here. Another good reason to get away from here: Tom's family, the fucking psychos. They would drive for hours just to have coffee. They must all know that he brainwashed her, they have to. Thankfully for her, there are no living relatives on her side left. Not that they were any good either, a drunk mom, cheating dad and several uncles who couldn't keep their hands to themselves.

Sick of daytime movies and talk shows, Sandy moved from the bed and headed for the window seat Tom had installed for her as a welcoming present to the new house, just like Lilly's. Outside, the police were doing a decent job of keeping the camera crews off her yard, but they couldn't do much about them setting up across the street. There only seemed to be three stations set up, yet there were dozens of cars.

A makeshift flower and candle vigil had also been set up at the end of the walk that led to the front door. Sandy couldn't understand how people who had no idea who Lilly or anyone else in this family was could set up a vigil outside their home? Why would you bother? Christ, it was her own daughter and the only time she cried today was when she watched some cheesy movie on the Hallmark channel.

Annoyed with the moronic crowd holding hands below her window, a siren sounded as she stood up to leave.

Why would they put on the siren? She looked out to see where it was coming from. At the mouth of the street a motorcycle cop had his lights on. Sandy laughed, not realizing this town had one. Then she saw a familiar car following it. It took a few seconds for her to realize it was Shawn.

Slowly, but surely, the cop moved everyone out of the street; several others cleared his driveway. Once Shawn was completely in and the garage door was shut, the cop turned off his siren and drove off. She wondered if she should call him and invite him over for coffee. She was terribly lonely and he was the only person she had ever met that understood her, well, besides Mark.

She had wanted to call Mark earlier but realized that they had tapped the phone downstairs. Though she was innocent of everything, she still didn't want the accusations that she was planning something with her lover. The pain of missing him was so much that it actually made her feel a little guilty that she missed him more than her own flesh and blood. But, as Shawn said, that's only because society makes you believe that's how you should feel.

Some people started noticing her in the window. The vigil group shouted words of encouragement while the camera crews scrambled to get a shot. Panicking, she dropped the shade down and backed away as if it was about to explode. She was starting to feel like a prisoner here, nowhere to go but this one room. It was too much to take, all because of that little bitch.

A genius he was. Shawn cracked open a beer and sat down on the couch buck-naked. It took him a while to figure out what to do to avoid the media. Then it hit him, have the people he has been running from for seventeen

Shawn was sixteen, a typical teen in Dunlap, Tennessee, when he started working at a local day care owned by his aunt in order to make some spending money. At the time he always thought about girls, girls at school, few grades below, usually. Then the first day at Tiny Tots, his true lust was discovered.

The job was supposed to be easy, take out trash, help with the snacks, clean up, and basic odd and ends. But, on that first day, Aunt Tina was shorthanded and asked Shawn to help watch the kids in playroom A while she watched the younger ones in playroom B. At first he sat in the corner watching the seven kids, four boys and three girls, play in their separate groups. Then two of the girls told him they needed him to play the Daddy since they were playing house. Grudgingly he agreed.

It was definitely the clearest memory Shawn had of his youth. Sitting at the table Indian style, watching the two girls, Toni, who was a tan eight year old with dark hair, and Bonnie, who was nine and blonde. For some reason he couldn't take his eyes off Toni, who was pretending to be the Mommy. To this day Shawn still believes that Toni was the one person he had ever fallen in love with, and it was right at that moment. The actual game of house he didn't remember much, except for one part.

"Honey, you're home from work," Toni had said to Shawn in a pretend mature voice before going to hug him. First she kissed him on the cheek, then she gave him a big hug. Standing up she was the same height as he was sitting, so he wrapped his arms around her whole body and squeezed. It was the best hug of his life, a hug that released the demons of a tortured childhood into the world.

After seeing how good he was with the kids, Aunt Tina asked him if he would mind watching them everyday instead of taking out trash. Of course, he didn't mind. Starting the next day, he worked on Toni as if it was instinctual. Over the years since then, he had learned many, many techniques from practice and from other pedophiles on how to pick up kids, how to make them trust you, how to keep them quiet, but Shawn still believed that most of it was instinctual.

Three weeks into his job, Shawn had gotten Toni to get naked in the bathroom for him. Four weeks in, he started to touch her. Five, she was touching him. By the sixth week, the girl's childhood and innocence were completely destroyed. By the eighth, Shawn was caught.

Being just sixteen, he did only nine months in Juvenile Detention. The press never even got wind of it. Being the decade it was and where it was, society just didn't want to admit those things happened then. His family, whom he hated anyway, disowned him by the time he got out. He was alone from there on out.

Now, thirty-nine years later, Shawn was masturbating with his newest victim's underwear. Just about to finish, finally, he removed the underwear, terrified of getting them dirty, and went back to the task at hand, just as the phone rang. He had ignored all the calls since he got home - almost forty from stupid reporters and good citizens trying to help - but he couldn't help but glance at the caller ID each time. This time was no different. *Tom Boyer,* it read. Knowing it was the father of the girl he was about to come to distracted him. Pissed at losing what should have been an amazing orgasm, Shawn answered the phone in a huff.

It wasn't Tom who was calling, it was Sandy, a pleasant surprise. Though he had almost no desire for a normal-aged woman, he could still have sex with one and on occasion think of one. So, while listening to her voice begging him to come over, he resumed the task at hand, picturing Sandy and Lilly together.

"So, can you come over? I'll have one of the officers go out and get us dinner."

Shawn couldn't respond. He was too close to the point when nothing can stop you.

"Shawn? Are you okay?"

The comment almost distracted him since she probably thought he was crying by the quickness of his breathing. With a loud grunt, he finished on his leg.

"Sorry, San, I was just trying to squeeze my foot in a boot that I haven't worn in years."

It was an odd comment and he had no clue where it came from. Whether she thought it was odd or not, she didn't comment.

"I'll be over in a half-hour. How about Chinese?"

For a few more seconds they discussed what was the best Chinese place around, before hanging up.

Shawn took a shower, wishing he were at the apartment with his love. Letting the colder than hot water beat on his back, he wondered if he had made the right decision to take his neighbor's daughter. It wasn't the moral concept of it that was bothering him, it was the fact that it was too fucking risky.

In the past he had let himself slowly get more and more lazy, risking more each time, just to get his rocks off. But to him and other of his kind that he had talked to, it was more than just getting off. It was an obsession, no, a necessity in life. Just like air is to everyone else. Little girls are just as important as air to Shawn.

At the age of twenty-two, he was living in Michigan and truthfully couldn't remember how he made his way there. Being young and not caring much about life, he would just go to the local play ground, sit in a car and offer candy to little girls like in those stupid safety videos they play in school. You'd be surprised at how many would take a Kit-Kat from a stranger, or how many kids would offer to help you find your lost puppy. It was too easy. And Shawn got too lazy.

By twenty-three he was arrested again. Being his first offense - since his juvie records couldn't be used against him in his adult life - and it was only for molestation, he got mandatory counseling, restraining orders to stay away from any playground, three months in jail and two years probation. It was the best thing to ever happen to him.

Court ordered therapy, he was surprised to find out, consisted of group sessions twice a week, as well as the one-on-ones three times a week. At a group session he met Craig Singleton, a veteran child molester. The two hit it off right away. After each session they would go for coffee and laugh about how hard everyone was trying to "fix himself". They didn't want to. Fuck, they loved little bitches and had no intentions of stopping.

They toyed around with joining NAMBLA (The National Association of Man Boy Love) but it felt too open, it made you suspicious, and, besides, they liked girls (though Craig occasionally dabbled in boys). So, instead, they made a club of two. Together they would seduce, molest, rape and photograph kids from all over. Sometimes their trips would take them three, four hours away from where they lived, just to be safe. It was great for a while, until Craig got too rough too often.

It's easier than pie to not get caught. Just leave no marks, no semen, no torn clothing, just no evidence. Then it's only a kid's word, and ninety percent of the time they are too scared to tell. Then the other five percent of the time if they do tell, people brush it off as just a kid's imagination. Or if they don't they can never give a good description. So, if you followed the rules you really only had a five percent chance of getting caught and they both knew that. But when you feel like you're invincible, you get sloppy.

Shawn never got sloppy. In fact, he found himself cleaning up Craig's messes more often than he would have liked during those three years. Actually, after the first year, he wanted to break up their club of two, which he would have if it weren't for one thing. Craig was rich. Filthy rich. So much so that he insisted that Shawn didn't work. He paid him a four hundred a week to just hang out and seduce girls with him. He even gave him the guesthouse at his six-bedroom mini-mansion. At first it was a bit awkward, but try having someone pay you to do nothing but get off. It was a nice deal, a non-stop party and damn hard to stop.

Shawn didn't know and didn't care what Craig did to make all that money. All he knew was that he would go to work for ten and come back at four. During those hours he was supposed to go to playgrounds and work on potential victims, which he did. They would have at least one girl a week. Usually they would try to keep using the same girl a few times so they wouldn't have to go through the whole grooming process each time.

The major difference between the two was Craig liked to do rough stuff. It started as light slaps to the kid's bodies, not hard enough to bruise. But it got worse and worse. For a while Shawn was able to stop him and talk sense to him. They were opposites in that department. Shawn liked to make love, to feel and touch the bodies. They are too beautiful to mess up, that was his philosophy. After a while Craig was impossible to stop. Punches, kicks, and burns began.

Shawn knew he had to get out fast or else they were going to get caught. Hell, he was amazed they weren't caught already. After one particularly bad beating, which made Shawn throw up, Craig ordered him to take the kid and dump her in the woods. Something they had never done. Connie was her name, a little Asian girl. Craig wouldn't even let him touch her.

Not having the heart to let Connie die, Shawn dropped her unconscious body on a curb, two blocks from the hospital. On the way back he knew there was no choice but to leave. The cops would somehow find their way back to them. And he wasn't stupid. He knew Craig was setting him up for a fall in case something happened. Never being on camera, yet taking pictures of Shawn like crazy. He was furious as he headed back to the house.

Getting back to the house, he found Craig sleeping naked right in the place he left him, right in his own dry semen. He wanted badly to kill him, but he didn't. Stuff like that wasn't in him. Instead, he went up to the study and into the safe. He knew the combination since he had set up a hidden camera of his own, in case of such an incident. Opening it, he laughed to himself, knowing that this whole time they had been using each other.

The safe had over one million two hundred thousands dollars in it. Shawn nearly fainted after counting it in his hotel room two states away the next day. Seems Craig traded foreign currencies, and knowing he was a child molester, who someday might have to go on the run, he kept almost all of his savings in his house. A stupid mistake for Craig, a miracle for Shawn, who still to this day only worked if he got too bored.

Shawn came to find out that Craig was indeed arrested five days after the little girl was found. Craig did only five years for the crime since Shawn was the one on the videotapes and in the pictures. Ever since that day, he has been a wanted man, well, not Shawn Daggerty, but a man named Lou Stone. Connie is now in her late twenties, and still in a coma.

After getting dressed, Shawn put on a hat and a high-collared fleece to cover his face for the quick dash next door. An officer even covered him as he skipped over. So nice to be treated this way! Sandy was waiting inside the door with a big hug for him. It was a bit awkward having never been hugged by the woman before, but he liked it.

The two ordered Chinese, Kung Pow for him, General Tso for her. Sandy was smiling at him so much that he had to hug her again to whisper in her ear to cut it out around the cops. She hadn't even realized it. Sitting around the table waiting for the food to arrive as the sun was setting, the conversation was non-existent. Shawn was bored to tears, but this was a vital part of the plan. To be here, make his presence known. Show concern. What a perfect cover.

5

It was an odd feeling. Sort of like coming out of a deep sleep and not knowing where you are. At the same time it was like having a blank mind; the emotions came from nowhere, the answers from somewhere else.

All the while Mr. Bluestick watched from the back corner of this new dark world. He watched Sue's eyes look in at him. Tearful, he wondered if she could see him in here. Her words were muffled and hard to hear. He strained to make them out but it only frustrated him more. This new place was so dark, why not just sleep.

"You did great, Edward, just great. Why don't you get some rest. I need to cuff you back up, but I'll get you some pillows."

Leaving the room, Sue felt as if a vise had been put on her chest and someone was tightening it every second. She just knew no one was going to believe her. Not even three feet out of the door, she ran straight into someone, her face almost squishing against his chest. Apologizing profusely she backed up to see it was Tom. Instantly she felt awkward. She wanted to blurt out that it was his neighbor that took Lilly, but that would just cause panic. First she needed to figure out who would believe her here.

"Sue, I believe him."

She blinked in response, not really understanding.

"The door, it was unlocked. I saw it all. I can't believe it, but I believe him. Should I?"

The vise started to tighten at a rapid pace. Not only was she going to be in trouble for talking to the suspect without supervision and for uncuffing him, now she let a civilian, the victim's dad nonetheless, sneak into the surveillance room. For a few seconds she couldn't think of anything but how she was going to lose her job. What would she do then?

The smile cleared all of that. The smile that graced Lilly's face in the picture that was being played on all of the Amber Alerts. Nothing mattered but getting her back safely, if it wasn't already too late.

"Tom, OK, listen, don't tell anyone what you just saw. It will cause too much unnecessary trouble that will detract from your daughter's case. I believe him, too. I just need Rudder to listen to me but there's no guarantee he will." Sue stated with a go get them attitude. She tried to convince Tom to go into her office and rest while she tried to talk to Rudder but he refused. Instead he asked her a question that made her mind shoot in ten different ways.

"Can I bring him in a pillow. I want to talk to him myself. You won't have to worry, I trust him now. I just want to thank him."

Sue's first reaction was obviously a huge NO, but then she thought about how it could help. If he saw how distraught the father was, he might even come out with more information. Then, again, what if Tom is lying and just wants to beat the shit out of him? The safe bet was just to repeat the no, which made tears come to his eyes when she said it.

"Please, Sue, I need to feel like I'm doing something. Then, at least, let me talk to Rudder with you, if I say it, too, maybe he will believe us."

"Actually, he'll get more pissed, he'll think that I tricked you. It's better I do it alone."

Sue disappeared quickly. Tom stood there feeling defeated. Then a few seconds later she returned with a pillow and blanket, handing them to him.

"Two minutes, and I go in with you!"

The tightening stopped for a brief second when she saw Tom's smile of hope. Sue looked around for a good thirty seconds before opening the door with a sigh. Mr. Bluestick had his head down on the cold desk; it looked terribly uncomfortable. Tom walked like a scared cat over to him. It took a few seconds before he looked up and noticed Tom. Instantly he perked up and slipped right back into Mr. Bluestick.

"Thomas, dear Sir. I'm terribly sorry for all of this, I swear. I tried my best to keep Lilly safe. Gave your neighbor a good licking, but he tricked me just the same and took her away."

It seemed almost rehearsed but Tom appreciated it. In a tiny way, he still blamed the man, for if he didn't let Lilly hang out with him then none of this would have happened. This was no time to hold grudges now, though.

Tom slipped the pillow between his hands. Mr. Bluestick looked at it, clearly nervous. Did this man still want him dead? Or, for some reason, did he finally believe him?

"Do you swear on Lilly's life that Shawn took her?" The question was said through such tightly gritted teeth that Mr. Bluestick thought he was about to hit him.

"Sir, I swear to you, it's the truth. I love Lilly, not in a bad way, I swear. I want her to be safe."

Tom's face quivered as he sat down. As crazy as Mr. Bluestick might be, and as crazy as it might make him, Tom believed him. "Do you think . . ." Tom tried to control his breathing, tried to calm down. Even though he believed this man had nothing to do with Lilly's disappearance, it was still amazingly hard.

"Do you think . . . Oh God, do you think he killed her?" Mr. Bluestick's face went slack, as if the thought had yet to cross his mind.

Sue, who had been looking at her watch, changed her focus to the two. "Thomas, I believe your neighbor is a sick, sick man. But I do not believe he will do such a thing. I think he is sick . . . in ways I don't want to imagine."

Tom let the blanket he had been wringing fall to his lap so he could rub his eyes. It was relief, yet pain at the same time. Getting a sliver of hope that she was alive, but then again thinking that someone might be touching her in ways he wouldn't let his mind picture. It was horrible.

After a long pause, and well after the two minutes were up, Tom stood, walked around Mr. Bluestick and placed the blanket over his shoulders and left.

"The next time you bother me with this shit I will have you tossed in the cell yourself for interfering with the case! We are trying to save a girl here. Now let me get back to my job,"
Rudder bellowed.

"I'm trying to save her, too, damn it, and not so I get on the eleven o'clock news."
Sue's lip quivered as she spat her final rebuttal. She was out of options. What next?

The conversation had stalled after she finally broke Rudder down enough to call Shawn and ask if he could search his house again. Shawn had responded with, "Oh, dear God, please go right ahead. Whatever will help get Lilly back, anything you need you let me know. Do you want me to go unlock it now?"

No guilty man would react like that. Rudder was pissed that Sue fell for the crazy old man's lies. Having such a bad history to begin with didn't make his judgment any easier. He had ordered every officer to ignore her, if any officer were to help her, he would be put on suspension.

Sue tried to grab her best friend Meg, but she just gave her sad eyes and mouthed, "Sorry" to her. She was on her own now. Well, not completely, Tom was with her. She wondered if having Tom plead the same story to Rudder would help. She wasn't willing to take that risk. If he didn't buy it, he would have her thrown out of the station.

Back at the office, Sue found Tom once again looking out the window. He turned anxiously at her arrival. Instantly he could tell it was bad news. "He won't buy it. Said if I brought it up again, he'll lock me up as well."

Tom pursed his lips, he wanted to go knock out the bastard, to give him some of the pain he had. "I'll talk to him!" Tom declared as he puffed up his chest and headed for the door ready for confrontation.

"Tom, no! If you go to him, all he will do is send you home and get me fired. He's not going to believe us. We're on our own here. We just need proof."

Tom finally snapped. For almost twenty-four hours now, he had been holding everything in, doing his best to be composed. But now his next-door neighbor and best friend might be raping his daughter. And no one was going to believe it.

With a loud thump, Tom kicked the wall next to the door and followed it by a low growl of a yell. As he cocked back his arm to swing at nothing, Sue grabbed him. He tried to fight her off for a few seconds, but it was useless, he was exhausted.

Sue originally grabbed his arm because she was scared he might punch a hole in her Fordham diploma, but now she was scared he was going to hurt himself. First, she held his arm as he fell to his knees, then to his ass. Finally, she caressed his head as he lay in the fetal position. It was something she had seen many times before, in movies and in therapy sessions. It was what she liked to call a second birth because when the patient reached this point of complete frustration, he would usually revert to this position, the safest and most comforting one. Then, slowly but surely, he would calm down and come out of it, usually a different person, a person who was past the hard part and ready to take on what was next. She didn't want to waste any time but she knew the next hour with Tom was going to be very important, especially since she needed him for her new plan.

Lilly stared at Dumbo flapping his ears. Did Shawn really think she was this little? Dumbo is for like four year olds? Why would he get that? Then again, out of the five movies, it was the first one she put in, even over "The Goonies." Maybe she just wanted something else to focus her anger at for a few minutes. Who knows?

It was the first time in her life that she didn't take going out for granted. Lilly wanted nothing more than to just be running through the woods heading to Mr. Bluestick's. He was the one person who actually did love her. Right? He wouldn't lie to her. That's what she should do - get out of here and go live with him. It would be so much fun.

The images of last night, the fight between Shawn and Mr. B, the fire, were all too confusing. Every few seconds she would question herself. Did this or that happen? Is Shawn lying to me? He couldn't be, I saw the letter. Then why did he fight last night and say those nasty things? They would all thunder through her head, forcing her to grow up too quickly. Maybe that's why she picked "Dumbo" to watch, she didn't have to think.

It had already felt like a week in this tiny box. Hopefully, next time Shawn comes back, he'll let her at least wander around the apartment. Or, heck, at least just let her have cable TV. Hopelessly bored with the big-eared elephant, Lilly got up and paced back and forth. She had so much energy in her that she started doing a few jumping jacks, but those too quickly became boring. Trying to figure out a new exercise to keep her occupied, she tried to grab the clothing rack that was way above her head. No way. Unless…

With the ease of a gymnast – well, more like one of those bears in a circus that pretends to walk the tight rope - Lilly climbed up onto the TV, hoping it wouldn't break. Though it creaked in protest, it did not. Balancing dangerously on top, she was able to grab hold of the bar and hang there. Now what? With all her might, Lilly did what she had not yet been able to do in gym class, a pull up.

With her sweating brow just barely above the shelf, she could see what was up there. Dust, lots of dust. Wait, in the far back corner was an old metal hanger. Not having a clue why, or maybe it was just for the challenge, Lilly knew she had to have that hanger. It might take her a few hours to get it, but what else did she have to do?

No more, not right now. Tom wiped away the last of the tears, determined not to let any more out until he got his daughter back. Lilly needed him right now. Looking at Sue, he saw the same face she had on with Mr. Bluestick, a tiny fake smile, kind eyes and a furrowed brow of concentration. Was it the look she put on with everyone she thought was crazy? Did she think he was crazy? What did it matter, she was helping him. Nodding his head at nothing, Tom was past it. He was ready.

"Well, what do we do? I could just go and . . . and kick Shawn's ass. I'm in much better shape than he is. Well, except for the arm, but then again it works like a weapon, too..."

Sue cut off his ramble. "Tom, you can't do that. There are so many officers there that you would get one punch in and you'd be the one getting arrested. We need to do this in a roundabout way."

Tom watched her face go through the calisthenics of concentration. If she wore a bit more make-up, maybe changed her hair, she really could be quite beautiful. Tom couldn't help but think of that while waiting for her to speak.

"We need to go to your house. We can say I'm there to make sure everyone is okay. Then, we get Shawn alone; I'll work him over in a subtle way, see what I can learn. It's a good starting point. We can work more on the plan on the way over."

It took Tom a second to realize that Sue was getting ready to leave as she scurried about the office gathering some objects. He quickly joined her.

Sue had to drive her almost new gold Altima since Tom had been driven to the station by Rudder himself. Luckily, no one saw them leave, well, no one of importance. Tom sat watching the world go by, wishing he were anyone else at this moment, while Sue tapped one finger wildly on the wheel.

The silence was broken by the loud crackle of the police radio. Sue had no clue why she even had the damn thing. She never had to go to the scene of a crime. It was useless to her, yet when Rudder offered it to her as a friendly gesture, she took it without a second thought. And, in truth, she enjoyed listening to it over the radio on most days. Real life drama over sugary pop songs. Instinctively her hand went to go shut it off so it wouldn't bother her passenger, but when the nasally whine of the dispatcher chirped, "All units be advised." she let her hand drop back to her lap. That was something she had never heard before.

Tom looked away from the outside world to look at the radio as if a screen would suddenly pop up and show him what was going on. Tom had no clue what the code numbers the woman was repeating over and over meant. He just knew that it must be serious by the look on Sue's face. The color drained out a bit and her lower lip stuck out, sort of how Lilly would pout.

"Sue?" Tom said for fear of his own life. It seemed to snap Sue out of her shocked daze. Keeping her eyes on the road she nodded.

"What did the dispatcher just say?" Tom asked for fear it might have something to do with Lilly.

"Well, it's not good, Tom."

He felt like they drove into a wall, yet they were still moving. His legs curled up at the same time as he hunched over to cope with the churning in his stomach. "Did they find Lilly?"

Sue's eyes opened wide and turned to greet Tom's. "NO! Oh my God, Tom, I'm so sorry. I'm such an ass. It had nothing to do with her. Jesus, what is wrong with me?"

Though she let him know, Tom didn't feel any better. Even though he was bracing for the worst, in a tiny way he was excited that it might have been over, that it would all just stop.

"I said it wasn't good because it sounds major. A hostage situation... Shit."

Tom felt horrible that someone was being held hostage but he had his own situation to handle right now. Did Sue always get so upset when something happened?

"I just hope it goes quickly because, being a small town, a situation like that is going to take every officer. Tom, this means your daughter's case is going take a backseat."

Tom was glad he hadn't left his defensive curl, he needed it more now than before.

Sue pulled over at a Dunkin Donuts about a mile from the house. They still needed to go over a few things. The two went inside; Sue ordered for them, black coffee for her, cream and extra sugar for him. Sitting in a window booth, Sue wanted to tell Tom to sit up more or else he was going to attract attention. She fought the urge and looked out the window just in time to see several news vans speeding away from Tom's street, obviously heading to the next big story. She couldn't help but wonder if this was a good thing since no one believed her.

"Tom, I can't stress this enough. You cannot say or do anything to Shawn. I know this is going to be incredibly hard, but it could mean all the difference in finding Lilly or not."

Tom fingered his coffee cup, resting on one elbow. What the fuck did she know? She's just a shrink. He should just barrel in there, take Shawn down and beat him until he told him where Lilly is.

"Listen to me. This Shawn is probably incredibly mentally strong. Violence and threats don't work with people like that. They're too smart to give anything up that will convict them. So we need to keep emotions out of it."

Tom shut his eyes, doing his best to just fight back his emotions and just listen to her. If she was wrong and they weren't getting anywhere after a few hours, he could start his plan of attack.

"Now we're in a better situation since the media will back off the case for right now. We won't have to watch our backs as much. But you still need to be the best actor you can be. Are you ready for this, Tom?"

He sat up, rubbed his eyes, and opened them to look at her dead on. "Thank you, Sue. And, yes, I'm ready to get my daughter back."

As they pulled into the street, both of their hearts were thumping. If the radio hadn't been on to ease the tension, anyone in the car would have been able to hear them beat. The area around the house looked much calmer than before; just a few strips of yellow tape and only one police car was left along with some petering out candles. It looked like the case was over.

Tom kept opening and closing his hands into tight fists, like a fighter before a big match. It made Sue nervous so she stressed once again the importance of keeping calm. The two got out of the car and started to walk the short distance to the door.

Tom looked at the house in a way he never had before. Though he had only been there a short time, he had loved it; it was the home he had always dreamed of. Now it just looked like a shell. He wondered if it would feel like a home again even when Lilly came back to it. Then he looked at the house next to his. Amazingly, it had taken on an ominous look and feel. It now felt like a witch or Dracula lived there.

Frozen, looking at the house that filled him with rage, he felt someone take hold of his hand. It was warm, felt nice and reminded him of holding hands in fifth grade, back when holding hands was the greatest thing in the world. He closed his eyes and squeezed the hand tight for a few seconds, forgetting whose hand it even was. Feeling a second hand wrap around it, he opened his eyes to see Sue smiling. This time the smile looked real. It made him smile, it made the anger and rage melt enough to make him ready to go into the house. Letting go of each other's hands, they did just that.

Halfway to the Boyer house, Rudder and his battalion of men got the call. For the first instant he was pissed. He had organized every available man, forty-three in all, to do a new full out search along with the neighboring town's sniffing dogs, which weren't available to them earlier in the day. The news crews were already at the house. Rudder had called ahead of time so they would be ready to catch the impressive convoy he put together. Now he had to turn around. But soon as he realized that hostage situation could get live coverage, he started to smile.

The only thing he could do with the Boyer case was to leave a patrolman at the house for comfort. Hell, the girl was probably dead anyway; a few hours wasn't going to hurt anyone. Besides, a hostage situation needed immediate and thorough attention. He listened carefully to the details from the three officers already on the scene. Seems some guy got dumped by his wife and was now holding her, her lover and two kids hostage in their house. This was an amazing day! For years Rudder has been waiting for something to propel his career into the spotlight and nothing had happened. Now, two things in one day? What the hell were the odds? Who cared? It was wonderful.

After getting all the details he could, Rudder made five anonymous phone calls to the news channels, even though he knew most likely they would already be on their way. He wanted to make damn sure they were. A few miles from the house, Rudder started to panic. Did he look good enough? He had put on some light make-up before leaving earlier, but he needed to make sure it was perfect. Swerving ever so slightly in his lane, he glanced at himself in the mirror, checking and re-checking every inch of his face. Perfect.

All he needed now was for this event to go smoothly. Ideal situation: several hours of a standoff, some good footage of Rudder giving commands, maybe on the bullhorn. Then, finally, after everyone was tired, the suspect gives up. No one harmed. Then he could give a quick interview, brush it off as if it was nothing and end with a great line like, "Excuse us, but we still have a missing girl that I plan on getting home." Man, this was all too good!

Sleep was a glorious torture for Mr. Bluestick. His body recharged, yet his mind burned with images of long ago and not so long ago. Breathing in and out like a hyperventilating puppy, face flinching every few seconds, with subtle moans and words escaping his lips, his head lay on the cheap pillow in an uncomfortable manner.

Officer Jackson, who had just come on duty, held a tray of food, made up mostly of vending machine junk, including a sandwich, as he watched the old man. Still in his first year, he felt like the bitch around the station. "Jackson, get us some coffee. Jackson, get us some more paper. Jackson, the toilet is overflowing." It was an endless array of shit he had to put up with, definitely not what he signed up for.

Being extremely large, by far the most muscular on the force, weighing in at two hundred seventy-three pounds and reaching six-four, he was a menacing sight. Regardless, the other men on the force treated him like the scrawny freshman nerd. They had the right to push him around. He put up with it for now. Soon enough someone new would come along and he would be just one of the guys, so he hoped.

Not sure if he should come back with the food or just leave it, Jackson teetered back and forth on his heels, thinking of how much it sucked to be a rookie. Everyone left him here alone with only the front desk guy - he could never remember his name - to go handle the hostage situation. He tried to imagine how exhilarating it would be to be outside of the house waiting to rush in and save the day. God, he couldn't wait for that.

After imagining being the hero and carrying out children in his arms from the hostage situation, Jackson decided to put the tray down on the table for the man. The guy did look like a weirdo. Actually, he reminded him of a circus performer with that beat up old tux on. With a gentle clink, he set the tray down in front of his head. Then he wondered if he should wake him or not? Probably not.

He started to leave, but stopped and went back when he realized that with the man's hands cuffed like that, he wouldn't be able to grab the food. Shit. So, now what? Wake him up and feed him? Un-cuff one hand? What was the protocol for a thing like this? Asking was out of the question. He already took enough abuse as it was, and, besides, no one was here anyway. Might as well wait for the bastard to wake up, then un-cuff one hand. He wouldn't be able to get away. And what the hell could he do to a rock like him with only one hand?

With a noise loud enough to make himself jump, Jackson pulled back the chair in front of Mr. Bluestick, whose head jerked up a few inches and stopped. A few seconds later, he started to roll his neck around. Jackson watched, not envying how much pain the bastard's neck must be in from sleeping like that. How could you even sleep like that? As the white dirty hair on Mr. Bluestick's head started to lift, Jackson felt his heart rate rise a bit as he realized that this was his first time alone in a room with a suspect. This was going to be great practice. How should he play it? Good cop? Bad cop? Middle of the road?

Seeing Mr. B's eyes open groggily, he was surprised. They didn't look like a child molester's. That's what they taught him in the academy, though. No suspect ever looks the same. And almost no one looks like the monsters they really are.

"Food is here." Jackson boomed in his toughest voice, maybe a bit too loud, judging by how the suspect's eyes widened. A slight pang of guilt came over him as he watched the old man instinctively try to rub his eyes, only to end up tugging at the chains.

"Look, I'm going to uncuff one hand, only one. That way you can eat. If you try anything, anything at all, so help me . . ." It was definitely the tough cop he went with. It felt good having power over someone. Isn't that the secret reason why all cops become one?

"I'd appreciate that."

The old man's voice was gravelly yet filled with an air of knowledge, Jackson thought. With his giant hand, he nervously uncuffed Mr. Bluestick. It took him three attempts to get the key in properly. He was a bit embarrassed.

The old man instantly rubbed his eyes and whispered another thanks. This was it. This was the opportunity he had been waiting for. Mr. Bluestick decided to work out his plan while slowly eating the sandwich. Whatever it is going to be, it will work. It has to.

6

Sweating hard, dusty and exhausted, Lilly could feel the cold steel tapping the ends of her fingers. Just a tiny bit farther. Pushing to the tips of her toes, the way she hated to do in ballet class - the reason she quit - she could just about get it. One last push and she should be able to get it. One, two, three . . . jump. With a quick thrust, her fingers glided past the rod. Slapping them down past it, she fell backwards, pulling the ancient rod with her.

Landing on her back was nowhere near as painful as she thought it would be. Maybe she was just too excited that the coat hanger came down after what felt like two hours of trying. Feeling as if she accomplished something important, she just lay there smiling at the bare burning bulb above her.

After a good ten minutes of basking in the glow, she replaced the overturned TV and tested it. It still worked. Then she claimed her prize. After all the hard work, it felt as if it was made of solid gold. But it only took a matter of seconds before the feeling faded. What the heck could she do with a coat hanger anyway? Tossing it aside, she went back to being bored. At least it occupied some time. She almost wished that there was something else up there to go after.

Lying back down on the makeshift bed, she picked up the hanger once again. Looking at it made her think of the time that her Dad took her to a flea market. At first he kept teasing her that there were going to be fleas everywhere and that he was going to go buy some. She believed him for a while. When they got there, she was so confused. It was just a huge field with a lot of junk on it. When she asked why he wanted to go, he explained to her in the classic way that "one man's junk is another's treasure." After hearing that, Lilly made it her mission to find her treasure.

Table after table, she searched the endless, old, half-broken toys. Some were cool, some were lame, but she was on a mission to find a treasure, not just a toy. Dad bought some stuff: an old hand eggbeater, an extra hubcap for his car and a few tools that he still hadn't used. Then, in the back corner near the hotdog stand that Dad said was too dirty to eat at, Lilly found her treasure.

On the old rickety table sat a dozen handmade planes, cars and trains made out of various pieces of trash. Most of the planes were made out of old soda cans. The trains were made from popsicle sticks and the cars were made of coat hangers. They fascinated Lilly. How could someone make these things? Dad crouched down and whispered into her ear, "See, one man's trash . . ." Lilly found her treasure: a propeller plane made from Mountain Dew cans.

The ancient man who had glossy, dyed, jet-black hair made Lilly laugh as he flew it into a plastic bag for her. At home, Dad hung it in the corner of her room, and there it sat gathering dust for over three years until she redid her room. Not wanting to throw it away, her dad took it to hang in his workshop. Every time she walked through there, it made her smile.

After thinking about how that old man made such cool things with junk, she thought, why couldn't she? Carefully, Lilly tried to undo the hook end of the wire. It hurt her little hands to force it to turn, but turn it did. It was going to take a while, but what else did she have to do?

Swinging the door inward, Tom quickly scanned the room. No one was in the kitchen. It was a mess though. Cluttered with half full Chinese food containers, napkins half used, dirty plates, forks, and a few half full glasses of flat soda. It almost looked like a scene from a Stephen King movie where everyone just disappeared in mid-dinner. Tom was nervous for a few seconds until he heard the voices coming from the living room.

Sue followed him into the kitchen and shut the door quietly. It felt as if they were sneaking into a house. Why hadn't Tom announced his entrance? She watched as he crept to the corner to peek into the next room. The second his nose passed the wall, a short jittery man burst out of the room, making them both jump back.

"Freeze!" At the sight of Tom, the young cop's eyes shot open as if he'd won the lottery. His shaking hand fumbled to put his gun back in the holster.

"I'm sorry, Mr. Boyer! I heard the door and I . . . I, realized I forgot to lock …Oh, I'm…"

Tom put his hands up to calm him down. The cop stopped his banter and put his narrow head down like a child anticipating his punishment. Tom ignored him and walked into the living room, ready to face Shawn.

With a deep breath and full confidence, he sturdily walked through the doorway. Sandy was sitting on the couch, hugging a pillow and looking frightened. Tom was so relieved to see her, even though she caused so much pain lately. God, he needed to hug her, to hold her, well, someone at least. But first - Shawn. He looked around the room, confused when he saw no one else was there.

"Where's Shawn?"

Sandy looked at him with a disgusted look before standing up in one swift motion. Her pink flower-covered pajama pants and matching long sleeve shirt made the only sound by swishing hard.

"Where is Shawn? I've been home alone all day, ALL DAY! And the first thing you say is 'Where is Shawn?'

What is the matter with you?" Sandy raised the green-frilled pillow above her head, ready to throw it at him when the strange woman appeared in the doorway. Not knowing what to do, she slammed the pillow on to the couch and stormed up the stairs, two at a time.

"Sandy! No, no, wait; I can explain!" Tom was about to race after her when someone grabbed his arm. Thinking it might be Shawn, he balled his cast-covered hand into a fist, ready to throw a punch. It was Sue. He had almost forgotten she was here. She gave him a look that said "wait." Tom just wanted to hold his wife, though. As nicely as possible, he pulled away from her grip and started for the stairs.

With one hand on the railing, Tom lowered his head and looked to the officer who was standing in the doorway pretending not to be watching. Tom addressed the obvious rookie, who was still shaken. The officer nodded, ready to oblige Tom, whatever his request was.

"Officer, my neighbor Shawn. Do you know where he is?"

"Oh, uh, he had a phone call about twenty minutes ago. He had somewhere to go, said it was important."

Tom looked to Sue; she nodded for him to go ahead to his wife. Waiting for Tom to fully ascend the stairs, Sue turned to the officer and identified herself. Her title made him nervous. Sue knew she had some power over him now. After several easy and quick questions, she found out that the officer thought the mother's relationship with the neighbor was sort of odd. They seemed to have been laughing and having a good time. He couldn't understand it having a child of his own.

Sue's mind went to work trying to figure out whether or not Mrs. Boyer had anything to do with the girl's disappearance. But from what Tom said earlier on in the day, she didn't like him much. Why the sudden change? Or had she just been hiding it? Maybe she had him kidnap Lilly so she could leave and the two of them could raise her. No, that was stupid. The only way to find out more was to talk to her, which she planned to do once Tom had some time to calm her down.

The shotgun stuck out the window just enough to make everyone within a hundred yards duck. Perfect. You can't get more photogenic than that, Rudder thought, as the taste of iron filled his mouth. He kept himself from smiling by biting his cheek so hard it bled. The poor fucking bastard came home to find his wife banging some random guy she met at the grocery store while shopping for baby food. From what he could gather so far, she was getting it from behind, holding onto the kid's crib for support, letting him cry. Fuck, that could drive any man insane.

It was still unclear whether or not the gentleman caller had been shot or not. A shot blew out the front bay window an hour earlier, alerting the neighbors to call the cops. So far, Mr. Joyce, age 33, had only yelled into the phone about how disgusted he was with his wife. Now the phone was off the hook. That made this even better. Rudder would now have to use a megaphone! That would surely get on the news.

Arriving at the scene in high fashion, Rudder had stopped only for a quick comment, stating, "Please, everyone for your safety, please listen to the officers and stay back. I promise, soon as we get a handle on the situation, I will update you all." With that, he turned his back on them and started to point at things randomly while talking to other law enforcers to make it look as if he was giving orders. Not bad at all!

This was a first for this town. A hostage situation . . . never. At first Rudder thought that maybe Sue should be brought in to talk to the man, but then realized that they normally would use a negotiator, like in that Kevin Spacey movie he loved so much. Not having one, they would have to bring one in from five towns over. Supposedly he was already on the way. He made a mental note to give hell to whoever ordered him over here. He could only hope to talk this guy out himself before the big city guy arrived.

Getting caught up on all the details, Rudder totally forgot that Lilly even existed. With one quick order, every man from on-duty to off-duty was ordered here, leaving only two officers to protect the rest of the town. And they already had their hands full.

The door was shut, of course. Tom knocked lightly, speaking in his best soothing voice, aching to get in. She didn't answer his constant pleading. Leaning on the doorframe, he could hear the rustling inside. Odd. Usually she would just lie on the bed and hide in her cocoon of anger. What was she doing? Another good knock. No answer. Slowly, as to not be too much of an intrusion, Tom swung the broken door inward. At first he saw nothing. Moving it a bit farther, he was completely confused when he saw Sandy packing a suitcase. Why would she be doing that? Was she leaving him? The fear of his wife walking out made his mind blank. He wanted desperately to ask why she was packing but he couldn't find the words. Instead, he just sat down in the not so cozy decorative chair, the same chair that Shawn was sitting in not long ago, and just watched her.

Sandy packed in a confused state. She could feel Tom's eyes boring into her back but she just ignored them. Fuck waiting a few days. This was the perfect opportunity to take off, perfect. Hopefully he will be too worried about Lilly to put up much of a fight. But it doesn't matter how big it is, she wasn't going to stay.

After packing enough stuff to hold her over for a few days, Sandy shut the case and locked it, ready to go. With her hand on the handle, she went over a mental checklist to make sure she didn't forget anything. She had only packed toiletries and clothing; she didn't need any damn keepsake. It would be a false, painful memory of this damn place anyway.

"Why?" Tom's voice cut through her thinking like a sharp knife. She had almost forgotten he was there. With a few seconds' delay, she grabbed her bag and headed for the door.

"WHY?"

Just as she was about to make it out, Tom jumped in front of her with a look in his eyes she had never seen before. She wondered if it was the real Tom finally showing through, the Tom that had manipulated, used, and brainwashed her for so long.

"I'm leaving, Tom. I can't take this."

Tom was filled with the rage of not understanding. What the hell did he do wrong? Their daughter was missing, damn it! Nothing in the world should matter right now except for that. "Take what, Sandy? Take what? Lilly is missing, what is wrong with you?"

Sandy stared at the ceiling trying her best not to make eye contact, in case he was trying once again to brainwash her. She wasn't going to let that happen again. "Please move."

Out of all the hard times she had given him over the past few years, Tom had yelled, but always kept his cool. This was the first time he wanted to hit her, to tell her to shut the fuck up, that for once something wasn't about her. This was about Lilly! "What the fuck is wrong with you? Did you stop taking your medication? Is that it?"

Sandy tried to push her way past Tom but he stood his ground. Pushing him with one hand did nothing. Tom grabbed it and squeezed enough to show he meant business. It broke his heart to be doing this to the woman he once loved. But what other choice did he have?

"Get your hands off me! I'll scream, you son of a bitch! There is a cop just down the stairs. He'll have you in jail in a fucking second. It's where you belong anyway after everything you have done to me, you sick fuck!"

Tom let go of her hand, trying to figure out what the hell she was talking about. Did she mean this? She had to be going crazy. Maybe the added stress of Lilly being gone had made her crack.

"Sandy, what are you saying? I don't understand what you are doing. Please, baby, talk to me." Tom choked, holding back tears, desperately wanting to figure out why she was saying such things.

"Oh, stop the goddamn act, you shit bag manipulator. You know exactly what I'm talking about. From day one - day one - you have brainwashed me and just used me for your own sick purposes. I never loved you; I never would have loved you. You just used whatever scientific methods you know to trick me into having your fucking cunt daughter. I hope you never find her. You deserve it after . . . "

Without even thinking, Tom slapped Sandy hard and firm across the face. She needed something to snap her out of this. Seeing her hold her face, guilt washed over Tom as never before. It was the one thing he vowed to never do in his life, hit a woman, let alone his wife. What had he done? What could he have done?

Maybe Sue has something on her that could calm Sandy down? Tom backed out of the door, trying not to watch the woman crying in pain in front of him. He turned and headed down the hall to get help but more so to run from what he had just done.

Reaching the bottom of the stairs, Tom felt himself becoming frantic. Sue wasn't in the living room. Damn it! He raced to the kitchen to find her sipping a coffee and chatting with the young officer who now looked calm, until he saw Tom's face, that is. Tom's first thought at seeing the two was this man felt at home enough to make someone else coffee in my fucking house? It was an odd thought but was his first reaction at the sight.

Sue abandoned her coffee and rushed to Tom, instantly grabbing his arms, the way a good wife would. "What is it Tom, did Sandy do something to herself?"

The thought of Sandy hurting herself seemed impossible once, now who knows. Now he was worried that he left her alone. "She's just talking all . . . crazy. She packed a bag and said she is leaving me. I have no clue why."

Sue looked off into the distance as if looking for an answer to be floating around somewhere. Then, instantly, she headed for the stairs. Not even looking back, she told Tom not to worry.

Tom desperately wanted to follow but was too scared to. What if she did something stupid. It was awfully quiet up there. What if she screamed at him more. He just couldn't take that again. Standing at the bottom of the stairs, Tom waited for something . . . yelling, Sandy storming down, anything. Instead, all he could hear was the officer, whose name he still didn't know, in the kitchen trying quietly to sip his coffee.

It was probably the fact that he hadn't eaten in hours but Mr. Bluestick thought the sandwich was delicious. Purposely he took his time with each bite so he would have a longer time to have his hand free and to think his plan through. It was going to be tough but he had to do it.

"Pardon me, Mr. Jackson, but where did everyone go?" Jackson, who looked really bored watching him eat, raised an eyebrow to show it was none of his business.

"Look, I'm here to make sure you eat, not to chitchat."

"I'm terribly sorry to have bothered you; it just makes me nervous."

Jackson's eyebrows went from raised to scrunched. "What makes you nervous?"

Mr. Bluestick held back a smile, the fish was biting. "Well, it seems to be important. It just bothers me that no one is looking for the poor girl."

Jackson rubbed his chin, loosening up a bit to him. "I know, pisses me off, pisses a lot of guys off. But what can you do? Something bigger comes along, you got to take care of it."

Mr. Bluestick chewed another bite, savoring the mayo, nodding his head before responding. "It's a shame. Time is of such essence in cases like these. Involving a life, that is."

Jackson seemed to be starting to lose interest as he leaned back in the chair. Time to go in a bit deeper. "They left you to watch me? Why didn't you get to go to the more important thing?"

The line seemed to sting him a bit. He shrugged his shoulders and raised his eyebrows, trying to act as if it was no big deal. Mr. Bluestick took another bite to let it sink in a bit. He watched Jackson's face flinch with thought before he finally responded.

"Technically, I am the new guy here. That's why they left me to baby-sit you. Why the fuck do you get off on little girls anyways? I never understood sickos like you. You know, we learn about your kind in psych class, but still, I just don't get it man."

Mr. Bluestick took his time putting down his sandwich and wiping his mouth. He had to be careful now. He was close to losing him, yet even closer to winning him over.

"Officer Jackson, I know I must look like a freak to you. Heck, look how I am dressed and, yes, I do live in an old burnt-out factory, but, I assure you, I am no . . . sicko." Pausing to think a minute, Mr. Bluestick for the first time in ages voluntarily stepped aside and let his real persona take the lead. He had to. Edward Cotter needed to speak to this man if he wanted a chance to get Lilly back.

"Sir, I have never told anyone why I am so, well, eccentric. But I need your help tonight to save Lilly. I love her like a daughter and I would never harm her. That is why I'm going to tell you everything."

Jackson's eyes immediately opened wide. He looked around the room, wondering if he needed to turn on any recording device but didn't want to waste time. Instead, he pulled out his pen and pad, pulled his chair up close to the desk and gave the man his full attention.

"Thank God," Mr. Bluestick thought, "thank God." He was going to listen. He had the innocence needed to believe someone enough to help.

7

Makeup! Goodness, she needed a lot of it to cover up that slap. That fucker. How was she going to look good for Mark with this stupid red, swollen cheek. Damn it. She'll just have to get a hotel tonight and wait for it to go down. The bastard must have had this all planned out. He must have known she was going to leave so he sabotaged it like everything else. She only wished she could take some revenge. Too bad that fucking cop is here.

"I'm sorry, Mrs. Boyer, I'm Sue."

The voice came from nowhere yet it didn't startle Sandy. She kept her eyes focused on her face in the mirror as she applied makeup.

"I'm terribly sorry to bother you, I'm the police psychologist. I was wondering if I could talk to you."

Satisfied with the application, Sandy turned to the woman. She was expecting to see some butch Dyke type with a gun but instead she was a young and pretty little thing. "Sorry, but I have to go. No time to talk, I'm leaving." Sandy was hoping she would move from the door but she held her ground. Tough little thing. Must have had police training. "Look, I'm not talking to anyone else. I have to get out of this house before I go nuts!"

Sandy approached her but Sue didn't budge. She couldn't let her leave. "Ma'am, I know how hard this is for you with your daughter being missing. It causes a lot of stress. I just want to talk to you about it. I can help, I really can."

"I don't need help. I need to get as far away from this fucking loony bin as possible."

With that Sandy pushed her way by.

Sue did not want to get physical. That would ruin all chances of helping this poor woman. She moved to let her by. Sandy grabbed the suitcase that was in the bedroom and headed back into the hall to find Sue still there waiting.

"Ma'am, we found out who took your daughter. It's not the old man. We're going to get her back."

Sandy paused for a second. "Please move."

Sue crossed her arms, showing she wasn't letting her by. "Look, this might be hard to hear, but your neighbor took your daughter."

Sandy started laughing. Sue couldn't understand it; the stress must be incredible.

"He fucking got to you, didn't he? That manipulative cocksucker! All I can tell you, sweetheart, is get the fuck away from him as fast as you can or else you're going to end up with a whore daughter and half of your fucking life gone!" With that, Sandy gave Sue a hard shove in the shoulder before storming down the stairs.

Tom was still waiting at the bottom of the stairs as Sandy came down fast. He, too, tried to block her. She paused and gave him a look that would send any child crying.

"Tom, if you do not get out of my way, I will have you arrested for assault, and, no, I'm not fucking joking."

Defeated, Tom moved aside, tears filling his eyes once again. "Why, Sandy? Our daughter is missing! I've never done anything but love you," Tom whispered to her as she passed.

Sandy spun around with the same killer look. "I never loved you, not one day. You tricked me all along. And it's your daughter. I never wanted anything to do with that little brat. I should have left years ago. I'd say good-bye but you don't even deserve that."

Tom's hand went to his chest as pain shot through it. Was it just mental or was this what a heart attack felt like?

The sharp pain turned to a burning sensation as he watched Sandy disappear into the kitchen.

The hapless officer looking at him wondered what to do. Tom wanted to scream at him to stop her but words, let alone air, weren't coming out. His vision starting to blur, he could sense Sue coming to his side, even though he couldn't see anymore.

The hot throbbing in Lilly's hand reminded her of the time a bee stung her palm when she was fishing with Dad. It was the first time she had ever been fishing and it was wonderful. Just she and Dad sitting on the edge of the dock on the big lake. They had been using balls of bread for bait since she had cried when Dad tried to show her how to put a worm on the hook. It was funny eating the sandwiches with holes all over them. It made her giggle thinking of it now.

After taking a big bite of the ham, cheese and mustard sandwich, Lilly went to take a big gulp from her Dr. Pepper and that's when it stung her. The little bugger had been feasting on the sugar drying on the lip of the can. After crying for a few minutes Dad pulled out the stinger and put some ice from the cooler on it. It made it feel much better for a little while. Then, on the way home, it started to burn and swell.

By the time they got to the hospital, her hand was the size of a baseball. Luckily, she thought it looked funny and Dad even took a few pictures! After a few shots, which hurt more than the sting, it started to go down. The doctor told them that she wasn't allergic to bees, that the bee just had a dirty stinger. Her Dad still teased her about being careful near bugs with dirty butts.

Looking down now at her red palm, she worried it would swell up. But she knew it wouldn't. It was just sore from straightening the dang hanger. She did it, though! It was almost as satisfying as getting it, but not as much since her hand hurt. The only question now was what to do with it?

Stiff from lying on her back while she straightened the wire, Lilly got up and stretched. With her good hand, she held the wire out in front of her like a sword and started to pretend to fight an evil monster. Swiping it from side to side, she yelled and growled as in a tough battle. Spinning around to do a jump kick, not too successfully, the wire screeched across the back wall, leaving a long scratch. Instantly she was worried she was going to get in trouble.

Cautiously, she walked to the wall to inspect the damage. It wasn't too bad, but definitely nothing she could hide. Would Shawn be mad at this? God knows Mom would be if it happened at their house. She'd probably yell for an hour, then follow that with a few spankings before locking her in her room the rest of the day.

Lightly she touched the scratch to see if somehow she could rub it to clear it up. As her two fingers brushed furiously over it, flecks of the ancient paint dropped to the ground. Her eyes followed them as some floated and others dropped fast.

She expected the chips to be strewn all over the carpet, but for some reason they weren't. With her childish curiosity, Lilly dropped to her knees to see where they had disappeared to. There seemed to be a tiny space between the carpet and the crack in the wall that they had fallen into. Lilly crammed her tiny fingers into the small crack. It took some effort but the carpet pulled back just a tiny bit. There, under the carpet, Lilly found a whole new project to keep her occupied.

Pretending not to be home was harder than he thought it would be. Every time he went to put on a light he had to think twice. That would be the easiest way to get caught. Even the TV would give off too much light. What was the purpose of this anyways? Because of a stupid feeling in his gut? Right after they had finished eating the Chinese food with that dork of an officer, Shawn got a feeling in his gut. At first he thought it was the food gurgling, but soon enough he realized it was the old feeling of panic.

It was the same feeling he had all those years ago when he knew the cops would come after Craig when he went too far. He had it a few other times and it was wrong, but with so much up in the air right now, it would be stupid to take a risk. So instead of sitting there with the cops, he opted to make an excuse and take off. At first he was going to head to Lilly's but again his gut gurgled at the idea. He could have driven around aimlessly but instead he opted to settle here for a bit until he found out what was causing his uneasiness.

As he sat in the dark, ready to go crazy, the phone rang. He wasn't even going to look to see who it was but his stomach churned, telling him he had better. The caller ID read *Boyer, Sandy-Cell*. As the phone rang, he turned it over a few times. Should he answer? He had watched with great pleasure at how she ran out of there with a suitcase about twenty minutes ago. Maybe she was having second thoughts and wanted to go back. He had better answer just in case he had to talk her out of it. After greeting her, he had to pull the receiver away from his head so as not to hurt his ear as she screamed.

"Woooohoooo! I fucking did it Shawn! I left the piece of shit!"

Cautiously Shawn put the phone back to his ear and cordially congratulated her. Thank goodness, he wasn't going to have to do any more work on her.

"Get this, he fucking hit me. Can you believe the balls on him! I wanted to deck his ass but it was too risky with the officer there. I know you said to wait a few days but, well, it was just a perfect opportunity!"

Shawn rolled his eyes in the dark while she rambled on and on about how she was going to have such a great life now. Then they shot open when she mentioned something he was hoping to never hear.

"Oh, and get this! You're going to fucking laugh your ass off! This shrink bitch was there, too. Well, Tom must have used his brainwashing tricks on her, too, because she tried telling me that you took that little bitch, not the fucked up magician guy! Isn't that a riot?"

Shawn's gut gurgled overtime as he pretended to laugh. Shit, the feeling was right. Plan B was definitely going to have to take effect now.

Jackson rubbed his eyes. What to do? Damn it. This guy seemed crazy at first but now he seemed more normal than half the guys who worked there. What if what he was saying was true? If it was, he could save the little girl on his own. That would get him the respect he deserved. Hell, it would get him a promotion. Well, if he didn't get into much trouble first. If he saved the girl, though, they wouldn't slap him with any charges, would they?

"Jackson, we . . . *you* can save her tonight. She needs you. No one else is going to do it." Still rubbing his eyes, Jackson raised his extremely large finger to hush the old man. He needed to think some more. What if the old coot was tricking him? Even if he was, one slap and the guy would crumble. All he had to do was keep him cuffed and keep a good eye on him.

Mr. Bluestick casually wiped the crumbs off the table, waiting for the man to make his decision. Please. Please, was the only thing going through his mind. Yes, he had lied to the man; he had no clue where Lilly was. But as long as he could get him to take him out of here, he could do something, damn it. He had to.

"Tell me again why you didn't tell this to Captain Rudder?"

Letting out a big sigh, Mr. Bluestick replied. "I told him everything, but he is too gun-ho to see the truth. I was set up and fell for it. Sometimes it is hard to see past things like this. He chose not to. Thankfully, you can."

Jackson's fingers moved from his eyes to his forehead. Was he really going to do this? If he was wrong he could lose his badge? Was it worth the risk?

"Jackson, she's only eight, for crying out loud."

That's it. He joined the force to help people, not feed them. Saving a life was worth risking his badge. And if they didn't find her, well, he'd cross that bridge when he got to it.

"Fine. But you stay cuffed and listen to everything I say. You so much as sneeze wrong and I'll break your nose. You got it?"

He watched the smile cross the man's face as he agreed and thanked him. His heart started to pound as he un-looped the chain through the I-hook and re-cuffed the old man.

"I'm going to go make chit-chat with Earl at the front desk, tell him I'm going to take a nap or something. I'll be right back."

Mr. Bluestick stood up for the first time in hours as he watched Jackson fill up the entire doorframe as he left. His body ached and disagreed with him as he stretched out. It was going to be another long night. He needed to be as limber as possible. Loosening up, he paced the room, forcing himself to think of what he could do.

There was no doubt that Shawn took her. Just where would he hide her? Obviously not in his own house. And being that he is still around giving support to the family, he has to have her somewhere close. Maybe he rented a storage shed somewhere in town. Or even had another place. How the hell could they figure out where, though? It was a small town but there were endless hiding places.

The only thing they could do was either follow Shawn when he left the house, or, if he could talk Jackson in to it, beat it out of him. That would be a tough sell, but he had to do what he had to.

Five minutes later, Jackson came back into the room. He looked pale and nervous as hell. Mr. Bluestick was worried that he might be changing his mind.

"You ready to go?" Thank God, he didn't change his mind.

He nodded his head and followed him out of the room. They took a sharp left down a hall and before he even knew it, he was hiding in the backseat of an unmarked cruiser pulling out of the lot.

"You can sit up now. Shit. My heart is pounding. I swear man, if you're making this shit up, I will beat the fuck out of you and have you back in that cell before anyone knows you were gone."

"You won't regret this, I swear, sir. You will be a hero." Mr. Bluestick could see the adrenaline running through Jackson's face; it brought back a lot of the color.

It was amazing, after who knows how many years of not leaving the woods, he still remembered his way around town. Jackson knew his way pretty much but Mr. Bluestick gave him directions anyways. Three minutes into the drive, he felt his heart skip a few beats, and suddenly Mr. Bluestick was forcing Edward back into the darkness that he had been in for years. It was a tug of war, back and forth. And seeing a certain house caused it all. A house Edward had lived in, but Mr. Bluestick had never seen in person.

With his eyes shut tight, he tried his best to push back the memories that hadn't been brought to his mind in years, memories that had been locked away deep, deep in his mind. Memories of his wife, his friends, all the innocent people that died because of him. Sliding down in the seat, it felt like a migraine was taking over his brain as everything rushed to the foreground. There was no more fighting them.

Broadway was fantastic, and Hollywood was calling over and over, but Edward wanted a break. He already made enough money to live off the rest of his life. And, with a baby on the way, he wanted to take a two-year break away from the big stuff and do something small, a dream project that was too off kilter for Broadway, and too odd for Hollywood.

Jessica, his wife of five years at the time, thought it was a splendid idea to move to the suburbs and build a theater of their own. They wanted to raise their child away from the chaos of the big city and still be able to perform and give back to the community. It was a dream come true. In her first trimester, they bought the house on Elm Street they always dreamed of - front porch, huge back yard, a two floor Victorian. Only a few hours from New York City, yet in a small enough town that they could keep their privacy.

It was all so quick, everyone thought they were nuts to leave such a huge career behind. Jessica, herself, was an up-and-coming Broadway star, but to her, a family was more important than applause. A month after settling, they bought the mill for a steal. It was old and needed work, but it had plenty of room and charm. Not only that, it would make an incredibly unique place to put a theater.

With a lot of work—backbreaking work (and many hired hands)—they fixed up the place pretty nicely. It only took three months to get the place good enough to start having rehearsals. Edward brought a lot of his friends from the city to work on and be in the show. It was nice having them all around. The set building was going smoothly, rehearsals were great and the pregnancy on schedule. They couldn't have imagined being happier.

The play was something Edward thought up when he was a kid. Sitting in his room one night, too scared to sleep from the thunderstorm pounding away above him, he played with his Lone Ranger flashlight and it just came to him. It was to be called "The Fantastic Journey of Tim Light." It was a working title, but he still liked it. Besides, it was geared more for kids anyway.

The plot involved a family of space traveling adventurers from the planet Malluminous. Visiting earth one day, they get stranded. They try to fit in but before they know it, the locals who are scared of them are driving them out. The only problem is their space ship, the Chrimsawheel, was broken and they couldn't get it to work. It was his homage to *Frankenstein* (which his Dad had read him the very night he thought of the story) and "Lost in Space," one of his favorite shows.

Edward, himself, was going to play the Dad, who always wore a Tux to fit in on earth since in the transmission (which little did they know were TV waves) they received they all seemed to wear one. Jessica, even though pregnant, was going to play the wife.

The set for the finale, for when they all made it back home, was an amazing array of lights that made up everything on their planet. It was late one night and everyone wanted to go home but Edward wanted to get the scene done, so he kept everyone there to do it a few more times. The finale called for all the lights to flash on at once. Edward wanted to see it himself from the audience to make sure it looked just the way he wanted. It just happened to be during that particular take that the temporary wiring sparked, causing the fire.

The fire spread so fast through the cheap curtains and plywood sets that by the time Edward got to the stage, half of his friends were on fire or already crushed to death by falling set pieces. Jessica, who was in her seventh month of the pregnancy, was near the front of the stage away from the horror. He pulled her off and headed for the emergency exit. It was blocked. The painters who were doing the ceiling at the time had left the scaffolding right in front of it. By the time they reached the back doors, the fire had beaten them there.

Edward looked back to see a horror. Several people were on fire, running around. Another half a dozen were lying still on the stage, smoldering. Only four people were still okay. They were trying to move the scaffolding. Edward and Jessica raced forward to help them just as it toppled back and crushed two of them. One lady, who was Jessica's best friend, backed away from the scaffolding and right into the fire, catching her hair ablaze. Jessica started to scream frantically and panic. Edward grabbed her hand and headed for the side door next to the stage. It led deeper into the mill, but it was a chance. Tony, who was part of the ensemble and the only remaining person alive, followed in a daze.

The hallway was clear of smoke and fire, so they stopped and coughed out all the black gunk they could to suck in some clean air. After a few more seconds, they started to race down the hall. Jess couldn't go too fast so Tony, whom Edward use to tease about being the smallest dancer in history, led the way. They passed half a dozen doors when suddenly one of them exploded open, smacking Tony against the wall, killing him instantly.

It took a minute or two to calm down Jessica enough for her to step over the shattered body. Down the rest of the hall Edward kept himself in front of the doors, but it was getting hard to navigate as the smoke filled the tiny space. Turn after turn, they got more lost, until finally Edward opened a door that led to an office. Taking an old desk, he smashed it through the window and looked out. Somehow they had ended up on the third floor, but there was a fire escape.

It took some effort but Edward climbed out first and tested it. It seemed safe. But they had to pass a window, which had fire licking out of it to get to the ladder. It was a risk worth taking, or so he thought. Carefully he helped Jessica out the window. He headed to the ladder, warning Jess to stay back while he tested it.

With slow caution, he climbed onto the ladder. It held. He climbed down three rungs to be safe. It still held. Then he looked up to tell Jessica it was safe. As she headed to him, the window blew out. It was an image that would scare anyone for life. Jessica's hair instantly vaporized, her pants melted, and her shirt turned to ash around her bulbous stomach. Raising her arms to swipe at the flames, she lost balance and fell backwards into the window.

Edward raced back up the ladder and reached in for her. The heat stung his eyes but he pushed on through the smoke, grabbing at everything. The skin on his hands burned quickly but he ignored the pain and pressed on. Finally, he felt her foot. He tried to feel his way up her body to pull her out just as something exploded, probably an old chemical can that should have been thrown out years before. The blast shot him back over the railing on the fire escape and down three floors to the moss covered ground.

The next few months he hardly remembered. All he knew was that he went from the hospital to being arrested for manslaughter and then acquitted. He then was admitted to a mental hospital and released to his home that he couldn't stand being in. The last clear memory he had was getting the show costumes delivered to the factory. He had started living there since he couldn't stop walking through what happened everyday, trying to figure out if he could have done something different. Everything after that seemed to blur. And now here he was, an old man in the back of a police car, still dressed in the costume of yesteryear, and trying to save a little girl.

The rest of the drive was a blur and, before they knew it, they were parked across from the end of Lilly's street, waiting, watching with the lights off. Jackson seemed to be a bit nervous about Mr. Bluestick's condition. He seemed almost like the drug addicts he'd seen - slumped to the side, slightly quivering, not seeming to be in this world. Jackson wanted to jump into the back seat and shake some sense into him. Christ, he had risked so much and now the guy was turning to mush. Maybe he should just head back now. If he did, no one would even notice they were gone.

Off in the distance the Boyer and Daggerty homes looked like Monopoly houses. Jackson had to squint when he thought he saw a car backing out of one of them. Sure enough there was. It seemed to be coming out of the Daggerty house.

"Hey, hey, snap out of it back there! I don't know what the fuck is wrong with you but here is our one chance. That Shawn fellow is leaving right now. Either you straighten up and we follow him or you go back to the station right now! What's it going to be?" Jackson's eyes shot back and forth from the approaching car and the backseat, nervous, anxious and waiting to figure out what to do.

Struggling with the memories, trying to push them down once again, he could feel Mr. Bluestick trying to take over and protect him as he had for the past few decades. Sitting up, finally, he shook his head trying to clear it.

"Follow him. I bet he is heading to her now." Wiping his eyes, he couldn't figure out who had said it. Was it Mr. Bluestick or Edward? He couldn't even figure out who he was anymore. None of that mattered right now, though. Lilly had to be saved.

Using all the tactics he learned at the academy but had yet to use (except for spying on ex-girlfriends), Jackson followed behind Shawn, his adrenaline running as he expertly trailed him. Occasionally, he checked on the nut in the back seat. He seemed to be a bit better now, thankfully. They drove in silence for over ten minutes before he realized that the guy was just driving aimlessly, probably to make sure he didn't have a tail. Jackson knew he had to drop back as far as he could. It was risky, but better than spooking him.

The ambulance arrived too late. Tom was just fine. Classic panic attack caused by the added stress. Sue had handled the dilemma expertly while the officer panicked and called the ambulance. He did manage to get him a glass of water, though. The medics checked him over, checking all the vitals, giving him the all clear, but strongly suggesting avoiding stress and getting some rest. Like that was an option.

Sue rubbed Tom's back as a good mother with a sick child as he sat hunched over on the couch, trying his best to relax a bit. He thought about how Sandy would never rub his back this way. She had been gone now for only thirty minutes or so and he didn't miss her yet. Of course he loved her, but, for the first time, he was realizing that maybe it was all a sham. Maybe his love for her had faded years ago when she started to grow cold. He always hoped it was a phase; obviously now it wasn't.

The biggest thing that bothered him now about Sandy was the fact that she didn't care about Lilly. Was she losing her mind or was she really just like this? No matter how many times he had asked her and talked about it over the past few years, she always swore that she loved her, even though she treated her like an unwanted stepchild. None of this mattered now. He had to get back to finding Shawn so he could get his daughter back. The rest can wait.

With each tug she grew more tired and annoyed at the horrendous tearing sound. It wasn't easy but little by little the carpet was ripping away from its ancient seal of glue on wood. Bit by bit, Lilly could see what lay beneath it. With six or so inches pulled up, she needed a break. With a soft thud, she flopped onto the makeshift bed and drank some of the warm water. Sure was a lot of work being locked up in a closet alone.

After a few minutes and half a bottle of water, Lilly felt a bit of energy come back into her. Yet she hesitated at going back to tugging at the carpet. What was the purpose? Why bother getting all tired trying to pull it up? If Shawn caught her, it would probably make him upset, and he has been pretty nice to her lately, even if he was still really creepy. But what else was there to do in here?

Still arguing with herself, Lilly stood up and paced the tiny space with her arms crossed. So what if there was a hatch under the carpet? Even if she could get out of here, where was she going to go? Dad didn't want her anymore. He . . . he hated her, just like mom did. What would be the point of running around alone? She might have the mind of an eight year old but she was smart enough to know she couldn't make it on her own. As that thought raced through her head, she realized there was one person she could go to - Mr. Bluestick. He'd want to take care of her. Maybe he'd even take her home with him once he fixed the Chrimsawheel.

Mind made up, Lilly went at the carpet with new enthusiasm. Cautiously, she folded it over a few inches and got a good hold on it, checking to make sure there was no more of those big scary staples like the few she threw into her toilet. None. Perfect. In her head she counted to three, dug her feet in, and pulled back hard as she could. The carpet let go with a loud cracking and tearing noise, sending Lilly onto her back once again. This time, though, she didn't stay there. Lilly bounded back up and screamed as if she had won a championship fight. And, in a way, she had. Little girl vs. carpet. Winner: little girl.

With the carpet now loose, Lilly immediately pushed it back to explore what lay beneath her all this time. It was an old wooden hatch, three feet wide by three feet wide. The side towards the door had hinges on it. They were small but Lilly still wondered why she hadn't felt them as she walked around earlier. The far side had a small black handle and a slide bolt in the lock position.

Shaking out her tired fingers, Lilly tried the slide lock. It didn't budge. It looked a bit rusted and she wondered if she was strong enough to do this. Dad would be strong enough, but he wouldn't help her anyway. With both hands, she grabbed the tiny knob and pulled. Nothing. A wave of defeat started to come over her until she looked at the carpet. Heck, if she was agile enough to get the hanger and strong enough to rip up the carpet, she could definitely do this. Brainpower was needed though.

It took a while but Lilly thought of something. The coat hanger. Maybe if she scratched away some of the rust, it will be easier to open. It was worth a try. With one tip between her fingers like a pencil and the other wobbling in the air, she scratched away, occasionally blowing the sharp rust pieces in the crack and down to who knows where.

After working up a decent sweat, Lilly was ready to try again. Both hands ready, she tugged hard. Nothing. Then she put her weight into a slow pull. It felt as if it budged a tiny bit. Did it? Yes! It was moving! With a quiet thunk, it slid back, unlocking it and sending Lilly back over the carpet. She couldn't help but laugh hysterically. It felt good.

She took another break, this time more to keep up the anticipation of what may lie beneath the door than to get back strength. A treasure? A way out? A secret fortress? The Bat Cave? Not being able to take it anymore, Lilly stood next to it, placing one hand on the handle and one on the wall for safety. It was a lot heavier than she thought it was going to be. Both hands were needed. It lifted easily, but the second Lilly saw what was beneath it, she dropped the door shut, scared.

It took her breath away, making her a bit dizzy. A treasure it wasn't. A way out, maybe, if she was Spider-Man. There was nothing below the door. It was a straight drop down onto a car that looked pretty old. To Lilly it looked about as deep as the Grand Canyon.

The next time she took a look she made sure to be lying down on the floor, so there was no chance of falling down it. Raising it up a few inches, she put a couple of the DVD's in the crack to prop it open. Through the tiny opening, Lilly surveyed what she could see. It was just a plain old garage with two cars, a red, beat up old one below her, a blue newer one next to it. The rest of the garage seemed to be just like any other she had ever seen - paint cans, hoses, trashcans, bug spray, boxes and other junk. Looking at the drop now, it seemed a bit less threatening, but still too high for her to jump down. She could land on the roof of the car though, but that was still too scary. The drop made her think of her friends at home. Toni and Sara would egg her on to do something like this. If she didn't, they would make fun of her, yet they wouldn't even do it themselves.

It didn't take much debating to decide not to try the drop. Defeated and not finding anything else to accomplish tonight, Lilly closed the heavy lid and placed the carpet back over it. If you looked closely at the wall, you could tell it had been ripped up but otherwise you wouldn't notice, she hoped. Lying back down on the bed, ready to get some sleep, Lilly heard someone coming into the apartment.

8

So many turns. So many that Shawn himself almost got lost. He could have sworn that a car was following him, so much so that he ripped off the eye patch and let the dull light burn his battered eye in hopes of not being recognized. Even then, every time he pulled down a street to see if there was someone tailing, he saw nothing, but the feeling didn't leave him. Maybe it was an expert tail. But then again he never had to shake one before so what did he know? Maybe it was just his nerves. All he knew was that after this many turns he wasn't only dizzy, he was sick of driving and pretty sure no one was following.

Turning into the apartment driveway, nerves already shot from all his plans being ruined, Shawn shut off the engine and waited. No one pulled in after him. A few cars zipped by, but way too fast to be following someone. With the car safely behind the garage, he made his journey up the stairs, trying to figure out what the hell to do. Inside the living room, he leaned against the door and tried to get hold of himself.

Was Sue wrong with what she said? How could they really think he was the one who took Lilly? Everything was so perfect, flawless almost. Yes, it had its bumps but it worked out even better than he thought it would. He had time, though, with that big-ass standoff going on, live on TV and everything. All the resources were there. It would give him time to get out of town with Lilly. But then the Feds would be after him. Of course, he had planned for that. He could easily disappear, but running was the last thing he wanted to do again. Was there a way he could cover this up still? Hell, of course he could. There was nothing linking him to Lilly, nothing. As long as no one finds out about this place, he'll be all set. So if that is the case, why come here?

This is what happens when you panic. Well, if he was going to lie low for a while, Lilly would need some more food anyway.

Yes. Yes, it was going to be just fine. Freshen up Lilly, tell her something has come up and he'd be back in a few days, maybe longer. Then head back home, ready for the firestorm. And, hell, maybe he could even get his first touch in tonight. Yeah, that is just what he needed to relax. Thinking of touching that cool, soft skin relaxed Shawn enough to move away from the wall.

With ease he opened up the heavily locked door and peeked in to see Lilly watching a movie. He couldn't tell which one it was, but she seemed engrossed in it. He did a good job! She looked so beautiful lying there half curled up. She even gave him a smile. Why couldn't it just be a few weeks from now. By then he will be able to crawl next to her and start caressing. But for now he still had to take it easy.

"Hey Lil-ster! How's it going here?"

Lilly carefully paused the video and propped herself up on her elbow. "It's okay. It gets boring and lonely some. Can't I go out into the rest of the place? I promise not to make a mess and I'll be quiet."

Shawn crouched down and placed his hand on her leg, slowly rubbing it. She probably didn't think a thing of it, just like a dad would do, but to Shawn, it was foreplay. "I'm sorry, honey. It's too dangerous. Your dad has sent people out to look for you, to make sure you are far away. He doesn't even want to run into you."

Lilly wanted to kick away from Shawn's slimy hand touching her. It was so creepy. For some reason she believed him before, but now she didn't know. Maybe Dad didn't want to see her around anymore but would he really go through all that trouble to get rid of her? She wanted to cry so badly, but he would think she was a little girl if she did that.

"Now, Lilly, you're probably going to get upset, but I have to go away for a few days and you're going to have to stay here. I promise you, the second I can, I'll be right back here. And then you won't have to stay in your room anymore."

Lilly wanted to scream. The thought of staying in this box alone for days, it just, it was unbearable to think of! She'd go crazy!

"Shawn, no! Please, please, no!" Lilly jumped up and did the most disgusting thing she could think of: she hugged Shawn. He hugged backed so tight she could hardly breathe. Feeling his body against hers reminded her of one of those scary movies when the big monster grabbed the girl.

"It's okay. You'll be fine, I promise."

She could feel his hands running all over her. She could have sworn he was grabbing her butt. Could it be? Just to be safe, she pushed back, wondering if she should throw a fit. Would it work?

"Lilly, I have no choice. I wish I did. Now, why don't you take a shower before I have to go so you're nice and clean and I'll make you up some extra food." He kissed her lightly on the forehead.

Lilly wondered if his lips would burn a mark into her head. It felt as if the last shower was just a short while ago but after all that work, she definitely needed one now.

Pulling away from him she gladly walked out of the tiny room. It felt wonderful to have so much space around her. In the bathroom she started the water and waited for Shawn to walk by before getting undressed. Starting to take off her shirt, she heard a loud bang. It startled her enough to put it back on and shut off the water to hear better.

Jackson couldn't believe he had lost the perp after such a long pursuit, but luckily Mr. Bluestick had seen where he turned. Jackson parked out on the street a few houses down and ran through the side yards like a commando. Creeping around the corner of the brown house that they thought he turned into, he smiled. There was the car parked way back, behind a garage. The lights were on up in the apartment. Maybe this guy wasn't so crazy. He was right about the neighbor, he had another place, and that meant one thing: He must have the girl.

Within a few minutes he was back at the car and letting out Mr. Bluestick who had a serious look on his face. He quickly briefed him with his findings, and then he did a daring thing. He un-cuffed Mr. Bluestick and gave him a weapon. It was just a baton but still enough to do damage. Jackson's gut told him it was okay. He knew calling backup wasn't only protocol, it was smart. But it wasn't an option. The guy could kill the girl by the time anyone got here, and, most likely, they'd make him go back to the station not believing his story. He was on his own, well, with a crazy guy at his side. Silently they both arrived at the bottom of the apartment stairs.

"Look, stay here until I yell for you. If you hear shots, go to that house and call the police. You can do that, right?" Mr. Bluestick nodded calmly and watched as Jackson unclipped his gunlock and headed up the stairs. At the top he looked down and nodded to him. Fear and nerves covered the young man's face as he lifted his fist to pound on the door.

Live on the news! This was fantastic, but if something didn't happen soon, they were going to lose interest and just become a headline instead of a live segment. What to do? Probably take some action, risk it all to save them. That's what the media would think, right? Rudder kept smoothing his hair, and plucking off lint balls from his suit while mulling over what actions to take next.

"Rudder! I have to talk to you!" A young officer out of breath ran over to Rudder who was clearly upset at not being called the correct handle in front of others. He'll rip into him later. First, he had to find out what was so important.

"Yes, Officer?" The man looked around nervously and motioned for him to move away from everyone else. Rudder was more than annoyed at this man. He made a mental note to have him on traffic duty for the next month.

"Sir, the suspect in the Boyer case, he . . . ."

Shit. He knew it, the fucker had a heart attack, just perfect.

"He's gone, sir. So is Jackson."

Rudder's instant reaction was to fix his tie and jacket. "What do you mean?" he said through gritted teeth, still fixing his tie, looking around to see if anyone was watching. There were cameras everywhere and he felt as if they were all on him.

"Sir, they, well, Tim at the front desk needed a bathroom break. He couldn't find Jackson so he checked and they were both gone. He tried radioing him. There was no answer. Do you think that crazy old coot could have overpowered Jackson? He's so big."

This was the last thing he needed right now. Every fucking thing was so perfect. This could mess it all up. What to do? If he sent off guys to go looking for him, the news would be all over it in seconds, calling him incompetent, that he let someone walk right out of his precinct. No. That was not an option.

"Listen to me, Jimmy. Who else knows about this?"

The seasoned middle-aged officer answered quickly as if it was a drill, "No one, sir. Just you, Tim and me. I made sure no one was told until you were briefed."

Rudder fixed his hair again. "That was good thinking, Jimmy. We need to keep it that way. Just for a little while, until we get this settled. Do you think you can do that?" It was Jimmy's turn to look around to see if anyone was watching them.

"What if Jackson is in danger, sir?"

"Trust me, Jackson can take care of himself, and if he hasn't, then it's his fault. If we let this out, the lives of the family inside there will be on the line. We can have this done in a matter of minutes. Soon as it is, I'll have every available man head out on this. Top priority."

Jimmy nodded and walked away, tripping over a crack on the way back to his post. Rudder wanted to look in the mirror to see if he looked all right before going back to the task at hand. He just hoped his face wasn't too flush for the cameras. Those things pick that up easily.

The pounding on the door almost made Shawn throw up. This was it. This was the end of it all. All the years of getting away with it, the good life over. He was going to end up in a cell with a dude who just happens to have a daughter. The fucker will beat the shit out of him and rape him on a daily basis. This couldn't be happening; he couldn't take that. He'd end up getting killed in a matter of days. And they were sure to find out about all the other girls he has had. That would put him away for thirty life sentences. This was not good.

All of those thoughts shot through Shawn's head like a bullet before the third pound even came. He had to calm himself. If he handled this right, he could get out of it. There were two options: If there were a lot of cops, he could pretend to find Lilly on a hunch and try to play the hero card. If there were only a few, he could manipulate his way out and go on the run from here. It would suck, but he'd be free.

Bolting to the front window, he peeked out ever so carefully to see . . . nothing. Not even one cop car was parked out front, or even on the side. Was it even the cops? Next, he darted to Lilly who was standing in the bathroom gripping a towel as if it was some sort of magic shield that would protect her. Without a word, he scooped her and had her back in the closet by the sixth pound on the door. Seeing the fear in her eyes tugged at his heart. God, he prayed not to lose her.

"Lilly, it looks like some of the people that your dad sent to make sure you left town have found us. You have to hide in here and not say a word. You've got to be silent. You understand that? And if someone opens this door besides me, you have to promise me not to tell them anything about how you got here. It might sound weird, but trust me. Your dad has even paid some guys to dress up like cops to trick you. So don't trust anyone but me!"

Lilly's eyes were locked on him, completely confused and frightened. He wanted to hold her but had to shut the door not even letting her make the promise. Snapping the locks shut on the door, he raced to the front, preparing to put on his acting cap again.

Opening the door, he acted surprised at the man's presence. The gigantic man, way too big to fight, had his gun more than half out, his other hand hovering between his mace and preparing to defend himself.

"Mr. Daggerty, we have suspicion to believe that you are housing our missing victim Lilly Boyer. Please step back from the door and put your hands in the air."

Shawn obliged as the man filled the doorway , not once taking his eyes off him. Shawn looked behind him at the open door waiting for at least another officer to follow. "Officer, I don't understand. I have been doing everything to help find Lilly. The girl is like a niece to me, just ask Tom." Shawn started to lower his arms, not for any reason other than they were getting tired.

It made Jackson whip out his gun and aim it right at his chest. It was a first for both of them. Shawn had never had a gun aimed at him, and, truthfully, as tough as he thought he was, he started to shake and felt tears in the back of his eyes lining up to come out like passengers ready to evacuate a boat. Jackson, on the other hand, had adrenaline rushing through his body so much that he, too, was shaking. His finger felt slippery on the trigger from the sweat that was starting to cover his body. The only situations he had ever been in like this were in training, and the man in front of him was always a cutout that didn't actually speak.

"PUT YOUR HANDS BACK UP!"

He did. Both trembling, they stood staring at each other, wondering what was next.

"Officer, I assure you, I'm not dangerous. Of course, you need to take precautions. You can search me if you want."

Jackson finally looked around the room. It should have been the first thing he did. Luckily, it was safe. "Up against the wall, hands raised high." With the gun back in its holster, Jackson clumsily but thoroughly searched his body and found nothing. His nerves settled a bit. Should he cuff him, though? Technically, if he found nothing and he did cuff him, Shawn could file a complaint. Then again, he was a suspect. Shit, why couldn't he ever remember the proper laws.

"Officer, if I'm a suspect now, where is your back up? You didn't come alone, did you?"

"Shut up! Only speak when I ask you something, got it?"

Shawn could sense the panic in the man's voice. He must be a loose cannon trying to make himself a hero. Shawn had to push him. It was dangerous but it was his only choice. Maybe this wasn't as bad as he thought.

"Officer, I'm sorry, but with all those reports you see on the news about people dressing up as cops, I'm having a hard time believing what is going on right now. Could you please show me some ID."

Jackson backed off him a bit allowing Shawn to turn around. He kindly showed him identification. Shawn inspected it carefully when something caught his eye. Another man was peeking around the corner of the door, a man who should not be here.

"What the hell is this? What is going on here?" Shawn screamed, startling Jackson as he turned to see Mr. Bluestick . "This is some sort of set up, isn't it? You're both in on it! You bastards kidnapped Lilly! How dare you do this!"

"I told you to wait downstairs!"

"I hadn't heard anything, I was nervous! Where is she, you sick bastard!"

301

Shawn and Mr. Bluestick started shouting at each other like a couple of school kids. Jackson stood in between trying to calm them. Neither would shut up until he aimed his gun at Shawn.

"Both of you shut up! I want to know where the girl is and I want to know now. I'm going to cuff you, Mr. Daggerty, so I can search the house." Jackson went to grab Shawn by the arm. He jumped back yelling about how this was all a set up and he wanted the real police. Jackson gave him his best death look and lunged at him. In less then a second Shawn succumbed to the burly man, who continued to handcuff him to the radiator in the living room.

Jackson seemed even more relaxed now that the perp was cuffed and couldn't cause any damage. The nut job almost ruined everything but luckily he hadn't. He surveyed the room for any clues, but it was barren of pretty much everything; even the couch was missing its cushions. Carefully he checked the one closet but found nothing but the stench of old mothballs.

"What are you doing in this shit-hole anyways, Daggerty? Needed a place to stash the kid, huh?"

Shawn rolled his eyes and tugged at the chain before responding. "Look, what you are doing is illegal. And since I, on the other hand, have not done anything illegal, I suggest you un-cuff me before you lose your badge." Jackson seemed not to notice the remark. He went about looking through the kitchen with the help of Mr. Bluestick. Shawn kept his eye on them, waiting for the right time to distract.

When they finished the search in the kitchen, Shawn knew he had to stop them. There were only two rooms left in the house, one of which would send him away for good. "Officer, I'll tell you!"

Jackson reappeared in the living room with his arms crossed waiting to hear what he had to say. Shawn waited a few seconds for Mr. Dickhead to appear but he didn't.

"If you must know, I have come on some hard times lately and I can't afford my house anymore. I was too embarrassed to tell anyone. I just got this apartment this week and I was going to start moving stuff here when this whole thing started. I should have said something but it was just embarrassing. I hope that nut job didn't trick you into thinking I was the sick one. He's sneaky, you know. He tricked the little girl's dad before, too. You'd better watch out."

Jackson's heart sank to the floor. It was a pretty good story. Shit, if he was telling the truth, then he had been duped pretty badly, meaning he would lose his job for good. He'd end up being a security guard at Wal-Mart for the rest of his life. Oh, this was bad. Did he still have time to bring back the nut job? He'd have to hurry.

Jackson sprinted at Shawn so fast he felt as if he was at the running of the bulls and about to be gored. He almost let out a yelp. Yet, instead of pummeling him as Shawn was expecting, he un-cuffed him and helped him up. What was going on?

"I'm sorry, sir, it's just that no one was doing anything about the little girl, and I just wanted to help her."

Shawn put a hand on his shoulder, fighting every urge to run out the door, or to run to the back room and stop that bastard from finding the closet. It was probably too late; the front door was most likely his best bet.

"It's all right, officer. I completely understand. I want to find her just as much as you do. You'd better go get him, though, before he gets away."

Jackson's eyes bulged, showing that he had clearly forgotten. In a flash he was gone down the back hall.

The second he disappeared, Shawn grabbed his keys and headed for the door. At the threshold he paused. Did he still have a chance that the old man hadn't found Lilly?

"SHIT!" The booming voice came from the back room.

Guess not, Shawn laughed to himself as he took the steps three at a time. He was in the car and turning the engine over before he saw the shadowy figure in the doorway. Not seeing the rogue officer's car anywhere near, he knew he was going to make a grand getaway.

Calmly, to not gain attention, he pulled out onto the street as he would any other day. No one around, perfect. He had a chance to get away as long as this risk-taking bastard hadn't called this in. Almost to the edge of the street, something caught his eye in the woods. Could it be? Impossible. Maybe God was on his side as he thought. He had to be if what he saw was true.

9

Mr. Bluestick's heart was racing. He was frantically trying to open the heavily locked door when Jackson barreled in and knocked him to the floor. It took more than one shout to get the burly man to turn and look at the oddly secured door. Seeing it, the man's eyes flashed with rage and he leapt off Mr. Bluestick and shot back out through the door. Shaken, he went back to try opening the locks, but what good were bare hands on locks that could withstand a gunshot? Besides, it might hit Lilly. And the baton? It was so thin it wasn't any use on a small object.

With an open fist he pounded on the door, quickly realizing it might have been so hard it could scare Lilly. He switched it to a gentle knock and put on a soothing voice. "Lilly, my darling! It's Mr. Bluestick. Are you all right in there?" No answer. He knocked again, getting worried. "Lilly, Shawn is gone, my dear; it's just me and the police. I'm trying to get you out. Are you okay?" Again, nothing.

He started to shake, fearing that Lilly was unconscious or even worse. Stepping back from the door, he had to force the horrible images out of his head. Was he too late? Like a chicken with his head cut off, he started to search the room, shooting from one spot to the next, trying to find something, anything to use to open the door. Nothing.

Ready to head for the kitchen to find something more useful, Jackson, out of breath, came rushing back. "Lost the fucker. Did you find the girl?" Grabbing Jackson, Mr. Bluestick shoved him to the door. "Open it! Open it! For crying out loud, she could be hurt!" Pulling out his Billy club he raised it high above his head, ready to whack it down on one of the locks.

Mr. Bluestick grabbed his hand to stop him. "Lilly, we are going to bang on the door to open it. Don't be scared, it's only the police and me. Just stay in the far back." Finishing his sentence, he let go of Jackson and nodded. With thundering force the Billy club came down, smacking the lock with a loud clank. Mr. Bluestick covered his ears and worried about Lilly inside. He hoped she was covering hers.

Ten cracks or so on each of the three locks broke them open. By the time they were ready to slide the door aside, Jackson was sweating and exhausted; Mr. Bluestick was a mess waiting to see Lilly. Finally, he placed his scar-covered hands on the door and pulled it aside slowly, hoping not to frighten the poor girl. Instinctively Jackson wanted to take the lead, to cover him just in case it was a trap, but Mr. Bluestick wasn't having any of that. He peeked his head in first, putting on the best smile he could to show Lilly all was safe.

The smile faded quickly, though, as his eyes scanned the room. It was definitely a holding cell of sorts, and no doubt it was made to suit a little girl. Only one thing, there was no little girl in it. His heart fired pain through his chest as he fell to his knees defeated.

Jackson popped his head in over him and practically mimicked the same response. "My God, if he had her in the car already, I'll, I'll never forgive myself," Jackson let out in a quivering voice.

Mr. Bluestick leaned forward, putting his weight on his hands, hardly being able to hold himself up. Opening his moist eyes, the edge of the carpet caught his eye. It was lifted a bit, sort of torn. He couldn't stop himself from crawling over to it.   Pulling back the carpet, he saw the handle and latch that Lilly had worked so hard to get to. A laugh burst out of his shaking lips.

Jackson looked confused until he peeked over the edge of the carpet.

"That Lilly girl, I told you she was special! She found a way out, that little bugger!"

Jackson was smiling now but it seemed forced as Mr. Bluestick opened the hatch to look below. "How can we be sure of that, though?" said Jackson.

Looking down onto the old car, Mr. Bluestick saw a tiny dent with some scuffmarks on the roof. The front window boasted many tiny finger smudges. "Look! She must have gotten scared with all the noise and jumped down. And we can be sure because I know Lilly! And besides, who would lock someone up so expertly if they knew there was a hatch in the room!"

Jackson's smile turned from fake to real as hope flooded back into him. "Yeah, that's true. The hatch must have been the old attic entrance before they turned this into an apartment. They must have just carpeted over it instead of bothering to replace it. Jesus . . . and the girl found it!"

Mr. Bluestick stood up and rushed by Jackson. "I know where she's headed! We've got to hurry, though. Shawn might be running scared, but I doubt he's the kind to give up."

While the entire town was in an uproar - missing child, crazy old man, and a stand off - Sandy went shopping. She had taken the essentials from the house but she needed a special outfit to go and see Mark. After all these years of being brainwashed, having her life taken away from her, she was finally free. And she damn well planned on celebrating it. Finally Mark and she could run off to Jamaica. No,

Bermuda? What would be the best place? It didn't matter. First she had to find the perfect dress; then it was off to the travel agent.

After trying on nine different outfits she finally decided on a tight, short green dress. It would probably be a bit chilly, but she looked fabulous. Keeping the dress on, she paid for it with Tom's credit card, making her feel all that much better. Luckily the travel agent was in the same shopping plaza as the dress shop. She hadn't been there since the time Tom saw her coming from it. That sure was a close one.

The small narrow store was decorated with dozens of posters with faraway places on them. They all looked so perfect to go to. There were only two agents left at the desks since it was late. Both were on the phone. The man she usually talked to wasn't there. She was a bit disappointed but it didn't matter. The young woman who was sitting at the desk closest to her waved her over, giving Sandy a silent smile while talking to someone about an Alaskan cruise. It sounded nice but she wanted something tropical.

The blonde woman hung up the phone and before she could even say hello Sandy spoke. "I need you to help me decide."

The woman looked thrown but responded anyways. "O . . . K, what are we deciding?"

"If you were to go away with your true love for the first time, where would you go? I talked to Ralph that works at that desk on several occasions. He showed me a lot but never really said what he would choose. So, what would it be?"

Connie, or so said her desk plaque, could sense that something was off in Sandy so she slowly started to form a response when Sandy once again cut her off. "I would . . . ."

"Oh! And we have to hurry. I want to leave tonight or tomorrow morning."

It seemed as if it shouldn't have been a hard decision for Connie. A woman is fleeing the country, running away from something. You should alert someone, right? Connie decided to make the commission instead of reporting it. Why not? She had a family to feed. Forty-five minutes after Sandy sat down, Connie had talked her into an all-inclusive resort in Santa Domingo. It was all booked and ready to go, Connie even pulled a few strings to make the return tickets open-ended. Sandy was beaming with excitement as she profusely thanked the woman and headed out.

The next stop was at the hotel. The flight was in the morning, might as well get a good night sleep. Who knows, maybe even some pre-eloping hot sex! It was the run of the mill Best Western but more than suitable for one night. Besides tomorrow she'd be in paradise with her true love, and all this shit will be left behind for good.

Putting on her make-up, she flicked on the TV to kill the silence. There was a live report in front of some house. For a quick second she figured it was hers and they had found Lilly. There was a spark of emotion, but a spark was all it was, gone in a flash. Besides, it wasn't even about Lilly, it was about some guy holding his family hostage. She felt for him. Maybe the same damn thing happened to him as her. Good luck to him, if it did.

Ignoring the news, she hummed as she made herself up, paying careful attention to the bruise on her face. It was the most she had been made up since her wedding day. Hell, she shouldn't even call it that, it should have been called her sentencing! Finally done, she checked herself out in the mirror. Amazing how someone can clean up so well. Mark's jaw was going to drop. Ready to go, she grabbed her keys and headed out the door, time to go get her man.

The phone rang, startling them out of their deep conversation about what to do next. So far they had figured out nothing except to wait for Shawn to come home and then to confront him. Sue answered it for Tom.

"Mrs. Boyer?" the vaguely familiar voice asked. Sue told the caller no and he asked for Tom. She passed the phone to Tom, who answered it, not even paying attention.

"Mr. Boyer, I know where your daughter is. We need your help to get her. She's in danger."

Tom immediately perked up, almost knocking over his coffee trying to get Sue's attention. He looked around the room for the officer but he was in the other room watching TV. Some cop.

"WHAT? Who is this? I swear if this is another prank, you'll be sorry! The phone is tapped and it's a felony!" Tom could feel his face getting hot with anger thinking it might be a prank and hoping that it wasn't.

"Sir, I'm a police officer. We accosted your neighbor Shawn at an apartment a mile or so from your house. He was holding your daughter there, but she escaped on her own."

Tom could not think of a way to explain the feeling that flopped on top of him like a blanket thrown over his head. "Where? Where is she?" he screamed into the receiver as he stood up. Sue, following his cue, stood up, too.

"Sir, we are about to enter the woods behind your house. We are entering from the Adams Street side. We strongly believe that she is heading for the old mill on her own. If you could head out there, we'll meet you there."

Tom was starting to head for the back door before the man was even finished speaking. "You sure of this?"

"Ninety percent, sir, but there is one other thing. We believe your neighbor is still pursuing her. You should take the officer that is at your house with you. I already called this in but they are too backed up right now with the hostage thing."

Tom was in the backyard, halfway to the tiny gate when the phone started to get static. It stopped him in his tracks. Not wanting to lose the call, he pulled out his cell and dialed the number from the caller ID on the house phone. Then he quickly hung it up so he would have the number saved on it.

"I'm heading in. I'll call you when I get there, Jackson, is it? And, thanks." He clicked off the phone and tossed it in the grass. He was just about to break into a run when Sue grabbed his arm. It startled him for a second. When he realized it was her, he explained the call. She urged him to go back and get the cop inside. Tom felt he would be more of a hassle than anything.

"What about a weapon, Tom?" He looked down at her belt. She thought for a second before handing him the baton. Then she cursed herself for having heels on. There was no way she could make it through the woods. "Tom, what size are Sandy's shoes?"

Staring at the woods Tom answered without even thinking. "Seven."

"Might be tight but should work. Wait for me while I go switch shoes." She started for the house, then looked over her shoulder to reassure Tom. She should have figured it, though; he was already racing through the gate. A scream gurgled in the back of her throat to try and stop him, but she stopped it, knowing it was no use. She was better off changing shoes as quickly as she could and getting the lazy moron cop to accompany her out there. She just hoped that losing a few minutes wouldn't mean losing a life.

Lilly heard Shawn shout for her but ignored it. He sounded far back and she knew if she stopped for him, he wouldn't let her go to Mr. Bluestick. Right now that was all she wanted. Every few yards she looked over her shoulder to see if he was gaining on her. He was. She did her best to move faster.

Stepping over burnt branches still dripping wet, Lilly did her best not to breathe in the pungent scent of wet ash. She could hardly believe how different the woods looked after the fire. It seemed like a whole new world, an alien world. Coming at the mill from a different angle made her nervous about not finding it. She felt as if she was on the right path though.

Walking around a particularly large branch, she wished she could stop and take a break. Her body was exhausted from all the work she'd done today. First, getting the coat hanger, then the carpet, now this. Thinking back through the day's events made her smile. For the first time in her life she felt independent. It couldn't be better timing since now she was alone in life. Most of all, she was proud at how she handled the situation at the apartment.

Hearing all the banging and yelling after Shawn scared her so much, she knew she only had one decision ; jump. If Shawn had been telling the truth, she didn't want to get taken away again, especially if they were as mean as Shawn said. And even if he hadn't been telling the truth, it was best to get out of there. And if he was trying to protect her, she didn't want to live like a prisoner forever. So she lifted up the carpet, raised up the hatch and set a video in the crack to keep it open. She sat with her legs dangling above the car. It looked so high she was sure that she would break every bone in her body.

Frozen, she sat there, debating whether to take the leap. Maybe it wasn't that bad where she was. But when she heard the loud thump right outside the door, she scooted off the ledge without even thinking. Landing on the car did hurt a bit but nothing like she thought it would. In fact, it was sort of easy. Looking up, she laughed to herself. From there it looked a much shorter distance. The video still in the crack was evidence of what she did. If she could get rid of it, it might buy some time. Being a genius again, she slid down off the car, grabbed a rake, climbed back on up and whacked it down. The lid shut perfectly. Dang, she was good.

After hiding the tape under the car, she ran outside. Sneaking around, running behind bushes as she did when she played hide and go seek. Reaching the road, she quickly recognized where she was. It was only a few streets from home, and if she cut into the woods right across from the house, it would lead her to the mill. Too perfect! And now she was here, tired, wanting to stop, but refusing to give up.

With Shawn yelling more and catching up even more quickly, Lilly was ecstatic to finally see the mill in the distance. It shot new vigor into her tired body, helping her step up her pace. She was so excited to see Mr. Bluestick. In a matter of minutes she was at the spot she had crossed so many times while yelling his name. Looking back, Shawn was only a hundred yards away. She had no choice but to go in and find him.

Once she found him, they were both going to have to hide from Shawn as well. They hated each other. What if he didn't give up, though, and kept looking for them all night? Or worse, what if he goes and gets her dad and he comes out here to send her away again? This was bad. Why hadn't she just stayed in the apartment. It would have been safer. She didn't want Mr. Bluestick getting hurt. Maybe she should just leave. NO! Mr. Bluestick was her only friend and the only person she wanted to be with. The only choice was to go in and find him.

Approaching the mill, Tom slowed down his run to a crawl as he saw a shadowy figure enter the building. It was too big to be Lilly. Was it Jackson? Should he yell? No, if it was Shawn, it would spook him. He flicked open his cell and dialed the number he saved a few minutes before. The deep voice answered almost immediately.

"Jackson, I'm at the mill. I just saw someone enter. Was it you?" Tom listened hearing only heavy breathing and crunching for a few seconds.

"NO! No, it's not us. Don't go in yet. I have no clue if he's armed. Wait for us. We'll be there in five minutes." With that the phone hung up.

Us? We? Wasn't he on his own? It didn't matter, what did was the man who just entered the building. It had to be Shawn. He should just run after him right now and crack him in the back with the baton. He's probably only a few feet in. He could catch up in a second. Though he wanted to do nothing more than kill the man who had taken away his child, the sane side of his brain got the best of him for the time being. He didn't want to end up being one of those guys in prison for life for committing street justice. Besides it could put Lilly in jeopardy. As hard as it will be, he had to wait. Maybe Sue will catch up by then as well.

Rudder was pissed beyond belief. This shit doesn't happen on *Law and Order*. The call came in ten minutes ago. This one from Jackson. The stupid fuck had let the prisoner out of the cell and was running around town like some commando trying to find the little girl. What could he possibly be thinking? It made no sense at all. So far the lid had been kept tight on it. And, damn it, he was going to keep it that way. As long as Jackson didn't do something so stupid that it drew attention, he could still get out of this mess and look great on TV.

The stand off was taking longer than he had hoped. Some affirmative action was going to have to take place. No more sitting and waiting. Flipping open his cell he snuck away from anyone's ear shot and put an anonymous call into the local news station that the police were about to go in with force. Of course the news crews were still there but they were all just sitting having coffee. The cameras were set up to catch anything that happened, but nothing would be live. He wanted, no, needed it to be live. Being almost nine o'clock, it was perfect timing, too. It would interrupt prime time TV, giving him the optimal number of viewers.

Less than a minute after he hung up, he smiled to himself as he watched the news crew scramble to get ready and then the others followed suit. Next, it was on to planning this out. If they were to storm in now, they would beat the negotiator as well. He was running late. It took only a few minutes to brief the team on the plan. It was a simple smash and grab. Shoot tear gas, smash the windows and doors and storm in. It should go smoothly. Rudder slapped on a bulletproof vest over his suit, knowing how cool it would make him look. He was going to go in, just to make this look even better. Hell, maybe they'll even have the girl back by the end of the night, too. Maybe this wasn't all that bad.

Sandy couldn't contain her excitement on the short ride over to the pizza parlor that Mark owned. Some people might look at a man working in a pizza parlor and think, "Oh, he must have no talents in life, or, Poor man, stuck working in a pizza place". Sandy didn't care though, because she knew the truth. Mark was amazingly talented. He made the best pizza in town, hell, the world probably. And not only that, he owned the place. It took in over a half a million a year. If people knew that, they wouldn't talk.

Pulling into the parking lot of Mark's Pizza Palace, Sandy checked her make-up again. Fucking Tom. The swelling was a bit noticeable, but Mark won't care, he loved her. Excited and nervous to start her new life, she headed for the main entrance. It was a busy night inside. Well, they all were since the food was so amazing. Most of the business was carryout, though. There was a line of five or so people waiting to get their pies and leave. A couple of the tables still had guests sitting and eating at them. As she walked in, a couple of the guests looked at her outfit and wondered what the hell she was doing here.

Looking through the latticework that separated the kitchen from the dining hall, she could see Mark in the back swirling sauce on fresh tossed dough. He was gorgeous. Not being able to contain her excitement any longer, she charged through the swinging saloon-style doors, right into the kitchen. The customers looked at her curiously; the workers were too busy to even notice her. Mark was starting to toss the cheese on when Sandy blurted out her arrival.

"I'm here, Mark! And, boy, do I have a surprise for you!" Turning his head to see who was talking to him, his hands kept making the pizza as if on autopilot.

"I'm sorry, what?" He looked her up and down, curious at her dress, curious at who she was.

316

"Mark, baby, I booked us a trip. And it has an open-ended ticket so we can stay as long as we want. Now I'm not going to tell you where we're going but I will say it's tropical!"

The pie was done being made. A short, tan man grabbed it away from him and tossed into an oven. The man Sandy called Mark wiped his hands on his apron, looking at Sandy with curious eyes. "Lady, I don't know you. And I'm sorry, but you can't be in the kitchen."

Sandy's face went slack but quickly shot back up. "Mark, you big tease. You're joking with me. Well, you'd better hurry up because we are leaving first thing in the morning." Several of the employees were now watching the conversation with this strange woman.

"Ma'am, I've seen you in here a few times, but I don't know you. And my name is not Mark."

Sandy was starting to get a bit confused. He had to be joking with her. He was a kidder! She looked at his gorgeous green eyes and smiled. "Stop it, Mark, it's not funny anymore! You're supposed to be excited."

The man started to roll up his sleeves some more, though they couldn't go up much farther, as he looked to his crew for help. An older woman who was wearing an apron like everyone else, even though she was working the cash register, scooted over to intervene. She was the typical Italian mother with big hair, big glasses and heavy accent.

"Miss, you can't be in the kitchen. What did my Tony do to you? Not call you back or something?"

Sandy started to back up, pursing her lips. "His name is Mark! Why are you all teasing me? It's not funny. Really, it's not! I took a long time planning this trip. I finally left my husband for you, Mark!"

The Italian woman nodded to a young girl at the counter who must have been her daughter since the resemblance was uncanny. As if being told through ESP, the girl picked up the phone.

Sandy could see that she dialed only three numbers. She couldn't believe this. TOM! He must have gotten to them, too! "Jesus Christ! What did he do? Pay you off? Or did he drug you all? Huh? What is it? Maybe he threatened you. Is that it?" The entire place was now watching her in an eerie hush. The only sound was the low hum of a Frank Sinatra song.

"Ma'am, I really suggest you leave. We are running a business here. I don't know what sort of drugs you're taking but . . ."

"MA! Be polite, would you! The lady might just be crazy or something. She can't help it." The man Sandy called Mark sniped at the older woman, bickering with her in rapid Italian.

Sandy took it as her cue to leave. She bolted back out through swinging doors. With everyone watching, she tripped on her heels and fell to the floor. It was the most humiliating experience in her life. And all because of Tom! That fucker needed to pay.

The Mill
Part 4

1

Tom hid behind a large tree, careful not to touch it since it was almost pure ash. Every few seconds he snuck a look around the corner, waiting for this mysterious officer. After five minutes he wanted to pull out his cell to call again, but he heard snapping noises in the distance. Edging around, he could see two figures coming from the opposite side of the mill. They were walking directly for it, not caring if anyone saw them. He figured it must be the cops. Getting a bit closer, he could see the moon shine off the badge on the chest of a man that looked like a body double for Arnold Schwarzenegger. The other guy was obscured behind him.

Feeling sure it was safe, Tom came out into view. The large man stopped instantly and went for his gun. Tom shot his arms up and cursed to himself. Was it a trap? God damn it! The bulky man edged closer to him. Tom hardly looked through his squinted eyes as he braced himself for a bullet.

"Jackson, no! That's Lilly's father, for crying out loud!"

Tom knew the voice but it didn't make sense. Opening his eyes in time to see the gun being put away, Tom was shocked to see Mr. Bluestick standing, un-cuffed and free in front of him.

"I'm sorry, sir. Can't be too safe, you know."

Tom nodded that it was fine, not taking his eyes off the man that only a few hours ago he wanted to kill.

"Thomas, we must hurry if you saw Shawn going in there. The man gives me quite a chill, I must say." The pair started walking to the entrance as Jackson grabbed both of their shoulders.

"Whoa there, tough guys. I understand you want to go in but I can't let that happen. I've broken enough rules to never work as a cop again. If either of you got hurt, I can kiss even security jobs at the convenience store good-bye. I've got to go in alone." Tom and Mr. Bluestick immediately protested at the same time. Jackson crossed his arms and stared at the two not budging.

"For crying out loud, no one knows this mill like I do. I know every single inch of it, short cuts, hallways, everything, for crying out loud!"

"What the hell. If it'll helped get the girl, none of the broken rules would matter anyway, right? Jackson mumbled to himself. "Fine, but you both stay behind me. Grab something to use as a weapon. The sick fuck is tiny and wiry but I have no clue what he is packing, if anything. You guys got it?" The two nodded like children listening to the playground rules from dad.

They followed Jackson as he pulled out his gun and walked to the door. Tom extended the club he had while Mr. Bluestick grabbed an old metal rod that lay right outside the door. Three against one, and the advantage of knowing the battlefield, Tom felt pretty confident walking through the doorway.

Lilly ran through the halls at a good pace. She figured it would be easy to find the door that led to Mr. Bluestick's room. It was darker than she thought it would be. A tiny panic started to fill her chest as she got more and more confused taking twists and turns. More than anything, she wanted to yell out his name so he could find her, but every time she took a turn, she was petrified to run into Shawn. Maybe it was this building or the dark but now she was scared of him again.

After what felt like an eternity, Lilly was ready to give up, to let Shawn take her back. No, no, it would be better to just hide until it was bright out. Then, in the morning, she could easily find her way around. That was the perfect plan. Only, where to hide? There were a million places but anyone with a flashlight would find her in most. And every room seemed to be scarier than the last.

Just pick a door, just pick a door! Each room was too dark, the few with handles were too spooky to open. Taking another turn, she wondered how much more of this she could take and then. . . there it was - brightly painted double doors. The paint was flaking, making the writing unreadable, but Lilly could tell, whatever it was, it must have been cool. It was the friendliest door yet, making it the only choice. The only thing that bothered her was the fact that she had never seen it. She must be in the other side of the mill that Mr. Bluestick always told her to stay away from.

Pushing it in, she was still a bit hesitant. It resisted a little but, after a tough shove, it gave in, letting a tiny cloud of dark dust fly up, making what lay beyond hard to see. The dust slowly faded; seeing inside relieved and fascinated Lilly. It was a huge room, almost lit up by the moonlight through several open holes in the roof. There were dozens of seats, all black and flaky. In fact, everything was black and crackly except for down in front of the seats. There was something amazing there.

Lilly walked down the middle isle towards the front of the theater. There it was, a giant tree with red leaves growing towards the ceiling. It was like a fairy tale, so beautiful, so out of place. Lilly touched the trunk. It was real. Walking around the back of it, she found that the roots had ripped up the floor, leaving a big gap covered in moss. Almost like a bed. A bed, just perfect. Not even thinking, Lilly immediately lay down in it, hidden from the view of the doors. She felt safe here.

Shawn crept through the halls, confident no one was there but him and Lilly. He also had the advantage of a flashlight that he had kept in his car. That was the one thing that worried him, the car. Did he pull it off the road enough so that rogue cop and loony old man wouldn't find it? If they did, then there might be some trouble. For right now though, he felt pretty confident. He just needed to hurry up and catch her so he could flee this place.

It was all just another test, wasn't it? God was seeing how he could handle this, wasn't he? He may have given him the prize, but, of course, he wasn't going to just hand it to him. It was okay, he gladly accepted the challenge. Anything to have Lilly. Room after room, he listened first then shined the flashlight in to see if there was any evidence of her. It was a bit annoying not being able to remember for the life of him how to get to that stupid room he had taken her from in the first place, but he pushed on anyway.

Ten, fifteen, twenty minutes went by searching for her. He had a few times yelled out her name, but, as time flew by, it made him too nervous. Someone else might hear it, or she might be running from it. Part of him was pissed to have to go through this, to have to lose his house and the life he was starting to get to like. But that was his life. He was prepared for it and could handle another move. It was simple, really, just stop by one of his safe deposit boxes – one that was under a different name - pick up a new ID set and some cash and head off to the next location of his desire, maybe somewhere warmer this time. That might be nice. Lilly would probably like that, the beach and sun. He could almost picture it now, lying out on the hot beach next to Lilly in a tiny bikini. It would perfect. Maybe that was why God did this now, to give him an even better prize.

Rounding a familiar corner, Shawn started to smile. There was yellow tape blocking off an entrance. With ease he snapped it out of his way, letting it fall to the filthy floor. A chuckle escaped his thin lips at the sight of the evidence marker on the floor, standing like a tiny cone, a number three on it. Guess the coat worked. The heavy door that he passed the day before was propped open, leaving easy access to the room. The lights were off this time, though.

Locating the stairs, he grasped the railing and clicked off the flashlight. With the light off, he couldn't even see his hand in front of his face. Perfect. The element of surprise was always the best. Making almost no noise he made it to the bottom of the stairs without incident. There he stood frozen, listening for any noise, and searching his memory for the layout of the room. He could recall the basic floor plan, but didn't dare move. First he wanted to listen for breathing. Nothing. He heard nothing, plan B then.

"LILLY!" He screamed at the top of his lungs in hopes of startling her enough to make some noise. He prepped his light to aim it at whatever he heard. Again nothing. Shit. Giving up on the waiting game, he slipped on the light, blocking the stairs in case she ran. Guiding the beam slowly around the room, he saw nothing but the odd machine and junk. Not satisfied with the visual check, he walked the room, twice. She wasn't here. Odd. Wouldn't a little girl go where she was comfortable? There must be another place; it's got to be near by.

Walking back up the stairs, he finally heard a noise. Yes! Coming from the hall, he scurried up the rest of the stairs quickly and silently. At the top he crammed himself in the corner by the door and clicked off the light once again. Crunching noises. They were a bit loud for such a tiny girl though? And there were a lot of them. Whispering too. Oh shit, this was not good, not at all. It had to be the nut job and the cop. Where the fuck could he go? There was no way out of this room except for the hatch in the back. And who knows where the hell that led?

Shawn tried to control his breathing. They were so close they might hear him. The crunching had stopped, but the whispering got louder. There were more than two voices? Odd. Tom? It couldn't be. Shit, they must have called him. What to do, what to do? He could try to trick them. Talk it out and explain that he ran because he thought there was a cop trying to set him up. Tom would believe him, wouldn't he? Then again, Sandy said Tom was after him, too.

Ready to curse God for putting him in such a tough spot, he calmed himself and realized no matter what, he'll get through it. He had to. God was pulling for him. He just knew it. Besides, he had two things on his side right now besides God: the element of surprise and the gun he got out of his trunk earlier that now sat snuggly at his waistline.

Sue tossed shoe after shoe aside. Damn, this woman had bad taste. In the back of the closet near a giant penny jar nearly filled, she found a beat up old pair of Nike's. They were beat up enough that they fit her feet pretty well. . As she was tying the laces loose enough so they wouldn't cut off her circulation yet tight enough to not come undone, the doorbell rang. She wondered if Justin, the most useless cop in the world, would answer it or if he would be too busy watching the Animal Planet.

Bounding down the stairs, she was relived to see Chip. He had a concerned but friendly smile on his face. Justin was sitting back in front of the TV once again. She wanted to yell at the kid but knew it was just his nerves paralyzing him. Better off leaving him be, he could mess things up more than help. Grabbing Chip by the arm, she ushered him into the kitchen and explained the situation.

"Did you call Rudder? Where the fuck is the back up?"

"There is none, Chip. Jackson did this off the books and from what I can get, I think Rudder is keeping it that way until the hostage thing is over. Bigger headline, if you know what I mean." Chip's face scrunched up with anger.

Turning away from Sue, he looked out to the woods and took a deep breath. "Well, let's get going then."

This was the sort of man you wanted running a force, not Rudder, Sue thought to herself as they walked toward the gate. The man had a family at home and still he was willing to risk everything to make sure someone else could keep his family safe.

The three men stood around each other whispering, yet not one of them looked at the other. They each looked behind them, down halls and into darkness, making sure they were safe.

"Lilly knows this area. Let's go in. We'll search the rest if she's not here."

Jackson listened to Mr. Bluestick with respect. It made sense but it still pissed him off that he felt as if he had no authority in this situation when he should have it all. "Fine. But I go first." Mr. Bluestick tried to protest saying he knew the place better than anyone and could find his way in the dark better than he could with a flashlight, but Jackson refused to listen.

"Follow ten yards behind, got it?" Jackson readied his gun and flashlight in the classic TV cop pose - gun held high in right hand, flashlight in left under the right arm for support. Though it looked cool, he still wondered if it was the best way to do it. Mr. Bluestick crossed his arms and watched him cross the threshold into the room that until this summer no one had entered but him for over twenty years. Tom kept his gaze fixated behind them. Without a flashlight it was hard to see much in the halls. He could feel the hairs on the back of his neck stand up. It had to be his mind playing tricks on him. Getting all-nervous for no rea . . . A loud scream, banging and finally a gunshot cut off his thought.

Tom readied the baton just as Mr. Bluestick raised his weapon. This was not good. Neither of them had a flashlight. Staying as far back as they could, all they could see was a streak of light in the far depths of the room. It looked as if it was on the floor and it definitely wasn't moving anymore. Both panicked. Not knowing what to do, they looked at each other. Someone had to do something.

"JACKSON!" Tom yelled then jumped back around to the corner, back into the hallway that only a few seconds ago was creeping him out. No reply. That was not a good sign. He waited a few more seconds and yelled again. This time Mr. Bluestick raised a finger to his lips to silence him. He was right. If he wasn't answering, then something was wrong, horribly wrong.

Tom wiped the sweat off his hand, then grabbed the baton with a better grip. Getting it ready, he looked to Mr. Bluestick as he motioned his head toward the door, asking if they should go in. For crying out loud, they had to do something. Mr. Bluestick nodded to agree before darting across the doorway to Tom's side. They both felt a bit better being closer to each other. Quickly they scooted a few yards down the hall so they could whisper.

"There is only one other way in or out of that room and it's no help to us. But I've got an idea. I'll sneak down the hall to a panel where I can switch on all the lights in there, catching the son of a bitch off guard. When they come on, we can see from the door where he is. There aren't many hiding places."

Keeping his voice as low as possible, Tom kept his eyes fixated behind them once again. "What about a weapon, though? He obviously has a gun. We've only got fucking sticks. What good will they do?"

"Thomas, it's all we've got right now. If anything, I'll rush him, take the hit, try to disarm him, then you follow in."

Tom turned his eyes to the man. He was willing to give his life to save his daughter. Christ. He wanted to thank him but knew it was an inappropriate moment. And besides, he didn't even really know who he was talking to at the moment, Edward or Mr. Bluestick. It didn't matter anyway, he decided.

Finalizing the plans, Tom took up guard at the side of the door as Mr. Bluestick disappeared. He counted in his head with *Mississippi's*. They agreed on one hundred. Of course they might be a bit off, but a few seconds was better than not having a clue. Getting to eighty, the chest pains he had earlier started to creep their way back up. Trying not to lose count, he did everything he could to push them back down. Ninety. Damn, they hurt. Ninety-three, click. Light suddenly blared out from the door spilling out into the hall. It felt oddly comforting to be able to see everything, yet it was terrifying not knowing what was going to happen next.

It was an odd sensation, fear. It was something he felt his whole life. But never had it been like this. It made Shawn's entire body weak. The gun in his hands felt like a hundred pounds. He hadn't fired it, though, yet he was still responsible for killing the police officer at the bottom of the stairs, if he was dead. Staring down at him, he could hardly see the black lump that was his body. It didn't move at all, not even a noise came from it. Desperately he wanted to shine his light on him to see what the damage was. He knew, though, that it was too risky. There were still two of them out there.

Why would God want him to kill a cop? It made no sense. Unless, unless the cop was evil himself. That must have been it. Rationalizing it in his head made the gun a bit easier to lift. He never hurt anyone in his life, especially his girls. He always treated them like angels. The thought of killing someone was sickening. Well, technically, he didn't do the killing, really. All he did was smack him in the back of the head. Well, that and a hard push sending him down the stairs. It was the stairs and his own gun that probably killed him, that is, if a bullet even hit him. It must have, though, because he heard no ricochet or impact.

What were the other two waiting for? Why aren't they storming in? They must not have guns. That's it! They didn't have them! Why would they? Maybe he should just go out there, then. A gun is one hell of a bargaining tool. Working up a plan to just burst out on them, he was suddenly blinded. Fabulously bright light shot on from every direction, stinging his eyes. Fuck! The old coot lived here. He should have been ready for that. Not knowing what the hell was going on, he raised his gun, ready to shoot at the first sight or feel of anything.

As his eyes slowly adjusted, he was surprised again. No one attacked him, no one was there. What were they waiting for? Realizing they might have found another way in, he spun away from the door, aiming his gun down the stairs. The sight made him gag. The officer was bent in ridiculous ways with blood spilling out from under him. The puddle was so big he could see the reflection of blinking lights in it. It was hard to look away. Too bad, too, because that is just when something struck him in the ribs, sending him towards the stairs.

Peeking around the corner, Tom couldn't believe his luck. There he was - Shawn, facing the other way. He wanted nothing more than to hit the gun out of his hands but there was no clear shot to do that. So he chose to take a rib shot. It was a direct hit. It felt incredible to finally take out some frustration. There was enough force in it that if he didn't break some bones, he'd be amazed.

Unfortunately, though, Shawn didn't drop the gun or even hit the floor for that matter. Bracing to take another whack, he was too late. Shawn already had the gun aimed at him. He wanted to risk it and take another swing, but he couldn't do that to Lilly. If anything happened to him, she would have no one. He lowered the baton, regretting that he didn't wait for Mr. Bluestick.

"Fuck, Tom! Shit, that hurts!" Shawn braced his side, wincing in pain but not wavering the gun's aim.

Tom looked around the room to see if Lilly was near. All he saw was Jackson's body lying still at the bottom of the stairs. His heart sank, letting the chest pains shoot up again. Was he dead? He sure looked it. "Where is my daughter?"

"I'd like to know the same thing myself, Tom. And where is the weirdo while we're talking about missing people?"

"You're lying!"

Shawn rolled his eyes losing patience.

"I'm not playing games here, Tom. I'm going to find Lilly and we are getting out of here. If you want to live, you're going to help me. Now throw the fucking baton down and turn around."

Reluctantly Tom threw it into the hallway, hoping that it would signal Mr. Bluestick enough to get the hell out of here and keep looking for Lilly. Turning around, he felt the butt of the gun nudge the back of his head. It was a bit cold. Next came Shawn's frail arm, right around his neck.

It was an odd feeling having a gun to your head. Seeing it countless times in the movies didn't lessen the effect it had on you. It was fucking frightening. Tom wasn't scared of dying, though. He was petrified of leaving Lilly alone in this world. Who would take care of her? Sandy sure the hell wouldn't. He had to take it easy, do what Shawn said until they found Lilly. Then, maybe then, he could fight off the bastard.

Seeing Tom's baton on the floor, Mr. Bluestick immediately backed down the hall once again. Why didn't he wait for him? Damn it. He ducked into the second room on the right. He knew in the back far corner was an old storage cabinet he could hide in. Hopefully he won't check there. Climbing in it he wondered if Shawn had Lilly or not. It certainly didn't sound like it. Once inside he crouched down but kept his makeshift weapon ready. He wouldn't be expecting him to be low. Luckily the cabinet was big enough that he could leave the other door open and still stay hidden. That way he won't think anyone could hide in it.

Several minutes went by until he heard the shuffling in the hall, followed by a quick flash of light. The shuffling continued on down the hall and again he waited for several minutes before silently creeping to the doorway and taking a look. Shawn had a gun to Tom's back. They were stopping and looking into each room. Soon as they disappeared around the corner, Mr. Bluestick made his break.

Standing at the top of the stairs that lead into what was once his safe haven, he stared at Jackson's body with horror. He never wanted to see another body again in his life, especially in here. This, too, was his fault, another life taken because of him. If he hadn't forced him to help, he would be just fine. Did he have a wife? Kids? Pinching the bridge of his nose, he tried to concentrate on Lilly. There was no time for regret just yet.

Rushing down the stairs, he checked Jackson for signs of life. There were none. There was his gun though. It was a few feet away from the body. He picked it up and examined it. He had never fired or even held a real gun in his life, only stage guns. It shouldn't be that hard to use though. After familiarizing himself with it ever so carefully, he shoved it into his belt line, making sure the safety was on. Next, it was off to the big cabinet in the corner that was locked yesterday, but since had been cut open by the police. He only hoped his stuff was in it.

Sure enough, it was. With great pleasure he plopped on a crisp yet dusty top hat and a cape dark as the night; finally, he chose a new cane. His mood wanted him to pick red but he knew Lilly would only respond to blue. So blue it was. With a flick it snapped on, illuminating his face as he prepared for the biggest fight of his life.

It felt wonderful to be back, Mr. Bluestick thought as he felt Edward slide away to the back of his mind. It was a nice vacation, but he knew he was the one who had to handle this. It was his fault, his responsibility. Time was of the essence so he wasted no more getting ready. The last delay had been to click on nine different switches. As he raced up the stairs listening to the humming, he wondered where Lilly would be hiding.

Quick as he could, Mr. Bluestick raced from room to room in the opposite direction from where Shawn and Tom had gone. He wondered if he should have the gun in his hand. Probably should, but it just felt so awkward, and, besides, he didn't want to get startled by Lilly and accidentally shoot. Using his cane for light, he swung it around, adamantly hoping to catch Lilly's attention. If only he could yell for her.

Leaving the wing that was his home, he crossed over into territory into which he had hardly ventured. This half of the building was covered in black soot almost everywhere. In fact, he could remember coming over here only a handful of times since, well, since . . . . It didn't matter. He still knew his way around it. But would Lilly venture into a part she didn't know, especially with it looking like this? Then again, if she didn't have a flashlight, she wouldn't even be able to tell it was like this.

Feeling uncomfortable, not wanting to be in this area of the mill, he hurried his pace even more. Abruptly he stopped at the end of a hall. He didn't want to take the corner. He knew what was on the other end. Lilly, Lilly, Lilly. He repeated over and over again in his head, building up the courage to take the turn.

Seeing the door, he felt terrified but didn't know why. Deep inside of him he could feel Edward cringing. He had only been here one other time since the fire, to plant Judy's favorite tree, a Crimson King Maple. They had planned on putting up several in the backyard. They take years to grow but they planned on keeping the house forever, so it didn't matter. When the trees were delivered to the house after the fire, Edward had two of them taken back. The third one he had brought here. Not wanting any help, he almost killed himself getting it in. It took the entire day to plant it.

Since that day he has never gone back in there. He couldn't bear having all those memories flood back. Heading for the door now, he knew it was a door that Lilly would be drawn to. With his hand on the push plate, he wondered if the tree would still be alive. He wondered if he would be able to handle going in. There wasn't a choice.

Keeping his eyes down, he pushed the door in. On the floor he could see the ancient dust had been disturbed recently. She must be in here! Forgetting where he was, his eye shot up to look for Lilly. Seeing the theater for the first time in decades sent his mind spinning, but then he saw the tree.

"My goodness," he mumbled to himself, calming down, it was gorgeous. Never in a million years would he have thought the tree would have grown, let alone stand so tall and strong as it is now. Not taking his eyes off it, he walked down the aisle to get a closer look. Standing under its long branches, he was speechless. Tears filled his eyes. Jessica would have loved this tree more than anything. Maybe she did? Maybe that is how it has survived here all these years. Touching the trunk of the tree he started to circle around it in awe, laughing and crying.

Reaching the back, he stumbled upon Lilly, sound asleep. She looked so peaceful. His heart swelled with love and relief. She was safe and looked unharmed. A tingle started to run over his body. Looking up at the tree again, he could see the moon shining through the hole in the roof. He really felt as if Jessica was watching him now. Maybe she even protected Lilly and that's why she was all cuddled up in between the roots. She would have been an amazing mother.

"I'm sorry, Jessica. I loved you so much." Shaking, he leaned to the tree and gave it a light kiss. He did his best to savor the moment, but, as amazing as it was, there was a lot of work still to be done tonight. The last thing he wanted to do was to wake Lilly. She looked so peaceful, but then again, there was no choice. Edward slipped back into the recesses again as Mr. Bluestick resumed his duty.

"Lilly, darling. Wake up."

She shuttered a bit, groaned and rolled over. Sleep was so amazing, no matter how traumatic the last few days were it could steal you away for a while. With his gloved hand, he gently rocked her awake. Lilly jumped up with a scream so loud his ears rang. It took her a second to remember where she was, then she saw who woke her. The screaming stopped and a smile replaced it before she dove into his arms for a hug.

"I couldn't find you! I've missed you so much!"

"I've missed you, too, my little darling."

The two embraced, savoring each other's arms around them. They both felt safe, comfortable and loved, until they heard the shout.

Hearing Lilly scream was relief to Shawn and Tom's ears. They both wanted to find her more than anything. They just wanted different results. It wasn't hard to follow the scream. It led them into a hall with not too many doors, one of which was wide open. It was an easy choice. Scurrying to the door, Shawn whispered in Tom's ear.

"I will fuck your daughter, then slit her open and feed her guts to dogs if you try anything." Shawn didn't mean it, but he had to say something to keep Tom in his control.

Arriving in the doorway, Tom and Shawn's minds both raced to figure out plans as they saw the touching sight below. Tom's plans were delayed as the chest pains, that had been getting worse since the gun was put to his head, disappeared at the sight of Lilly. When you have the possibility of never seeing your child again, yet you do . . . . It was a feeling that Tom could never explain. All he knew was that it gave him new vigor and hope.

Shit. Mr. Bluestick was with her. Shawn couldn't take this. He couldn't see a non-violent way out of this. Tom won't give up on his daughter; neither will the nut job. Why didn't he just leave before? He could have gotten away scot-free. Was this girl really worth it? In a way, yes. But it was more so to take on the challenge that God gave him. This was going to ruin, but it was the way it had to be.

The main thing he needed was to somehow get Lilly in his hands. From there he could back out of this place and maybe have a chance of getting away with no more bloodshed. If, that's if, they didn't try anything. If blood was to be shed, then it was God's will, not his.

"Lilly! Get away from him. He's going to hurt you. Your dad paid him to find and kill you! You've got to trust me. I have your dad here. Don't listen to him. Come to me and I will help you get out of here!"

Tom couldn't believe what he was hearing. What the fuck was he saying? Did he say this bull to her before? She wouldn't believe him, would she?

"Mr. Bluestick would never hurt me!"

Thank goodness she wasn't believing him. "Sweetie, I was so worried about you! I love you so much!" Though they were a distance away, he could still see Lilly's face scrunch up as it always did when she was angry.

"I know you hate me! You wanted to get rid of me!"

What? What the hell was going on? Tom wanted to elbow this fuck and run to his daughter more than anything in the world. Again, though, it was too risky. At least Shawn was now walking them down closer. Slowly he could see his daughter's face more and more clearly.

"Lilly, listen to me. I know you trust Mr. Bluestick, but he is lying to you, just like your dad lied to you. I saved you, for crying out loud!"

Lilly's head was now spinning. She didn't want to let go of Mr. Bluestick. He couldn't be on her dad's side, could he? No way. Shawn was lying, but if he was, then that would mean her dad didn't want to get rid of her? No, no, she knew he did.

"Tom, it's okay. I can handle this."

Huh? Lilly didn't want to believe what she heard. It felt as if her heart was being ripped out. He was really going to give her up to him? Hard as she could, Lilly shoved Mr. Bluestick in the chest and ran into the middle of the aisle between them both. Both her dad and Mr. Bluestick yelled, "No" at the same time.

Tom tried to tug away from Shawn but he stuck the butt of his gun harder into his head and whispered in his ear, "You don't want your daughter to be covered in your brains do you?"

It stopped Tom cold. Tightening his fists, he started to quiver. He had to make a move soon. And what did Edward mean that he can handle this? Did he have a plan? With his fingers digging into his palm, he remembered his cast. It had been nothing but an annoyance since the second he got it, but maybe tonight it could help him.

Lilly wanted to just sit down and give up. Who to believe? All this running. It was too much, just too much. The thought of running away again popped into her mind but then again she would have to find her way out of the mill. Then what? Where would she go? The answer was nowhere. After being on such a high of accomplishments, Lilly crashed, feeling like a failure. So, in protest, she sat down Indian style, crossing her arms right in between the bickering grown ups.

The three men in the room went silent as they watched Lilly sit down. They could all tell she was now playing the role of the stubborn kid. Whoever was going to get her was going to have to pull her kicking and screaming, no matter what.

Mr. Bluestick could see Shawn was looking around the room trying to plan something. Taking advantage of the moment, he grabbed the gun under his cloak, felt around for the safety, and switched it off. Next he stared at Tom until he got his attention. Having it, he did his best to silently tell him now was his chance to make a break. He seemed to understand. At least he hoped that's what the nod was for.

This was it. Time to be the person he had never been, the tough guy. Time to fight for his daughter and his life. The gun was at the back of his head, so he needed to drop away from that first and then attack. He did his best to give Lilly a heads up with a look, but she refused to look at anyone. Feeling Shawn getting fidgety, he sprung into action. Not even counting to three, he let his weight drop. The second his knees hit the floor, he swung his cast with all his might right around behind him, connecting directly with the ribs he had broken earlier. He could see the pain in Shawn's face, but chose to not watch it for long. Using all his energy, he dove towards Lilly. With a bit too much force, he landed on top of her and waited to see what happened next. Hopefully Mr. Bluestick could muster up some magic to go with the outfit.

The pain was blinding. Shawn wanted to drop to the floor and let the pain ease away. That wasn't happening though. Through wet eyes he could see Mr. Bluestick pull something out of his pants. What was it? A gun? Shit. Where did he get that? He wouldn't fire, would he? Suddenly a bright flash emitted from the tip of the barrel. Shawn instantly pulled his own trigger, firing back.

The second the blast struck Shawn's ears he could feel a hot stinging sensation in his leg. It felt as if a hot butter knife was poking around in there to get the last of the mayo out of the jar. It made him drop to the floor. Luckily he fell behind a row of seats. The pain was bad, but life threatening it wasn't. He could hear Lilly screaming and Tom trying to calm her down. He must have hit that bastard. Good, but what to do next? If the pain was bearable, he could drag himself across the row and out the side door, maybe make it back to the car. But what then? If he had hit the bastard, then why not crawl the other way and just shoot Tom. Then he could still take Lilly and all this would have been for a reason. It was a plan.

The bullet ripped right through Mr. Bluestick's left shoulder and out the back, landing somewhere off in the distance. The shot rendered his left arm useless. Lying on his back, feeling the blood leave his body, he stared up at the red leaves above him. It was beautiful. Did he do it, though? Did he protect Lilly? He tried to sit up to see if she was all right but the pain kept him pinned to the floor. The best he could do was lift his head. The sight relieved and overjoyed him. Tom was holding Lilly tight. All he could see of Shawn was his foot behind the chair. It wasn't moving. He laid his head back down and beamed with pride as he looked up at the leaves and thought of what his daughter would have been like.

Lilly did her best to fight off her dad but he was too strong.

"Lilly, for God's sake, stop it. I love you so much. Shawn is a very, very bad person. You have to believe me!" Having her completely in a body lock, not being able to move, she yelled back, "Then why did you send him to take me away!"

Tom kissed her head and she started to calm down a bit. "Sweetie, I would never do something like that. Shawn . . . honey, he kidnapped you. Remember how we talked about how bad people do things like that? Well, Shawn is one of them. He lied to you, I'm sorry."

"You promise?" The voice was frail and weak.

He was winning her back, thank God. It was so wonderful to feel her in his arms again, to hold her too tight, to feel her little lungs fill with air, to feel her tears fall down onto his wrist. She wiggled a bit. It made him nervous wondering if she was trying to get away. Instead, she was turning around to look at him.

"I'm sorry I believed him, Daddy. He showed me a note and said you wrote it. It was so mean."

Tom shushed her, telling her they didn't need to talk about it just now. After several moments of complete joy, Tom realized he should be more attuned to what was going on around him. Was Mr. Bluestick all right? Did he kill Shawn? Would he even be able to figure the way out of this place? Helping Lilly up, the chest pains came back as she screamed at the top of her lungs.

Shawn was just a foot behind them. With one quick swoop Shawn yanked Lilly to his good side. Limping, he backed away with her, grinning an evil smile. The only problem he had was he was holding her with his right arm away from the injured ribs, leaving the gun in his left hand. It was awkward, but sometimes you have to do what you have to do. His hand was shaking as he pointed it towards Tom.

"Sorry, Tom, but I have no choice now!" The gun fired, sending his untrained arm flying backwards. Concentrating on not dropping it, he had taken his eyes off Tom. Did he hit him? Looking back, he cursed himself for never training to use this thing. A large chunk of the burnt out chair near where Tom had been was missing. So was Tom. Instead of searching for him, he chose to flee. Lilly kicked and screamed but he still had a good grip on her as he backed out of the theater, limping severely.

Hearing the shot snapped Mr. Bluestick out of his daydream and pumped new energy into him. In a flash he was sitting up, gun in hand. Watching the door shut, he saw Tom pop up from behind a chair. It startled him. Tom was by his side in a second, amazed that he was all right.

"Give me the gun, I have to go after them!"

"Help me up first, then you can run ahead. I know some shortcuts so I can catch up."

Tom helped him up, grabbed the gun and sprinted up the aisle.

Fucking maze! Shawn was more than pissed that he hadn't paid attention as to how they got here. And now, with a shot leg, fucked up eye and broken ribs, he'll never make it out of here! After a few seconds he could hear feet pounding behind him. Tom, fuck! Lilly tried to scream but he had her mouth covered. Hopping down the hall, dragging his leg behind him, Shawn felt defeated. If only he could make it outside, then he could pop Tom on the way out and take his time heading for the car.

After too many turns, he found himself staring at a set of stairs. Either turn back and have a shoot out or head up the stairs. Fuck this. Shawn pulled Lilly's hair hard and whispered in her ear. It stung his heart hurting her.

"Listen up. You so much as make a peep and I will kill your father then beat the shit out of you. Do you understand me?" Lilly nodded to agree as he shoved her up the stairs. With a hole in his leg, it was like climbing Mount Everest, but he made it to the top. Exhausted, he shoved Lilly into the first room on the right hand side. He was amazed to see it had windows. Keeping the gun aimed behind them, he tried the window. Stuck. Of course. Wiping the grit off it, he could see a fire escape. Perfect. The only problem is he'd have to smash the window to get out there. It just might be worth it.

Tom had lost the sound of Shawn's footsteps. He was cursing himself at the same time as trying to keep his breathing steady to listen. It was a dead end, stairs. There was no way he would make it up them. He tried to search the ground for blood drops but it was too dark. Turning away from the stairs, he heard a loud smash. It sounded like glass breaking.

Tom reached the top of the stairs so fast that an Olympic runner would be jealous. Gun in hand, he looked in the right side door first. Nothing. Turning to look into the left door, he saw her instantly. Lilly was standing on the fire escape right outside the window. She was facing away. He must already be out there! Ready to sprint in, something down the hall caught his eyes, stopping him. It was a brilliant flash of blue light, the light he had seen from Lilly's room on several occasions. Mr. Bluestick. He would have ignored it if it hadn't been moving about so wildly. Was he trying to get his attention? It didn't matter, he had to get Lilly.

Tom barreled towards the window, racing through the doorway, only to hear a loud popping noise, then again and again. Flecks of something sharp hit his forehead. The wall was splintering apart next to him? Bullets? Shit. Lilly was screaming before he could reach the window. It was a trap! He should have waited for Mr. Bluestick again. Damn instincts.

Falling to the floor, not sure if he was hit or not, Tom aimed the gun into the darkness and fired three times. He was amazed at how much the recoil hurt his hand. Did he hit him? The shooting had stopped. The silence scared him enough to pull the trigger eight more times. Only three more bullets came out before the gun just clicked. Again there was silence.

Feeling his body, he was pretty sure he was un-harmed. Tom started to get up when he heard a crunching noise coming from the darkness that was the rest of the room. It was soon followed by a low chuckle. This was not good. Shawn was still moving. Squinting his hardest, he could still see nothing, but the hall started to glow with blue light. It gave him hope but then it suddenly disappeared. Less then a second later something slid across the floor. It had a tiny red light on it, blinking. What was it? A bomb? Flashlight? Was Mr. Bluestick trying to give him a weapon?

Not sure what it was, Tom started for it the second it flicked on. Six beams of light shooting from its disk-like shape lit the room up instantly like some sort of tiny alien spaceship landing upside down. The first thing he saw was Shawn aiming the gun right at him. He was temporarily distracted looking at the disk, confused. Tom wasted no time tackling him. He went down easily but still put up a fight.

Had the once show prop worked? He heard scuffling in the next room. He wanted nothing more than to help but knew what his job was right now. Saving Lilly. Just one problem. To save her he had to enter the room in which Jessica and his un-born child perished, the room in which her flesh melted to the floor. He stood frozen at its entrance. He could do this, he tried to tell himself as the image of Jessica falling back into the room played over and over again in his head like a broken record. Luckily it was stopped by Lilly's scream.

It was only six steps across the room to the window. That's it, and then the girl will be safe. The image that had haunted him started to play again, but this time it was different. Just before Judy fell back, everything froze, the horror on her face disappeared and a smile grew.

"Eddie, you have to do this. For me, for Sylvia." She turned her head back and looked at the fire.

"Hurry, hurry." The image resumed it's normal horror. Sylvia? So that was the name she decided on for his daughter. Sylvia. He had told her she could pick the child's name. She was giddy about it and swore not to tell him until the day she was born. He never found out what it was… until today, until this trauma caused him to remember for the first time that detail of that horrific moment.

Everything left his mind as he took the six steps across the room to the broken window. Ducking his head through, he peaked out onto the fire escape that once upon a time he had fallen from and there was Lilly holding on, looking in on her father, petrified.

"Lilly, my darling, surely you'd be much better off in here!"

Lilly's eyes shot open at the sight of Mr. Bluestick, thrilled to see he wasn't dead. Without even thinking, she clambered over to him. The familiar glow of his cane felt like home. She gave him a big hug before remembering that her father was in trouble. "You have to help my dad!"

It seemed they both had forgotten, for Mr. Bluestick spun around, his useless arm flapping behind him, and took the six steps back out of the room, not even thinking of Jess.

Feeling he could take Shawn down finally, Tom wrestled the gun from his hand and tossed it out the window, not even thinking if Lilly would grab it or not. Then he went for where it hurt most, the broken rips and gunshot wound. Punch after punch, Tom beat the two injuries until Shawn seemed to stop fighting back. Stopping, catching his breath, Tom braced himself to get off him, just as something slammed his into his head so hard he saw more lights than just the odd one on the floor.

Tom fell off Shawn with a hard thump, his hands instantly going to his head. Shawn laughed as he rolled over and pushed himself up. Tom wanted to jump back into his attack but couldn't move his hands from his aching head. He watched the thin man, amazed that he was still going. He had taken quite the beating yet he was still able to pull himself up and out the window in seconds.

An odd half yell, half gurgle emitted by Shawn when he saw Lilly was gone. He searched the ground for her but saw nothing. Fuck. Well, he was still alive; best get out of here and forget all of this happened. He knew what he had to do. Kill Tom and head out. If Mr. Bluestick came across his path, he'd kill him, too, but, if not, no one would believe his story anyway, if he was still alive, that is. A tiny twinge in his heart ached to keep looking for Lilly but his body told him it was impossible.

Leaning back against the railing for support, he took a breath and began searching for the gun just as the blue light appeared in the doorway.

Tom couldn't believe after all of this it was going to end with him dying. He was amazed that even with this imminent future he still couldn't move. He shut his eyes, preparing for the bullet. "I LOVE YOU LILLY!" he screamed what he wanted his last words to be. He only hoped she heard him and that Mr. Bluestick could keep her safe. Then the gunshot rang out.

2

Hearing the gunshot, Mr. Bluestick dove out of the doorway and scampered back to where he had left Lilly in the other room. She wasn't there. Instantly he knew what had happened. Walking slowly to the window he whispered her name. Hoping she was alright.

Poking his head out, she saw her on her knees holding the gun. It looked ridiculously big in her hands. Carefully he climbed out and pulled the gun out of her hand, hiding it in his pocket for safety. He wanted nothing more than to hug her but he couldn't move his arm enough to get it around her. Luckily Tom popped out of the other window, battered but alive, to take care of her. With out words she latched on to her father and he pulled her back in the mill.

Mr. Bluestick stood up ready to go back in, but he couldn't help but take a look down the at the man that almost ruined so many lives. His body was laid in unnatural ways on top of leaves, sticks and rocks. He moved a bit but Mr. Bluestick knew he wasn't getting up from this fall, like he did all those years ago. As he ducked to go back in the building he couldn't help but smile at the thought of Lilly being the one to stop him. He just wished he could have seen his face.

The three headed down the stairs and to the front of the mill. It was an odd, silent trip. They were all too emotionally drained to talk. Walking through the door into the night's cool air, Tom thought he might now know what it was like for an ex-con to be released from prison.

Sue raced to the small battered group that was exiting the mill. With a mother's concern, she looked each of them over quickly, checking for injury. She was relieved to see Lilly and Tom were all right. Mr. Bluestick, on the other hand, was a different story.

"You guys all right?" she said to Tom and Lilly.

Tom introduced his daughter to Sue, who said hello with a big hug. Tom looked around the woods still on edge. Chip came walking around the corner from the side of the mill. He had a grim look of pity on his face. He shook his head and they all knew Shawn was dead. Hiding his nerves he smiled before crouching down to see Lilly for the first time. Looking at her beautiful, tired eyes, he was glad she was safe.

Standing back up, Chip wanted to apologize to Mr. Bluestick for how he treated him earlier. He might have been nuts but he was a good guy. Opening his mouth to speak, Chip noticed he was gone. "Where did he go?" No one else seemed to have noticed he had left.

"He must have gone back inside," Tom said, turning around, confused. "For crying out loud! I'm amazed he hasn't fainted from the loss of blood as it is. He needs to get to the hospital now!"

Chip ran past them and into the mill, not knowing what name to call out. Tom wanted nothing more than to go and sit on the rock a few yards away to let the pain in his head ease while he hugged his daughter. But, of course, Lilly let go of his hand and followed after Chip so he joined them.

Many twists and turns later, the four of them arrived at the top of Mr. Bluestick's stairs. Lilly was amazed that there were more lights than ever swirling around the room. At first sight Sue thought it looked as if there was a rave being held here. Then she saw Mr. Bluestick, who was strapped into the large chair of the ChrimsaWheel.

"Please! You all must leave; it's too dangerous. I don't even know if this will work. It's still not finished, but I have no choice but to try it! You must go!" Mr. Bluestick screamed over the humming noises that were growing louder and louder. With his good arm he strapped on a large metal buckle across his legs.

"What's going on?" cried Chip.

Lilly quickly explained what the device was and that he was going home to his family.

"Christ, he'll fry himself! The thing is practically an electric chair!" Chip yelled out to no one in particular. Everyone wanted to help but no one dared go down the stairs for sparks were now flying out from several different areas.

"GO! GO! GO!"

"NOOOOOO!" Lilly screamed in response to Mr. Bluestick's angry yells.

"Lilly! Thank you for teaching me to love again! But you must go!" With his final words said, he reached for a lever just to the right of the chair, pulling it down.

Tom grabbed Lilly and Sue as the sparks headed toward them. There was no choice but to leave. Outside of the room Lilly cried as Chip shut the heavy door on the room, hoping any fire that started would not spread. Tom stared down the hall, not believing he was feeling so much grief for a man he wanted to kill such a short while ago and that's when it hit him - the power switch Mr. Bluestick hit earlier to turn everything on, he could shut it off and maybe save him!

Without a word he grabbed Chip's flashlight and sprinted off to the room he was almost sure he saw him enter earlier. Sure enough, in the back corner was an electrical cabinet. It was old and rusted but it had to be it. Using the light to guide him, he moved every switch in the opposite direction. Finished, he raced back to the three who were still standing curious about his actions. Without answering them, he swung the door back open. It was pitch-black inside except for a few small specs of glowing embers.

3

Tom carried Lilly in his arms while Sue strolled next to him back to the house. Chip stayed with Mr. Bluestick. It was touch and go but if help got there fast enough, he could make it. Walking back through the small gate, Lilly was asleep in his arms. Tom half expected there to be a media circus around the house, but there wasn't a soul to be seen. He was relieved

Entering the house Tom gently set Lilly down on the couch, letting her stay asleep. The officer was nowhere in sight. He must have left. Tom didn't want to let Lilly out of his sight, but he didn't want his talking to wake her so he reluctantly went back into the kitchen with Sue. Sitting down at the table, Tom stared at nothing while Sue stared at him.

"You did great, Tom. You got her back. The hard part is done. Things may not be easy after this, but just remember . . ." Sue's speech was cut off by a sudden laugh, a woman's laugh.

"Oh, giving a heartwarming speech, are we?"

The two turned to see Sandy coming out of the hallway holding a standard issue police handgun, just like the one Tom used only a few minutes earlier. Her hair was knotted and her face covered in black streaks from her running mascara.

"Sandy, what? What's going on? Where did you get the gun?"

"Let's just say men are pigs; they have a hard time resisting a pair of spread legs."

Tom couldn't believe what was happening. How did she get the gun? He prayed that she hadn't done anything to the officer. Sandy wouldn't do something like that, though, would she? Tom stood up and raised his hands. Slowly he approached his wife. After only two steps, Sandy fired.

The bullet cracked through the ceiling with magnificent force. Sandy screamed at the top of her lungs over and over again, a low growl of a yell, until Tom sat back down. Immediately his mind went right to Lilly. Sandy was in the way of being able to get to her.

"Fuck you, Tom! FUCK YOU! I can't believe you took Mark away from me! It wasn't good enough for you to take my life away, to ruin my body by making me give you that fucking bitch child of yours? No! Nooooo! You had to go and take away the one thing I wanted!"

Tom was baffled at what was happening. She'd been sick lately, not herself. But this? This was insane. How did she get like this? He turned to Sue for help. She was a brain doc. She could talk her out of this more than he could.

Sue saw his look and Said, "Sandy, why don't you put the gun down and we'll all talk about this over coffee."

As Sue finished her sentence, Lilly walked through the doorway. It was the last thing Tom wanted to see. Why didn't she just run upstairs to her room!

"Lilly, go upstairs now!" Tom screamed.

"Mommy?"

Sandy turned the gun, aiming it at Lilly, who was too tired to even realize what was going on.

"You took away the one thing I loved, I'll take away the one thing you love!" With that Sandy pulled the trigger.

4

It was the worst sight Tom would ever see - his daughter lying motionless on the floor, covered in blood. The rage of everything over the past few days built up in him and emitted from his body in the form of a primal scream. It all happened so quickly. His first reaction was to rush over to Lilly, but Sandy still had the gun in her hands. Her face was slack, the blood draining out of it.

"I shot her. I actually shot her." She turned the gun towards Tom, who was choking on his own tears as he tried to move from the seat. A banging came from the door, not a knocking but a crashing sound. Tom finally could move. It didn't matter anymore if he got killed, not with Lilly . . . not with her. . . . Tom stood up. As the door shattered inward, he slowly walked towards Lilly, hardly picking up his feet. Sandy kept the gun fixed on him though her grip on it made it look as if it might fall out of her hand at any second.

As Rudder and the other officers rushed in, they saw the sight and focused their guns on Sandy. "Put your gun down!" Rudder yelled as one of the heavily suited men grabbed Sue and pulled her back out of the room. Sandy stood there still, aiming at Tom who was almost to Lilly. Once again she yelled, this time tightening the grip on the gun.

As Tom dropped to his knees, he didn't even flinch as a barrage of gunshots went off behind his back. In fact, looking back at it, he hardly remembered hearing anything as he stroked Lilly's hair away from her face. She was pale but breathing. There was so much blood he couldn't believe she was alive. Life started to pump back into him as he saw she was shot in the hip, not the chest as it had looked from where he was sitting. Less than a minute later he was in the back of an ambulance holding Lilly's hand while two young men worked feverishly on her.

5

Two-weeks later Tom woke up in the same chair that he had been sleeping in every night since Lilly got shot. It was horribly uncomfortable but it was right next to Lilly's bed. The sun was shining in the colorful room as he rubbed the sleep out of his eyes. Shaking off the stiffness, he turned to check on Lilly.

"Morning, sleepy head!" said Tom.

"Today is my big day, daddy!" said Lilly.

Tom's smile grew across his whole face. The past few weeks had been a nightmare. Of course, compared to that night it was a vacation. Sandy was buried discreetly. Tom attended but told everyone he didn't. He had been losing her for years, but it didn't make it any easier to lose her completely. Jackson was also buried, a hero's funeral that was played live on TV. As for Shawn's funeral, Tom didn't have a clue and didn't care when or what happened at it.

With three people dead, one cop in a coma (Sandy had beaten the officer unconscious after she got him to take his pants off) and a child in the hospital, the media had been relentless. Luckily it had been dying down. Of course, with today being Lilly's release from the hospital, it was sure to pick up again. Tom didn't have to worry much though. Rudder, whom Tom had learned to like recently, was there to handle most of the media. Sue would be, too. She had been here almost as much as Tom had. It was nice. She helped Lilly and him cope with things and was just plain fun company. He was getting used to having her around and hoped she would keep visiting once Lilly was out.

"Sure is your big day, honey! And I've got a special surprise for you later!" Lilly's eyes were wide at the idea of a surprise. She had been spoiled the last few weeks with flowers and presents. There was so many they had to donate half of them to charity. She seemed to be coping pretty well with the loss of her mother. She cried at times but Tom always suspected that she would eventually be okay with it. It was sure going to be tough raising her without one though. She was tough, they were tough; they'd get through it.

An hour after getting up, Tom shaved at the tiny kid sink in the bathroom and got ready for her release. The staff was in and out all day saying bye to Lilly. It was really sweet seeing how loved she was. With all the flowers cleared and both of them dressed to go, Lilly asked when she was getting her surprise.

"In a few minutes," Tom replied, placing her in the wheel chair. She winced a bit but quickly wiped it off her face. Tom looked at his watch, then checked the hallway.

"Here it comes, honey. Close your eyes." Lilly closed her eyes but couldn't help but peek. It sure was a surprise, the best surprise she could have hoped for. Mr. Bluestick walked through the door! "Surprise!" Tom yelled.

Lilly was so excited she tried to get out of the chair. Tom held her back and let Mr. Bluestick walk over to her and give the best half hug he could with the arm brace on.

Lilly looked him up and down and put on a quizzical look. "Where's your normal clothing?" She was a bit disappointed to see him clean shaven, wearing jeans and a button-down shirt, but it didn't matter. It was still good to see him.

"Lilly, darling. Your father explained to you what happened, right?" Lilly nodded. Tom kissed her on the head quickly and patted Mr. Bluestick on the good shoulder before leaving the room to give them some privacy.

"He said you were sick," she said in a sad voice. He turned and looked over his shoulder, making sure Tom was gone.

"Naa! I'll let them believe that, but between you and me, Mr. Bluestick made it home. The ChrimsaWheel worked!" Lilly's face filled with excitement but then rushed to confusion.

"You see, Lilly, as your father told you, my real name is Edward. Mr. Bluestick was using my body while he was here. Like you see in the movies, since he wasn't from here, he couldn't let people see what he really looked like!" "He did contact me to tell you thank you for being his friend and for helping him. He said he hopes you and I can be friends."

Lilly nodded. She wasn't sure whether or not to believe his story, but it did make her happy thinking about it.

"He also sent a present for you. He heard about how your hip got hurt and that you will need a cane to walk, so he sent this for you." Lilly watched as he scooted out of the room only to quickly re-appear, hiding something behind his back. "Ta-Da!"

With the same flare that Mr. Bluestick had used, he produced the walking stick she loved so much. With a tap on the floor he lit it up and handed it to her. Tears started to fill her eyes. She had been so nervous about having to walk with a cane, what all the kids were going to say to her at school. But now, now she was going to be so cool!

About the Author

Michael, known to his fans as AuthorMike, is the author of seven books, including a number one bestseller and the star of a popular web series. He has done book tours in over five countries and twenty states, sold movie/television rights and his books have been featured in over one hundred media outlets around the world. All of which, he achieved independently.

Best known for writing legendary horror movie star, Kane Hodder's official biography, *Unmasked*, Mike also wrote a journal called *The Killer & I*, about the making of *Unmasked*. The original journals were read in over 50 countries thousands of times a week. It became so popular, it was released as a book… and is now the basis of a reality series starring both Kane and Mike! The first season has enjoyed tremendous success on DVD.

Arm Candy: A Celebrity Escort's Guide To The Red Carpet, which Mike co-wrote, was a number one Bestseller on Amazon for over two weeks and was featured on hundreds of media outlets around the world including *E! News, Extra, People, The Jeff Probst Show, Marie Osmond Show, US Weekly, OK! Magazine* and numerous others.

His other writing includes the novels *Fifty Handfuls* and *Mr. Bluestick* and the short story collection, *White Ash*. He also writes under the pen name, Michael Gore, having released a horror short story collection titled, *Tales From a Mortician* and *Skeletons in The Attic*.

With his MFA in Creative Writing and background in filmmaking, Mike has written several acclaimed short films and a dozen live action children's shows that have played around the world and has been commissioned to write several feature length scripts.